COMBAT SHIFT

WORLD OF COMBAT DYSTOPIA BOOK 5

MISTY ZAUGG

For my beautiful Brooke:
My daughter, best friend, singer and artist extraordinaire.

CHAPTER ONE

"R is for Radiation. Radiation from the Blast makes the
world outside of our city unlivable."
— Chikara City Elementary Primer

"This is it," said Eigo in a voice just a little too loud and
animated. The lanky figure of Kiriai's best friend practically bounced next to her in the crowd instead of walking. His
mop of blond hair was disheveled as usual and his pale blue eyes
fairly danced with excitement. He had none of the decorum one
would expect from a member of a brawler crew.

"Oomf."

Eigo's soft grunt of pain made Kiriai turn, and she smiled
when she saw him aim a glare at Shisen and Mikata, who walked
just behind him. Both pretended neither of them had just
elbowed him. Kiriai's friends sported identical smirks, but the
two women couldn't look more different. Shisen's dark hair
framed her pale skin and piercing eyes as she strode through the
crowd with an innate poise. Mikata, on the other hand, fairly

dwarfed her friend with a stocky figure, brown hair and average looks. Instead, her athletic grace and natural cheer made the fighter stand out in a crowd.

Smiling, Kiriai felt the knot of tension inside her relax at the antics of her friends. Brawler Initiation started today, and she couldn't decide if it was nerves or excitement that had her insides jumping. Probably a bit of both.

"Crew for Brawler Dento Kiriai," Aibo said up ahead, to a clerk who had waved her over. Aibo, the youngest and most exuberant member of Kiriai's crew, handled all the tedious minutiae for their crew in her job as their aide. Kiriai especially appreciated her work during events like this.

Facing her, the officious clerk wore a Southern Burb armband and seemed tired of her job even though it was barely mid-morning. The rest of their group stopped while Aibo presented their papers. Kiriai wanted to just ignore the formalities and hurry through the huge doorway she could see at the end of the hall. Instead, she let her eyes roam over the ornate calligraphy scrolls on the walls and the rugs under their feet that probably cost more than the entire home she shared with her grandfather back in Jitaku Hood. Kiriai forced herself to breathe and relax as the clerk checked each of them off a list.

"You're missing your trainer," the clerk finally said as her eyes moved between their group and the paper in front of her.

Kiriai stiffened. She had decided to talk to the rest of her crew about this tonight, after putting off the subject multiple times. She'd seen questions in Mikata's eyes, but everyone had given her space and not broached the topic of her crew trainer. Well, to be honest, Kiriai had kept delaying, hoping for an answer, still conflicted about who she really wanted. No, after their trip here and their first day in Southern Core, she still didn't have an answer.

Before Kiriai could stop her, the clerk went on. "Trainer Mosa Sento? Will he be joining you?" she asked. Disapproval filled her tone as she continued. "The doors close after the last person here enters. We allow no late arrivals."

Eigo's head snapped around at Sento's name, his expression a mix of shock and outrage. Behind him, Aibo gave her a helpless shrug. She'd kept Kiriai's secret, but neither of them had expected the clerk's involvement.

Eigo pulled her to the side, into a small nook created by a display table, and she let him. This was her own fault. She was the one who had put off this discussion until it was too late.

"You chose Sento as your trainer?" Eigo hissed, keeping his voice below the sound of the crowded hallway. "After everything he put you through?"

"None of that has anything to do with his fighting and strategy talent," she said, hating how defensive she sounded. This was her decision, not Eigo's. "Besides, at the end of the brawler tournament, he stepped in to protect me from the chief. It's not as black-and-white as you're making it seem."

Eigo stared at her, speechless for a moment. An expression of dawning realization spread across his face.

Kiriai swallowed, wanting more than anything to not do this right here, right now.

"You're actually considering getting back together with him? Not just taking him on as trainer?"

"No!" She shook her head, one hand raised in protest. "Being willing to learn from him and salvage a friendship isn't the same as getting involved again. In any case, he hasn't taken me up on the trainer position, if you haven't noticed." She waved back at their group and the missing Sento.

Eigo relaxed a fraction and let out a harsh breath. He looked around and seemed to suddenly notice the awkwardness of the whole situation.

"Our trainer is indisposed at the moment, but I wanted to thank you for being so attentive to the details of our paperwork, M. Clerk." Tomi's voice boomed from beside her with its usual cheerfulness as he threaded his large figure up toward the clerk, drawing the gazes of those nearby. Their crew 'ranger tended to do that. His ready smile, bright shock of red hair and ability to remember the personal details of everyone he met, made him welcome almost everywhere. "None of this would be possible without the hard work of people like you. We should all acknowledge the clerks and all they do more often."

Tomi then folded his considerable bulk into a bow to the surprised woman, whose frown disappeared. She smiled and preened at his attention. Without another objection, she waved them on, and they rejoined the throng heading toward the towering entrance at the end of the hall. They had slid the doors wide open to accommodate everyone. While there were only eight new brawlers this year, together with their crews and a smattering of household members, they made an impressive number.

Passing through the doorway, Kiriai stifled a gasp as she saw how vast the training space was. She should have known it would be impressive based on the opulence of the entryway, but she'd never imagined anyone spending so many credits furnishing a practice area.

"Keep walking, little one. Can't have you looking too new to all this," a cheerful voice prodded her, quiet and near her ear so only she would hear it. Startled, Kiriai looked at 'Ranger Tomi with a grateful glance before picking up her pace. Despite his mop of red hair and easy smile, Tomi's prodigious bulk ensured that no one got too close or jostled their group.

As the crowd filtered into the large space, clerks directed the traffic, giving Kiriai the chance to take everything in. Her head swiveled from one sight to another, some of them making her drool. Against one wall stood practice dummies in pristine condition, padded and wooden, lined up like a small, frozen army, affixed to their heavy bases and awaiting orders. A far corner had walls covered with mirrors, an expensive but invaluable tool when training to hone skills. And the equipment . . . Kiriai couldn't identify half of it. They had filled shelves and tubs with weights, balls, padded bats and everything Kiriai could imagine being used in practice.

"Well, that's the most sensible thing I've seen yet," Isha said under her breath as she tipped her head. Kiriai glanced to the left where her crew fixer was looking and saw a row of alcoves with padded tables and shelves filled with an orderly assortment of fixer equipment and treatments. She smiled.

"Don't worry. I'm sure as soon as I get started, you'll get to use all kinds of the new fixer gear to patch me up."

Isha let a quiet sigh escape, and Kiriai felt a twinge of guilt. Isha had treated her after some hefty damage and didn't consider the topic a joking matter. Her tone was more clinical as she continued. "Having treatment alcoves right here, in addition to the rooms in the fixer hall, saves having to transport the injured." She aimed a frown at Kiriai. "Though I'm not sure it bodes well for you. How hard is this brawler initiation going to be?"

Kiriai swallowed and didn't answer. Her tingling nerves slipped a bit from excited toward worried. She didn't know any details and despite asking around, the initiation seemed to be a well-kept secret. No one who'd endured it was willing to share. Even Boss Akuto, who'd opened up more and more lately, had just shaken his head and changed the subject.

Isha must have sensed her worry, because she reached out and gave Kiriai's hand a squeeze. "We're all here to help you through this, Kiriai-chan. Besides, I promised your grandfather I'd take care of you until he can come join us after graduation. And everyone knows it's a bad idea to break a promise to Fixer Ojisan."

Kiriai gave Isha a small smile and squeezed her hand back, thinking of her own promises to her grandfather. Protect the secret of the gifted and help get reinforcements for Jitaku, but above all, make sure she and her crew stay safe.

"Brawlers on the mat. Crew and household members, please find a seat," said a short clerk, her sharp orders interrupting Kiriai's thoughts. The man waved an impatient hand, directing Kiriai toward the center of the vaulted training space while motioning with his other hand for her crew to move to the seating area. Kiriai turned to follow his directions, but paused, surprised by the sudden desire to cling to her friends.

"Try not to hurt the other brawlers, dear," said Mikata in a droll tone. Kiriai's training partner startled a chuckle out of Kiriai and her heart lightened as Mikata waggled her fingers before turning and following the rest of her crew toward the seating area. Feeling more upbeat, Kiriai followed the clerk's directions.

As she emerged out of the throng, her eyes widened and her step stumbled for a beat. With all the people, she hadn't been able to see the welcome awaiting the new brawlers until now. Arrayed in a line at the front of the central space stood a line of senseis, men and women, experienced fighters, all wearing the brown belt instructor rank and staring straight ahead, still as statues. It was intimidating and made Kiriai want to run to her position and snap to attention. She settled for a quick walk and stopped on the spot pointed out by another clerk.

She couldn't help reaching up to feel the familiar shape of her medallions under her shirt. Eigo had given her one, a duplicate of the virtual symbol only she and Yabban could see. And Boss Akuto had given her the other, a token that let her request help with his backing. Steadied, Kiriai found her place and with the ease of long familiarity, snapped to attention, her feet together, back straight, eyes forward and face expressionless. In her peripheral vision, she saw the rest of her new class find their places and follow her example. To either side came soft, murmuring voices from their crews and household members as they took their seats.

This is happening. Kiriai felt a wave of disbelief and awe at the notion. She was living one of her childhood dreams and only a year after first making scrapper. That made her younger than everyone here, something she usually didn't pay attention to. Right on the heels of that thought, though, came another that punctured her excitement. Her hood was losing the war, and if she and her crew couldn't find a way to send reinforcements, she might not have a home to return to.

"Welcome to this year's brawler initiation! I am Sensei Hisho." The booming voice came from a lean, middle-aged woman who stepped forward from the center of the line of senseis. All eyes snapped to her, and every voice fell silent. The other senseis kept their eyes on the new brawlers, except for a woman on the far right. Her demeanor caught Kiriai's attention, and she wondered why a sensei so obviously bored with the proceedings was even there.

"This is the first day of your new lives," said Sensei Hisho, and Kiriai focused back on the leader. "You are like children, leaving your homes behind and starting adulthood. You are no longer scrappers from different hoods. You fought long and hard your whole lives for this opportunity. This initiation will rip away your past and rebuild you as part of a group of elite fighters, one only a select few ever join . . . the Southern Burb Brawlers!"

A resounding cheer met her short speech and Kiriai felt the thrill sweep away some of her reluctance.

Before the sensei's words faded, a loud bellow came from both sides of the large hall.

"Oda!" yelled a whole cadre of voices in unison.

The brawler next to Kiriai flinched. Only long practice kept Kiriai's gaze forward and body still as the noise of what sounded like hundreds of bare feet pounded in their direction. Then she saw them.

Brawlers jogged forward in lines, steps in sync and faces impassive. They wore identical black uniforms, blue belts around their waists and Southern Burb patches on their chests. But their clothing wasn't the only similarity. It was their movement, light and quick with a smooth efficiency, that suggested they could break out into violence at any moment. They filed into neat rows in the large space behind the senseis and snapped into ready stances with uncanny precision.

Not only that, she saw familiar faces she had only seen on the screen before, brawlers she'd admired as they fought in burb battles.

Was that Brawler Haran? He'd been a finalist in last year's City Warrior Tournament. Kiriai's heartbeat quickened, and she worked to steady her breathing. These were her heroes, and she was joining them. These men and women radiated power on a level she hadn't seen before. A stab of doubt hit her. Was she good enough to do this?

"Chief Kosui has given you an honor that not all of you merit," said Sensei Hisho once the ranks of brawlers behind her had stilled. It was as if she'd been reading Kiriai's thoughts.

"During the next month, you will prove to us and to them"— she paused to indicate the brawlers behind her—"that you deserve to join them. If you show yourself worthy, at the end of your initiation month, you will celebrate your graduation with your first official fight as a Southern Burb Brawler. However, we know this life is not for everyone and there is no shame in choosing something different."

Kiriai stifled a scoff of disagreement as the sensei reached into her gi top and pulled out an armband and held it up like a limp snake. Squinting, Kiriai recognized the pattern as Chief Kosui's with an additional embellishment she didn't recognize running along the bottom.

"Chief Kosui is always looking for new talent in the ranks of his 'forcers, and as the top fighters from your hoods, he offers you a top rank should you decide the brawler life isn't for you. The pay is excellent, and from what I hear, while the training is intense, injuries are mild and rarely happen."

Kiriai didn't know why the sensei was droning on about 'forcers. Her attention wandered to the rows of brawlers still standing motionless behind the senseis. These would be her new colleagues, opponents when chosen for the disputes of the rich and powerful, but team members in battles against enemy burbs. Like the territory tournament fought by brawlers from different burbs, with ownership of an entire hood as the prize.

Kiriai shuddered. That was exactly what everyone back home fought to avoid. With a handful of scrapper reinforcements, they could hold on to a majority of their home property and keep Western Hood from initiating a territory tournament.

Her anger flared at the stupid politics and power plays that were leaving her home in danger of being taken.

"It is your choice and yours alone."

What? Kiriai berated herself for letting her attention wander. What choice? She couldn't raise her hand and ask for the sensei to repeat herself. Definitely not the way to make a good first impression. Yabban?

There was a hesitation before her AI answered. I am not an in-game personal assistant, Kiriai. That is something you unlock and pay for in an entirely different game path.

But you know what she just said?

Of course.

Kiriai thought for a moment. She needed to frame the request in Yabban's training language. A sudden idea made her smile.

When I leveled up your autonomy, you could offer unsolicited strategy advice, right?

Correct.

Could you advise me about the upcoming training, my choices and which you think would be the most beneficial to my martial art skills?

Kiriai felt a pulse of amusement along her mental link to the ancient gaming AI. Sometimes she still felt a flash of surprise at how normal the trainer's presence in her mind felt now. Yabban's accidental addition to her fighting implant so long ago had turned into the best thing to happen to her fighting career.

As your martial arts trainer, I would recommend not quitting the brawlers during initiation by walking up to that stand, taking the armband and choosing to join Chief Kosui's 'forcers instead.

What?

Kiriai glanced at the ornate wooden stand two assistants had just set down in front of the sensei. With a flourish, the imposing woman connected the armband to a gold clip at the top and let go. It fluttered down, hanging there, taunting. Behind the row of senseis, the ranks of brawlers looked on, impassive. They must have all refused the same offer during their own brawler initiations.

Sensei Hisho turned and spoke, her voice almost friendly as she addressed the spectators to either side. "Crew and household members, you will be sorted and escorted to orientations discussing your roles, and responsibilities and resources available. You will attend classes and at times participate with your initiate's training during the next month."

Then she turned back to the short row of initiates. Her expression hardened. "Initiates, we will give you your gear and an orientation of our facilities. Afterward, I suggest you make an early night of it. Tomorrow we will find out what you are truly made of."

Complete silence greeted her pronouncement. Kiriai knew there was no way she would ever quit and take a 'forcer position. Now she just had to prove it during the next month of training.

"Dismissed!"

The room erupted into sound and movement as everyone relaxed, and officials began calling and sorting various crew members. Kiriai went up on her tiptoes to try to see her people.

Tomi was the only one she could easily pick out. When he saw her, he gave her an encouraging wave before turning back to the official addressing his group.

"Initiates! Follow me, please." An impatient man holding a clipboard barked the command and, without waiting for a response, spun on his heel and began marching toward a smaller exit door on the other end of the hall from where her crew had been sitting. Kiriai hesitated before hurrying to fall into line.

What exactly will tomorrow be like? she wondered, trying to quash her growing feelings of trepidation.

Will you remember me tomorrow? Yabban suddenly asked in her mind.

Kiriai cocked her head to the side as the crowd parted to let their group pass.

What kind of question is that? Of course I will.

Knock, knock?

Kiriai felt a half-smile emerge as she followed the other initiates and left her crew behind. At least she had Yabban with her to face whatever torments they had in store for her.

Who's there? She humored her AI trainer's penchant for telling jokes.

See? You already forgot me!

Kiriai snickered. The burly man in front of her looked back at her, and she quickly schooled her expression.

Tomorrow wouldn't be all bad with at least one friend along for the ride.

CHAPTER TWO

"Up! Up!"

Adrenaline surged through Kiriai, and she leaped out of her cot. She almost stumbled, one foot getting tangled in the bedding as she fought to her feet, fists raised before she was fully awake. Chaos filled the spacious barracks the new initiates had been assigned for the month. Kiriai blinked, trying desperately to figure out what was happening. Her fellow initiates were scrambling everywhere, the white of their identical sleeping clothes a stark contrast to the black of the intruders. Without warning, something smacked the back of her head at the same instant her feet were swept out from under her. She barely managed to catch herself before her face hit the polished wooden floor of the barracks.

"Push-up positions! Now! Why can't you initiates follow simple commands?"

Kiriai shook her head to clear away the last cobwebs of sleep from her mind and made a snap decision to fall into line until she knew more. She placed her hands shoulder-width apart, straightened her back and held her position. She scanned the chaos that had invaded their peaceful barracks so early that it was still dark out. Light from lanterns made shadows flicker across the figures in the room. Some, like her, were holding a push-up position. One initiate kept trying to get up and multiple attackers knocked him down with ease, as they continued yelling at him to comply. A woman wasn't getting out of bed fast enough and two men heaved the edge of the mattress, dumping her to the floor in a heap. It didn't take long before every initiate was holding a plank position. Invaders stalked around them in circles, using hands and feet to adjust small imperfections. It was obvious now that she was fully awake. These were senseis or other brawlers enlisted to help with the initiation.

Kiriai felt small tremors in her arms, a mix of tension and the rush of adrenaline from the unexpected attack. To either side of her, she heard the other brawlers in similar states, some quiet, others breathing raggedly. Kiriai clenched her teeth before letting out a slow breath. After yesterday's introduction, she'd suspected this would not be easy. And it was just getting started.

"At ease," said a droll voice from the direction of the entrance to the barracks. The invaders moved back and arrayed them-selves into a straight line a few feet behind the line of shaky initiates.

"You too," the woman said. No one moved.

"She means you, idiots. Stand up," hissed someone from behind Kiriai, and she felt a foot smack into her lower leg.

Without second-guessing herself, Kiriai jumped to her feet and stepped into a ready stance, hands held low with fists clenched loosely in front of her.

Walking toward them was a woman who looked so unimpres-sive that it seemed far-fetched that the line of invaders would obey her with such alacrity. Something about her seemed famil-iar. Her sandy hair was tied up in a sloppy ponytail, the impatient kind used to keep hair back instead of for appearance's sake. She looked less than pleased to be here this early. Kiriai could empathize with that.

Her plain black gi looked to be made of a superior fabric, but it was hard to tell for sure. It lacked any of the subtle embellishments that went along with expensive tailoring. She dragged the wooden stand from yesterday behind her with complete disregard. When she came to a stop, she tipped it to a standing position and let go, making the 'forcer armband swing wildly for a moment.

As Kiriai's gaze moved up to her face, she found startling blue eyes staring back at her, one eyebrow raised. Kiriai flushed at being caught. As she dropped her gaze, she saw the other initiates had quickly followed her lead and were also standing at the ready. With a start, Kiriai suddenly remembered where she'd seen the woman before. She was the sensei from yesterday who'd seemed so bored at the opening ceremony.

"I am Sensei Nigai. Not that it matters much to you. Your job is to hate me and especially my trainers. Their job is to pummel you into submission so you'll grab this armband here and join the 'forcers. My trainers have instructions to pay special attention to those of you who've managed to irritate powerful people." The woman stopped and sighed with a tired expression. "Pummeling newbies into submission doesn't require much talent, but like you, I have to obey those who have more power than I do, and this is what they want out of me. Your job is to do everything I want, and everything my trainers tell you, because we have more power than you."

Kiriai tried not to let her shock at Nigai's words show in her expression. The eight of them had fought the best fighters of all four hoods to make it this far. They were officially brawlers, for ancestors' sake. The initiation was supposed to hone their fighting skills and give them a chance to integrate with the other brawlers, not make them want to quit. First the push yesterday to join the Chief's 'forcers, and now this sensei was blatantly mentioning prejudices and power plays?

Either Kiriai didn't succeed in masking her reaction, or her fellow initiates felt the same, because Nigai started laughing. It was a chilling laugh, without hope, and it made Kiriai shiver.

"What?" said Nigai with a bark. "Don't tell me you've made it this far without having the facts of life explained to you? Those with power get to do what they want to those with less. Ask anyone who's been around Chief Kosui during his recent rampage, if you don't believe me. Everyone with any sense is hunkering down and following orders." The woman moved with a feline grace as she spoke, pacing back and forth in front of her captive audience. The glimpse of the warrior under the unassuming clothes was scary. She stopped and the glint in her eye made Kiriai hope someone else had attracted her attention.

"Here, let me show you. Brawler Gebi, get up here," Nigai said with a bark of command in her voice.

A woman raced past them and snapped to attention three feet in front of Nigai. Brawler Gebi executed a perfect bow and straightened with a snap, ready for orders.

Nigai looked back at the initiates. "See? I have more power than Gebi here and she knows it. So she has to do whatever I want without complaint, just like I have to obey those above me. Consider this your first lesson. Welcome to the brawlers, kids."

Kiriai relaxed, thinking the show was over. But Nigai turned back to Gebi, expression hardening. "Sit down, Gebi."

The woman dropped to the floor instantly, legs crossed and back straight.

"Stand up," said Nigai, and Gebi obeyed just as quickly.

Kiriai held herself still, uneasy about where this was headed. She heard someone shifting next to her and knew she wasn't the only one.

"Hands up, above your head," said Nigai.

Gebi's hands shot up without hesitation.

"Don't move, except to breathe."

And then with no warning the sensei punched Gebi directly in the stomach. Hard.

A grunt escaped Gebi. Kiriai could see her torso flex and tighten, but the woman's stoic mask didn't budge. And to Kiriai's surprise, she kept both hands in position above her head.

"Aww, so well-trained, don't you think?" Nigai asked with a smile as she turned back to the initiates. "Now, as the brawlers behind you will attest, while I'm not the nicest person, I try to be fair."

Sensei Nigai turned back to Gebi. "Fighting stance, Brawler Gebi."

In a flash, Gebi was in position and she suddenly looked dangerous.

Nigai scanned the room with the row of beds along one wall and backed up with lazy movements to the large open space on the other side of the room. Then, she stopped, tipped her head side-to-side and let out a sigh. One foot stepped back into a shallow stance and Nigai waved a hand at Gebi. "Come try to hit me back, Brawler Gebi. I'll give you a fair chance."

Kiriai saw Gebi's mask slip as a familiar eagerness filled her eyes. The other brawler wasn't much taller than Kiriai. Gebi probably outweighed her by half and moved with a fighter's economy of motion. Her dark chestnut hair was cut in short spikes that made it easy to see her blue fighter's implant on her neck with two black stripes that matched the ones on the belt tied at her waist. Her high cheekbones framed eyes that focused on the sensei's figure across from her.

It seemed as if the rest of the room's occupants held their breath as Gebi stalked toward their instructor. Nigai barely moved. She didn't even have her guard up, and Kiriai wondered why Gebi was exercising so much caution.

"If you take any longer . . ." Nigai began.

Before the sensei could finish her sentence, Gebi lunged forward with a kick that flicked up from the floor. She followed it with a lead hand punch moving so fast, an invisible string seemed to have yanked it forward. Nigai waited until the last moment to respond, and Kiriai was sure she would see their instructor's head snap back from a punch at any moment. Instead, Sensei Nigai leaned to one side followed by a turn and spin that made all of Gebi's attacks miss their marks. Kiriai could have sworn one of Gebi's punches brushed against the sensei's cheeks. Kiriai's eyes widened. She'd only seen this kind of fighting on the screens, never in person.

Before the younger brawler's foot had even landed from her kick, she stumbled forward, hands flailing. Kiriai didn't even see what Nigai did, but the sensei didn't pursue her advantage. In a moment, Gebi caught her balance and spun back to face her sensei. She attacked again, lightning-fast but just as unable to land a blow against her sensei. The more experienced woman was untouchable in a way Kiriai's eyes couldn't follow.

Watching the amazing display of skill, desire and worry clashed inside Kiriai. If she could learn moves like that, she'd be unbeatable in the ring. Too bad there wasn't time to learn them and then take them home to teach the Jitaku scrappers. This kind of skill would have helped them hold on to the territory Raibaru had been whittling away at over the year-long war.

Now, her home had the two options that she and her crew had been endlessly debating. The first, and best, plan was to find reinforcement scrappers to send home so they could spell Jitaku's weary scrappers, who were being beaten into the ground by Raibaru's seemingly endless supply of fresh fighters. Or, if the worst happened and Raibaru won a majority of Jitaku Hood, the fight would move to the burb level. Then the Southern Burb brawlers would be the only ones left to defend her home from conquest by their enemy, Western Burb.

But she was nowhere close to the skill of these brawlers and would have little if any role if it came to that. Kiriai's heart sank. Fighting had always been her talent, and she rose to every challenge, excited to improve. But now, how could she get to this level of fighting in time to help save her home?

Kiriai clenched her jaw. Somehow, she and her crew had to make their first plan succeed. They would force the other hoods to send reinforcements by any means necessary. And soon, before time ran out.

Nigai had straightened with a chuckle and made a pushing motion with one hand. "That's all you get, Gebi. One chance to hit me back. You failed, but"—the older woman brushed one hand across her cheek—"you came closer than anyone has in quite some time. Nicely done. Back in line, now."

"Thank you, Sensei," said Gebi before spinning and jogging back to her position. Kiriai caught the glimpse of a tight smile as she ran past.

When everyone was in position again, Sensei Nigai moved back in front of them and . . . yawned.

It took great force of will for Kiriai not to follow suit.

"I hate getting up early and am only here because it's required of me. But I have taught you a lesson and demonstrated fighting skills, which means my responsibilities are done. Back to bed for me." She stopped and looked at the back row of brawlers. "Brawler Gebi, with your show of skill today, I think I'll turn these babies over to you for the rest of the month. You are now officially the Head Trainer. Try to find out if they have what it takes to join your ranks." Sensei Nigai aimed a cheerful look at them and then added, "Oh, and make them hurt."

Without another word the strange sensei turned and meandered out of the room. By the time she had disappeared, Trainer Gebi was standing in front of them, and Kiriai groaned inwardly at the look on her face.

CHAPTER THREE

"Why does everyone keep blaming machine intelligence for the end of the world? Human beings built those machines and programmed them with specific instructions. Then our enemies figured out how to hack in, to bring the entire world crashing down around us. AI weapon systems, nukes, guns, they are all tools used by us. We're the ones who destroyed our world, and we're the ones who have to rebuild it."

— Journal of Elliot Tucker, Leader of Idaho Compound and future Founding Father of Chikara City. Oath Keepers Archive of Truth, Volume 2

Trainer Gebi waited until Sensei Nigai exited the far end of the barracks before she turned back to the row of initiates staring at her, silent and waiting.

"Well, now that that's over, it's time for us to have some fun," she said and waved at her fellow brawlers to join her. The other fighters sauntered around to take their places on either side of her. Gebi's smile was the opposite of reassuring. "As you heard, my name is Brawler Gebi, but to you, for the next month, you will address me as Trainer. You will answer, 'Yes, Trainer' or 'No, Trainer' when I ask you a question. Do you understand?"

The beat of silence after her question seemed to enrage her.

"I repeat: Do you understand me?"

Kiriai wasn't the only one who flinched, but she readily joined in with the other initiates in yelling, "Yes, Trainer!"

"Follow me to the training hall. Now!" Gebi spun on her heel and jogged toward the doorway.

Taken by surprise again, none of the initiates moved . . . until the yelling started.

"Move it! Move it!" One of the brawlers stepped forward, spit flying as he screamed. Kiriai's pulse jumped and her first instinct made her want to drop into a fighting stance, hands raised. As soon as her mind caught up, she knew it would be a bad idea. Even worse would be to let a hint of her humor at the situation show on her expression. Now that she was feeling more awake, the haranguing felt familiar. Kiriai sent a mental thanks to Trainer Kakyo from the youth arenas, who'd used similar tactics to prepare them for the stress of fighting.

A lean man next to Kiriai had already moved, racing after Brawler Gebi. Face carefully blank, Kiriai fell in right behind him.

"What? You don't know how to run?"

The screaming continued behind her as the rest of the initiates moved.

"Go! Go!"

The short line of eight initiates ran through the hallway, still in their sparse sleeping clothes, bare feet soundless on tightly woven rugs. This hallway was much more spartan compared to the entrance they'd taken yesterday. Moments later, they followed Gebi through a smaller doorway that dumped them into the far side of the large training hall. Lanterns barely lit the vast space, which swallowed the sounds of their movement. Everything looked much more menacing and eerie compared to yesterday's celebration. Gebi led them in a run past shelves and containers filled with training equipment of every sort. Kiriai wanted to stop and look closer but knew that she'd have plenty of chances soon. The corner of one side of her mouth turned up at the thought. She'd never been afraid of hard work, and if the brawler organization would help her hone her fighting skills . . . well, the thought sent a thrill through her. Fighting had always been her first love.

Kiriai was happy to leave the political maneuvering to Tomi and Shisen. They would pump their contacts for information and wrangle advantages to help Jitaku's quest for reinforcements. Kiriai would much rather ignore all that, including the powerful people entangled in the mess, and focus on her fighting. Her excitement wavered as she remembered the skill level she'd seen in the short confrontation between Sensei Nigai and Brawler Gebi. Could she improve that much in the time she had?

"Toes on the line! Arms out! Space yourselves until your fingers don't touch!"

The man she'd been following ran and stopped on the line indicated. He snapped to attention before holding both of his arms out in a T-shape while staring straight ahead. Kiriai decided he'd be a good one to follow and mimicked his actions. Frozen in the requested position, she didn't look as she heard the rest of their group fall in. It took only moments. It wasn't as if they were new recruits. Everyone here had been fighting for years, and obeying a demanding sensei was child's play now that they were all wide awake.

"Attention!"

Feet snapped together and hands slapped against the thin fabric of their shorts.

Brawler Gebi paced in front of them, staring at each of them.

When she came to Kiriai, a look of derision flashed across her face so fast, Kiriai thought she might have imagined it.

"So maybe not all of you are worthless," Gebi said as she returned to front and center. She was looking at Kiriai when she said *worthless*. Kiriai forced herself not to react. What was going on here?

"The ability to follow an order well," said Trainer Gebi as she moved her gaze up and down their line, "while a beginning skill, is one you will need every day of your new life as a brawler." She stopped and smirked before continuing. "If you make it, that is. Sensei Nigai gave you a small taste of your new life. We brawlers belong to one man, Chief Kengen Kosui of Southern Burb, and anyone he delegates control to. We obey absolutely and we do this willingly. Willingly! Why?" She stopped to look at her fellow brawlers, who had lined up on either side of her, four on either side. When she looked back, her expression was fierce and a touch fanatic. "Because Chief Kosui keeps our burb, our hoods, and our families safe from our enemies." She paused and her statement echoed in the huge hall that dwarfed their small group. Then she grinned. "And because he shares all the credits and power with his loyal fighters."

A handful of the brawlers chuckled at her words, grins of agreement on their faces.

Gebi clapped her hands together, face stern again. "The 'forcer armband will always be here waiting for any of you who want the easy life. Feel free to quit at any time." She pointed toward the doorway they'd come through, and Kiriai saw that someone had placed the post in a prominent position just inside the hall. Kiriai pursed her lips. Like she would throw everything away for the power offered by the limp armband that hung there.

"Now, let's get started honing your bodies into something close to the condition expected of Southern Burb brawlers." Gebi turned to her fellow trainers. "T-drills. Grab body shields, then positions!"

The other brawlers sprang into action, moving as fast as Gebi had under Sensei Nigai's orders. Kiriai held her attention stance as each brawler ran to equipment shelves, grabbed a shield and raced back to line up facing the initiates, leaving about ten feet between each other. As they stepped back into stances, the brawlers slid their arms into the straps on the shields and braced them against their forward legs. The shields looked much better than the ones Kiriai trained with back home. Burb craftsmen had made them out of a tight canvas weave with double-reinforced stitching. No fraying fabric or straps for burb brawler equipment. Randomly, Kiriai wondered what they filled them with. Probably something better than the lumpy mishmash of rags shoved into the ones she normally used. They definitely didn't stint on credits for their fighters here.

"Spread out to face one of your trainers. Now! Move!" barked Gebi. Kiriai responded quickly, ready to get to work. Talking was overrated.

Once the initiates were in position, Gebi stepped up and took the pad from the man closest to her. "Brawler Akumu, let's show the newbs how this is done."

The lean man grinned and moved across from Trainer Gebi, giving the initiate there a none-too-gentle nudge out of the way.

"Reverse punches. Move!"

The brawler surged forward across the open space and slammed a solid fist into Gebi's shield as soon as he was close enough. Without pausing, he moved with fast lateral steps to his right until he reached the next trainer in line. Another solid punch and he was returning to the left, where he hit Gebi's pad again as he passed. Kiriai saw the muscles of her body flex with the impact and marveled at how hard the man was hitting while moving so fast. He reached the woman to Gebi's left, punched her shield and reversed his motion so fast his body leaned at a sharp angle. A final punch to Gebi's pad and he was churning his feet to run backward back to his position, where he snapped to attention, drill complete.

Standing next to him, Kiriai could hardly hear him breathing much. Not only were these brawlers a few levels above her in skill, they were in amazing physical condition. How long had it taken them to get that good?

"That is the T-drill. It will improve your stamina, agility and foot speed. You better be fast or your neighbor will run into you. Your turn. Ready?"

"Yes, Trainer," Kiriai yelled with the others and pushed her worries aside for another time.

"Move!"

Kiriai ran as fast as she could, her bare feet gripping the polished wood floor as she changed directions while trying to settle her weight to put a decent power behind her punches. Out of the corner of her eye, she saw two initiates barely avoid a collision. She didn't let it distract her, pushing herself to move faster. Back at attention, her knuckles stung and she could feel the skin on the bottom of her feet burning after only the first repetition.

"Again!"

Kiriai launched herself forward again.

And again.

"Faster!"

Her lungs burned and she could taste copper at the back of her throat.

"Is that all you've got?"

The trainers yelled and jabbed their punching shields forward as her arms tired and her punches lost power.

"The armband is right over there if you want to quit already."

The initiate at the end of the line to Kiriai's left broke first, bending forward, hands on his thighs, sucking in deep gulps of air.

"Again!"

Kiriai forced her legs to move despite the wooden feeling of overused muscles. She managed yet another repetition. Barely.

When the initiate didn't move forward with the rest of the group, Gebi charged at him, yelling. "Move it! Again! Don't just stand there. Do you want to be a brawler?"

The man's head lifted and he gave her a faint nod.

"Then move it! Now! Go!"

He moved forward at what could only generously be called a jog just as the rest of the group was running backward in the final movement of the T-drill.

And then it happened. Whether it was her burning muscles, exhaustion or the distraction of the yelling trainers, Kiriai lost focus for a brief second and didn't pick her foot up far enough. Her heel caught on the floor and the slight stumble was enough to send her falling backward to the floor. At the last moment, she curled her back and turned to hit with her shoulder, instinctively working to protect her back and arm.

"What are you doing?" Gebi leapt forward to yell at her.

Kiriai tried to scramble back to her feet, but her body was happy right where it was. The thoughts running through her mind weren't any help either. She had already failed after the first exercise on the first morning of brawler training . . . all before breakfast. This was much harder than she'd expected. How was she going to survive a month of this, much less excel? And here she'd thought she was in decent condition.

"Any time now, initiate. Stand up!"

Kiriai rolled to the side and got herself to one knee.

"How did you even make it here?"

Gebi was leaning forward, yelling so close to Kiriai that it made her ears ring.

"Who did you pay off to get here? Did you cheat to get here? What? You want to quit now that someone is making you do some real work for once?"

Kiriai's gaze snapped to Gebi's at the personal attacks and saw only malice there.

"Aw, there is a little fight in you after all. More than I heard."

Kiriai clenched her teeth, pulled her feet under her and pushed to her feet. She wasn't imagining this. Gebi had a problem with her, a personal one.

Lionel Sosa's opinion was that, "Anger does not solve problems— anger only makes things worse." Practicing your Centering during these conditioning drills would help you level up multiple skills at the same time.

Yabban's calm statement punctured the emotions building up in Kiriai. She sucked in a breath, turned from Gebi and aimed her gaze straight ahead. Kiriai focused on calming her breathing as her lungs heaved from the effort she'd been expending.

Thanks, Yabban. I thought I had kicked this anger thing. Guess not.

Why was the apple mean and angry?

I'm not an apple, Yabban.

Gebi was yelling something next to her ear, but Kiriai held her position, using the easy banter with her AI to distract her.

It was a crab apple.

Kiriai smiled inside, and the last of her anger fizzled away. Her pulse was slowing, but the rest of her body was slipping into that shaky stage that came after pushing too hard.

"Line up! Attention!"

Glad that she seemed to have lost Gebi's attention, Kiriai tried to psych herself up for whatever was coming next.

"Trainers. Line up for the gauntlet."

The initiates watched as the brawlers ran back to the equipment racks and returned with padded clubs in addition to their shields.

That couldn't be good.

The trainers split into two lines, four on each side and facing each other, ten feet between their rows. When they were all in place, on some unspoken signal, they all yelled "Oda!" and dropped back as one into fighting stances. The practice bats sat on their shoulders while they braced the shields on their forward legs.

Gebi moved to stand at one end of the gauntlet. "Initiates! Line up behind me now."

Everyone quickly obeyed. Kiriai stifled a groan when one of the other initiates slowed at a crucial moment, leaving Kiriai to be the first in line behind Gebi. Kiriai made a mental note to remember that trick.

"Pay attention! I will now demonstrate the gauntlet. I will attack each of my opponents with a front kick as fast as I can while still maintaining my form. Move fast. Hit hard. Don't get hit. Do you understand?"

"Yes, Trainer!"

Kiriai's inner rebel wondered briefly what would happen if she yelled "No, Trainer!" instead.

Shaking off the distracting thought, Kiriai focused on breathing to her usual slow count and pushed her emotions and body to settle as she used the small break to center herself.

In front of her, she watched Gebi fly through the gauntlet, her kicks slamming into the shields with powerful thuds. She maintained a perfect fighting stance, her upper body swaying and moving to let the padded clubs whistle past her head without landing. The other brawlers were grinning, their clubs moving as fast as she did, whipping in deceptive patterns to try to catch the wily trainer with the single attack allotted them as she sped by.

A younger man whooped with glee when his pad grazed Gebi's shoulder, and she tipped her head with a grin in passing.

Mere seconds after starting, Gebi reached the end of the drill and turned to face Kiriai, who stood lined up at the head of the initiates. Her grin disappeared and her expression hardened.

"Initiate Kiriai. Let's see what you have."

Steeled against whatever grudge Gebi had against her, Kiriai focused on pushing her tired muscles to respond despite the short recovery time.

"Back to your barracks! Get cleaned up and dressed. Eat breakfast. You have exactly one hour and I expect you to be back here in the exact same spots. Do you understand?"

"Yes, Trainer," they all yelled. Kiriai wasn't the only one whose voice had an undercurrent of relief to it. At least the last drill had been for one initiate at a time, giving the others a chance to recover between repetitions. Kiriai barely noticed the crawl of sweat that ran down the side of her face and neck. The hour of early morning training had felt like ten, and Kiriai didn't dare think about surviving the rest of the day. Her lungs no longer burned, and her face felt hot enough to fry an egg on. Plus, her hair, tunic and shorts were sweat-soaked. She'd never trained this hard. It was becoming obvious that the brawlers' skills were on a different level than she was used to, and they worked extremely hard to get that way. How was she supposed to measure up? Jitaku Hood didn't have much time.

Without another word, the group of trainers turned and jogged away, heading to a different doorway.

Left alone, Kiriai felt her body sag. She wasn't the only one.

"Well, that was fun," said the man who had been the first to fail at the start of their training. He turned and headed back the way they had come. "We only have an hour," he said as he looked back at them over his shoulder and waved one hand at the time on one of the wallscreens. "We'd better hurry."

CHAPTER FOUR

"Initiates' table is over there," a woman said with a dismissive glance and pointed to her right when Kiriai, tray in hand, tried to sit at an empty spot at her table.

Flushing, Kiriai looked across the bustling eatery and saw that, yes, there was a large, mostly empty table in the center of the room. Two of her fellow initiates already sat, eating with single-minded focus. All she could see was the tops of their heads, damp from the shower, as they leaned over their trays. Kiriai hurried in their direction, knowing how little time they had. She reminded herself not to eat too much, especially considering what tortures Gebi might have in store for them.

"I'm Brawler Kiriai," she said as she set her tray down next to the dark-haired man, whom she recognized as the one who had tired out first. She was pretty sure his name was Jimu. She knew how he fought, from analyzing him last month in the brawler tournament, but she was embarrassed to admit she hadn't spent too much effort remembering names.

His head popped up, and he forced a swallow down before replying. "Don't let any of them catch you saying that," he said with a tip of his head to the rest of the room. "Apparently they don't consider us brawlers like them until we suffer through the next month without quitting." He shrugged a shoulder and gave her a half smile. "Misery always loves company. They had to suffer through it when they started, so somehow they enjoy making sure we do the same."

Kiriai set her tray down and pulled back a chair to sit. He reached out a hand. "*Initiate* Jimu here," he said, injecting a hefty dose of sarcasm into the title.

Kiriai relaxed and shook his hand, letting her defenses drop a little for the first time since Sensei Nigai shocked them out of bed this morning. "*Initiate* Kiriai," she said with half a grin before reaching for her spoon and shoveling a big bite of a colorful egg-and-vegetable dish into her mouth. She tried not to moan at the burst of flavors and textures. At least their initiation didn't bar them from the brawlers' food. That in itself almost made up for the rest of it.

Jimu smiled and nodded at her reaction. After he swallowed, he paused for a second. His expression sobered and he leaned in to speak quietly. "You seem to be a decent sort. Don't let all the nastiness get to you. All of us fought and earned our spots here." He waved a hand at the rest of the table. "We're brawlers and they can't take that away from us if we don't give it to them. Just remember that, no matter how bad it gets. We're brawlers."

"And we'll learn to fight as good as them?" Kiriai let the words and doubt slip out before she could stop them.

His eyebrows shot up. "Them? Of course. They all sat right where we are sitting when they started. Just give it some time and we'll be just as good."

Kiriai forced a smile in thanks for the encouragement as a painful knot tightened in her chest.

Time. That was one thing she and the people of Jitaku Hood didn't have.

A tray clattered down across the table from her, jarring her from her thoughts. The tall woman didn't even look at her. She was eating almost before she'd fully sat down. She'd tied her light cinnamon hair back, revealing features a little too rugged to be pretty and now filled with a focused intensity. Kiriai recognized her as the first brawler Chief Kosui had chosen at the end of the tournament. She'd seemed friendly enough from the short interactions they'd had a few weeks ago.

"Good to see you again, Initiate Jiseki," Kiriai said, aiming for a cordial tone.

The woman looked up and stared at her, silent as she chewed. When she finished, instead of answering, she let out a short disgusted huff, shook her head and returned her attention to her meal.

The unexpected rebuff stung, especially after Jimu's friendliness. More than that, Kiriai had no idea what had prompted it. She hardly knew Jiseki.

"Rumors are the bane of Southern Core. Just ignore them," muttered Jimu without looking at her as he stood, tray in hand, plates empty. Before she could ask for details, he strode quickly toward the cleanup area.

His fast pace reminded Kiriai to hurry, and she followed suit, polishing off her single plate of food. Across from her, Jiseki remained silent as she ate. The rest of the initiates now sat at the table. Like Jiseki, they kept to themselves, eating with none of the camaraderie, or even the friendly challenging, Kiriai was used to among a group of fighters assigned together.

A sudden wave of homesickness washed over her. She wanted her friends and family around her instead of these touchy strangers. Even the battles in her home arena with fellow scrappers took on a nostalgic glow compared to this new world of skills that made her feel like a beginner again. She prayed that Tomi and Shisen had good news when she met with everyone tonight. By tonight, she'd really need some.

CHAPTER FIVE

"We'll probably never know how it all started. Was it a
concerted effort by a powerful country or the focused work
of a small group of fanatics? Does it matter? What we do
know is that by the end of the first month, almost all of
mankind's deadliest creations had been released."
  — Journal of Army Reserve Captain Jasmyn Starks, Army
Research Lab, WSMR, New Mexico. Oath Keepers Archive
of Truth, Volume 4

"Ah, at least the lot of you can be relied on to be punctual,"
Gebi said as she paced back and forth in front of the stiff
line of initiates, all standing in ready stances, eyes forward. "I
hope you enjoyed your break and are fully recovered from this
morning's little warm-up."

There was an almost inaudible snort from Jimu's direction to
her left, and Kiriai barely restrained a smile. Good thing, because
Gebi's head snapped in their direction as she examined faces,
looking for the culprit. No one moved.

She charged in Kiriai's direction. "You think this is funny, Initiate?"

"No, Trainer!" Kiriai belted out in the loud voice that Trainer Kakyo had instilled in her.

"Do you think being a brawler is something easy?"

"No, Trainer!" Kiriai steeled herself to keep yelling until Gebi tired of harassing her.

"Is protecting Southern Burb from Western Burb a game to you?"

"No, Trainer!" Jimu's words from breakfast echoed in her mind. Being a brawler might not be a game, but this initiation was . . . a mind game. They couldn't do a thing to her, though, if she didn't quit.

"During this month, we will train your bodies to be faster and stronger than they've ever been before. We will also drill basic principles into your thick heads until they are instinctive and require no thought." Gebi stopped and looked at them with a warning glare. "If you think too much during a fight, you will lose. You will practice every one of these skills until you can do them in your sleep. Do you understand?"

"Yes, Trainer!" they all shouted in unison.

Kiriai was just happy to listen to Gebi drone for as long as possible. It gave her overused muscles more time to recover from the morning.

She is making some good points. Perhaps you should listen to her and focus on improving your foundation.

Yabban's words startled Kiriai. She forced herself not to dismiss them out of hand just because she disliked the head trainer. While her crew worked to get reinforcements, Kiriai needed to do her best to improve her fighting abilities. If the battle for Jitaku made it to the burb level, she didn't want to be left out of the equation because she wasn't good enough. Besides, she'd seen a tiny sample of Gebi's fighting, and she didn't have to like the woman to want to move like her.

"All right. First things first. Let's learn how to stand," said Gebi with a smile that didn't reach her eyes. "Left forward stances. Whichever style you favor. Move!"

Kiriai barely stopped herself from rolling her eyes as she dropped her right foot back and braced her heel against the ground. She shifted her weight forward in the style of the beginning stance Yabban had taught her. Next to her, the other initiates all moved into their versions of the stance, weight shifting forward and feet turning at slightly different angles. Fighters of any caliber rarely used this type of stance in actual fighting because with the back foot braced firmly against the ground and the weight so far forward, it was immobile for all practical purposes. It was a perfect example of being caught flat-footed. Maybe Trainer Gebi wouldn't teach them anything valuable after all.

"Trainers, grab shields. Line up facing the initiates." The other brawlers hurried to obey and in seconds there was one in front of each of them.

A woman about Kiriai's size faced her with a stony look on her face that promised little mercy.

"Your job, Initiates, is to stand there. Do you understand?"

"Yes, Trainer!"

"Do not move backward or sideways and whatever you do, do not fall down. Understand?"

"Yes, Trainer!"

"Well," she said in a softer, smug voice, "let's see how well you can follow simple instructions. Trainers, attack."

The woman in front of Kiriai lunged forward and bashed her padded shield into Kiriai almost before Gebi had completed the order.

Taken by surprise, Kiriai felt the shield smash into her, the brunt of the force hitting into her front knee and lead hand. Thankfully, Kiriai had bent her knee and her foot gripped the ground. But it wasn't enough. The force threw Kiriai back, her stance breaking as she flung her hands up for balance. She kept her feet at least. Barely.

"What kind of stance is that? Why can't you hold a simple stance?"

Ignoring the yelling as best she could, Kiriai quickly moved into her forward stance again, raised her hands and braced her legs.

"Attack!" yelled Gebi.

The woman didn't hesitate to slam the pad into Kiriai again with tremendous strength. This time Kiriai kept her feet in their position, but her whole body bent backward under the force of the blow. Her lead hand snapped back so fast she hit herself in the lip.

"That's better. At least you didn't go flying back like the first time," said the trainer, facing her, already back in position.

Without hesitating, Kiriai shifted her weight forward, dropped her center of gravity lower and gripped the ground with her toes and edges of her feet. She sucked her lip into her mouth and tasted blood. She was determined to keep her stance intact this time.

"Attack!"

The canvas of the padded shield burned the skin of her forearm with the force of the blow. This time Kiriai barely moved under the bashing attack, but she felt the power of it ripple through her body and muscles, driving her rear heel into the ground.

"So you can learn! After only three attacks, you're up to a beginner level of maintaining a solid base," said Gebi, who had come up beside the other trainer, unnoticed.

Kiriai ignored the malice in the head trainer's expression, instead keeping her focus on the trainer in front of her. She wouldn't let her take her by surprise.

"Attack!"

Again and again the hated shield slammed head-on into her

body. Whatever padding the shield had seemed to harden into something painful with each successive blow.

A different kind of weariness from this morning's seeped into her muscles as the unrelenting blows continued. Kiriai's rear knee wanted to bend, and her arms struggled not to droop with each subsequent attack. Just as her resolve wavered, Gebi called a halt, but not for a much-needed break.

"Neutral stances. Move!"

There wasn't much pep in the initiates' movement, but Kiriai saw them all obey, shifting their weight back to center and changing their foot positions.

"Trainers, move and shift. From the front and behind. Continue until I say halt. Attack!"

Like predators, the trainers circled the line of initiates, and Kiriai felt a blow slam into her back. She fought to keep her position, but couldn't help letting her feet take a short step forward. Immediately, she moved back into position and worked harder to strengthen her stance. Kiriai bent her knees farther and pushed down with her legs, almost as if she were trying to drill her bare feet through the floor. Every muscle in her legs shook with tension, poised to resist the next blow.

The next one hit from the front, thrown by a female trainer who, while she hit fast, lacked the bulk of the others. It stung, but Kiriai held her position, unmoving.

She smiled inside, but was careful not to let it show on her face. There was no need to antagonize the trainers. This wasn't that hard of a skill, after all.

Blow after blow slammed into her. The ones from the front weren't so bad, because there was plenty of warning. But with the trainers jogging around them mixed with the grunts and blows all along the line, it was difficult to anticipate the ones from behind.

Kiriai snuck a quick glance behind herself, hoping for a little more warning.

"Eyes forward, Initiate!" came the command from the angry face of the trainer directly behind her. "If we wanted you to be looking back, we would have told you. Do you understand?"

"Yes, Trainer!" Kiriai yelled as she snapped her eyes back to the front.

A split-second later, the trainer's shield slammed into her back, throwing Kiriai's torso forward and making every muscle in her back and legs object.

So maybe not so easy after all.

Smash!

Again.

The incessant punishment of the drill made her earlier strategy unsustainable. She couldn't keep every muscle tensed and flexed indefinitely, waiting for the next blow. This was stupid. She never fought like this—standing still and letting someone hit her. It went against every one of her fighting instincts. Her strengths were in her speed, movement and making sure she never stayed still long enough to take this kind of beating. Kiriai's strength slipped, every muscle in her legs down to her toes, burning and hot.

Out of necessity, Kiriai let her legs relax and straighten just a fraction. The relief was instant, and she almost groaned aloud. At the same time, she put her senses on high alert, striving for as much warning as possible to react when the next blow came.

Her break was short-lived. One trainer bashed into the initiate next to her and without pause jumped sideways to slam into her. By the grin on his face, he was enjoying himself much more than the initiates were.

Kiriai bent her knees, tightened everything to absorb the force and still felt her feet shift a few inches. This time, though, she kept her posture erect and stance balanced. As soon as the blow's power was spent, Kiriai relaxed everything again and grinned at the discovery. If she stayed poised for action, she could save energy and brace herself only when the threat materialized. Her movement felt like a young sapling that absorbed a blow but immediately sprang back into place. Even as tired as she felt, Kiriai couldn't wait for the next hit to see if she could do it again.

The trainer stopped and stared at her expression. Kiriai froze. His grin widened, and he tipped his head at her before jogging on to his next victim.

A quiet creak of a pad behind her and the quick intake of breath were her only warning for the next attack from behind. She was ready and coiled her muscles just in time. The pad drove into her back, but she absorbed the blow with her legs and feet, keeping her hands up and back straight. As soon as the incoming force stopped, Kiriai relaxed again and struggled not to smile. Sure, she hurt everywhere, bruises forming and muscles overused, but this was fun on a level only another fighter could understand.

She knew she still had a huge talent gap to overcome, but taking the first step gave her hope.

Another blow rocked into her as she flexed with it.

If I survive the training, that is.

CHAPTER SIX

Everything felt numb and Kiriai's teeth were chattering as the training assistant held up a big towel and finally indicated she could step out of the deep pool of freezing cold water. She would have thought it was a torture technique for the new initiates if she hadn't seen other brawlers pop in after a workout, strip down to underthings and step into the cold water with barely a wince.

The young man wrapped the towel around her with quick efficiency and put a mug of something hot in her hands and nodded toward the curtained alcoves. "Dry off. Take one of the mesh bags for your wet things. Put on a robe and grab your belongings. You're off to fixer room five, next hallway to the right and third room on the right. Five minutes."

She barely had a chance to nod before he scurried off to grab another towel for the next fighter. Trying hard to pretend this was all familiar to her, Kiriai headed to the row of cubicles and hooks to grab her bag, sandals and robe. Arms full, she pulled aside a curtain and stepped into an alcove and followed directions. Goosebumps popped up all over her body and the room-temperature towel felt heated against her cold skin as she rubbed herself dry. The frigid water hadn't been fun, but Kiriai had to admit that her sore muscles felt soothed and less inflamed than they had earlier. Moments later, she emerged, the cozy softness of the provided robe so luxurious, she barely felt the straps of her own bag or the mesh one she had slung over her shoulder.

Tossing the towel in a bin by the door, she walked out into the hall. There were locker rooms, the pool, and she thought the steam she'd seen escape an opened door indicated a sauna. It was disconcerting to have so many expensive resources there for the taking. It was a dream come true for a fighter. And she hadn't even seen the private training areas yet.

Is this a good time to update you on your improvements? Yabban asked in her thoughts.

Improvements? I've only been doing conditioning stuff. I thought the main game computer keeps track of stuff like stamina and agility, not you. Has that changed?

No. The main computer monitors those statistics and remains inaccessible to me. I still have no answer for the lack of connection. Perhaps we are playing in an isolated section of the game. Hacking is also a possibility. I will inform you as soon as I find new information.

Kiriai didn't correct her friend. They'd come to an impasse on the issue. Yabban insisted that the main-game AI would eventually make contact and fix everything, but Kiriai didn't force the truth on Yabban that her game, with all its programming and support, had turned to dust centuries ago in the blast.

Perhaps. But you mentioned improvements? Kiriai prompted as she exited the hallway back into the main training space. She turned and strode along the wall until she came to a hallway to her right. The faint smell of healing herbs confirmed she had the right place.

Yes. Congratulations, you have unlocked and learned the fighting principle Solid Foundation.

Kiriai stopped walking and frowned. *What kind of principle is that?*

Your ability to hold your position against outside forces. Surely you remember the trainers hitting you from all sides?

Kiriai snorted and started walking again. *Of course I do. But that's a basic principle. Surely I've used it and unlocked it before now.*

You may have accidentally used a version, but to unlock a principle, you must focus on and execute the most fundamental form of it. Cheer up, though. At least it's already leveled up to Learned with all the work you just did. Yabban's words stopped for a second and Kiriai felt a sense of satisfaction along their link, or was it glee? *I think this training will be very beneficial to your fighting skills.*

Kiriai groaned as she reached the correct door with the number five carved in strong, black relief into the rich cherry wood.

I think you just enjoy watching me suffer and even more so when it's focusing on the basics like you keep insisting I do.

No pain, no gain, said Yabban with just a touch of pleasure.

Kiriai laughed. *Now that's a wise saying I can agree with. And I need to improve as fast as possible. If this is what I have to do to get there, then pain it is.* Kiriai stretched and let out a soft groan before knocking on the door. The sooner the fixer helped her heal, the better. She'd rather have Isha's fixing help, but any help after the first day of training would be more than welcome.

The door slid open and Kiriai stared, surprised.

"Get in here already," Mikata said as she grabbed Kiriai and pulled her forward into the room.

Kiriai yelped as Mikata's hand hit a mass of bruises that had collected along her forearm today.

"Sorry," her friend said, immediately letting go. Mikata reached behind Kiriai, slid the door shut and engaged the ornate latch.

Kiriai barely noticed as her emotions threatened to overwhelm her at the full room. Tomi and Eigo sat together in a lounge against the left wall, though Tomi took almost all the space on the medium-sized sofa. A second couch held Aibo and

Shisen, whose hand on the younger girl's knee looked to be the only thing keeping Aibo from leaping up when she spotted Kiriai

To Kiriai's right stood a padded table with Isha nearby, obvious concern etched onto her face. She'd arrayed herbs and poultice supplies on the counter behind her. A pot of tea steamed on the small cast-iron stove in the corner and filled the room with a familiar aroma.

It was almost too much. Kiriai sucked in a sharp breath and ordered her eyes to stop watering. She'd just seen them all yesterday. There was no need to get so emotional.

"Looks like they cooled you down, which will help with all the damage I'm sure they did to you today. Get over here so I can finish fixing you up for another round tomorrow." The touch of command in Isha's words helped. Kiriai gave her a grateful look and strode across to the fixer's table. She began to pull off her robe and suddenly remembered her audience.

"Quit dawdling, Eigo, and bring that byobu over here," Isha said.

He jumped up and grabbed one of the standing screens along the wall and slid it across the floor until it stood between the fixer table and the sitting area. Kiriai gave him a quick nod of thanks before he slipped back behind the screen, leaving her and Isha shielded from view.

"Up on the bed, child. Let me see what they did to you."

Isha helped Kiriai out of her robe as she lay face down on the table. A sharp intake of breath made Kiriai wince.

"Ancestors," said Isha in a soft voice. "I'll never understand why you do this to yourself. If I didn't know how much you love it, I would never stand for it."

Something inside Kiriai relaxed at the familiar love and outrage she heard in Isha's voice. Kiriai let herself sink into the padded table as she felt a cool sheet drape over her back and legs.

"Can we talk now?" Tomi's deep voice asked from the other side of the byobu, making Kiriai's smile widen.

"Go ahead. Kiriai might be happy for the distraction while I work on her. She only has an hour here before she's expected at dinner and then back at her barracks for lights out."

"All right," said Tomi, "before you ask, no, it isn't normal for your entire crew to join you in your fixer appointment. But even though we've only been here a day, I decided we needed a planning and information meeting." A touch of humor entered his voice as he continued. "I cleared it with a clerk who thought it was a great idea to offer emotional support to our new brawler who was so far from home."

Kiriai chuckled and would have shaken her head if she could. Tomi was a master of sweet-talking his way into almost anything, and his skill had come in handy. Her thoughts sobered. All of Jitaku might depend on that skill now.

Tomi's next words echoed her thoughts. "Today Shisen and I have been making contacts in the offices and households of the top officials of the other three hoods. It's not looking good. We have powerful enemies and no idea who they are. In addition, I just received the results from Jitaku's battles yesterday against Raibaru. We won one and lost four, which gives Raibaru ownership of forty-five percent of our territory, the most they've controlled in the last five years. We are only a handful of losses from having Jitaku's fate become the responsibility of Chief Kosui and his brawlers."

Silence greeted his words, and suddenly Kiriai's bumps and bruises didn't seem so important anymore.

CHAPTER SEVEN

"Overwhelming force is the only way we will survive. No warning. No talking. Whenever you come across anyone weaker than you, move with decisive force. Capture them if it can be done safely. If not, kill and loot anything we can use. ZJaps rule!"

I nstructions from Kado Tagami during a ZJaps gang meeting. Week One after the Blast. Las Vegas, Nevada. Oath Keepers Archive of Truth, Volume 3

"Then we just have to work faster. How long can it take to figure out who wants to hurt us and who will help us?" Eigo's question broke the silence. "There aren't that many possibilities. They have to be leaders at the top of the three hoods or someone powerful in the burb."

"Yes," Shisen said with a scoff. "That's all. Just the leaders, their seconds and large portions of the upper staff. It might as well be thousands of possibilities given how hard it will be to get close to or spy on any of those people."

"And it's also difficult to get close to the servants and under-lings because everyone here knows exactly what we want and how desperate we are," said a soft voice.

The room quieted and Kiriai could imagine everyone staring at Aibo.

"What? Just because I'm the youngest one here doesn't mean I don't understand what's going on." The affront in her voice was easy to hear.

"No, no," said Shisen. "We know how much you do to keep everything for the crew running smoothly. It's just that you rarely join in these kinds of discussions." Without giving Aibo a chance to object, Shisen continued. "And you make a great point that we all need to think about. It explains the responses I've seen in just one day of asking questions. People have either refused to speak to me, or I've seen the greed in their eyes. They're thinking of all the demands they can make of a desperate hood."

Isha began humming quietly as she gathered items. Kiriai let out a breath along with the tension that had crept into her shoul-ders and neck listening to the crew's discussion. She couldn't really help with any of this now. Maybe once her training eased up, or she came into contact with some higher-ups—

"I can't believe Chief Kosui won't just step in and tell the hoods to send us a dozen fighters each," said Eigo, the disgust in his tone clear even without seeing his expression. "Then no one could complain about losing an advantage against their neigh-bors, and we'd have a chance to save one of his hoods. Doesn't he care about all the territory and taxes we give him?"

Kiriai focused on her Centering skill, letting her breathing and emotions calm together under her mental direction. It wouldn't do to let Eigo's anger inflame her own. Her breathing calmed further as she moved her attention to physical sensa-tions, the padded leather beneath her, the cool sheet and Isha's practiced movements. A moment later, Kiriai felt the distinctive vibration and cool metal of the fixer wand pressed against her shoulder. She relaxed further when Isha moved the device in gentle circles over Kiriai's worst bruises. Unlike her grandfather's distaste for the devices and the average fixer's tendency to rely on them exclusively, Isha was pragmatic. She usually started with a wand treatment, followed it with herbs and manipulations and finished with another wand session at the end.

"Chief Kosui's motivations and actions aren't always clear. Even Boss Akuto can't always decipher the powers in play," said Tomi. Then he stopped speaking for a moment. When he continued, his voice was uncharacteristically grim. "Before I continue, remember to keep everything we discuss here about these topics private. I trust each of you implicitly, but a reminder doesn't hurt. No sharing with anyone else, even by accident."

Kiriai heard murmurs of agreement to his request as Isha pressed the wand a bit too hard along Kiriai's lower back. When she flinched, Isha pulled back immediately. "Sorry, child. I just hate that we have to resort to all this to defend our home. Does no one know the meaning of the word *ally* anymore?"

"Isha has a point," said Tomi, making Isha's hand twitch again. Kiriai flinched at the increased pressure. Maybe combining Kiriai's fixer session with this discussion wasn't the best idea. "I believe at least one of the hood bosses is a willing ally and would help us if there was a show of support from the chief or the other bosses. When Boss Akuto met personally with the chief after the brawler tournament, he seemed to be ambivalent about losing our hood to the Westerns."

"How is that possible?" Eigo's question was full of disbelief.

Tomi's answer was tinged with resignation. "While our hood brings him income, taxes and new brawlers every year, the idea of being exempt from war altogether might be what is tempting Chief Kosui. At least that's Boss Akuto's current theory. If Southern Burb loses Jitaku and is reduced to three hoods total, City law prevents all attacks by the other burbs until he regains a hood. That would allow him unlimited time to regroup and build his strength for a comeback."

Someone scoffed in disgust. Probably Shisen.

"He'd abandon us? Just like that?" asked Aibo.

"Why would you expect anything different?" said Shisen, her tone sad, not condemning. "We are all just insignificant game pieces to those in power who do what they want with us."

"Well, don't count us out yet, my young dissident," said Tomi, his humor back in full force. "The boss reported that Kosui didn't seem to have chosen a path yet. If we figure out a way to win, he'd likely consider it a triumph of strength and fate."

"That makes little sense," said Shisen. "Does he want us to lose or not?"

"It's the fighter's way, dear," said Isha as she raised her voice to be heard through the curtain. "Tomi is saying that if we can win on our own, we will prove our strength and worth to Kosui. If not, he has pragmatic ways to take advantage of our loss."

"Yes," said Tomi. "He told Akuto he didn't plan to help or hurt, that our fate was our own."

"Also," said Mikata. "I know we haven't been here long, but have you been hearing the newest rumors about the chief?"

"Some," said Tomi. "What have you heard?"

"I noticed the fighting staff has been a little cagey if I bring up the chief," Mikata said, "but I just figured some kind of disciplining or punishment had happened."

"Well, maybe, but not between the chief and his brawler like you're thinking," said Shisen. "One of my contacts said the city founders are angry at the chief about something and he's taking it out on everyone around him."

There was silence and Kiriai's stomach turned sour. For the moment, Kiriai was glad her face was pressed into the treatment table and she didn't have to control her expression. She knew exactly why the city founders were angry with the chief and so did Shisen, Mikata and Eigo. Their ability to play innocent in front of Tomi and Aibo, who hadn't been in on the craziness during the brawler tournament, impressed her. Her friends had risked everything for a copy of the list . . . a list of gifted teenagers the city families wanted rounded up and delivered. Most of whom Ojisan and his gifted had snatched away just ahead of hood 'forcers across the burb.

Kiriai still felt sick visualizing agents of the gifted council, taking the children away from their families to start new anonymous lives. Hard as that was, it was worlds better than the slavery and abuse awaiting them in the city.

But now her crew would be right in the middle of the tumultuous consequences as the City Families focused their ire on Southern Burb and Chief Kosui for his failure to deliver the youth. Kiriai shuddered and vowed to work even harder to keep her head down and not attract attention.

"Business between the chief and the city is way above our level. If we're lucky, it'll distract him and maybe we can negotiate some reinforcements from the hood bosses ourselves," said Tomi. "Keep an ear out, however, so we can avoid getting entangled in the mess if at all possible."

Kiriai felt the first plop of the herbal mush of one of Isha's poultices cover her forearm in a sticky, wet heat. The pungent smell made her smile and helped take her mind off their dangerous predicament and the unfairness of the Chief's treatment of Jitaku. Raibaru, their enemy, constantly received reinforcements from their burb and allied hoods, while Jitaku had only received a handful of rejects that were more trouble than they were worth. How was it fair when Jitaku scrappers, injuries and all, had to keep facing fresh Raibaru fighters every battle? Just refusing to give up should prove their strength to Chief Kosui. Kiriai almost said as much, but stopped herself. Stoking anger wasn't going to help anything. Besides, she needed to relax under Isha's ministrations.

"You have another fifteen minutes," said Isha as she made her way down to Kiriai's legs and began digging into the muscles, searching for the most exquisitely painful spots. Kiriai's focused breathing did double duty, holding her emotions under control while also working to keep her from yelping and squirming under Isha's treatment. This was the best and worst part. Once the painful massage stopped, Kiriai knew her limbs would feel loose and fluid. It was just getting there that really hurt.

"All right. We all know what's at stake here. Enough discussion," said Tomi. "Time for assignments. I'll be contacting the top 'rangers from each hood that are here at the core as well as the burb 'rangers. I'll also drop in to each hood rep's office and see what I can glean. Boss Chusei from Seidai Hood is in town and I'll see if he'll agree to see me."

"Wow," said Eigo, his tone light and teasing again. "Don't feel like you need to leave anything for the rest of us to do."

Tomi laughed, a delighted sound that further helped the mood. "Oh, you all get to do the fun part. While I'm stuck in boring meetings with people too arrogant to see the world around them, you get to go on adventures and explore all that Southern Core has to offer. Our job right now is to collect information. We can't act until we know who the players are, for and against us. Once we know who our true allies and enemies are"—he stopped and his voice dropped, sober and a little scary—"we get what we need and give our enemies everything they deserve."

A chill trickled through Kiriai and she thought once again how glad she was to have 'Ranger Tomi on their side.

He continued as if he hadn't just threatened a whole host of powerful people, the smile back in his voice. "I was thinking Eigo could spend his time with the servants and builders. Shisen, you go find your dissident contacts skulking around the core. Mikata, how about feeling out the other fighters and trainers, while Aibo sees what the clerks in the core headquarters are thinking? And Aibo, why don't you make the rounds of the youth arenas, too. Get a little training in while keeping your ears open." Tomi paused and must have turned toward the curtain because his voice got louder. "Isha, you'll be starting the extra training Ojisan set up for you at the fixer's college. I'm sure the other fixers will tell you everything they know. Just aim that motherly concern their way."

"As you wish," said Isha with a chuckle. Kiriai stifled a groan as Isha's hands found another painful knot.

"And Kiriai . . . well, your job at the moment is to survive." He raised his voice and projected the last instruction with more force. "You got that, kid? Unless you've already found an ally or enemy in that torture you call training?"

The smile that had formed at his words faded as she thought of Gebi and Jiseki's unexpected reactions to her. Were those directed at her personally or because she was a Jitaku initiate? "Not yet, but I'll keep an eye out," she said, doing her best to project her voice through the curtain.

"Anyone want a different assignment?" asked Tomi. When no one answered, Kiriai heard a loud creak from a sofa. A moment later, Tomi spoke again. "In that case, let's get to work and let Isha finish torturing our young brawler initiate."

Kiriai heard the door open, but instead of the usual noise of friends taking their leave, silence descended on the other side of the screen with a suddenness that made every instinct insist she jump to her feet, ready to fight.

Isha laid a warm hand against her back and pressed her down. "Don't get up and ruin all my work. Let me check first," she whispered.

Before Isha could move, Kiriai heard Eigo's voice filled with a rarely heard anger. "What are you doing here?"

"Why don't you ask Kiriai? She's the one who invited me."

All semblance of calm centering fled. Tension returned to her muscles and Kiriai's throat felt tight as she recognized the voice.

Sento was here.

CHAPTER EIGHT

"Tell me what you want, Kiriai-chan, and I'll make it happen," Isha said in a calm voice. "I can ask him to leave or halt your treatment if you want to deal with him now."

Her friend's calm words gave Kiriai the touch of control she needed to think straight. She'd known the risk she was taking when she'd penciled Sento's name in the trainer's spot on her crew requisition form. Her heart still ached from the loss of their relationship, but enough time had passed for Kiriai to resign herself to it and know they couldn't make their relationship work. Sento had not been prepared to compromise on his ambitions when they collided with Kiriai's needs. He'd more than proven that during the brawler tournament.

She stiffened her resolve before speaking.

"Are you here to find out why I wrote your name down, Sento?" The words slipped out before Kiriai could reconsider them. Isha's hand patted her shoulder with encouragement, but Kiriai's breath hissed out through clenched teeth. This discussion might go easier if she could have it later . . . especially when she wasn't lying on Isha's table, mostly undressed and covered by herbal treatments.

She tried again, aiming for reasonable, or her best attempt, while lying prone on a treatment table. "This isn't really a good time."

Complete silence greeted her words on the other side of the temporary curtain, and Kiriai realized Sento and Eigo must have been engaged in an argument too low for her to make out. The absurdity of the situation struck Kiriai, and she started laughing. It wasn't a pretty laugh and came out sounding a touch panicked and hysterical.

"We're done with our discussion for now, so we can leave so you can talk with your"—Tomi hesitated with an awkward pause —"trainer?"

"No, I can find another time," said Sento, sounding much more reasonable than Kiriai had expected.

The absurdity of the entire situation made Kiriai want to laugh even more, but she tamped down the impulse. A soothing, heavy heat pressed down on her as Isha draped damp towels across her body. The comfort and care were just what Kiriai needed to regain her emotional footing. She could get past lying on a fixing table with her crew and ex-boyfriend on the other side of a thin curtain. She was a fighter who trained for all situations, and this was just another conflict she needed her skills and control to handle.

"No. I changed my mind. Now will work fine. Besides, I don't know when I'll have everyone in one place again. You are my crew and this affects you too. This won't take long. If you don't mind sitting back down for a few minutes, I'll explain."

Soft noises carried through the curtain. Kiriai felt Isha removing the herbal treatments and beginning her final pass with the healing wand under the warm towels that ensured her muscles stayed loose and relaxed.

When quiet returned to the room, Kiriai gathered her thoughts and cleared her throat. She focused on keeping her voice and words practical and unemotional. "As you all found out yesterday, I wrote Sento's name down as my trainer. I had two reasons to do this, and neither has anything to do with us breaking up a few weeks ago. Nothing has changed on that front and I have no plans to start our personal relationship back up again."

Kiriai heard a murmur of sound from the other side of the room, but she couldn't tell who it was. If it was Eigo, he was probably bouncing with a silent cheer at her words. If it was Sento . . . well, the only thing she knew for sure was that she was terrible at reading him. Besides, that wasn't her problem anymore. "First, Sento is one of the best fighting strategists I know, in and out of the ring," she said.

"He still lost to you, despite all his dirty strategies." Mikata's words and angry voice brought back a sudden rush of memories. During their brawler fight, Sento's hurtful words, based on his intimate knowledge of her insecurities, had stabbed so deep, she'd almost lost the fight. That had been his intention, of course, and afterward, he'd excused the nastiness as a simple tactic, nothing personal. Kiriai hated that phrase. Anyone who said "nothing personal" meant just the opposite.

Kiriai focused on the wand moving over her legs to help her swallow back the hurt threatening her composure. "And we will need as many of those *dirty* tactics as possible to fight the corruption here, even if it's just to detect the ones being used against us. Besides, we are all willing to do whatever it takes to save Jitaku."

Silence greeted her words, and she continued before anyone else could start arguing again. "Second, I trust Sento as a friend who will help us save our home. That has never been in question, despite our differences. He risked himself to protect all of us and our safety. That's all that matters."

Kiriai didn't feel her crew needed any further explanation. She had chosen Sento as her trainer for practical and loyalty reasons, nothing more. There was no way she would discuss the hurt and frustration that had ended their relationship. She didn't have time for that, anyway. One positive about the initiation month: Kiriai expected exhaustion would prevent her from even thinking about a relationship.

Mikata was the first to speak, her voice full of disbelief. "So you'll join the crew as Kiriai's trainer, as if an apology will make up for everything you did?"

Mikata's anger didn't surprise Kiriai. While she'd once considered Mikata an enemy, the woman had proven herself to be the staunchest of allies. Mikata's opinion of Sento's actions had been clear all along.

"Yes, I am joining the crew. No, I'm not apologizing to you." Sento spoke in such a mild manner that it took a moment for anyone to react to his words. Someone sucked in an outraged breath.

Before anyone could speak, Sento continued, his voice hardening. "I will do my best to help Kiriai advance as a brawler and help Tomi and all of you in our quest to get reinforcements to Jitaku. It's my home, too. I want to save my family and friends just as much as you do. Those are my jobs as a member of this crew and all I'm willing to discuss with you." He paused and when he spoke again, his voice was softer, a touch uncertain. "As for an apology, that's between me and Kiriai."

"Well, I have to admire your fortitude in facing everyone here without flinching," said Tomi with his usual cheer and a bit of laughter in his voice. "And we can use someone with your talents in our work to save the home we all care about. Mikata—" Tomi's voice stopped. "Never mind. I can see it is too soon to ask you two to work together. Sento, we'll assign you to gather information from the other trainers and turn over the sparring partners and other fighting support staff to Mikata. Is that acceptable?"

"Yes," said Sento, just loud enough for Kiriai to hear.

Mikata must have nodded, because Kiriai could hear Tomi

standing and moving to the door. "Good. Let's stop bothering our brawler so the experienced hands of Fixer Isha can get her patched up for her next round of training."

Shuffling noises filled the room, and Kiriai was relieved to hear Tomi say, "You, too, Trainer Sento. You've had your say. It's time for us all to get to work. I'm sure Brawler Kiriai isn't in any condition for a confrontation at the moment . . . or an apology."

Kiriai tried not to hold her breath as she waited for an explosion or objection. Nothing. It seemed Tomi was persuasive enough and Sento was willing to comply. Kiriai let out a breath and felt tension drain from her muscles as she heard the door slide shut.

"We're all here for you. Don't forget that," said Isha quietly as she moved to treat Kiriai's forearms. Her strong, warm hands helped Kiriai relax further.

"Yep. You're safe as long as I'm alive. I'll fight everyone off so no one hurts you," said a cheerful voice that made Kiriai start in surprise. She'd thought everyone had left.

Eigo popped around the curtain, his hands raised in a mock fighting style that made Kiriai smile. He looked over his shoulder, back into the sitting area, and then leaned forward with one hand next to his mouth to keep his words quiet. "Especially him. I know he's here because of how nice you are . . . and his mad fighting skills . . . but we won't let him hurt you like that again. I promise." Eigo's teasing expression turned serious with his last words.

Isha smiled and made a shooing motion. "Thank you, Eigo. I'm sure Kiriai is happy to have such a good friend. But I need to finish here so she can get dressed and go back to her schedule."

Kiriai was smiling at Eigo's antics when he finally made eye contact with her lying on the table, covered in a few towels. His smile froze and his face reddened, making Kiriai laugh. "What? You've seen me in a lot less than this. We've grown up together, for ancestors' sake."

Eigo made a few more unintelligible sounds and then vanished back behind the curtain. The noise of the door shutting came a few seconds later.

"No need to tease the boy, Kiriai. Be nice."

"Tease him?" Kiriai was confused. "We've been teasing each other our whole lives, Isha."

"But you aren't children anymore. That boy will do anything for you and always has. Maybe you should give him a little more consideration."

"But I do—"

"Stop and think, child. You'll figure it out," Isha said as she whisked the towels off and smacked Kiriai's leg. "Now you're done. Get up. Time to eat and sleep before they throw you back into the grinder tomorrow. I have it on good authority that your training will start early again." Isha tossed the used towels into a bin. She grabbed a fresh one from a nearby stack and handed it to Kiriai.

Kiriai groaned at the news as she took the towel, dried herself and rubbed away any last remnants of the herbal poultices.

"How do you feel?"

Kiriai straightened and took a moment to assess. She bounced lightly on her feet, moved her shoulders and then turned to Isha and grinned. "You're a miracle worker, Isha. Yes, I still have a few twinges of soreness, but I feel worlds better."

"You should feel even better by the morning—at least the bruises and torn muscles will, after they've had a few hours to benefit from the wand's accelerated healing." Isha reached out for the towel, and Kiriai traded it for her bag of clothing. She tipped her head and pursed her lips. "I don't suppose there is any way to keep you from undoing all my hard work again tomorrow, is there?"

Kiriai took the question seriously as she pulled on a clean set of loose training pants and shirt. For some reason, she didn't feel like joking anymore. The discussion with Tomi had made it impossible to ignore the danger facing her home and friends. It overshadowed her problems with Sento, how hard her training was with Gebi, making it all seem insignificant. When would she learn to be grateful for small problems and remember there were always bigger ones waiting to crash down into her life?

"Isha, I don't have your healing skill, Tomi's diplomacy, or even Aibo's enthusiasm. But one thing I have is the ability to fight better and train harder than anyone around me." An image of the trainers' skills flashed in her mind. "Well, the brawlers here completely outclass me, but that's the point of training harder and taking more punishment than everyone around me," she said, trying to explain it to both Isha and herself at the same time. "It's what I've always been good at, and it's the only way I can help save our home. How much it hurts or the damage it does to me comes second to that. I just don't know if it will be enough this time . . . if I can get good enough, fast enough, in case Western challenges the chief for our hood."

Isha had stopped, giving Kiriai her complete attention as she stood still and listened. The towel hung, forgotten, from one hand. It was something Kiriai had always loved about Isha. When she listened, she did it with such a focus that it felt as if you were the only person who mattered to her in that moment.

Kiriai looked at her friend and gave her a shrug. She'd run out of words.

Isha broke the moment with a soft sigh as she looked up briefly to meet Kiriai's gaze with a smile. "We all believe in you. Try to remember that all you can do is your best. It's something I know and respect about you. You fight for the people you love, despite any obstacles. And not that I object, I just love you and hate to see how much pain your chosen path brings you." Isha reached out and pulled Kiriai into an embrace. In a quiet voice, close to Kiriai's ear, she said, "Just promise me you'll take care of my young friend and keep her as uninjured as possible, deal?"

Kiriai nodded and took a moment to cement the embrace and

caring moment in her mind. She'd need every bit of encouragement and support during the difficult month ahead. The thought made her wince as she considered the early morning start tomorrow. She stepped back with a sigh. No point in worrying beforehand.

CHAPTER NINE

"Evil people rebelled against their rightful leaders, which caused the Blast. They destroyed themselves and the rest of the world with them. It's up to each citizen to be loyal, to be diligent at rooting out rebels before they destroy our new world, too."

— Chikara City Elementary Social Studies Text, 1st edition

Tired, but with her thoughts still racing, Kiriai sagged back into the plump feather pillow. She slipped her hands behind her head and looked up at the ceiling of the barracks room. The wooden beams above were just visible in the dim light cast by the last lantern lit by the doorway. A few of the other initiates stirred as they fell asleep and someone on the far end of the barracks room snored softly.

Her body and muscles had never felt this drained before, but her belly was full of delicious food and the bed . . . well, the life of a brawler seemed a whole level above what she was used to. Not that she couldn't have passed out on a cold dirt floor after her first day of initiation, but the silky feel of expensive sheets and warmth of the puffy comforter were a treat.

Kiriai's thoughts muddled in the first stages of sleep, and she hoped the trainers wouldn't wake them as early again.

Would you like to train before sleeping?

It took a moment for Kiriai to order her thoughts again. *Yabban? Now?*

Yes, this is an ideal time to train. You finished your daily tasks. Your body can rest and continue to heal while your mind trains with me in our virtual dojo.

Kiriai smothered the groan she wanted to let out. It wouldn't do to wake up any of the other initiates who were mostly asleep by now. They were the smart ones without an ancient gaming AI to harass them into one last workout, even if it was a mental one.

Yabban waited patiently for Kiriai's answer. That consideration tipped the scales. Yabban really understood her and wanted the best for her.

All right. I'll give you one hour to do what you can. Run me through as many basic, repetitive drills as you can fit in an hour. Deal?

A thrill of anticipation resonated along her emotional connection from Yabban, making Kiriai smile.

And you'll do any exercises I choose? As many repetitions as I think necessary?

Kiriai's smile froze as she had second thoughts about her impulsive words. But it was only an hour. Yabban couldn't be any worse than Gebi, right? Besides, Yabban's dojo was virtual, so no real physical damage could be done. After a year of training together, her mind had even adjusted enough that she didn't get the splitting headaches that had plagued her at the beginning. *Yes, Yabban.*

Relax and get comfortable so your body can continue to recover while you're with me.

Kiriai followed instructions, though a wave of tiredness

tempted her to change her mind. The flash of Gebi's and the other trainers' skills made her purse her lips and close her eyes instead.

Ready, Yabban.

Without further warning, Kiriai's world spun and a brief twinge of nausea fluttered through her. Then she felt her bare feet land on a familiar surface, the hardwood floor of Yabban's dojo. Kiriai opened her eyes and couldn't help the grin that spread across her face. She tipped her head back and blew out a breath, enjoying the huge benefit she'd almost forgotten about this place: A virtual body was a pain-free one.

The sweeping beams above her held up a well-sized training space outfitted with supporting pillars covered in intricate carvings and an entire wall of expensive glass windows that overlooked more open green space than Kiriai had ever seen in real life.

"Take a moment to review your current levels and then we'll get started," said Yabban from behind her.

Kiriai let her focus soften as the familiar grid of her fighting abilities appeared in bold letters floating in front of her.

Character Name: Kiriai

    Level: Error. Inaccessible.

    XP: Error. Inaccessible.

    Character Traits: Error. Inaccessible.

    Training Statistics:

    Beginning Moves: Unlocked: all. Learned: all. Proficient: all. Mastered: Stances 5/12, Strikes 4/20, Kicks 6/20, Blocks 7/10, Foot Maneuvers 4/8.

    Novice Moves: Unlocked: all. Learned: all. Proficient: Stances 3/6, Strikes 12/16, Kicks 2/20, Blocks 4/10, Foot Maneuvers 2/7.

Mastered: Stances 1/6, Strikes 5/16, Kicks 0/20, Blocks 0/10, Foot Maneuvers 2/7.

Intermediate Moves: Unlocked: Stances 0/6, Strikes 1/14, Kicks 0/16, Blocks 4/10, Foot Maneuvers 2/8. Learned: None. Proficient: None. Mastered: None.

Fighting Skills:

Will Power Level 4 (80% progress to Level 5)

Resilience Level 4 (95% progress to Level 5)

Observation Level 5 (10% progress to Level 6)

Strategy Level 1 (90% progress to Level 2)

Injury Healing Level 5 (0% progress to Level 6)

Evasion Level 4 (30% progress to Level 5)

Meditation Level 3 (20% progress to Level 4)

Centering Level 4 (20% progress to Level 5)

Berserker Level 3 (60% progress to Level 4)

Fighting Principles:

Unlocked: Marriage of Gravity, Line of Attack, Moving up the Circle, Solid Foundation.

Learned: Marriage of Gravity, Line of Attack, Moving up the Circle, Solid Foundation.

Proficient: Marriage of Gravity, Line of Attack, Moving up the Circle.

Mastered: none.

Training Aids Activated: Demonstration, Overlay Training, Corrective Stimulation, Surround Mirror Training, Opponent Training, Realistic Demonstration, Replay Training.

Kiriai squinted at it, trying to figure out what had changed. "What happened to the fighting sequences?"

"Your focus has shifted to learning better principles and applying them to all your moves, instead of learning specific sequences, so I removed them. Would you like them back?"

Kiriai shook her head. "No. You're right. I fight by feel and was never good at following specific sequences." She paused and looked at the other numbers before frowning. "So the only things that have changed are a few of my fighting skills and that new principle, Solid Foundation? Though I guess the new level 5 in Injury Healing will come in handy."

"Yes, your Healing at level 5 is significantly faster, which will be very useful during your brawler training," said Yabban, and Kiriai couldn't disagree, though she had no idea how that would translate into the real world.

"Now, why don't we see how much we can add to that list in an hour," said Yabban as she swiped one hand in the air, dispersing the list of stats. "Left neutral bow," she said with a sensei's commanding voice.

Kiriai instinctively obeyed, before giving her trainer a half smile and ignoring the stern look on her face.

"What?" Kiriai asked. "No informal chatting before jumping right in?"

Yabban didn't respond. Instead of her usual easy smile, her expression was intense. She stood taller than Kiriai and moved with a fighter's grace that radiated warning to those who knew what to look for. She'd pulled back her straw-colored hair and tied it off with a black slip of silk that matched the severe cut of her plain uniform. The worn instructor's brown belt wrapped around Yabban's waist was the only spot of color against the black.

"I only have an hour and I plan to use every second," she said.

Picking up on Yabban's determination, Kiriai bent her knees and took in a long, slow breath before releasing it. She was ready to see what they could do in an hour . . . and then she would crash for as many hours as Gebi gave her.

"We will start at the beginning and then jump to the more advanced," said Yabban.

Kiriai stayed silent, knowing Yabban would explain. After

more than a year together, it was times like this that made Kiriai realize how little of Yabban's potential she'd tapped.

"You've been neglecting your basic principles, and with a little focused practice, you should be able to unlock a whole set of them quickly," Yabban continued without waiting for Kiriai to acknowledge anything. "First is the clock principle, a simple technique for me to give you accurate descriptions and to help visualize movements that are more sophisticated than simply moving forward and backward."

Yabban pointed at the ground in front of Kiriai and, as if by magic, the glowing number twelve appeared on the burnished wood surface in front of her lead foot. "Straight ahead is 12 o'clock, to your left is 9 o'clock, to your right is 3 o'clock and behind you is 6 o'clock." Yabban pointed, and Kiriai's gaze jumped from one glowing number to the next. After the six appeared, she turned to look back up at Yabban with a grin. "This is why I love you so much better than the regular senseis. None of them have magic like you do."

Yabban gave her a brief smile then barked out a command that made Kiriai jump. "Push-drag forward to 12 o'clock."

"Drag-step reverse to 9 o'clock."

"Step-through forward to 3 o'clock."

The commands came rapid-fire, and then Kiriai got her numbers mixed up and moved in the wrong direction. A mild shock zapped up into her lead foot, making her jump and aim a glare in Yabban's direction.

Yabban repeated herself. "Again. Step-through reverse to 6 o'clock."

Kiriai couldn't argue since the shocks forced her to focus, which resulted in fewer mistakes, even when Yabban added diagonal directions into the mix.

The commands came faster and Kiriai's focused tightened until she moved in a complicated dance of foot maneuvers all across the training space.

"Attention stance," said Yabban.

Kiriai was so focused on responding to the next direction that it took her a moment to let go, relax and straighten into an attention stance.

"Congratulations, you have both unlocked and learned the Clock Principle. This will help during instruction and improve your ability to think about fighting in the full range of directions instead of only forward and backward," said Yabban with a satisfied smile on her face.

Kiriai's eyebrows shot up. "Wow, up to Learned in only half an hour? Maybe I'll stop fighting you on training the basic principles."

Yabban smirked. "Fifteen minutes, Kiriai, not half an hour."

Kiriai started to speak, but Yabban beat her to it.

"Left Neutral Bow!"

Kiriai shut her mouth and obeyed. She'd promised Yabban an hour and would give it to her.

A bulky man in a plain gi materialized in front of her. The canvas-wrapped kicking shield he held at the front of his body was similar enough to the ones used by the brawler trainers that it startled Kiriai.

"Push-drag and reverse punch. Move!"

Kiriai sank into her stance a fraction. She pushed forward, snapped her hips and slammed her back fist into the shield. Her lips pulled back in a fierce grin as she felt her knuckles burn and force ripple back through her arm and body. It was a good punch.

"Not good enough," said Yabban, bursting her moment of enjoyment. "Your timing is off. The point of this new principle, Back-up Mass, is to time your strike to hit simultaneously with the greatest forward momentum of your entire body. The idea is to hit him with all of your weight, not just this little hand and arm here." Yabban reached over, a bamboo stick suddenly appearing in her hand that she used to tap Kiriai's arm. "Watch."

Yabban dropped back into a fighting stance and the stoic man turned to face her with his shield.

"This is what you did. Pay attention to the timing." Yabban exploded forward with a punch that hit hard enough to rock the man's weight back. It looked pretty powerful, in Kiriai's opinion.

"This is what you're supposed to do," said Yabban once she'd reset herself. Then with minimal effort, the AI pushed forward and hit with what looked like an identical punch.

The results were anything but identical.

The man staggered back, both feet forced to move to stay standing under the power of the blow.

"What did you do?" Kiriai asked excitedly. "You're not just messing with me, are you? This isn't one of your jokes, is it?"

"No, Kiriai. You already occasionally used a form of this principle, but more by accident than design. It's all about the timing, just like using Marriage of Gravity. Think about that one and this time I'll demonstrate it on you."

"You know how much I love when you use that realistic demonstration on me," Kiriai said with a groan, but she stepped sideways into a horse stance, pulled her hands back out of the way and braced herself.

This is going to hurt.

To distract herself, she thought about the fighting principle Marriage of Gravity. It had become almost second nature to time the drop of her weight with the exact moment a kick or punch landed. Yes, timing was crucial. Too early or too late and the power of the attack would fizzle. She watched Yabban line up in front of her and after tightening her core, Kiriai gave the AI a nod.

Kiriai shouted a short kiai as the punch landed low on her torso with an immediate stab of pain. A dull ache radiated out from the impact, but it wasn't difficult to handle.

"That punch landed a split-second after my forward momentum had slowed. This one I'll time right."

"Great," Kiriai said, not bothering to suppress her sarcasm.

As Yabban readied herself, Kiriai narrowed her eyes, determined to see what she did differently this time.

The power of the punch slammed into her torso again, and Kiriai's shout had an undercurrent of surprise and pain as she folded forward and had to shuffle her feet back to keep from falling. Kiriai groaned as she straightened, but a big grin spread across her face when she caught her breath.

"It's the same thing, just moving forward instead of dropping," Kiriai said, her voice full of excitement as she ran a hand across her stomach. "But dang, Yabban. That hurt." Kiriai kept count in her head, knowing that the pain would disappear in a few more seconds.

Yabban returned her smile and nodded. "Feeling is not only believing, but it is also learning." The AI said nothing more until the final seconds ticked away, and Kiriai let out a sigh of relief. Another thing she loved about the virtual dojo.

"Your turn," Yabban said, moving out of the way. "I'll activate Overlay and Surround Mirror to help you visualize the correct movements. Even a small amount of error can make a difference. And I'll turn off Corrective Stimulation. For now." Yabban's stern look assured Kiriai that painful jolts would be added again if she didn't improve quickly.

Kiriai dropped back into her stance and waited for a heartbeat as green light washed over her, leaving a thin layer covering her from the neck down. Four other virtual Kiriais popped into existence, one on either side, and two next to the man holding the punching bag. One faced away from her, allowing her to see herself from behind, while the other faced her, mirroring her movements exactly. After a quick mental review of her goal, Kiriai pushed forward and punched.

She didn't need to see the orange flash of color over her arm and fist or the ghostly image of a punch moving just an inch ahead of hers to know her timing was off. Sometimes all of

Yabban's fancy training aids were insignificant when compared to *feeling* that a move wasn't quite right.

Again. This time her punch landed a split-second too late, when the forward movement of her body had already slowed. She jumped back, her four mirrors mimicking her movement, and tried again.

And again.

Kiriai alternated between being too late and too early, the perfect timing frustratingly out of reach. Her overlay flickered between green and a hint of yellow as she improved. She was so close. Her entire world narrowed to a single goal, all her other worries and concerns forgotten as she focused on attaining this skill.

Definitely more than ten minutes later, she did it. It was perfect. Her fist, arm, hip and leg all coordinated together, timed to strike perfectly with her forward momentum. When she hit the bag, she felt it in her entire body, as a single unit, not just a clenched fist striking. Instead, the force rippled through her body, all the way down to her rear foot.

Even better, her untiring bag holder had to take a step and adjust his feet as his weight rocked back from the punch.

Kiriai turned to Yabban and got the reaction she'd been looking for.

"Nice, Kiriai!" she said with a wide grin on her face. "Congratulations, you've unlocked and learned the fighting principle Back-up Mass."

Kiriai sucked in an exhilarated breath. "I know I've done this before, hit with coordinated power," she said, trying to explain why she was so excited. "I recognize this feeling of everything coming together to generate a powerful move. I've just never done it so deliberately, understanding exactly what and how I'm trying to do it. Does that make sense?"

Yabban nodded. "So you won't give me a hard time anymore about training the foundation moves and principles?"

Something between a laugh and a groan escaped Kiriai. "No. I guess not," she admitted. "But I can't promise not to complain a little, especially when you demonstrate on me. Deal?"

"Deal," said Yabban. "Now with our last fifteen minutes, I'd like to unlock as many intermediate moves as possible."

Kiriai let out a real groan this time.

"Don't forget," Yabban said in a chipper voice, "you get another attribute point to spend on me once you unlock them all."

Kiriai decided to just ignore that. She didn't want to imagine what other upgrades Yabban might get with another attribute point. Emotions, jokes, autonomy and an archive of wise sayings were plenty for an AI martial arts trainer, in her opinion.

"I'm pleased you're finally progressing past the bird stage," said Yabban as she motioned for Kiriai to get back into a training stance.

"What does that mean?"

"Well," said Yabban, as her face lit up with a grin, "Birds like to wing it. And that doesn't always work in the ring, does it?"

Kiriai laughed. She couldn't argue with that.

CHAPTER TEN

"I think it's time to make this a little more challenging for all of you. What do you think, initiates?" Gebi asked the group as she stalked in front of their line. "Are you up for a challenge?"

"Yes, Trainer," they all shouted. They stood facing a bank of mirrors lining one wall of the main training dojo. Examining the group's reflection, Kiriai saw the signs of strain as the eight of them stood in ready stances, fists held low and forward. They had been training hard since the early morning roust out of their bunks, and it showed.

"Are you ready to push yourselves?"

"Yes, Trainer!" The group shouted louder. Kiriai fantasized about a meal, a session with Isha and a nap, in that order.

"Become brawlers for real?"

"Yes, Trainer!"

Gebi stopped pacing back and forth and turned to face them. A smile emerged across her face, and Kiriai suddenly felt nervous.

"Each initiate will take a center position in a marked ring on my command," she said with a wave toward the space at the center of the immense dojo. The morning sun had finally risen

enough to send light streaming down from the skylights high
above them. When they'd first entered hours ago, the lanterns on
the walls made shadows leap and dance, giving the space a
spooky feel. Trainer Gebi had made it clear initiates weren't
worth the expense of using the tech lights. There were only eight
initiates, after all, and a wall of lanterns was plenty.

"Move!"

The initiates bolted for the center and Kiriai forced her
muscles, which had cooled, to respond as she joined them.

"Now!" yelled a trainer running behind her.

"What is wrong with you?"

"Can't you follow simple directions?"

Kiriai wasn't sure exactly where the marked rings were and
saw she wasn't the only one as the group of initiates reached the
center of the immense space and slowed, looking confused.
There was nothing like lack of sleep and continuous berating to
make mental processes slower than usual.

"Get in your ring!"

Kiriai saw Jimu moving again, his eyes glued to the floor
beneath his feet.

"Pick a ring! Any ring. Move it!"

Duh! Of course the floor would have embedded markings for
arena practice.

"The lines in the wood," she hissed at the initiate nearby as she
made her way into the area marked by the lighter-colored inlaid
wood.

A surprised inhale made her look up. Jiseki gave her a suspicious glare. Kiriai pointed at the floor with a shrug before
turning to hurry to the center of the ring she had stepped into. If
the other fighter wanted to let some imagined slight interfere
with practicalities, it wasn't Kiriai's problem.

She slid to a stop and snapped into a ready stance on one of
the two starting positions. Now that she was looking for them,
the standard arena markings were obvious. Frozen in position

with eyes forward, Kiriai tuned out the yelling until it diminished along with the other initiates' movement. Everyone must have found a ring.

"Time for a little group training. Brawler Akumu? Get the door and bring them in."

"Yes, Trainer Gebi," said a male voice with an undercurrent of sadistic pleasure.

Kiriai barely kept from turning her head. She would find out about the newest form of torture soon enough. No need to attract more attention by letting her form slip.

A door on the far side of the dojo hit its stops with a boom that echoed in the vast space. Chattering voices filled the air, spiking Kiriai's curiosity. One stood out from the other. *Was that—?*

"Initiate crew members," yelled Gebi. "Pick up a crate, find a place on the out-of-bounds markings of your initiate's ring and wait for further instructions."

Kiriai wanted to shake her head, unsure if she was hearing what she thought she was.

"One of my trainers will join each initiate's crew members," continued Gebi. "Move it!"

"So you just stand around like this all day? I thought this was supposed to be some kind of brutal training?"

The edge of Kiriai's mouth turned up as she heard two familiar voices behind and to her left, followed by a thump and clatter of items being dropped to the wood floor.

"Be quiet," hissed another voice to her right, and her smile slipped. Was that Sento, in addition to Eigo and Mikata? Was her whole crew here?

She was about to break form and sneak a quick look when she saw one of the trainers strutting in her direction. Kiriai held still.

"Nice little reunion you have going here," said the trainer as he stopped at the edge of Kiriai's circle and set a wooden crate on the ground. He was taller than Kiriai but didn't look to outweigh her by much. Ropy muscles wrapped around his forearms, and the lazy way he moved made Kiriai think of a snake—slow, but able to strike without warning. "I'm Brawler Akumu, but you will all address me as Trainer. Understand?" His dark hair was short enough to see his scalp on the sides, and Kiriai was immediately wary of the cruel light she saw in his eyes. She'd had plenty of experience with bullies. Why did they seem to gravitate toward her?

"Yes, Trainer!" she yelled. It didn't cost her anything to play their games.

Behind her she heard assent from her friends, but they didn't yell their answers out like she had.

Akumu sent a pointed look at them. "I don't control the trainers and sparring partners as I do the initiates, but during group training sessions like this one, we require you to follow my orders. Is that clear?" His expression promised unpleasant conse-quences for defiance.

"Yes, Trainer," they chorused a little louder this time. Kiriai breathed a sigh of relief when she heard Eigo's voice too. Sento and Mikata were old hands at handling bossy senseis, but Eigo might get them all into trouble with a poorly timed joke.

"Attention!" Gebi's voice from the front cut through the chatter and everyone went silent immediately. A pleased smile crossed the woman's face at the quick response. "I will demon-strate the drill"—she stopped and scanned the initiates closest to her—"with Initiate Jimu. Everyone move so you can see."

A few people changed positions and Kiriai sensed movement behind her. She kept her eyes forward as Eigo and Mikata moved to either side of her. Sento kept more distance between them, which was just fine with her.

"I'm not going to like this, am I?" whispered Eigo out of the side of his mouth.

Akumu's head twitched in their direction and Kiriai didn't dare answer.

"We will start with your crew members and assigned trainer throwing sequential kicks moving clockwise like this."

Gebi nudged aside the trainer standing by Jimu's ring, took a fighting stance and nodded at Jimu's crew to spread around and encircle their initiate. When everyone was ready, she moved without warning, skipping forward and throwing a speedy front kick at Jimu.

She almost caught him flat-footed, but they'd had enough time with these trainers to keep on edge around them. Jimu leaped back, his front hand blocking the kick with enough force that Kiriai was sure they'd both be sporting a bruise later.

Gebi glared at the crew member to her left and the woman flinched before she turned to face Jimu in a fighting stance. She copied Gebi, though her kick wasn't anything like the one Gebi had thrown. The four fighters around Jimu followed suit, doing their best to kick Jimu while he blocked.

"Yame!" called Gebi as she stood and relaxed out of her fighting stance. She turned to face the rest of the group. "Next, I'll call 'Random' and you'll alternate around the circle, doing your best to catch your initiate off guard. I will also call specific attacks and finally random ones." Gebi stopped to scan the group. "Any questions?"

She obviously didn't expect any because she clapped her hands a second later. "Positions. Ready? Sequential front kicks. Hajime!"

Kiriai had barely moved back to the center of the ring when Akumu's kick flashed toward her from the left. She jumped and got her front hand down just in time to meet it. She bit back a yelp of pain. Blocking his kick felt as if she'd hit a tree trunk with her forearm. She didn't have any time to recover as Eigo's kick came a second later, though Kiriai could tell he pulled it at the last second.

"Do you *want* your initiate to be weak?" Akumu rounded on Eigo, who flinched, but kept his cool and stepped back into an awkward fighting stance. Kiriai hoped Mikata would work with him more so he didn't look so clumsy. The sparring partner on a brawler's crew was usually a seasoned fighter.

"No, Trainer," he said firmly, eyes front.

A flush of pride sparked through Kiriai at her friend's poise.

"After everything she did to get here," said Akumu in a quieter voice that would go no farther than their group. "You might want her to improve enough to deserve to be here."

The trainer's words caught Kiriai flat-footed . . . and her crew, too, if their expressions were anything to go by. Before any of them could respond, Akumu stepped back and reverted to his loud trainer's voice. "Then try to hit her next time. Tough training builds tough fighters. Do you understand?"

For a split second, Kiriai thought Eigo would object, but he'd been reading dangerous situations on the streets since they were both young.

"Yes, Trainer!" he answered back. Kiriai recognized the mocking glint in Eigo's eyes. She knew exactly what he really thought of the bossy trainer. They both had plenty of experience with bullies.

As soon as Akumu turned away, Eigo winked at her. Distracted by the first friendly face she'd seen that day, Kiriai didn't see Sento's kick barreling from her other side soon enough. Her former boyfriend didn't pull his kick. In fact, he committed so fully, he caught the edge of her hip with his kick, forcing her to spin back with a chopping block to keep from getting too hurt. Pain stabbed through her hip, making her wince, as she pivoted to catch Mikata's incoming kick, which was almost as powerful as Sento's.

From the corner of her eye, Kiriai caught Eigo glaring at Sento. However, even though she bore the brunt of the attacks, Kiriai had to agree with Akumu. The ring was vicious and her training had to match that if she hoped to prepare for life as a brawler.

It didn't take long for Kiriai to feel dizzy, constantly moving clockwise, blocking kicks that continued to hammer into her with an almost regular cadence.

"Yame!"

Everyone paused, and Kiriai sucked in a deep breath and shook out her hands.

"Random front kicks. Hajime!" yelled Gebi. The pressure on Kiriai escalated because randomizing the attacks changed the nature of the drill completely. No longer able to anticipate where the next kick would come from, it was like fighting four people at once. Kicks flew at her from every direction.

"Faster!"

Her forearms ached and burned, parts going numb with the continuous hammering. Kiriai sensed movement behind her as she blocked a kick from Akumu. When she spun, Eigo deliberately missed her with his kick, giving his eyebrows a little waggle that loosened a knot of tension inside her she hadn't noticed forming.

During the next hour, Gebi moved them through a host of different attacks. Despite glares from Akumu, Eigo continued to go as easy on Kiriai as possible. Mikata's attacks were fast and sneaky, forcing Kiriai to ratchet up her awareness of her friend.

Kiriai couldn't distinguish between Sento's and Akumu's attacks. Both men seemed bent on getting past her defenses and landing telling blows. While she expected it from Akumu, a pain tugged inside her to feel like Sento's adversary again.

"Yame!" said Gebi and everyone in the whole room seemed to sag like puppets with their strings cut.

Kiriai let her hands drop and focused on drawing in long, measured breaths instead of gulping at the air as her body urged her to do. Her legs shook with that loose, weak feeling of overexertion. Her forearms throbbed from all the blocking, and they had hit her so many places on her body that the pain just blended together. The only consolation was that Gebi had declared no head shots. Though for a moment, Kiriai wondered if getting knocked out might have been preferable.

She felt as if she'd been fighting in a real battle, like the ones taught about in the histories from before the Blast. Back then, huge groups of fighters would enter combat right out in public instead of arenas. Not only did they threaten the 'zens who couldn't get away safely, they tried to kill each other, instead of stopping when a victory was obvious. They fought these ancient *wars*, resulting in untold death and destruction, all to resolve disputes between individual, but powerful, leaders. It seemed crazy, but so did the Blast and the plagues that followed. Kiriai was glad she lived in today's age instead of back then.

"Next. Any attack. Random," called Gebi.

Everyone reset themselves, though arms sagged and knees weren't bent as much as they should be.

"Hajime!"

The next block of time blurred as a whirlwind of feet and fists attacked from every direction. Kiriai could barely keep up just defending. Blows landed, and she stumbled, only for someone to attack from another direction. She was the center of a storm, buffeted on all sides.

Pain was an effective teacher. Too stubborn to quit and without a blow to the head to end her misery, Kiriai improved. What was more pain when everything hurt? Her senses turned on overdrive, reaching out in the noisy training room to distinguish just which swish of cloth or grunt of effort meant one of her attackers was on the move out of sight. Her battered forearms blocked faster. She spun and met attacks a split second sooner. She improved.

"Yame!"

It took a second for Kiriai to register the command. Only when she saw Eigo and Mikata drop their hands and straighten did she realize Gebi had halted the exercise. She dropped her hands, too, when a sound behind her made her spin out of reflex.

She was a fraction too late and grunted in pain as Akumu's roundhouse kick slipped under her elbow to land into her ribs.

"Hey," said Eigo, his face furious. "She said *yame*—that means 'stop.'"

Kiriai tried to wave off her friend, but was too late.

"That was a jerk move!" he yelled at the brawler with no regard for his own safety.

His words echoed in a space suddenly gone quiet, and Kiriai could feel every eye turn in their direction. The sudden spike of worry that filled her drove all her exhaustion and pain to the background.

She turned, and sure enough, Gebi was stalking toward their ring, her face full of retribution.

This would not be good.

CHAPTER ELEVEN

"Ransacking warehouses is fine, but we need to plan for the
future. Breeding stock, seeds, fruit-tree cuttings, fruiting
vines, collect it all, bring it all back to the greenhouses and
protect it with your lives. We need to be producing our own
food before the packages run out."

— Instructions from Yolanda Cortez to her scroungers.
One month after the Blast. Phoenix, AZ. Oath Keepers
Archive of Truth, Volume 3

Kiriai tried to step in between Gebi and Eigo, but one
furious glare in her direction had her sidestepping and
letting the woman past. Making a stand here would be ill-advised
until she found out what Trainer Gebi had planned for Eigo.
Kiriai hoped it would only be more yelling and screaming. A
dressing down was something Eigo could handle, especially if he
wasn't trying to protect her.

"Crew member. What is your name?" demanded Gebi when

she stopped in front of Eigo. Her voice was commanding, clear enough for everyone to hear.

Eigo's eyes darted to the side, and Kiriai could see him realize the gravity of his situation. Thank the ancestors!

"Sparring Partner Eigo, Trainer," he said and even snapped to a passable attention stance.

Something loosened inside Kiriai. Maybe this wouldn't be too bad.

"Sparring Partner Eigo. Why am I not surprised to hear such blatant disrespect from one of Initiate Kiriai's crew?" she said with a drawl before turning her gaze on Kiriai. "Is this how you've trained your crew, Initiate?"

Kiriai scrambled for an answer that would defuse the situation even as anger urged her to snap back.

Gebi didn't give her time. "You are initiates because you haven't proven to us that you are brawler material," she said, as she turned to address the rest of the crowd. "Initiate Kiriai and her crew member are good examples of why we lack confidence in you. You have one month to change your ways, learn, get better, and prove that you deserve to join us." She turned back to fix her gaze on Kiriai but kept her voice loud, projecting to everyone listening. "Tricking and cheating your way into the brawlers will not happen, even if it worked for you in the past. Understand?"

"Yes, Trainer," came the loud response of many voices, including Kiriai's, even though she had to force the words out past a choking anger. What did Trainer Gebi have against her? And was she implying what Kiriai thought she was? A glance in Eigo's direction showed he'd clenched his fists despite the obedient mask he had plastered on his face.

Trainer Gebi rounded on him. "Apologize to Brawler Akumu for your disrespect."

Kiriai saw Eigo struggle, obviously wanting to defend his

actions and call out Akumu's dirty blow after the command to stop.

Please don't. Kiriai sent a silent plea to her friend. Now wasn't the time, and it would only cause more trouble.

Eigo turned to Akumu, his expression suddenly clear and calm. "Brawler Akumu," he said with a tip of his head. "I apologize for my disrespect. Please forgive me."

Akumu's eyebrows shot up, and Kiriai couldn't tell if he was mollified or disappointed.

It didn't matter. Eigo's apology was enough for Trainer Gebi.

She turned away and started yelling commands at everyone. "Circle around. One big circle, so everyone can see. Trainers, join me here in the center."

Everyone scrambled to obey, and Kiriai was more than happy her people were no longer the center of attention.

A few moments and yelled orders later, the initiates along with their crew members stood arrayed in a circle around Gebi and the eight other trainers.

Seeing everyone was in position and paying attention, Gebi smiled. It wasn't a nice smile. "Now, before I dismiss you for a break, I'd like to show you what it means to be a brawler. I mentioned that there are no shortcuts to joining us and I meant it. We fight so our people don't have to and we're good at it! Oda!"

"Oda!" yelled the other trainers.

One unfortunate initiate tried to join in the response and all the trainers rounded on him, glaring. "That is the battle cry of the brawlers, Initiate!" yelled Gebi. "Don't defile it by using it before you've earned the privilege. Understand?"

"Yes, Trainer," he said, face ashen. Kiriai tried not to feel relieved that someone else had drawn Trainer Gebi's ire.

His quick acquiescence seemed to mollify the dangerous trainer, who moved back to the center of the circle, her smile back. This time it was an anticipatory one.

"Now, I will demonstrate the correct way to do the exercise you just did. You four," she said, selecting half of the trainers. "Line up around me."

The other four moved to stand with the observers while the chosen brawlers quickly surrounded their leader and dropped into fighting stances, poised with energy that looked ready to explode on command.

"All attacks, random," said Gebi as she cracked her neck, shook out her arms and stepped back into her own fighting stance, every muscle loose and springy.

"Hajime!"

Her barked order sparked a flurry of movement. The surrounding attackers still took turns as the exercise required, but they left almost no time between attacks, their eyes sharp, ready to spring forward as soon as they spotted an opening. Punches and kicks flew without warning, driving with uncanny speed at the center figure so fast that Kiriai was sure they would be impossible to block.

Instead, Kiriai stared in shock and dumbfounded fascination as Gebi transformed from a belligerent instructor to a fighter full of deadly grace. The attacks came fast, but she moved faster. She spun and shifted by small but crucial amounts that let kicks slip by and fists punch harmlessly through the air, close enough to brush against her gi. She hardly even blocked, using open-handed moves that looked almost gentle as she met and guided attacks onto a trajectory that passed her by and left the attackers stumbling.

I need to learn to move like that . . . and those open-handed blocks. Kiriai felt a flush of jealousy rise and mix with her earlier doubts.

You've unlocked the parries, mostly by accident, but you can improve them during our next training session.

Kiriai had a vague memory of parries during all the intermediate moves Yabban had drilled her on.

And you just unlocked the fighting principle Environmental Aware-

ness during the exercise because of your singular focus on the principle. With enough practice, you can become as skilled as she is.

That's the problem, Yabban. Time is the one thing neither I nor Jitaku Hood has. Kiriai scanned the fighting implants of the attacking trainers. Only one of them had a single black stripe compared to Gebi's two, while the rest glowed the plain blue of the first brawler rank. So while they were extremely good fighters, Gebi might not fare as well if she had four attackers of her own rank coming at her.

Still, the fluid skill of the demonstration was mesmerizing, and Gebi wasn't even fighting back, only defending. Kiriai let out a quiet sigh. How was she supposed to succeed when every new exercise just reinforced the skill gap between her and the real brawlers? But she had enough determination and stubbornness for two fighters, and she had Yabban to help her improve faster than her peers. That would have to be enough.

CHAPTER TWELVE

"I can't believe all of you got to train with Kiriai," said Aibo, eyes alight with excitement that was tinged with jealousy.

"It wasn't too hard," said Eigo, preening under her admiration. "I don't know why she's always complaining. It's not as if she has to spend all day learning about training equipment, facilities and uses."

Kiriai aimed a mock glare at him across the dinner table she shared with her crew. They sat in the luxurious dining room of what would eventually be her quarters if she made it through the next month intact. Trainer Gebi had given the initiates two hours to meet with their crew and evaluate the progress of their various members. Kiriai hadn't realized just how extensive the crew training was until she'd spoken with her friends. Their instructors drilled them in their crew jobs for almost as much time as the initiates' training.

Instead of being put off by Eigo's description of his sparring-partner training, Aibo looked even more interested. She let out a sigh. "That sounds much more fun than the aide training. Would anyone like to learn about financial planning and average expenses for an active brawler?"

A chorus of groans and exaggerated waves of denial greeted her words.

"I didn't think so," she said sourly before taking a mouthful of the rich stew they were eating.

Kiriai copied her and almost swooned at the mix of flavors that exploded in her mouth. A bite of warm, crusty bread spread with butter enhanced the stew even further.

"At least they feed us really well," Kiriai said. A chorus of agreement greeted her words, and a comfortable quiet settled around the table as everyone took a moment to focus on the meal.

Aibo finished another bite and then raised a hand with a smile. "I know. How about maintenance expenses and when and where to file appropriate forms?"

A handful of laughs, but more grimaces, met her suggestion.

"I'm probably the only one that would find that interesting," said Tomi as he tipped his tea cup in her direction. "You're welcome to join me with some of my 'ranger training if you find that interesting."

Isha let out an unexpected laugh that drew everyone's attention. "I was just imagining some bureaucrat burb 'ranger trying to teach Tomi anything," she explained.

"Ah," said the large man as he raised one finger in her direction, "that's where my 'ranger skills shine the most. I made an officious woman feel as if her 'ranger knowledge was so much more extensive than mine, and I was grateful for her help. Sometimes it isn't what you know or want that is important, but how you treat people."

There were chuckles of agreement around the table. Even Sento's expression softened a bit at the words of the cheerful man, despite the invisible space the rest of the crew still seemed to give him.

But Kiriai just stopped, fork half raised as Tomi's words struck her. Was it really that simple? She'd always admired his people skills and likened them to her own well-honed fighting skills, assuming he had a talent for the social arena that he'd honed with years of practice.

She glanced over and saw him looking at her, one eyebrow raised. Whatever he saw in her expression made him smile again and nod before turning back to his food. Kiriai let out a huff and shook her head with a half-smile. She planned her next words with Tomi's comment fresh in her mind.

"I'd like to say something," she said after putting her spoon down and clearing her throat. Heads turned in her direction and the laughing camaraderie stilled when they saw she was serious. "Tomi's words reminded me of something I don't say nearly enough. I really appreciate all of your help and support. There is no way I could do any of this"—she stopped and made a gesture at the room and the expansive compound seen through windows behind them—"without the support of each of you." Kiriai ran out of words before she ran out of emotion. She wasn't very good at this and didn't know how else to communicate her feelings. Isha gave her an approving nod. Aibo ducked her head, but not before Kiriai saw the pleased look on her face. It was obvious to Kiriai that she needed to offer her thanks more often.

Tomi came to her rescue. "And we feel the same about you, young brawler. You inspire us to do our best for those we care about just like you do."

Now it was Kiriai's turn to flush with pleasure.

Sento cleared his throat from the end of the table, and the sound seemed to sour the mood instantly. He must have sensed it because he raised his hands defensively. "I am just as grateful to be here as all of you and know I owe that to Kiriai and her alone," he said as he caught her gaze and ignored everyone else in the room, including the glaring Eigo. "However, Kiriai chose me for my strategy skills and pragmatism, which tell me we are burning through our planning time before all of us have to go our separate ways again. We need to share what we've all found and come up with a plan."

Kiriai hated that he was right, even if it was exactly why she'd written his name on the crew page . . . well, one reason. And while she'd much rather spend the meal relaxing with her friends and recharging before going back to the strenuous atmosphere of brawler training, they needed to get in some planning too.

No one spoke for a moment and Kiriai thought many of them felt the same way she did and were reluctant to change to more serious topics.

"It's Mabbai Hood that's the problem," said Aibo into the silence. Startled gazes turned in her direction, and she shrugged. "At least, I think so."

"Explain, please," said Tomi from the head of the table. He took a roll and waved at Aibo to continue.

The young aide swallowed and then seemed to find her words again. "As aides, we often deal with the prickly and uh"—she hesitated, but after a quick glance around at the encouraging looks, continued—"arrogant personalities of leaders and their underlings who enjoy lording it over those in their power. So aides will share information with each other to try to help all of us avoid the worst offenders when they are on a rampage. Word right now is that Boss Ryuin and her people really have it out for Jitaku people, and I should stay clear."

Tomi nodded, his expression thoughtful. "Very good information, Aibo. Exactly what we're looking for."

Aibo flushed at the praise and ducked her head.

"Again, only insiders know this," continued Tomi. "Boss Akuto and Ryuin have a history that goes back decades. And it isn't a pretty one. She has hated him for years. But is her personal hatred enough to target an entire hood of innocent people?"

Shisen scoffed from the other side of the table. "When has the welfare of the average 'zens swayed a hood boss from their course?"

Kiriai started to speak, but Tomi held a hand in her direction before turning back to face Shisen's angry face. "I'll be the first to agree with you that the world isn't fair and the gap between those with and without power is filled with abuse. However, I've spent many years serving Boss Akuto and if there is one thing I can honestly say, it's that the welfare of Jitaku's 'zens weighs significantly into his decision making."

Shisen's glare softened, and after a pause she sighed. "I still hold to my point, but from my recent experiences hanging out with the likes of you all," she said with a wave at the table's occupants, "I might have a slightly less negative opinion of Akuto as compared to the other bosses."

Tomi smiled. "Well, I will count that as a victory for our hood leadership, if we've swayed your opinion even that much." The large 'ranger looked around the table at the others. "We've heard from Aibo and Shisen. Does anyone else have more information about the disposition of the other hoods toward Jitaku?"

Suddenly, Gebi's angry face and personal attacks came to mind. "This might not be significant," Kiriai said, "but Brawler Gebi from Rinjin Hood has been making nasty comments to me right from the start of training."

"Are you sure that isn't just part of the initiation?" Sento asked. "We know part of her job is to try to break you down, and that might be the tactic she's using against you."

Kiriai tried hard not to bristle at what sounded like criticism from him. "There is something unusual going on. She's attacking me personally, which she isn't doing to the other initiates. But what made me bring it up is her belittling statements against Jitaku Hood. I don't know if it's relevant, but it's unusual enough to mention."

Sento looked thoughtful, as if he were giving her words serious consideration. She felt a little mollified. Maybe he was really analyzing the intrigue instead of just doubting her.

"Anyone else?" Tomi asked, glancing around the table.

Mikata lifted a hand and Tomi nodded at her.

"Like Aibo, I've heard talk about Boss Ryuin's hatred of Akuto, but not anything direct she's doing against sending reinforcements our way," said Mikata. "The problem is, while the support staff are huge gossips, they are more interested in personal stuff than anything affecting the hoods at large."

"How is this going to help us get reinforcements sent to Jitaku?" asked Sento. "What is your plan, 'Ranger Tomi?" Sento's voice was much more respectful speaking to the 'ranger than it had been when he addressed Kiriai.

"Aren't you known for saying that much of a fight is decided outside the ring?" Tomi asked with a smile as he accepted a plate of pastries from Shisen. He kept his eyes on Sento as he added one of the delicacies to his plate and passed the dish on to Mikata.

Kiriai was surprised to see a hint of embarrassment in Sento's expression as he nodded.

"Yes. Well, this 'ranger business is much the same. First, we identify who exactly is working for and against us. Then we figure out what they want or need. Once we know all that, we try to give them what they want in exchange for what we need. It's all simple in theory, but it can be difficult to execute . . . much like your fights, I'd expect."

Sento was nodding along with Tomi, his eyes alight with consideration. Kiriai suppressed a groan. If the two connected like this, their crew would never do anything straightforward again.

"What?" Sento turned toward her and asked from across the table. Apparently her groan had been audible. "Do you have a better idea?"

"Yes," she said, with a flare of irritation at how convoluted their simple task had become. "Why don't I just challenge someone for the reinforcements and skip all this sneaking around?"

A shocked silence greeted her words, followed immediately by a mix of protesting voices and at least one person laughing.

Kiriai smiled and leaned back. "What?" she asked Sento as soon as the noise calmed down a bit. "Did you think I'd have a different solution? It's worked perfectly fine in the past, so why would I do anything else? I'm not any good at all the 'ranging, favor-trading, or secret-gathering that you all excel at. But never quitting a fight until I win, that I can do pretty well."

Instead of arguing, Sento gave her a half-smile that made a spark of loss stab her. "You're right," he said with a nod. "That's worked great in the past, but despite how much we'd like it to, it won't this time."

"Why not?" It had been an impulsive idea, but now it was growing on her: a simple and unexpected solution. "No one will expect me to challenge the bosses, and surely I can win at least one fight with all of your help. Reinforcements from one hood would be better than none. And maybe the other hoods might even follow suit."

"First," said Mikata, "you aren't allowed to make challenges until you finish your initiation month. And once you graduate, Chief Kosui will own you and control your challenges."

"But she didn't need Boss Akuto's permission to challenge the chief himself, last year," said Aibo. "The whole point of our system is that everyone is equal in the ring."

Shisen scoffed and gave the younger girl a pitying look. "I know that's what they teach us, but you have to have seen enough of Southern Core by now to know that's not true."

A mulish expression crossed Aibo's face. "I'm not an idiot. It's not a perfect system, but even the chief can't argue when a fighter beats his champion in the arena. The most powerful still have to submit to that, regardless of what they do outside the ring."

"But those same rules prohibit Kiriai from challenging anyone until she graduates initiation," said Mikata with an apologetic look Aibo. "And once she graduates, well, she'll belong to the

Chief then and you know he has ways of keeping her from going rogue. He won't go along with it like Boss Akuto did."

"Kiriai might not be able to make a challenge, but there is one man who might—" Tomi's musing words silenced the rest of the crew. All eyes turned to him. He gave a small shake of his head and then seemed to decide. "I normally wouldn't consider doing anything of the sort, but with our young Kiriai, the impossible seems to happen with regularity." He returned the looks aimed at him. "Do any of you know the details about the brawler graduation?"

Mikata sucked in a breath, and Kiriai saw Sento's eyes widen slightly.

"What?" she asked, suddenly eager for a solution to all their problems. "Can I challenge the bosses after graduation?"

"Not after, but during. And you can't be the one to issue the challenge," said Tomi. He paused and seemed to gather his thoughts. Everyone quieted and Kiriai clamped her mouth shut, knowing patient silence would get Tomi to explain faster than a demand.

CHAPTER THIRTEEN

"This is exquisite," said Jaaku as he set the glass with a finger
of amber liquid on the patterned wooden coaster with a
smile of enjoyment.

"I knew you'd like it," said his old friend, reclining in an
armchair with his own glass held in a loose grip. "I saved the
bottle for your visit. It's a waste to share it with someone who
can't fully appreciate it like you can."

Jaaku's bulk dwarfed the slight man who would blend in
easily among a crowd of more average-sized 'zens. His friend's
salt-and-pepper hair and skin were just beginning to show wrin-
kles. Jaaku briefly wondered where all the years had gone since
they'd been boys growing up on the same Rinjin street. His friend
was a successful businessman in the upper echelons of power in

his hood. It made Jaaku occasionally wonder if his friend had made the better choice of paths to power.

Jaaku covered his thoughts with another sip of the potent beverage. Now was not the time to second-guess himself, especially not with what he'd come to discuss.

"So what's the word on the brawler initiation? How is the first week progressing?" asked Jaaku, feeling that their earlier chitchat was of a reasonable length to discuss business now.

His friend's sharp eyes didn't miss a thing, and his half-smile made Jaaku a little nervous. "Are you going to tell me what you have against this scrapper?"

Jaaku stiffened and ran through approaches in his mind, searching for the one most likely to get him what he wanted.

"No, I don't mean it like that," said his friend with a wave of his empty hand. "We've been friends long enough and owe each other more than simple favors with no explanations needed. Don't worry. I've already instructed my daughter to make the training personally difficult for your initiate. It just sparked my curiosity. What does Boss Akuto have against his only brawler candidate this year—?" His friend's words cut off abruptly and his gaze narrowed.

Jaaku kicked himself for letting his friend's flattery lull him to relax his normally tight control on his reactions.

"This isn't a request from your boss, is it?"

Jaaku let out a sigh and gave his friend a conceding shrug. There was no point in pretending now.

The man across from him leaned back with a broad smile and clasped the glass with both hands in front of his chest. "Now, I really want to know the story. Come on, Jaaku. Distract me from the boring business of working with credits all day. Even a tidbit or two, please."

Jaaku hesitated. But if anyone would understand what he was doing, his childhood friend would. They both intimately knew the sacrifices required in pursuit of a goal. In fact, his friend was probably responsible for more pragmatic brutality than any hood boss Jaaku had met. And he would take Jaaku's secrets to the grave with him. He'd proven that many times over the years.

"I'm sure you're familiar with an underling reaching a position for reasons other than their skill," said Jaaku.

His friend laughed. "Is there any other kind? At least when you get to where we are. Devious maneuvering will trump skill every time."

Jaaku tipped his head in acknowledgment. "Yes, but the arena requires a modicum of skill that no amount of scheming or favor from above can substitute for."

The man across from him waved a hand for him to continue.

"This *girl*"—Jaaku's voice dripped with derision—"somehow caught the interest of Boss Akuto—"

Eyebrows rose across from him.

"Not in that way," Jaaku flinched back at the thought. "Boss Akuto was just getting bored with the usual day-to-day operations of running a border hood. And not that I blame him. I, too, miss the finer things in life." Jaaku gestured at the opulent surroundings in the spacious den. "In any case, this upstart reminded him of himself at a younger age, hungry and willing to fight tooth and nail for every advantage."

"Sounds like an ideal scrapper," said his friend. "What's the problem then?"

"She's subversive," said Jaaku, and tried not to clench his jaw. "She has no respect for her superiors and blatantly ignores direct orders if she doesn't agree with them. Ancestors! She's barely been a scrapper for a year and has somehow tricked and schemed her way to brawler status. Even if Akuto refuses to see it, her actions are tearing at the stability of everything we've built in Jitaku. If there are no consequences for her reckless and rebellious actions, we'll lose control over the next generation of fighters that come after her."

"One bad seed can have far-reaching consequences," said his

friend. "But surely, with her now in Southern Core, she isn't your problem anymore, right?"

"And have the other fighters watch her achieve brawler status? Something all of them dream of but only a lucky few achieve?"

"True," the man across from him said with a slight nod. "And she doesn't have the skill to be where she is now?"

Jaaku scoffed. "After only a year of training? What do you think?"

Without waiting for an answer, Jaaku continued pushing. He needed his friend to keep pursuing this for him. "Do you know of any fighter making brawler in a year without strings being pulled or special favors? She's no different. Besides, I'm not asking for you to get her dismissed. That's not possible and would ruin our system just as much as what she's done. I'm just asking for your help to make her initiation a true test of her mettle. If she is truly brawler material, extra push-ups and some harsh name calling shouldn't bother her a bit, right?"

Across from him, his friend chuckled and his smile had a touch of cruelty to it. "Jaaku, I can guarantee you she is going through more than a few extra push-ups and name calling. Southern Core is a hard place and our Chief deserves to have only the strongest fighters in his arena."

"I know this may not seem like such a big thing to you," said Jaaku, holding his friend's gaze. "But it's something that has been bothering me for over a year now, and I really appreciate your help in the matter."

"Then consider it taken care of," said his friend as he lifted his glass and leaned forward. "In fact, I'll make sure the pressure on the upstart increases even further. She'll either crumble under it or prove that she deserves to be one of our core's brawlers."

Jaaku clinked his glass against his friend's in a silent toast and didn't bother hiding his pleasure at the promise. *Finally!*

CHAPTER FOURTEEN

"Now, Tomi," said Isha from her end of the table. "Don't tease the poor children by being so cryptic. Spit it out already."

It surprised Kiriai to see the large man actually flush at Isha's chiding. He always seemed so confident.

"Sorry, ma'am. I wasn't trying to be coy. My thoughts were busy sorting through what I know about the brawler graduation customs, trying to determine which ones are actual laws or simply tradition." He paused and glanced at Kiriai. "Because we all know someone willing to flout tradition, if she has a good enough reason."

That elicited a guffaw from Eigo and a few smiles from others, making Kiriai unsure if she should feel flattered or insulted.

"Well," said Isha, after a glance at the time on the wallscreen, "we have enough time for a story. If you keep it short, we'll still have time to run through the crew business so Kiriai can report back on how well she is managing us."

Isha's words brought Kiriai up short. It was strange to think that was how the rest of the world saw her relationship with her crew. She was the brawler, and they were supposed to serve at her pleasure.

Instead, they were family, caring for and watching out for each other. Kiriai felt the soft warmth of gratitude for what she had as she watched Tomi take a sip of his steaming tea before leaning back and clearing his throat.

Kiriai exchanged a knowing look with Eigo, who was grinning at a fellow storyteller's antics.

Yes, I have the best crew anyone could ask for, she thought. The pulse of agreement she felt from Yabban made her smile widen further.

"They instituted the brawler initiation to ensure that fighters who had reached that level were truly committed and worthy to protect and serve our burb, and by extension, all of us. We all know that cheating and manipulation is part of our dispute system." Tomi stopped and aimed a look of acknowledgment in Shisen's direction, who nodded back. He shrugged. "As much as we might like to believe it isn't. The initiation is the final gateway to ensure that only skilled fighters become brawlers, those with the will to withstand everything thrown at them"—this time, he stopped and glanced at Kiriai before continuing—"and never, ever give up. The chief wants to cull any weaknesses before they make it to the arena where important issues and territory are on the line."

His description made Kiriai look at the last few days with new eyes.

"Also, the offer of an easy, lucrative position in the top echelons in the 'forcers weeds out those who are more interested in power and money than fighting."

"At least some of them," said Sento, his tone pragmatic.

Tomi nodded. "It's not a perfect system. But by the end of the initiation month, the trainers have hopefully taken a group of fighters from disparate backgrounds and forged them into a unified group. They are more determined to serve their burb and also in better fighting shape, giving them a jump on reaching true brawler skill in the arena."

"And the graduation? Is it a big party to celebrate? Does the chief recognize each of them?" asked Aibo, the questions bursting out, her eyes alight with fascination and craving.

Tomi smiled and waited until she finished. "Yes, our young aide. It is a celebration, welcoming the new brawlers into the fold. But the crowning events, and the idea I'm considering, are the first-fights." Tomi paused for another interruption, but everyone was quiet, hanging on his words. "It is a tradition, not a rule or law as far as I know, that halfway through the initiation month, the boss of each potential brawler issues a challenge to another boss on behalf of their fighter. The prize is usually a token object or service, like drinks or a party arranged for the winner's group, a month of submissive bowing . . . there is even a trophy for the occasion that has changed hands many times and the winner will display it prominently until the next year's graduation fights."

"Then at the end of the month, the initiates fight each other?" Kiriai asked, already seeing where Tomi was going with this, possibilities flying through her mind.

Tomi's expression sobered, and he looked at her with an expression that froze her excited thoughts midstream. "No. That's the problem. The challenger is the new brawler, while the chief appoints the defender from among the experienced brawlers. That's another reason they do the challenge at a ceremony halfway through the month. Part of the initiate's training will be how to prepare against a specific fighter."

Kiriai swallowed hard.

"'The point of the first-fight is for the experienced brawlers to crush the new ones, despite all their preparations. This will cement in the new brawler's mind how much harder they need to train to be worthy of their new position."

"It sounds like just one more sanctioned beating to me," said Isha, a touch of condemnation in her tone.

Tomi nodded and shrugged. "You're not wrong. After the fight, which they almost always lose, the new brawlers have proven that they can withstand adversities and are very aware of how much more they need to improve and train. It's not a system without its flaws, but it is effective."

"Almost?" asked Mikata, speaking for the first time in a while, her gaze sharp and considering.

Kiriai had latched onto the word, too, but was still feeling unsettled about how quickly the new idea had morphed into something close to impossible.

"It hasn't happened since I've been a high enough 'ranger to be privy to the first-fight outcomes, but I've heard rumors. These fights aren't public, which is why you probably haven't heard of them. Core 'zens hear a few details, but in the outer hoods . . . " He shrugged.

The table went quiet as everyone digested the new information.

Sento broke the silence. "So you're suggesting Boss Akuto challenges one of the other bosses in two weeks, and instead of fighting for something of token value, you want him to challenge for enough reinforcements to make a difference in the war back home?"

Tomi nodded without speaking, his raised eyebrows indicating he knew what a long shot it was.

"And the chief would choose the brawler Kiriai has to fight? I'm guessing he can choose from among any of his brawlers, from no stripes ranking up to three stripes?"

"Which adds another large variable to the equation," Tomi said. "If the chief is predisposed to send us reinforcements, he could increase Kiriai's chance of winning by choosing someone closer to her skill level. If he chooses someone from the top tiers, it would waste the whole effort. Boss Akuto would lose whatever valuable prize he put up to match the reinforcements in value."

"And I would get an epic beat-down," said Kiriai, and blew out a frustrated breath.

"That isn't the only risk," Isha said in a quiet voice, her eyes sad. "Death isn't out of the question, especially in a fight out of the public's eye. I've heard rumors."

"Well, we live in a society where our leaders can arrest anyone, anywhere, without warning, and send them to the farms. How are we to know which ones they kill?" Shisen's voice was more resigned than angry.

"Hey, not all of them are like that," said Eigo. "Boss Akuto isn't."

Both Sento and Mikata let out sharp barks of laughter at the same time. Mikata turned and glared at him, but he ignored it.

"I'll agree that Boss Akuto doesn't arrest and conscript 'zens on a whim or power play like others might," said Sento. "But if he decides it's in his or the hood's best interest, he won't let fairness stop him."

Mikata gave a reluctant nod of agreement without looking at Sento.

Kiriai sighed internally. No matter how much she achieved, there were powerful leaders who could snatch it all away in an instant.

"Since they have all the power, then why don't we fight back?" Kiriai asked, angry frustration clashing with concern for her hood inside her. She turned to face Tomi at the head of the table. "Contact Boss Akuto so he can prepare to issue a real challenge for my first-fight." She turned and looked at the rest of the table's occupants. "It's up to us to figure out which boss he needs to target. It isn't likely to be Seidai with how loyal they are to the chief. That leaves Boss Ryuin in Mabbai and Boss Yakara from Rinjin. We don't have a lot of time, but it should be enough to identify our opponent, don't you think?"

Silence greeted her, and after half a beat, Eigo let a snicker slip out.

Kiriai glared at him and he raised up a defensive hand, waving his spoon as if it could deflect her anger. "I'm sorry," he said. "But you just sounded so official and commanding right then, almost like a boss."

Kiriai's anger morphed to embarrassment, which was worse.

"I think what Eigo is trying to say is that you are correct in your assessment and your plan is a good one," said Tomi, giving Kiriai a chance to recover. "In fact, if we're able to pull this off and challenge the boss working against us, a win might impress the chief and other bosses enough for them to follow suit and add their own reinforcements. There's nothing like strength to impress or scare others into cooperation."

Tomi's words seemed to wrap up their planning, and Kiriai refilled her bowl with the last of the savory stew.

A short knock made everyone look up as the door to the dining room slid open and a young servant boy pushed in a cart with refills of drinks and food.

From Shisen's flinch at the boy's appearance, Kiriai knew she wasn't the only one wondering how much the servant might have overheard. She tried to remember exactly what they'd been saying and if any of it was incriminating.

The boy worked for the brawler food service department and had delivered the catered food at the beginning of the hour. He'd mentioned something about returning with more, but Kiriai had expected some kind of warning beforehand. She'd talk with Aibo about making better arrangements for their privacy as soon as he left.

"I am training mornings with senior fixers as they treat brawlers," said Isha, interrupting Kiriai's thoughts as she watched the boy finish up and leave, closing the door behind him. "I'm learning a lot more about handling acute injuries caused by combat, which I apply on Kiriai during her noon treatments. In the afternoons, I have permission to attend class at the Southern Core Fixer Academy." Isha's smile widened further, and she looked a little sheepish. "The problem is there are too many classes I want to take, and I'm having a hard time choosing. But I'll head over after lunch and decide. Your turn," she said, turning to Aibo.

The younger girl looked surprised, before understanding filled her expression. "Oh, right. We're reporting in on our crew duties so Kiriai can practice management. Um, I also have lessons in the mornings, some of them together with Shisen. Clerk and aide work overlap a lot. It's only been two days and most of what we're covering is how to establish your household here, so it will be ready for you at the end of the month." She waved a hand at their surroundings.

Kiriai had a hard time keeping a calm expression. She still felt overwhelmed that this mansion was destined to be hers in a month's time.

"It's mostly learning how to handle Kiriai's income, hire the appropriate staff, order supplies—" Aibo stopped, blushed and looked down. "You probably aren't all that interested. At the moment it's mostly handling income and expenses. I'm sure I'll learn more interesting things soon."

"Aibo," said Kiriai before any of the others could respond. She waited and on a whim focused on the word *friend* and did her best to mentally shout it at her aide. The girl's head snapped up with a hesitant look. Kiriai made a mental note to speak to Shisen sooner rather than later about the young girl's emerging 'path gift. Now was not the time, though. Instead, she smiled and nodded at Aibo. "The work you do is just as important as what any of us do." Kiriai gestured to the others at the table, and her heart warmed when she saw them nod in agreement, all aiming supportive looks at Aibo. "And we appreciate it. Besides, what-ever you did to get this amazing food here on the table for our lunch is worth more than anything these guys have been doing lately," she said with a wave at the training members. Kiriai was rewarded by a beaming smile from Aibo and chuckles from the rest of the table.

The rest of her crew gave succinct reports on their progress with no surprises. Kiriai made a mental note of enough details she hoped would help her with the inevitable interrogation, when she got back under Gebi's thumb.

The thought prompted Kiriai to put down her spoon, though she could probably have finished a few more bites. She'd learned long ago not to go into training with an overfull stomach. At least she'd had a treatment from Isha before lunch. Otherwise, she would be in no shape to do anything else strenuous this afternoon.

And Gebi had said something about blindfolds during training this afternoon.

Kiriai was pretty sure it was dread, not excitement, that fluttered inside her.

CHAPTER FIFTEEN

"When the warnings came streaming in and images of nuclear horror on American soil filled our screens, we didn't have time to stop the AIs from executing their doomsday programming. Would we? If we could have?"
— Journal of DMCCC Alex Stevens, Missile Launch Control Center, somewhere in South Dakota

"Your crew will make or break you," said Gebi as she stalked up and down the line of Kiriai and the other initiates, in what seemed to be her favorite method of intimidation. "Pay attention to your crew, and they will take care of you."

"Brawler Akumu," she said, looking over their shoulders at the row of trainers arrayed behind them.

"Yes, Trainer," barked Akumu, who'd seemed to have the same personal grudge against her that Gebi did.

"What would you do without your crew?"

"I'd lose in the ring, Trainer Gebi."

"How often?"

"Every time," he answered, but this time his voice was softer, as if he cared about the members of his crew. The thought surprised Kiriai. She hadn't considered the idea that other brawlers might have something similar to the family feel of her group.

Gebi stopped directly in front of Kiriai and spun to face her. "What is the status of your crew 'ranger, Initiate Kiriai?"

The demand caught her off guard for a split second and Gebi took advantage of it. "Did you spend your lunch stuffing your face or sleeping because all this training has made you *too tired*, Initiate Kiriai? You couldn't remember your assignment over a lunch break?"

"No, Trainer," Kiriai said, back straight and eyes forward. She could play this game all day.

"Then answer the question, Initiate. What is the status of your crew 'ranger?"

"He is meeting with the senior brawler 'rangers for training, Trainer."

"And what specifically is he learning?"

Kiriai's thoughts scattered. She couldn't very well say he was learning to let the other 'rangers think they were better than he was when they weren't.

"Come on, Initiate. Thinking fast and under pressure has to be second nature if you're going to be a brawler. I knew you didn't belong here. Now, answer the question!"

Gebi was so close, Kiriai could feel her breath hitting her cheek and could guess what she'd had for lunch.

"They have nothing to teach him," Kiriai said, unable to generate anything but the truth. "He's *handling* the other 'rangers so they think they do."

Gebi straightened and took a step back, her expression blank for a full second. Kiriai braced herself for the expected explosion, keeping watch in her peripheral vision. Instead, Gebi let out a scoff followed by a half smile she quickly covered.

"Maybe he can give you some lessons then," she said, back to her growly demeanor as she turned to harass someone else.

Kiriai was just glad her words hadn't set Gebi off again and quickly ran through each of her crew members, determined to be ready with quick answers if the trainer circled back around.

Instead, after interrogating the last initiate about the details of her crew, Gebi returned to the front and clapped her hands. "Listen up. I know you are all probably feeling tired and hurt after this morning's beating"—she smiled when she said the word —"I'm under instructions to give you a chance to heal so we don't break the little baby initiates. So while we'll continue teaching you to respond faster to attacks, this time you shouldn't take as much damage . . . if you learn fast enough. Pair up!"

Kiriai pulled on her centering skills and forced her muscles to relax as the brawlers behind them moved to pair up with an initiate. She suppressed a groan when the familiar wiry figure of Brawler Akumu stopped in front of her. What was his problem with her? Remembering their planning session at lunch, Kiriai decided to do her best to find out.

"Right-foot forward stance," said Gebi. "Cross your lead arms at the wrists and put your other hands behind your backs."

What kind of instruction was that? Kiriai hesitated, not too thrilled about getting that close to Akumu. He stepped forward with an impatient huff and grabbed her front arm. He moved it into a blocking position and then mimicked her position, angling the outside of his wrist so it touched hers, like crossed sword tips.

"Brawlers lead. Initiates follow their movements. You will maintain contact with your partner's arm at all times. Your job is to learn to feel and sense the movement of your partner as soon as or even before it happens. Understand?"

"Yes, Trainer," they all chorused, though Kiriai didn't think she was the only one a little fuzzy on the point of this exercise.

"Hajime!"

Akumu's hand whipped up and slapped her cheek so hard her eyes watered. Kiriai had been so focused on parsing Gebi's instructions, she had been completely unprepared. A flare of anger and rush of adrenaline had her jumping back, fists already moving to hit the smirking face right in the teeth.

"If you could follow simple instructions and maintain contact with my arm, Initiate, I wouldn't have been able to hit you," said Akumu with a sneer as his hands moved in fast, light touches, deflecting her punches with ease.

"What do you think you're doing, Initiate?" Gebi appeared by her side, voice blasting Kiriai out of her anger. "Get back into position, cross arms and maintain contact. Am I clear?"

The yelling wasn't helping her anger any. Kiriai knew a few deep breaths would help her calm down, but she didn't really want to calm down right now. She wanted to hit her tormentors. Hard.

Her feelings must have been obvious because Akumu let out a mocking chuckle.

"Stow the attitude, Initiate!" said Gebi. "Only when you've put in the time and training will you get the chance to face off against either of us. For now, you have one job and one job only." Gebi paused and then yelled, "Do what I tell you! Do you understand?"

"Yes, Trainer," she said, knowing that doing anything else would be foolish and could jeopardize everything. She couldn't fight in her first brawler challenge if she didn't make it through initiation.

Back in position, jaw clenched, she focused on keeping her forearm in contact with Akumu's. It wasn't easy. Sometimes he'd push closer to her, other times pull away, always switching the speeds to throw her off. As soon as she lost contact with his arm, she'd overcorrect, and move too fast, usually banging into his arm with a jarring thud that didn't seem to bother the man in the least. Her forearm, however, quickly thrummed with a dull ache that spread into her bones.

After an embarrassing moment when she lost his arm again, he flicked her forehead with a finger before she could reconnect. Kiriai clenched her jaw but kept quiet, using her wrist to push his arm back to the center position between their bodies.

"You'd make a great 'forcer," he said in a mocking voice. "Why suffer through all this, when you can go grab the armband over there and be on your way to a cushy life?"

Kiriai bit back a reply and focused everything on staying connected, mirroring his motions, fast with fast and slow with slow.

"The tricks that worked for you back in your little hood won't work here, Initiate. Just quit already." Akumu alternated the pressure as he pushed his arm against hers. After a hard forward shove, he backed off quickly and Kiriai almost lost contact again before following his movement.

"You'll never be as good as we are. Can't you see that?" The man's words kept coming, even as Kiriai tired. Her shoulder was on fire from the concentrated movement of her arms without a break. How did he have the breath or energy to keep speaking?

"You don't deserve to be here and no one wants you," he said and with hardly any effort, he slipped away from Kiriai's hand and patted her on the same cheek that still felt hot from the earlier slap.

Kiriai's control frayed, her anger and frustration sawing at it. "What's your problem with me?" she demanded through gritted teeth.

"Oh, so she speaks?" Akumu's face lit up with mocking surprise, before he leaned forward with a malicious glint in his eyes. "Gebi told me all about you. There is no way we will let someone like you cheat their way into the brawlers. Our job is to keep out anyone who isn't good enough." He shoved his arm hard into hers. "And you aren't good enough."

His words hit Kiriai harder than his slap had. Who did he think he was saying things like that? He knew nothing about her.

She'd given everything to get where she was, more than this pampered idiot in front of her had, no matter how skilled he was.

She knew her anger played right into his hands, but her earlier doubts let his words shoot past her usual defenses. It had been a while since anyone had dismissed her fighting abilities with claims she'd cheated her way to the top. Or at least had the guts to say it to her face.

But others had tormented her like this in the past, and she couldn't afford to lose control this time. With as much resolve as she had, Kiriai pushed herself, her arm stuck to his with all her tenacity. She refused to give him another chance to detach and get a free swipe at her.

"I knew it," he said. "You don't have any fight in you. I'll document your calm control in my notes after training today. I'm sure that'll impress everyone."

"Thank you," Kiriai said in a calm voice as sweat trickled down the side of her face. Her right arm and shoulder were a mass of burning pain, and tremors ran through her legs from holding the same stance for so long.

Her response seemed to bewilder Akumu for a heartbeat. Then Kiriai saw a new idea occur to him. A flicker of dread began inside her.

"Is your crew as bad as you?"

"My crew?" Kiriai asked, with a mix of worry and anger before she could stop herself.

The satisfied light in Akumu's gaze made her groan inside. He'd just been looking for another way to get at her and she'd given it to him.

"Hah. I think your crew could use more intense training to make sure they will be up to the strenuous life of serving a brawler." He punctuated every other word with pushes and pulls. Her arm screamed for a break.

Kiriai felt sick. Images popped into her mind of her friends being targeted. Her control slipped again. It was one thing for her to take this punishment. She was used to it. Her crew wouldn't be.

"After we're done here," he continued in his nasty voice, "I'll speak to the crew trainers. Your people will get the best *attention* we have available." Akumu stopped moving, his expression turning thoughtful as Kiriai's thoughts swirled in a dangerous mix of worry and anger. "Don't you have a scrawny kid as one of your sparring partners?"

Everything inside Kiriai went cold.

"Ego or something like that?"

"You stay away from him." Kiriai didn't recognize her voice. It dripped with cold threat.

Akumu looked taken aback for a moment before he laughed and moved again, probing her defenses and forcing her to follow. "Gebi and I can do whatever we want, even if it means harassing one of your crew to make you quit."

The trembling rushing through Kiriai now wasn't from fatigue.

"You should save you and your friends a lot of hurt and just quit now."

"Never," she said through gritted teeth.

Akumu shrugged, looking unconcerned. "Then don't come complaining to me when your friends are hurt."

The image of someone hurting Eigo was the final straw. Kiriai's control stretched to its limit and part of her tried to hold back and maintain control. But he'd threatened her crew, her family.

She snapped.

Rage flooded through her.

With an angry yell, Kiriai ignored the stupid exercise and punched as fast and hard as she could straight at Akumu's face. Even surprised and so close to Kiriai, Akumu still got his arm in front of his face to deflect Kiriai's angry punch. The first one, at least.

Rage blinding her, Kiriai's rear fist followed the jab a split second later. It slammed into Akumu's jaw with a satisfying crunch. His head snapped back, his eyes wide and astonished. Kiriai didn't hesitate, her fists driving to take advantage of her enemy's weakness. She hit his arms, ribs and torso because he'd raised both his arms high to protect his face from further damage.

Kiriai's world turned upside down a second later. Her feet flew out from under her, her back slammed into the floor and her breath choked to a stop as she stared up, stunned.

Trainer Gebi held her down, kneeling across her center with all her weight and hand pushing down on Kiriai's throat. The trainer's furious expression consumed Kiriai's vision as black crept in from the sides and her chest struggled in vain to suck in air.

Gebi looked even angrier at having to ease back, but she did, a fraction. Kiriai sucked in a gasp of sweet air and only then noticed the complete silence, except for her labored breathing and thudding heart.

"What in ancestors' name do you think you're doing?" Gebi's words sliced through the silence.

Kiriai didn't have an answer that would make a difference.

CHAPTER SIXTEEN

"We don't want it said that we don't appreciate fighting spirit," Gebi said to the brawlers and other initiates standing in a large circle around her. Next to her, Kiriai stood in a ready stance, inwardly vibrating with anger and also fear. Had she ruined everything? Still, she wouldn't stand by when they threatened Eigo and her crew. Forget this whole brawler business. She and her crew would just go back to Jitaku and find a way to win the war from there. She was done dealing with these arrogant idiots.

"However, attacking a trainer like you did during initiation has severe consequences," Gebi said as she turned her full focus on Kiriai. Kiriai kept her eyes up and forward, expression carefully blank. "Unless you are challenging your instructor. Are you challenging your instructor?"

"What? Challenging?" Kiriai asked before she could stop herself.

Gebi laughed with delight. "Don't they teach you anything out in the border hoods? Everything in our world depends on your fighting ability." She turned to face the other initiates arrayed around them. "Would anyone like to explain to Initiate Kiriai what I'm talking about?"

Initiate Jiseki's hand shot up, her eager expression stoking Kiriai's anger further. Did everyone here hate her?

Trainer Gebi gave a nod in the woman's direction.

"At any time, an initiate may challenge the trainers to combat. Winning proves that the initiate has the necessary skills to join the brawlers, and he or she is then exempt from further training and allowed to join the brawler graduation at the end of the initiation."

A sense of self-preservation tried to snuff Kiriai's anger, but the chance to fight the smug Akumu without anyone stopping her sounded really good.

"So, Initiate? Are you challenging Trainer Akumu? Or shall we move on to the consequences of an unprovoked attack on an instructor?" The smug look of triumph on Gebi's face made Kiriai hesitate, giving her common sense a moment to intervene. She knew what she should do: apologize and fall back in line. This whole thing was a mind game testing her ability to submit to authority. But knowing that didn't make it any easier.

Tomi's face came to mind as did the easy way he pretended to submit to get what he wanted. Shisen would kick her if she were here, and even Sento would be quick to caution her to back down and stay under the radar.

Gebi's gaze narrowed at Kiriai's silence, and Kiriai knew that submission was the right choice. Whatever this challenge was, it couldn't be good if Gebi was so eager for her to do it.

"Just as I thought," the trainer said, derision dripping from her voice. "You don't have the heart of a fighter when the stakes are important. When it comes to protecting those you care about."

Gebi turned, her words leaving Kiriai equal parts angry and worried.

"Initiate Jiseki. Why don't you inform our backwoods initiate here what the penalty for an unprovoked attack on a trainer is?"

"Yes, Trainer," said Jiseki, with a bit too much satisfaction in her voice. "The head trainer can impose any consequences that focus on improving the skills and abilities of those being punished, with the restriction that no permanent damage be done."

Gebi turned back to Kiriai, malice in her expression, and Kiriai realized how disastrous her brief loss of control had been.

"Since you weren't challenging Trainer Akumu, I will document your attack as insubordination. You will be assigned double conditioning routines starting tomorrow." Gebi stepped closer and glared directly at Kiriai. "I will personally make sure you are too tired to even lift a finger in defiance for the rest of the month if that's what it takes."

Kiriai swallowed and stayed silent, determined to take any consequences the trainer wanted to heap on her. She'd been the idiot that let Akumu goad her into losing control.

"And since Akumu has pointed out some deficiencies in your crew," Gebi continued, "we will remedy that starting tomorrow. I find pain to be a great motivator when training."

A dawning horror grew in Kiriai as she realized what Gebi planned.

"Don't worry, Initiate," she said with a mocking tone as she reached up and patted Kiriai's cheek. "We'll have that little Eigo of yours in tip-top shape in no time."

And just like that, she lost control for the second time in an hour.

"I challenge Trainer Akumu," she said, feeling the flush of anger making her face hot and her voice crack. She steadied herself before continuing. "That's why I hit him. It was a challenge."

A brief beat of silence filled the large hall, empty but for their relatively small group. Gebi smiled widely. It was a cruel smile.

"Trainer Akumu," she called over her shoulder, keeping her

eyes locked on Kiriai's. "It seems we have an initiate who thinks she doesn't need any more training. Care to prove her wrong?"

"Gladly," he said, and strode to the center. Her punch had reddened his jaw, and he looked more than happy to return the favor. He moved with a lupine grace that might have made Kiriai second-guess her decision if she hadn't been so angry. No one threatened her crew. She'd beaten bullies off Eigo the first time they'd met as children, and there was no way she would let some arrogant brawlers pick on him now, if she could help it.

"Positions," said Gebi with the snap of command used by judges to officiate a fight.

The order slammed into Kiriai's emotions like a cold bucket of water. She was about to fight a full brawler. Right now. Her feet moved unbidden to her mark as she scrambled to order her thoughts. What did she know about Akumu, his fighting style, his strengths and weaknesses? She'd been so focused on his words and implied attack on her crew, she hadn't even considered him as an opponent.

Gah. She gave an internal moan. *I will get slaughtered here.* At almost the same moment, satisfaction replaced her resignation. She'd be happy to take a beating to protect her own. They were family.

"Stances," Gebi said.

Feeling as if events were running away from her, Kiriai dropped back into her stance and forced her strategic mind to think of something . . . fast. She knew Akumu was quick, which negated many of her own strengths. She'd felt the power in his arms just moments before, so she didn't want to go toe-to-toe with him. That left his arrogance. She mentally gathered tactics she'd used in the past. She had faced many opponents who'd underestimated her. It was a small chance, but better than nothing.

"Hajime!"

Without hesitation, Akumu launched himself forward, his lead hand rocketing toward Kiriai's face, followed by a kick moving just as fast. But Kiriai was already slipping sideways with a mental thanks to Yabban for insisting she practice Moving up the Circle and getting off the Line of Attack.

"Ah, the rabbit can move," said Akumu as he came to a halt and circled to face her. He glanced at the spectators with a wide grin of enjoyment. "Good. I don't like my hunts to be too easy."

A few of the other brawlers chuckled while the initiates looked on with a wide range of expressions. Kiriai ignored them and stared at her opponent, watching every movement while searching her memory for a scrap of information that might help her.

Come on, Observation skill. Was his lead hand dropping a bit? His rear foot seemed to be turned on an angle he'd have to adjust before attacking.

Then time for thought was over. She barely noticed his intake of breath before Akumu exploded in another series of attacks. This time he turned and twisted to follow her evasions, not letting her put any distance between them, even though he seemed to expend hardly any effort.

Kiriai caught most of the blows with teeth-jarring blocks, but one of his kicks slipped under her elbow, landing just above her hip.

Despite tightening her core and letting out an explosive breath, the kick slammed her back. Pain blossomed in her side as her feet churned to keep her from going down. Looking at Akumu's relaxed stance, easy breathing and smile, Kiriai changed her goal. She was completely outclassed. But if she could get a repeat of her early punch, that would have to be enough. A random memory made a hint of a smile appear on her face. This was how her scrapper career had started. She'd been fighting Sento at the time and her goal had been to land a single attack against a much superior opponent. It would not be as easy as a punch to the foot this time, but she had improved a lot since then.

Akumu stood in the center, waiting for her. He tipped his hand and made a come-here gesture. She ignored him and concentrated on her breathing like she should have done much earlier. The familiar calm of her centering state filled her and the pain faded into the background. Her plan was simple: evade and watch for an opening, then throw everything into a counterattack.

For the next minute, they engaged in an intense cat-and-mouse game with Kiriai taking more hits than she would have liked while Akumu charged with bursts of blinding speed. She kept her eyes wide and her focus soft, to take in as much about her opponent as possible. Small signs of frustration showed in Akumu, and Kiriai knew she'd already be finished without her centering ability to help her ignore part of the pain.

"Stop playing with her, Akumu," said Gebi from the left, her tone irritated. "Finish this already."

Akumu's mouth tightened to a thin line, and for a moment, Kiriai thought he would snap back at Gebi. The moment passed, though, and he plastered on a smile that looked forced. "Yes, Trainer," he said before turning back to Kiriai. "Let's finish this."

"Everyone, one step forward," said Gebi. In the next moment, the size of their ring had shrunk, severely hindering Kiriai's ability to stay out of Akumu's reach. By the smirk on his face, she could tell he'd realized the same thing. This was her chance, probably her only one. A calm calculation ran through her mind, and she switched her stance with a fast twist of her hips. Akumu usually led with his left, keeping his more powerful right side to deliver the final blows. His attacks were often straight on, instead of roundhouses or hooks. Until now, Kiriai had evaded back and to the left, on purpose. She only hoped it had been enough in the short time for him to expect it again.

Akumu sucked in a short breath, and Kiriai charged almost

simultaneously with the trainer. Knowing she needed every advantage possible, she pulled on her gift, the unwanted skill that let her slow down time for a second or two and then rewind it back to the start. After months of practice, she could reliably summon it twice a day, most of the time.

Thankfully, it responded this time. Time slowed. Kiriai relaxed her mind, watching and marking Akumu's attacking punches, a lead jab followed closely by a tight hook. Her lead hand intercepted his jab, barely, but his hook flew right behind it, her rear hand too far back to intercept it. Kiriai winced mentally as she experienced the explosion of pain in her jaw during long, excruciating moments. But the information she gathered was more than worth it.

As the world around her rewound back to the start of the pre-cog episode, Kiriai already had her plan in place. The fight started again, motion full-speed and sound jarring after the calm of the pre-cog phase.

But Kiriai was ready. She aimed slightly to the man's left, both her hands high and braced to intercept both punches this time. Surprise flashed in Akumu's eyes as his lead jab ricocheted off her forearm with a stinging pain, and she immediately hammered down on his hook.

And then she slammed her rear elbow forward, twisting her hips and dropping her weight so it landed with a solid thud that reverberated through her arm and shoulder. She had timed it perfectly, everything channeling power into that single strike. Akumu's breath burst out in a pained gasp and a fierce surge of vengeance filled Kiriai . . . for a very brief moment.

She tried to follow her elbow with short chopping punches. But even though Akumu had curled protectively around his ribs, his feet carried him back and to Kiriai's side, easily evading her punches.

And then he was on her, unleashing a fury that easily tore past her defenses. *He really had been holding back earlier,* she thought amidst the overwhelming assault. Blows slammed into her jaw, head, stomach, ribs, everywhere. She lost count. Desperate, Kiriai focused, and her mental skills helped push the pain back, where it clamored for attention but didn't threaten to overwhelm her. She kept her hands up, eyes blinking past new swelling as she fought back. Her knuckles stung, and she knew she had landed an attack or two. But it was nowhere near enough. Pain from one blow merged with another in a full-body agony that made her legs shake and threaten to collapse.

Voices raised in anger didn't penetrate the pulse that thundering in her ears as a final punch, one almost tame compared to previous ones, tapped against her chin with almost negligent force. Kiriai's arms and legs went limp, no longer obeying Kiriai's commands.

The cool wooden floor was a relief, if only because the blows had stopped. Everything inside Kiriai urged her to close her eyes and leave the world for a while, at least until it turned into a nicer place.

Instead, after a ragged cough followed by a full breath of air, Kiriai pulled her hands under herself and pushed. She refused to lie at the feet of the trainers, if she could help it. When she raised herself to a sitting position and looked up, she saw Akumu glaring at her, looking flushed and upset. Gebi was standing between them, almost as if she were holding the man back. But that made little sense.

Thoughts dulled by pain and operating on instinct, Kiriai gave up on interpreting the scene around her and focused on getting her legs beneath her. She made it to her knees. Her actions seemed to prompt a reaction from the spectators, so she stopped and glanced up again. Akumu was smiling, and something that might have been concern or respect flicked across Gebi's expression.

"Stay down, already," Gebi said, her voice lacking its normal bite.

Kiriai just shook her head wearily and moved again.

"Let her stand, if she wants." That was Akumu, and he sounded delighted at her struggle to stand, which couldn't be good.

"She's had enough." A quiet voice came from her right. In her haze, Kiriai thought it might have been Jimu, but couldn't be sure.

Instead of rounding on the speaker, Gebi took a step closer and looked down at Kiriai. "If you stand, the challenge isn't over, and I have to let Akumu loose again."

Kiriai stopped moving. No wonder the bully was smiling.

"If you stay down, the challenge is over." Gebi shrugged. "It's not like you'll change the outcome anyway by standing up again."

But Kiriai wasn't trying to win. She was making a point, her point. Nobody would ever force her to quit, and she would get up and fight as long as she had a breath in her body. It might not mean much now, but she vowed that it would in the future. If she had her way, word would get around to leave her alone. Everyone would know that threatening her crew would result in an unrelenting enemy.

"Everyone will know to leave me and mine alone though, won't they?" Kiriai mumbled as she went back to the simple task of standing. It required all of her effort. Her arms shook as she shifted her weight to get one foot planted on the floor. And her head . . . this was even worse than that first trance-state headache she'd had visiting Yabban's virtual dojo.

A solid hand clapped on her shoulder, almost sending her back to the ground. Gebi crouched down and leaned in close. "What will it take for you to stay down?"

The question confused Kiriai. Why did Gebi even care? Wasn't this what the woman had been aiming toward this whole time? Didn't she want to tear Kiriai down and force her to quit? And did she want an honest answer to her question?

Kiriai tried to read the woman's hard face. Any bit of emotion Kiriai had thought she'd seen earlier was gone, replaced by the usual trainer's face.

"Leave my crew alone," Kiriai said with as much energy as she could inject in her voice. "Pile all the *training* you want on me, but don't go after them. That's what it'll take."

Gebi didn't answer for a moment as she scanned Kiriai's face. Around them, everyone was quiet. Kiriai wondered how much of the short conversation they'd been able to hear. No one spoke. They'd all learned over the last few days not to break rank or speak without permission.

"Maybe I was wrong about you, Initiate," Gebi finally said, her expression softening by the barest fraction. "And we were never going after your crew."

Of course they weren't, Kiriai realized as she sagged back to a seated position, all of her energy drained by Gebi's concession and her revelation. Kiriai couldn't believe she'd fallen for it. Next time she felt prompted to center herself and get her emotions under control, she would not ignore it.

Gebi pulled back, and Kiriai realized she was about to lose the opportunity that Tomi had tasked her with. "Wait," she said, almost reaching for the trainer, but pulling her hand back at the last moment.

Gebi stopped and looked down at the hand before glancing back up at Kiriai. Whatever softness she'd shown a moment ago had disappeared.

"Do you have a problem just with me or with Jitaku Hood?"

"Why would I have a problem with Jitaku Hood?" asked Gebi, genuine confusion on her face. Then she seemed to relent briefly. "Regardless of what you may think of me, I am committed to making sure only the best fighters become brawlers. That is all I care about." Then the gruff trainer shook her head. "I'd rather shove a nail in my eye than get involved in hood politics."

Gebi straightened, and Kiriai watched all hints of friendliness disappear.

Gebi turned and faced those watching. "Initiate Kiriai has lost her challenge against Brawler Akumu, but she showed a spark . . . a tiny spark, but one nonetheless . . . of the true fighting spirit that it takes to join the brawlers. In addition, her first concern was for her crew. As we've discussed today, your crew will become the foundation of your brawler career."

Gebi turned toward Kiriai and gave her the barest of nods before looking back up. "Initiate Jimu. Initiate Jiseki. Come help Initiate Kiriai to a chair against the wall," she said, pointing a finger at the two fighters, who hopped to obey. "Runner!" she said, yelling toward the desk by a far entrance that always had someone in attendance. A young boy popped to his feet and ran in her direction. "Find a fixer and an assistant to get Initiate Kiriai into treatment. Then get someone to find where her crew fixer is and have her join them." The boy skidded to a stop, spun on a sandaled foot and ran off in the opposite direction.

Kiriai clenched her teeth to keep from crying out as the two initiates pulled her to her feet and helped her across the workout area to one of the spectator chairs along one wall. Breathing slowly and deeply, Kiriai reached for her calm and centered state. She hurt everywhere and needed something to take the edge off. As her body and mind calmed, her pain immediately dropped a notch. She sighed in relief before shaking her head. After using her centering to help manage her pain, she'd get to see if her new game level in healing translated to the real world as well. She certainly hoped so.

Jimu moved at a slow pace, ignoring Jiseki's impatient noises. It wasn't long before they had Kiriai settled in a padded chair and left her to rejoin the other initiates. Training restarted with only an occasional glance in her direction.

But it wasn't the reactions of the other initiates at the forefront of Kiriai's thoughts. Struggling to stay centered against crashing waves of pain as her adrenaline faded and injuries swelled, she worried about something else entirely.

What was Isha going to think?

CHAPTER SEVENTEEN

"Two things we need to get out of new captives . . . well, call them recruits. Find out what skills they have and information they have about food, guns or survival goods. Make them think they'll have a place in our gang if they help us. We'll keep a few of the lucky ones."

— Miya Tagami's instructions to ZJap members on processing captives during the first weeks after the Blast. Las Vegas, Nevada. Oath Keepers Archive of Truth, Volume 3

"I don't care," said Eigo, his voice enraged as he paced back and forth, vibrating with so much energy he looked ready to explode. "We're going back home." He stopped and stared at Kiriai, propped up in the softest chair in the living room. Despite Isha's best efforts, multiple fixing wand sessions, guzzling every bitter potion Isha gave her and a good night's sleep, everything hurt even worse. They had given Kiriai two days off and permission to recover back in her brawler's home instead of the barracks. It was a practical decision by Trainer Gebi, as Kiriai would have access to her personal fixer and would recover faster without the interruptions in the barracks.

Kiriai, however, didn't care how logical it was. She was just happy to be in what passed for home until everything stopped hurting. At least this time, she'd been fighting back on her own two feet, unlike the brutal ricing instigated by Second Jaaku earlier when she was a new scrapper. Kiriai shuddered. The cruel memory still raised its ugly head to haunt her occasionally, despite how much time had passed.

Eigo's face was red as he struggled with words. "We can pack up and just leave, Kiriai," he finally said, his voice full of pleading. "You never wanted to be a brawler, anyway. You can go back to being a scrapper." His eyes flashed, seeming to visualize the new reality. "You'd still be doing your part to help Jitaku in the war. And you'd probably be much more effective than letting idiots beat on you here."

"Kiriai can't—" Sento spoke from where he sat in a straight-backed chair across the room.

"You," Eigo yelled, spinning and pointing at Sento as if he wanted to punch him. "You don't get to speak. You're the one responsible for everything that happened to her. I wish to the ancestors she'd never met you in the first place. All of us, but especially her, would be much better off!"

Sento flinched back at the verbal attack, and Kiriai's mouth dropped open. Neither of them spoke as Eigo stood, shaking and glaring daggers at the room.

"Eigo—" Kiriai said in a soothing tone. Apparently that was the wrong thing to do.

"Don't," he said, spinning back to face her. "Just don't. How many times—" His voice cracked and stopped. He dropped his gaze and sucked in a shuddering breath. Kiriai's heart broke, and if the poultices and pain hadn't kept her immobilized in her chair, she would have gone to him.

No one spoke as he struggled for control. Eigo brought both

hands up to rub at his face before he turned and sank into the couch behind him.

Kiriai exchanged a look with Sento, silently urging him to give them some privacy.

"Um, well," Sento said as he stood. "I just needed to get details of Kiriai's status to report back to the trainers this afternoon. I got a prognosis from Isha earlier, so I can leave you to get back to recovering."

Kiriai nodded, relieved that Sento had picked up on her request.

Instead of leaving immediately, however, he walked over to her and then paused awkwardly. Did he want to shake her hand? Hug her? After everything they'd been through together, Kiriai felt a stab of pain in her heart that blended with everything else that hurt.

"I wanted to say something to you," Sento said in a quiet voice.

She looked at him confused. "Now?" she asked in a whisper.

He gave her a wry smile with a one-sided shrug. "You're a hard person to get a private moment with, you know," he said, his voice equally quiet. "I've been trying for days. It'll just take a minute or two."

Kiriai hesitated. With everything going on, she really didn't want to deal with anything messy in her personal life. She examined him without answering. He looked sincere. Against her better judgment, Kiriai nodded agreement before she could think better of it.

Sento looked over in Eigo's direction, where Eigo looked at the two of them, gaze glinting with suspicion.

Kiriai let a sigh escape before she turned and caught Eigo's gaze. "Would you mind getting me more of Isha's tea while I talk to Sento for just a minute?"

Eigo sucked in an angry breath. He leapt to his feet and pulled himself to his full height. Even though he was taller, Sento probably had twice the mass. "There's no way I'm leaving you alone with him," he said, looking ready to launch himself across the room to attack her ex-boyfriend.

Instead of responding in anger, Sento turned and held out both hands in a placating gesture at Eigo. "I just need a minute, man. I'm trying to apologize here, all right?"

Eigo stopped and stared, examining Sento with the same scrutiny Kiriai had just used. Then he seemed to deflate, though he still looked unhappy. Glancing one last time at Kiriai, he gave her a nod before spinning on his heel and walking through the doorway that led to the kitchen.

Sento turned back to her, and Kiriai reminded herself to stay strong. She'd already played the back-and-forth game with Sento, and he was only here now as a friend and because he was one of the best strategists she knew.

After a glance around, Sento grabbed a nearby chair and pulled it over so it faced her. He sat down across from her, but instead of speaking, he looked down at his hands as they rubbed up and down on the tough fabric of his training pants.

Did she make him nervous? For some reason, the idea pleased Kiriai and she bit back any words she might want to say. If he wanted to apologize, she wouldn't make it easy for him.

Sento looked up and the obvious regret that filled his gaze touched her, despite her resolve. "I just wanted to apologize for how our relationship ended. I was an idiot. I didn't take you seriously and didn't think you would really break it off regardless of how I acted. I ignored your concerns and even if we disagreed on some things, I didn't give you the respect of listening to what was bothering you." He sat back, ran one hand through his hair and let out a frustrated sigh before he looked back at her. "I don't have an excuse, except for the fact that I was so close to making brawler that I couldn't see anything else, even you." He stopped talking and shrugged.

Kiriai didn't know what he wanted from her and regardless,

she couldn't offer him anything more than a professional relationship. She just couldn't.

When she said nothing, he continued. "When I got the notice that you'd put me down for your crew trainer—" He stopped and let out a slow breath. "Well, let's just say I was in a bad place after everything. And doing that for me—well, you can't know how much that meant to me."

Kiriai finally relented and gave him a wry smile. "It's probably not how you imagined making it to the core."

"No," he said, with an ironic chuckle. "But it's more that I deserved after everything I did—after trying to force you to step aside for me and my dreams."

He stood and shot a quick glance over his shoulder in the direction Eigo had disappeared. His expression turned serious. "I didn't just come to apologize. I also have something to say as your trainer."

She waited, unsure what to expect.

"I wanted to say that you deserve to be here, to be a brawler," he said. "You fought for this and won it with pure skill and that ancestor's-cursed stubborn refusal to back down, even when common sense says you should."

The words hit Kiriai with more impact than she would have imagined. Had Sento known she'd been doubting her abilities and comparing herself to the other brawlers? Yesterday's brutal fight had made it very clear that she wasn't on the same level as these fighters.

"Thanks," she managed to say. "That means a lot."

"It's true. And you have to believe it, because you know I'm brutally honest about that kind of thing." He waved a hand toward the kitchen doorway. "And despite what your friend wants, we both know there is no going home. We're stuck here, and all of us are depending on your skill and stubbornness, so we'll keep you training as hard as we can, all right?"

Kiriai nodded, enjoying the renewed feeling of hope Sento's words gave.

"And next week, you'll have time to train with your crew. That's when we'll focus on making you deadly enough to win your first brawler fight. Deal?"

"Deal," Kiriai said as she heard noise coming from the kitchen.

Sento must have heard it too, because he turned to leave.

Kiriai had just settled back into her chair with a soft groan as she tried to figure out how she felt about everything when Sento turned back, lips pursed.

"One last thing—"

She gave him a questioning look.

He ducked his head, but not before Kiriai could see the remorse in his eyes.

She waited.

"And if I could take one thing back, it would be what I said to you during our last fight. Using the personal things you shared with me like that was unforgivable." The words were low, barely audible, but clear. "I'm so sorry and hope you'll forgive me someday."

Kiriai looked at him and saw he understood how much his personal attack and betrayal had hurt her. His true remorse loosened something inside her, easing a deep pain.

She nodded, blinking at the sudden rush of emotion that choked off her words.

"Thank you," Sento said, looking relieved but also uncomfortable with her emotion.

Before she could say anything more, he left. His admission staggered Kiriai. He'd always maintained the excuse that his hurtful words during the fight were just a strategy, nothing personal. And he was apologizing for them? Why now? When their relationship was beyond saving?

Kiriai let out a breath and leaned back, unable to sort out the mix of emotions in her heart. At his apology for his personal attack and his confidence in her fighting abilities, together—a broken, scarred part inside her began to heal.

"Is the ugly brute finally gone?" Eigo came in with a tray of soft foods and a fresh pot of herbal tea that gave off the familiar bitter and spicy smell she knew so well. His grin faded as soon as he saw her face. He put the tray down on the low table with a clatter. With a single movement, he sat in the chair Sento had just left and leaned forward, both of his hands moving to her knees.

"What did he say? If he hurt you again, I will kill him. I don't care how good of a fighter he is, I'm sneakier. He'll never see me coming."

"Eigo," she said with a tired smile and covered one of his hands with hers. "He didn't hurt me. He apologized, just like he said, that's all."

Eigo flinched at her touch, but didn't pull his hand free, though it seemed to take him a minute to gather his thoughts again. When he looked back at her, she could see he was still suspicious. "Well, I should hope so. He's an idiot."

"He admitted that, too," she reassured him.

"Really?" Eigo asked before glancing over his shoulder at the door. He squeezed her knee when he looked back at her with a dawning smile. "Well, maybe he's not all bad, then. Did he get down on his knees and grovel? Promise to be your slave for the next decade if you'll only accept his abject apology—?"

Kiriai leaned back and held up her hands to stop him. She stifled a giggle that made her wince in pain. "Now you're the one being the idiot. Don't make me laugh. It hurts."

Eigo looked contrite, but only a little. "Laughter is the best medicine. Just ask Yabban."

"No," Kiriai said, pressing her lips together to dampen her smile. She hurried to intercept any attempt by her AI to join in the joke telling. *No, Yabban. No jokes right now.*

Of course not. Laughter might help improve your mood, but the injury to your torso would make that action painful right now. I would never cause you unnecessary pain.

"See," Kiriai said, pointing a finger at her friend. "She has much more sense than you and promises to never cause me—" Kiriai stopped, replaying Yabban's words. *Hey, you said "unnecessary" pain. Does that mean you'll hurt me if you think it's necessary?*

Of course. What do you think our training consists of?

"What?" asked Eigo.

Kiriai gave him a sour look. "She will only cause me pain if it's *necessary.*"

Eigo sat back and laughed. "I enjoy her more and more. Tell her that for me."

Kiriai ignored him, closed her eyes and tried to relax again and just enjoy the moment. If she didn't move too much, her pain stayed at a dull throb. Eigo's easy company kept her entertained and feeling cared for.

When a few moments passed without a word from Eigo, Kiriai cracked one eye open to see if he'd left. Instead, he sat right in front of her, his gaze searching and expression pensive.

"What?" she asked. "Are you the one needing cheering up now?"

His smile was soft, not joking as he shook his head slightly.

She waited, but he didn't answer.

He inhaled slowly and, as he let out the breath, he seemed to come to some kind of decision. "Kiriai, I have something I want to talk about with you, too."

She waited a beat for him to explain.

"Something important."

CHAPTER EIGHTEEN

His declaration seemed to use all of Eigo's resolve and he lapsed into silence, making Kiriai's worry flare up.

"What's wrong?" she asked. "Are you sick? Bad news from home? What? You can't say something like that and not explain."

Instead of smiling or joking, Eigo just looked a little sick. "Maybe this isn't a good idea," he said and shifted his weight to stand.

Before she thought better of it, Kiriai reached out to stop him. Pain shot through her shoulder, making her wince.

Instant concern flashed on Eigo's face as he leaned forward, took her hand and lowered it back into her lap. "Don't move. I'm sorry. I don't want to cause you more pain. It's nothing important. We can discuss it another time." He sat back and dropped his gaze.

"No," Kiriai said, trying to make her voice soothing. "Eigo, just spit it out. We share everything with each other. Just take a minute, get your thoughts straight, and tell me, all right?" She tried to catch his eye, but he wouldn't look at her.

At least he didn't leave. After a few minutes, he finally gave a small nod.

Relief swept through Kiriai. Eigo rarely spoke about himself, and she knew how hard it was for him to open up.

He finally looked up, nervous energy fairly radiated off him, and Kiriai tried to keep from imagining the worst.

"First off," he said, "can I start by saying that our friendship is the most important thing to me, and I would never do anything to jeopardize it." He stopped and waited.

Kiriai felt a knot form in her stomach. Was he going to abandon her and go back home? Could she do all this without him? "Of course, Eigo," she said trying to keep her voice steady. "Nothing you could say to me would ever affect our friendship. Good or bad, we will always be together, just like we've been since we were kids."

Instead of looking relieved at her words, Eigo looked even more nervous.

Frustration bloomed, pushing out her worry. "Just say it, Eigo. Whatever it is. You can tell me."

Eigo pressed his lips together and then a handful of words burst out in a rush. "I like you. A lot." He clamped his mouth shut and looked at her, waiting desperately for something.

"Um," she said, drawing out the word as she tried to decipher what he meant. "I like you, too? A lot." It came out more of a question than she meant.

"No," he said, shaking his head in frustration. "You don't understand. You aren't with Sento anymore and I was going to wait until life settled down more to talk to you. But with you, life never seems to settle down. So I figured if I ever wanted a chance with you, I'd better say something soon, especially since Sento just came sniffing around again, and how would I feel if he got a second chance with you just because I didn't have the guts to speak up and tell you how I feel, so I came in here, and now I have, and what do you think?"

The deluge of words stopped, and Eigo stared at Kiriai. She

sat across from him, unable to keep the dawning comprehension off her face.

"You mean, you like me like a boyfriend? Like you want to date me?" Even she could hear the disbelief and incredulity in her voice. Eigo flinched back as if slapped, and she immediately regretted not controlling her reaction better.

"I don't know why I thought I even had a chance," Eigo said in a dull voice as he stood. "Forget I ever said anything. How could I be so stupid?" He said the last in a low voice to himself as he turned, one hand rubbing at his forehead.

"No, Eigo. Just wait," she said and cursed her injuries that she couldn't stand and grab him. "You just surprised me, is all. Give me a chance to think about it, all right?"

He stopped but didn't turn around.

"You've obviously been thinking about this for a while." Kiriai tried again. "Give me a minute to digest it myself, before running off. Sit back down and we can talk."

He still didn't move.

"Please?"

Another moment passed before he moved back to the chair and sat. He wouldn't look up at her, and she didn't blame him, remembering her own embarrassment over a year ago in a similar encounter with Sento.

She tried to remember what she'd felt then, but the mix of friendship and worry made it hard for her to think. "Eigo, you know how much I care about you. It's just—" She stumbled and tried again. "I haven't really thought about that kind of relation-ship with you."

Eigo made an indistinct noise, but didn't speak, eyes still downcast.

Kiriai winced and tried again. "You never said anything before this. How was I supposed to know?"

That got a reaction, and for a moment, Kiriai was glad.

Anything was better than seeing her normally vivacious friend so subdued.

Until she saw the anger in his eyes as they snapped up to look at her. "How were you supposed to know? Really, Kiriai?"

The anger morphed to disappointment and then to such sadness that Kiriai flinched back, feeling her eyes sting at seeing her best friend full of such raw feelings.

"I have been by your side since we were both children. Everything I do, I do to take care of you, to make you happy. How can you not see that? Why are my actions not enough to let you know how I feel?" A flash of realization crossed Eigo's face, and then his brow wrinkled, and his head shook back and forth in disbelief. "Is that all I needed to do? Just tell you how I feel? Would that have kept you from chasing after Sento? Who, by the way, doesn't deserve you and is an idiot for throwing away what he had with you for his ambitions." Eigo stopped talking, but Kiriai could see he still had more to say. Even now, he was thinking of her and giving her a chance to respond.

But she couldn't. Still stunned, she sat without speaking, hoping a flash of inspiration would give her the words to fix this.

Eigo's gaze fastened on her and he took in a breath and straightened in his chair. Kiriai held her breath.

"Then I'm telling you, Brawler Kiriai, I have loved you for as long as I can remember. Yes, it started with the family kind of love, because you and Ojisan showed me what true family was like." He stopped, his eyes softening with fond memories before continuing. "I don't know when that changed, but I know it has. For a while now, I've known that you are the one person I care about more than anyone in the world. I'm happy when you're happy. Your successes mean more to me than my own. I don't really know what love is but with you—" He stopped again and searched her face as if trying to gauge how she felt.

Well, she wished him luck, because she didn't have a clue herself. It was a huge mental shift to see Eigo in the new role he was proposing. And he was right. As soon as she gave it some real consideration, tons of previous interactions took on a completely different light. She really had been an idiot. He might not have said the words, but her best friend had been giving her plenty of clues she'd been too dense to notice.

"—I want to give this a try," he finally said, making a motion with one hand between the two of them. "So I'm saying it. Kiriai, will you spend time with me and see if we can build a relationship that is something more than friends?"

The perfect words still hadn't magically occurred to Kiriai, and she floundered mentally for what to do. What she wouldn't do for an hour or even a few minutes to think about this, without Eigo sitting across from her looking so vulnerable. He was the one person in the entire world she would never willingly hurt. Especially not when everyone else had abandoned him since he was young. They'd both desperately needed a friend that day years ago when she'd thrown herself at the bullies chasing him.

A *friend*. Her mind latched onto that word.

"Eigo, you know you are and always have been my best friend. And we both love each other—would do anything for each other."

His expression closed off and he shifted his weight back, away from her.

"No," she hurried to explain. "I'm not saying no. But our friendship is probably the most valuable thing in my whole life, Eigo. And I don't want to do anything to risk that. You saw what happened between me and Sento. We started out as friends, colleagues helping each other in this fighting business. And when we gave ourselves a chance at something more, it was amazing."

Eigo scowled.

Kiriai hurried, trying not to botch everything. "Hey, we're being honest with each other. If you want to open up to me, let me do the same, all right?"

He gave her a grudging nod.

"I didn't tell you a lot about my relationship with Sento

because I know how much you didn't like him—" She stopped as more pieces fell into place. "Oh."

Eigo tipped his head with a wry smile of acknowledgment.

"Anyway," Kiriai said, needing to get this out if they were going to move forward. "Sento and I were fantastic together for quite a while. We meshed well as fighters, helping each other with strategies, training plans, encouragement to each other when we needed it. I really thought we might make a life together. One that lasted." The loss still hurt, but Kiriai pushed the sadness back down. Now was not the time.

Eigo looked like he wanted to object, but he stayed silent.

"And then the brawler tournament happened, and we both found out how our relationship measured up against our ambitions."

"You mean his ambitions?" Eigo snapped.

"And mine. I had things I wouldn't compromise on either," Kiriai said, able to admit now that it hadn't all been one-sided. "If our relationship had been more important than my stubborn insistence of having my way—it doesn't matter. But look at where we are now." Kiriai let out a slow breath, surprised how emotional she felt. "We aren't even friends anymore. At most, Sento is a professional advisor keeping his distance, sticking to his job as my trainer, but nothing further. And I don't even know if I want him to rekindle our friendship. I don't know if I can handle just being friends without it turning into more? Do you understand what I'm saying?"

It was her turn to feel vulnerable as she put into words the pain that had been living inside her the last few weeks. And now she shared this with her best friend, who wanted to take Sento's place. Crazy.

She sniffed and let out a shaky breath. "What a mess," she blurted out with a harsh chuckle.

It was the perfect thing to say. A matching, rueful smile emerged on Eigo's face, and the tension that had been holding him stiff and straight visibly drained out, leaving her friend sitting across from her again.

"You're saying you're worried a relationship will ruin our friendship if it ends badly, right?"

"You said it, not me." A flicker of relief built inside Kiriai. Maybe Eigo would drop this, and they could just go back to the way things were.

"What if I promise to keep our friendship unchanged, no matter how the relationship part turns out?"

Kiriai tried not to groan at Eigo's hopeful expression. "You can't promise that. No one can."

Eigo leaned forward and this time, she saw a strength in him that he usually hid beneath his lighthearted humor. "Kiriai, you said it earlier. Nothing either of us says or does could hurt our friendship. We are family for life, right?"

"Yes, but—"

"No, buts," he interrupted. "Let me in. Give me a chance to show you what it's like to be taken care of by someone who puts your interests first instead of his own. All I'm asking for is a chance, nothing permanent. We can just try it out, see where it goes, and if it doesn't work—" He leaned back with a shrug and a smile. "Well, then I'll go back to pestering you with jokes, making you laugh and watching out for you, nothing more."

Kiriai narrowed her eyes, trying to read his intent. "You would really be all right with that? If I decide it just isn't working and call it off? You'll be fine with going back to our friendship? No hard feelings?"

Something flickered briefly across his expression, but was gone before she could identify it.

He leaned forward and took her hands in his. The gesture took on an entirely different meaning than usual to Kiriai. It wasn't the quick rush of attraction she'd felt for Sento from the beginning, but it wasn't the same sense of calm friendship she'd have felt just minutes before they'd had this conversation. Kiriai stared down at their hands, torn. The pull to have someone hold her again, care for her and love her was stronger than she would have thought. Could she really feel this way about her best friend?

He squeezed her hands, and she looked back up at him.

"Kiriai, you are the most important person in my life. If this doesn't work out and we go back to being friends, I will treasure our friendship just as much as I do now."

"No hard feelings?"

"None," he said. And he sat back, let go of her hands and raised one hand up. "I swear upon my ancestors." His tone of voice was more serious than Kiriai had heard in a long time.

Then a smile crept onto his face as he continued, "I will not run off and pout if you reject me. I will not curl into a ball and cry in the corner. I will not wail to the world that you abandoned me—"

Kiriai smiled, too.

"—and I will definitely not choose my multiple careers as sparring partner, tech genius and jokester extraordinaire over my relationship with you." He said the last with a bit of a bite to the words.

"Hey," Kiriai said. "No bad-mouthing Sento. He's still my friend regardless of how mixed up our situation is. Agreed?"

"Agreed," Eigo said with only the slightest hesitation.

The silence that followed was awkward as Kiriai waffled, still not sure what to do.

"Well," said Eigo, with a smile that was equal parts hopeful and fearful. "What do you say?"

Looking into the eyes of the boy she'd grown up with, there was only one answer Kiriai could give. She took a breath, sent a prayer to her ancestors that this would turn out well for both of them. And then with a small smile she nodded.

"Yes!" Eigo jumped out of his chair, whooped and pumped a

fist into the air, startling a laugh out of Kiriai. "You won't regret this, Kiriai. We will be amazing together."

His enthusiasm was infectious, and Kiriai welcomed the new hope that filled her.

Still smiling, Eigo swept forward into a mocking bow. "I have to run now, so I will leave you to your recovery and be back later to serve you in any manner you desire."

"Where are you headed?" asked Kiriai.

"Oh, I think I know where Sento is right now."

"But—" Kiriai only got the one word out as Eigo headed to the door, a swagger in his step. He looked back over his shoulder with a grin. "I think the relationship between us will be much better once I inform him you are now my girlfriend."

And then he was gone.

Kiriai stared after him, mouth open, no words coming out as she envisioned him doing exactly that. What had she done?

Steps from the direction of the kitchen made her turn her head to see Isha looking at her, a mix of concern and compassion on her face.

"I hope you know what you're doing, Kiriai," she said, her eyes on the door Eigo had closed. "That boy cares more for you than you know."

Kiriai let a little of her emotions peek through when she answered. "I'm trying to do the best I can, Isha. I don't want to hurt either of them."

Isha gave a small shrug and moved forward with a tray wafting with tantalizing odors. "Well, that's all you can do then, isn't it? And don't forget, they're grown men themselves. You're not responsible for everything and everyone around you now, are you?"

Kiriai pushed herself up better with her good arm and tried to let the delicious food cheer her up. "Tell me how to stop feeling that way, Isha, and I'll do it."

Her friend chuckled as she helped position Kiriai's food tray in the most accessible position. "I'll let you know when I figure it out myself."

The two exchanged a smile and Kiriai focused on her centering techniques to push her worries aside for a later time, even though she knew they'd be back.

CHAPTER NINETEEN

"The ability of our machines to calculate faster and better than us might have doomed us all."
— Journal of Dr. Leah Campbell, Professor in Computer Science at MIT. Cambridge, MA

A medium-height woman dressed in sharp business attire looked up and down the deserted hallway. Her hair was jet black, cut short but stylish, and she moved with the grace of someone accustomed to power. She hesitated briefly before sliding open a door and moving into the small meeting room. She blinked and let her eyes adjust to the gloomy room, its single window so close to the neighboring building that little of the late afternoon sun could enter.

A rustle of clothing came from her left and she forced herself to take her time turning to face the man awaiting her. He sat at a chair behind a small table clad in dark, nondescript clothing and a simple hood that cast a shadow across his features.

"I don't appreciate your insistence that I meet you here and especially not in person," she said, her voice dripping with an arrogant tone that made her own 'zens shake in fear. "Consider this a one-time concession."

The figure in the shadows had the audacity to snort. "While your power might eclipse mine," he said. "It doesn't intimidate the man I represent. You need him more than he needs you, Boss." He paused. "Otherwise, you wouldn't have come. Please sit." He waved a hand at the chair across the table from him.

More than anything the woman wanted to call on her 'forcers to beat a little humility into the man, but moved to take a seat instead. "We both have interests that are aligned in this matter. If you will respect my wishes as much as possible, I will do the same for your boss. Then perhaps we can both achieve our desires."

"Are you still pretending this is about revenge for you instead of power and credits?" he asked. She was close enough now to see some of his features and could easily recognize the disdain on his face.

"Why can't it be both?" she asked. There was no point in denying anything when it was just the two of them. "You want Jitaku Hood and I want Boss Akuto destroyed. If that helps advance my business interests, all the better. And as far as I can tell, everything is going according to plan. Why the emergency meeting?"

"Is it?"

"Of course," she answered, refusing to let an underling rattle her.

"And you don't see the problem with Boss Akuto's chief 'ranger campaigning around Southern Core attempting to gather reinforcements for Jitaku?"

She kept her surprise from showing. Barely. How did he already know that? The crew with that upstart new brawler had only been in the core for a few days. "It's nothing to worry about —" she said.

"Nothing?" he interrupted. "They say 'Ranger Tomi can convince a mother to give up her children. What are you going to do if he finds a group of reinforcements to send to Jitaku?"

"It won't happen," she said, finally letting some of her anger into her voice. "I've worked on this for a year and have everyone here under control. Jitaku Hood will fall to Raibaru Hood as soon as your fighters step up and finish the job. When is that going to happen? How hard can it be to win a few more battles to gain a territory majority?"

"Under your control?" he asked, completely ignoring her challenge. "Even Chief Kosui? I wonder what he would think if he knew you considered him to be under your control."

"You wouldn't dare," she hissed. "You have just as much to lose—" Then she saw the self-satisfied smirk on the man's face and clamped her mouth shut. Why did she let this topic rile her up so easily? After a pause, she continued, her tone back under control. "I obviously don't control Chief Kosui. However, a problem with the city families is consuming all his attention at the moment. Funny how a threat to your life grabs your focus." She smiled at the visual of her arrogant chief being forced to kowtow to the city families. She shook her head and told herself to focus. "He's been ambivalent about fighting to keep Jitaku or letting the burb drop to three hoods. With his current difficulties, he is paying little attention to the issue."

The woman saw the quick flash of interest in his eyes and kicked herself for letting information slip for free. "A problem with the city?" he asked.

She wasn't going to make the same mistake twice. "I'm happy to trade that knowledge for something of similar value to me. What do you have?"

"Would a current disposition of Akuto's scrappers be worthwhile to you?"

Now it was her turn to snort. "I have my own people who can tell me what each of them ate for breakfast. But if you want to give me a disposition on the Raibaru scrappers—" She let the question hang open.

He shook his head despite his visible reluctance to give up on the juicy info about city troubles. "Sorry. While our objectives align for the moment, we both know we'll return to opposing sides once this is over."

A brief silence filled the room, and the woman reviewed the ins and outs of their mutual plotting.

"Why insist on meeting me personally today? It can't be just 'Ranger Tomi's presence."

"My boss wanted to emphasize that we will do everything possible to prevent any last-minute tactics from disrupting our plan and strongly urges you to do the same. I believe his words were, 'a cornered rat can be dangerous—'"

The woman didn't bother suppressing the smile that emerged on her face at the mental image of Boss Akuto as a small, angry rat cornered in her kitchen . . . right before she smashed him under her heel. Ancestors, the defeat of that man had been out of her reach for so many years, it would feel amazing to finally crush him.

"—and that he doesn't want his hand forced into using more drastic measures to ensure our success."

Her smile disappeared and her eyes narrowed. "What does he mean by *drastic measures?*"

The outsider leaned forward, and a trickle of warning crept up the back of the powerful woman's neck. "We have spent years, many credits and a lot of fighters on conquering Jitaku Hood. My boss will stop at nothing to ensure the plan goes through. Nothing."

"Are you threatening me?" Her voice was low. Her hand slipped into a hidden pocket on the underside of her pouch. At the same time she calculated all the consequences of a crack in their shaky alliance.

"No. No," he said as he leaned back and waved his hands. The smile on his face would have looked natural on a snake. "We have enjoyed working with you this last year and still have aligned goals. My boss wants to ensure that you are still committed to the plan. Also, he'd like reassurances that you are able and willing to remove any last-minute obstacles, whatever it takes."

She didn't relax and looked directly into his eyes. "Please reassure your boss that I am more than capable of removing any obstacles to my goals . . . our goals."

To her satisfaction, she saw the man swallow hard, though he kept any emotion from showing on his face.

With an abrupt nod, he stood. She followed suit, not comfortable with the dangerous man looming over her.

"Please keep us informed of any progress Jitaku makes in their recruiting efforts," he said and reached out his hand to shake hers. "And we will happily assist you in foiling them. Our alliance still stands."

She couldn't help her instinctive flinch back from the spy's hand.

"I apologize, Boss," he said and let his hand drop. "In Western Burb, shaking hands is the custom among allies. Besides, not every spy uses poison and subterfuge. You need not to worry as long as our goals remain the same."

The woman didn't flinch again when he raised his hand and held it out. Instead, she bent her body forward in the slightest of bows, maintaining eye contact the entire time.

He shrugged and dropped his hand with a half-laugh. He turned toward the door, adjusting his cloak and hood as he went. "Until next time, Boss," he said over his shoulder.

"No," she said. "Next time, you deal with my agent as usual. Don't summon me again without reason or I may reconsider whether we really have the same goals."

The cloaked figure stopped at her words, but didn't turn around. "I will carry your message to my boss."

And then he left.

"See that you do," said the woman as she forced herself to breathe slowly and contain her anger. If there were any other way to achieve her goals . . .

CHAPTER TWENTY

"Ouch," Kiriai said as Isha ran strong fingers over her face, cheekbones and jaw, searching out troublesome spots that had been slow to heal. Kiriai's brawler home had its own dedicated treatment room right off the private dojo on the lower floor. It was roomier and better stocked than Ojisan's was at home, where he treated a large portion of their neighbors and other 'zens. The expense of it all, just for her, made her feel a little embarrassed. Bare to the waist, Kiriai tried not to wince as Isha continued her thorough exam, checking the progress of her healing two days after the beating. Trainer Gebi expected her back tomorrow, and Kiriai didn't plan on disappointing her.

"You're healing faster than I expected," Isha said in her no-nonsense fixer voice. "These bruises are in their last stages as well as the ones on your shoulder and ribs."

"Really?" Kiriai's interest perked up. If she was healing faster than usual, did that mean the healing skill in Yabban's game affected the real world? Or was it just her own belief? Both Ojisan and Isha always harped on patient attitudes and how much it affected outcomes.

At Injury Healing level 5, your recovery will speed up by 5 to 10% depending on the severity of the injury.

Really, Yabban? So not as much as a fixing wand, then? But similar?

Your wands of healing aren't in my database, though based on watching them used on you, they seem to speed recovery time by half.

Kiriai thought about it and had to agree. But only for injuries your body would heal on its own. They don't do much for long-term illnesses. So did Yabban's healing boost stack with the fixing wand, or did one cancel the other out?

I will attempt to monitor your progress and let you know.

Thanks, Yabban!

"Ouch," squeaked Kiriai in pain. Isha had hit a tender spot between two ribs that still hurt and pulled Kiriai from her musings.

"Oh, be quiet," Isha said, her tone bossy but still kind. "Besides, nothing I do to you could possibly hurt more than getting these in the first place."

Kiriai let out a wry chuckle. "It doesn't make sense, but when I'm in the middle of a fight, I can ignore almost anything. But sitting here, waiting for you to find each sore spot . . . now, that's torture." Kiriai winced again, but held still as Isha probed behind her jaw on the right side.

"Then consider it repayment for forcing me to watch them hurt you on a regular basis," said Isha as her hands moved to Kiriai's bad shoulder.

Kiriai sighed and didn't answer. She couldn't really argue. Being forced to watch a loved one being hurt with no recourse was torture. She'd rather be in the ring herself any day.

"Speaking of torture—was this another retaliation because you wouldn't fall in line? Is that how this all happened?"

"Not exactly," Kiriai said, as Isha's question caught her without a good answer. "Ouch!"

This time Kiriai did flinch as Isha pinched the skin of her bare shoulder, hard. She reached up and rubbed the pain and glared at the woman standing over her.

"What part of 'mind games' did you not understand when Tomi briefed you on this whole initiation thing?" Isha asked, not at all affected by Kiriai's glare as she moved down and lifted each of Kiriai's forearms to examine the greenish yellow of the fading bruises. "You will do everything your trainers tell you, without questions and without fighting back"—Isha stopped and stared directly at Kiriai, her look brooking no disagreement—"no matter what they say to you. Do you understand me?"

"But—" Kiriai refused to make such a blanket promise. Who knew what else Gebi would threaten to do? Kiriai would not stand by and let them hurt her people.

"No buts!"

Kiriai's eyes widened in surprise. Isha rarely raised her voice.

"This isn't some rogue 'forcer group operating on the fringes of society, Kiriai. This is the brawler initiation for the best eight fighters in all of Southern Burb. Do you realize what that means?" Isha paused, but Kiriai was too busy parsing through all the implications to answer.

Isha reached and turned Kiriai's face to meet her eyes. "It means that regardless of how much they bluster, intimidate or even threaten your family and friends, they are powerless to do any of it, unless you fall into their traps!"

Isha held Kiriai's gaze. A sick feeling rose up in Kiriai as she understood Isha's implications.

Kiriai felt like an idiot. On some level, she'd known Gebi and Akumu probably wouldn't attack her crew, but she hadn't been willing to take the chance. Even Gebi's words at the end couldn't be trusted. But the power of the chief and the value of his new brawlers. Why hadn't she thought of that?

"Do you realize how much scrutiny they are under? How much you are under?"

Kiriai didn't have an answer.

"Their supervisors are watching everything closely. You know Sensei Nigai, who's in charge? She reports directly to Chief Kosui. If either of those bullies touched one of your crew outside of a sanctioned training exercise, they'd be in way more trouble than either of them wants."

"And this?" Kiriai waved at her body, still aching and covered with patches of healing bruises. Isha was busy rubbing an eye-watering ointment into the last of the painful areas. Kiriai was too wound up to even flinch.

"Sanctioned training exercises," Isha said, her voice resigned and sad. "Kiriai, if you hadn't attacked one of the trainers, they couldn't have done any of this to you."

Kiriai's shoulders slumped.

"Ah, my Kiriai-chan," Isha said as she helped guide Kiriai's arms into those of her tunic.

Kiriai barely noticed how soft the fabric of the high-end garment was.

"It isn't a secret that your first concern is often for your family, your friends, your hood. What better way to test your loyalty and obedience? Do you think the Chief wants a brawler with divided loyalties? One of the main points of this initiation is to break all of you down and rebuild you into a force whose first loyalty is to the Chief, not your crew and not your hood. Understand?"

Kiriai stood and faced the woman who long ago had become a rock in her life. When had she become shorter than Kiriai? With a shake of her head, Kiriai dismissed the random thought and addressed the matter at hand. "I won't let that ever happen. Ever. I might obey Chief Kosui, but he'll never have my loyalty over all of you."

Isha's smile wasn't what she expected. "Of course he won't," she said with a soft pat on Kiriai's cheek. "You and I both know that, but they don't need to." Isha's eyes unfocused for a minute before she spoke again. "Think of it this way. Just like you use a feint or play a part in a fight to fake out your opponent. This is the same. Buckle down, ignore their empty threats, make them think you are their obedient pet, and get through the initiation. When Tomi makes his move to challenge for reinforcements"—Isha's eyes went hard—"then you can let them see the predator inside. But not until then. Agreed?"

Kiriai nodded, her thoughts spinning, looking at her friend with new eyes. "Maybe you should be the one in the ring, Isha, instead of me."

Instead of laughing, Isha stopped and placed both hands on Kiriai's shoulders, her expression intense. "If it meant I wouldn't have to watch them carry your broken body into my suite again, I'd take your place right now, youngling." Isha's eyes sparkled with unshed tears.

Kiriai ducked her head in shame. Why did she keep leaping into danger with no consideration for what it cost those in her life?

Isha reached out, tucked a finger under Kiriai's chin and lifted her head. "Don't worry. I know exactly what motivates you to fight for those you love," she said.

Kiriai saw true understanding in Isha's gaze.

"All of us, your family . . . we do the same in our own way, because of your example. It's one reason you have our loyalty. We know that regardless of the dangers, we can count on you." Isha stopped and waited.

Kiriai gave her a shaky nod.

"But this one time, Kiriai-chan," she continued, her expression becoming stern again. "You don't need to protect us. This initiation month is all a mental game. They are messing with your head. We aren't in danger, regardless of any trickery they use to make you think we are. Your job is to fall in line and convince them you'll be an obedient fighter. Understand?"

Blowing out a slow breath, Kiriai straightened and nodded. "I won't fall for it again, Isha."

Isha smiled, put an arm around Kiriai's shoulders and pulled her into a side-hug. "Good. And when it's time to throw off the obedient facade, they won't know what hit them," Isha said as she led Kiriai out of the fixer room, through the dojo and into the hallway leading to the front room.

Kiriai let Isha offer support, but snuck a sideways glance at the normally demure woman. Perhaps she wouldn't fare half badly taking Kiriai's place in the ring.

Isha had just helped Kiriai get settled in a soft armchair and poured her a huge mug of acrid but healing tea, when loud voices drifted into the sitting room from the front of the house.

"I'll go see who it is," Isha said as she moved to place the teapot on a folded mat on the sideboard behind Kiriai.

"I don't believe you!"

The voice, though angry, was that of a young girl, and both Kiriai and Isha looked at each other in recognition. A moment later, Shisen walked in, expression closed off as she none too gently pulled Aibo into the front room. Shisen opened her mouth to speak to Kiriai, but closed it when she saw Isha standing off to the side. Aibo opened her mouth, but Shisen turned and shushed her. The younger girl clamped her lips shut, a mulish expression on her face.

"I was just about to head upstairs to my room for some study," Isha said in a soothing tone before she looked at Kiriai. "Unless you need anything else?"

"No, thank you, Isha," Kiriai said even though she felt reluctant to trade her fixer's calming presence for whatever conflict Shisen was about to dump on her. "I'm feeling much better and should be ready to jump back into training tomorrow morning thanks to you."

Isha smiled and gave all three women a nod before she turned and disappeared through a side door.

Silence filled the room until the fixer's footsteps faded away.

Aibo was the first to speak, standing across from Kiriai, her body stiff and fists clenched. "Shisen dragged me off today to tell me some crazy story about gifts and hearing"—the young woman spoke softer—"voices in my head." Aibo aimed a glare at Shisen, who quickly moved around the spacious room, peeking into hallways and rooms before shutting all the doors and securing their privacy. She ignored Aibo's words, which made the younger girl stiffen further and turn back to Kiriai with outrage. "At first I thought she was making things up, a story to entertain me, but she's claiming this is real. There is something in my head that lets me hear what others are thinking—" Aibo's voice broke off and one hand went to rub at her forehead as she paced in front of the low tea table.

Shisen plopped down next to Kiriai with a sigh, and when Kiriai aimed a frown her way, she simply shrugged and raised a hand slightly as if to say this was normal and to be patient. It reminded Kiriai of how she'd taken the revelations herself only a year ago. It had been confusing and outrageous. In fact, she had reacted similarly to Aibo right now.

"—and not only that, but she says you both have other gifts that let you do things that make no sense." Aibo had found her voice again. "Shisen can call on visions to see danger near her? And you can stop time?" Aibo's eyes were darting back and forth between the two women in front of her, panic building on her face.

Shisen opened her mouth to answer.

"I know!" Aibo said, holding out a hand. "You can only see danger really close by and only a few times a day. And Kiriai's only works for a second or two and not always on command, but still!"

Her eyes finally stopped and locked on Kiriai before she forced a weak smile to her lips. "Tell me this is all a big joke. Right?"

Whatever Aibo saw on Kiriai's face hit her with a blow. The young aide took a few shaky steps back until she bumped into a sofa. Without bothering to look back, she sank down, her eyes a bit lost as her head made small shaking motions she probably wasn't aware of.

"I'm going crazy," she said in a voice that sounded young and lost.

"No, you aren't," Kiriai said firmly and stood and stepped around the table. She sat next to Aibo and draped an arm over the shoulders of the young girl. A small smile played across Kiriai's lips as she realized Isha had done the same for her just moments ago.

"It isn't a joke. Your gift is real. When you feel as if you know what someone is thinking? That sense of the words in their mind? That's real. That's your 'path gift,'" Kiriai said in her firm instructor's voice. She waved a hand between Shisen and herself. "Both of us have one, too. Aibo, you're not alone. Each of us, each gifted, had to go through the same thing you're going through now. We all have to train our gifts to control them so they don't control us. But what you need to remember right now is that Shisen and I are here to help you with this. We'll always be here for you. Do you understand?"

Aibo turned to look at her, still a bit stunned. "The gifted? There are more? It isn't just the three of us? How did this happen? Why me? This makes no sense."

Kiriai aimed a helpless look at Shisen, and relief filled her when her friend stood and moved to sit on Aibo's other side. In a calm voice, Shisen recounted the history of the gifted, their exploitation and abuse, the absolute need for secrecy and the beginning training regimen that would help Aibo connect with and control her gift. Shisen's method of delivering the facts and details in a straightforward manner seemed to help Aibo regain control. By the end, she was asking questions and seemed on board, though reluctant, with the first steps specified by Shisen. When the two agreed to start with a short evening session after they finished for the day, Kiriai let out a sigh of relief.

"You'll be in good hands with Shisen, Aibo. She's the one who taught me when I was just figuring all this out not that long ago. I'll try to join the two of you if Trainer Gebi gives me a break, all right?"

Aibo's smile was tremulous, but she nodded.

Shisen gave Kiriai a look and tapped a finger to her chest.

Oh, right.

"We have something for you," Kiriai said, a smile on her face as she reached into her pouch and shuffled through the contents. It had been Shisen's idea, but Kiriai had loved the idea and happily chipped in the credits to have the gift made.

"We had this made for you, to let you know how much you mean to us," said Kiriai as she held a small cloth pouch out to Aibo.

"For me?" Aibo asked. She looked so surprised and touched that Kiriai resolved to be better about showing her appreciation in the future.

"Go ahead," Shisen said. "Open in already."

Aibo pulled a delicate chain out of the pouch, and her face lit up when she saw the small charm hanging from it. Shiny wire wrapped around a slender stem of amber-colored crystal that gleamed with gold flecks.

"It's not expensive enough for someone to steal it, but we picked the color to match your eyes," said Shisen.

"And the wire supports and holds the crystal, always close, always there," said Kiriai.

Aibo's eyes sparkled with unshed tears as she looked between the women on either side of her. "Like you?"

Shisen nodded, her expression as fierce as Kiriai's as she put an arm around Aibo and squeezed. "You're just as strong as this crystal, and with us here supporting you, we'll make each other stronger. Always. Got it?"

Aibo's head bobbed in happy agreement before she turned and wrapped Shisen in an exuberant hug. Shisen looked startled, but Aibo had already let her go and turned to launch herself at Kiriai.

"Hey," Kiriai said with a chuckle in her voice. "A simple thank you is plenty."

Aibo let go and sat back with a flush.

"But a hug is good, too," Kiriai hurried to add. "You're a full member of our crew and we just want you to know how much you mean to us. All right?"

Aibo looked back up, eyes shining with emotion. "Thank you. You won't ever regret bringing me on. I don't have a big family. Just my parents. And our crew, well—"

"They're family," said Kiriai, knowing exactly how Aibo felt. "You're family. We're all family."

Shisen nodded in agreement, and the moment felt like a small island of calm in the midst of all the chaos of Southern Core.

Kiriai gave her young friend's shoulder a squeeze and was just beginning to feel Aibo might be ready to handle her new gift when muffled but raised voices drifted through the closed doors. The three women looked up and fell silent.

"Not again," Kiriai muttered under her breath.

Kiriai.

Yes, Yabban?

The words of an ancient spiritual leader, the Dalai Lama, might help you now: "Do not let the behavior of others destroy your inner peace."

Kiriai sighed. Yabban was right. *This leader didn't by chance say how to do that?*

There was a brief pause. *I don't have that information, but I would suggest your meditation and centering skills would be helpful.*

A reluctant smile played across Kiriai's lips as she turned toward the door and the next problem.

CHAPTER TWENTY-ONE

"Q is for Quotation. Study the wise Quotations of our
founders and ancestors to learn and succeed."
— Chikara City Elementary Primer

"I'll just check to ensure that Initiate Kiriai is prepared for your visit."

Kiriai heard Tomi's voice just outside the closed door. She hadn't realized he'd been here. He must have just arrived with whoever the visitor was.

"I don't have time to waste on this nonsense. I'm a very busy man and have contracted to spend two hours training her for tonight's event. If she performs poorly, it will reflect on me. Let me in now!"

Kiriai didn't recognize the other voice, but she'd had enough of being bossed around. She might have to submit to Trainer Gebi, but whoever this pompous man was, she'd make sure he changed his attitude. She stood quickly and winced, reminding herself that the fixing wands and remedies hadn't completely fixed her injuries.

"M. Shuju, you are quite right to be careful of every wasted minute. I have no tolerance for it either. I will be very quick."

Hearing Tomi's words, Kiriai hesitated, her good sense coming to the fore. She trusted he would know how best to handle whatever this was.

The door slid open and Tomi moved into the room with a quickness that his bulk would seem to prevent. In just a second, he had slid the door shut behind him and moved to stand right in front of Kiriai.

"We have no time, so just listen and do as I say, understand?"

He was already speaking as Kiriai nodded.

"M. Shuju is an etiquette trainer sent by Sensei Nigai to prepare you for tonight's formal dinner. I apologize for the short notice. I will get better sources among the senseis after this. With you healing, someone was able to keep word of tonight's training from us until just now. Your colleagues have had an extra day to prepare, so we have to catch up, quickly."

Kiriai kept her mouth shut even though she suddenly had many questions. She trusted Tomi to tell her everything pertinent in the little time he had.

"Brawlers have social obligations. The most wealthy in our society won't take large risks without the opportunity to meet and evaluate the brawlers they are choosing to represent them. Tonight is supposed to be a practice session for the newbies, but those attending won't consider it a training exercise. The men and women you meet tonight can have a significant impact on your future and especially our current plans to save Jitaku."

Kiriai stiffened as she realized the implications.

"We have three missions tonight. Uncover our enemies, impress our friends and gain allies."

Noises behind the door indicated Shuju had run out of patience.

"Remember, Kiriai," said Tomi, his voice quiet and tense. "Treat this event like a battle in the ring. Follow my lead and may the ancestors grant us a victory tonight."

"And with M. Shuju here," Tomi said in his usual booming, jocular voice as he straightened and moved to slide the door open. "You will be ready in no time. He is extremely talented in teaching social niceties to new brawlers. He's an expert at preparing them for important social occasions."

As soon as there was clearance in the doorway, a short and pudgy man charged into the room as if he owned it. He had dark, curly hair that seemed frozen mid-wave and barely moved as his head turned, eyes darting around the room and seeming to analyze every object and person in view.

Tomi turned and held out his arms, one toward Kiriai and the other reaching to the intruder. Tomi gave a gracious half-bow to the man. "Initiate Kiriai, allow me to introduce M. Shuju. He has two hours to whip you into shape for tonight's etiquette training event." Tomi took a step to the side and swept one hand out. "She is all yours. Please help her become as skilled in this arena as she is in the fighting ones."

Kiriai struggled not to feel abandoned as the little man's eyes locked onto hers and he stepped forward to examine her. She felt like a particularly tasty bug under the eye of a hungry bird. The man moved around her, eyes missing nothing. She kept her mouth shut, remembering Isha's earlier counsel. Tomi knew what he was doing, and she resolved to follow his lead and keep from letting this man get to her.

"You won't be wearing this tonight," he said, distaste on his face. He held one hand in the air and waved it. Kiriai wondered what he expected to happen and sucked in a surprised breath when a tall, thin woman slipped through the door with a speed that would have been impressive in the arena.

"Majime, a solid, dark winter color to accent her pale skin. Make sure we get something to cover up these bruises." He waved a dismissive hand toward her face. The woman had a small pad out and scribbled furiously.

"The dress needs to hug her lines. With this figure, have it flare a bit at the bottom so she doesn't look too mannish. You know what to do," he said, turning to address the woman for the first time. "Off with you. We don't have much time. Get at least three choices back here before we finish."

Majime gave him a nod, spun on her heel and left the room moving at a good clip. Watching her leave, Kiriai was startled to see how many people had followed Shuju. They stood silent, arrayed along the edges of the room, some even back in the hallway. Not a single one was empty-handed. She saw clerk supplies, trays, dishes and . . . was that a roast? An army of servants had slipped unnoticed into her home, all apparently under the command of the bossy little man in front of her.

Kiriai shook her head, and remembering Tomi's words, forced herself to focus on Shuju and treat this like the important strategy training it was.

M. Shuju's eyes flicked up to the room's wallscreen and frowned before rounding on his workers behind him.

"Dinner crew, in there," he said and jabbed a hand toward the dining room. "You have thirty minutes to set up. Go!"

More than half of the people hurried to follow his instructions, including the one with the roast. Kiriai's stomach rumbled, reminding her it was lunchtime. Maybe this torture would have a bright side to it, if the food was as good as brawler fare usually was.

"Music, over there and start playing as soon as you're ready." M. Shuju flung a hand toward a corner behind the sofas. "Set up the bar over there where the teapot is." There was a bit of a mix-up as bodies moved in different directions until finally only a handful of well-dressed and empty-handed people were left.

"Guests, come in and begin socializing. And bring in the crew ones, too." He beckoned with an imperious hand and turned back to her without waiting to see if they obeyed.

Kiriai had turned her attention back to Shuju when familiar outlines in the hallway caught her attention. She looked over Shuju's shoulder and froze.

No!

Behind the other well-dressed *guests*, in walked a stone-faced Sento, followed by Eigo, who flashed her a sneaky grin when he saw her looking their way.

Why? Both her new and old boyfriend together? And stuck in a house full of people with no privacy to talk?

Kiriai plastered a smile on her face, hoping she didn't look too sickly as her insides twisted into knots.

CHAPTER TWENTY-TWO

Kiriai ignored the two of them as they approached and turned back to M. Shuju. She was just going to pretend her dating life didn't exist.

"M. Shuju, what would you like me to do?"

He looked almost startled when she spoke, but recovered quickly. What? Was she an object instead of a person to him? For a second, Kiriai wanted to go back to Trainer Gebi and her harsh regimen. At least she understood that.

The soft strains of a violin started up from behind her, and that triggered more calculation on M. Shuju's face.

"Can you dance?"

The question was so odd, Kiriai didn't have a ready answer.

"Dance? You know, music, with a man, move your feet, look pretty?" His last words were said in a loud, slow drawl, like she was a child.

Anger flared, and Kiriai spoke without thinking first. "I'm a fighter. The only dancing I do is around my opponents when I beat them!" She clamped her mouth shut with a clack, berating herself for letting someone push her buttons moments after promising Isha she wouldn't.

"Oh," said M. Shuju with a smile, instead of the anger she expected. "There's the brawler in you. Maybe this won't be so hopeless after all."

Her confusion must have been clear.

"Initiate Kiriai, your trainers may be drumming obedience into you, but in the social arena, you need the opposite to survive. Think about it." He stopped and waved at the small crowd that was already mingling and chatting, somehow giving the appearance of a wealthy and powerful crowd with their dress and mannerisms. "Do you think the power players want a passive mouse to represent them in the ring? Of course not. Hiring you to fight on their behalf, your brutal abilities, your raw emotions, all of that gets their blood pumping." He stopped and held up one finger. "Provided you don't turn any of that on them, of course. Finding the perfect balance isn't easy, but it's crucial to your career as a brawler. That's what I'm here to teach you. Understand?"

Kiriai looked at the odd little man with more respect and gave him an abrupt nod. Tomi was right. This was important. And if there was something she'd always been good at doing, it was learning from those who knew more than she did and would teach her.

"First, keep that superior attitude and bearing you just showed me, but don't speak until you are absolutely sure of who you are speaking to and the impact of your words. In fact"—he paused to rub his chin and look her up and down again—"you should stick with the strong and cold silence. For now, I want you to speak as little as possible while keeping this *intimidation* turned all the way up." He waved a hand at her before turning to face Eigo and Sento, who had paused behind him. Eigo had been grinning during the lecture, but quickly wiped the smirk from his face when M. Shuju turned to face him.

"You two. I'm praying you have at least a smidgen of social grace," M. Shuju said as he ran his intense gaze over the two men.

"At least my people found you appropriate attire in the little time we had."

Kiriai took a moment to look at the two and appreciate their appearance, despite the stark contrast between the two. They were both handsome in their own ways. Sento wore a silky shirt that brought out the blue in his eyes and tapered pants that accented his build. He looked unruffled, hair combed neatly while every line of his tailored clothing fell in clean lines, obedient to his wishes. Eigo, the taller of the two, stood thin and light, compared to Sento's stocky build and dark features. His clothing probably took half as much fabric as Sento's and seemed to showcase his flair for life. The top buttons of the patterned shirt gave the same carefree feel of his smile and he, or a dedicated someone, had used some kind of product to tame his hair into a semblance of order. Kiriai's eyes rose at the expense and effort that must have gone into getting them ready so fast. They cleaned up nicely, though she probably wouldn't have noticed if M. Shuju hadn't drawn her attention to their attire. The confrontation between her ex and new boyfriend was all she could think about. Who cared about clothing anyway?

"Come over here and each of you take a drink in one hand," said M. Shuju. He stepped back and a servant magically appeared just off his elbow and held out a tray of drinks and small finger foods to the pair.

As the men reached for drinks, Kiriai swallowed past a dry throat and racked her mind for what she should say to them.

For a moment, Kiriai felt the strong pull in opposite directions, insisting she move toward both men, the dark one who still made her pulse quicken if she let it, and her best friend who would always be her harbor in the storm of life.

Impossible.

Instead, she stepped up to the server, reached for a fluted glass of a sparkling amber liquid and took a drink.

"Sip, moron. Don't gulp!"

The berating voice almost made her crush the fragile glass and a bit of the fruity drink spilled down her chin. Eigo snorted back a laugh, and Kiriai turned to glare at M. Shuju. The odious man was impervious to her disapproval.

Instead, he smirked at her. "And don't let someone get to you this easily. Have you no sense of self-control? Do you let your opponents in the ring goad you this easily?"

His words struck her, drying up her retort before she could lash out at him. He was right. Suddenly it clicked for her. This was just like a battle in the arena. In fact, these opponents would be even more powerful and able to hurt her.

The shift in perspective was as effective as the technique Yabban had taught her to imagine how a situation looked from above. The reminder had her instinctively activating all of her control skills. She took in a slow breath, counting beats as she focused on her senses and the situation. Her irritation and anger were reluctant to subside, and Kiriai resolved to spend more time on centering and meditation amidst all the physical skills of brawler training.

Eventually, however, her focus had the desired effect. Back in control, Kiriai reached for a napkin from the server's tray, dabbed at her chin and then took the tiniest sip possible from the expensive glass. Without a word, she then looked at M. Shuju and raised her eyebrows expectantly.

The man returned her look, examined her for a moment before he smiled and clapped his hands. "Ancestors, bless me! Maybe this will not be the punishment duty Uwaki tried to stick me with."

Kiriai kept her expression polite, pressed her lips together and bit back any response. *Strong and cold silence*, the man had said. She could do that.

But something must have shown in her eyes, because his smile widened. "It's not an insult, lass. In just a few minutes, you've shown me arrogance, strength, the ability to reign in your emotions and most importantly, that you can learn." His gaze shifted to 'Ranger Tomi. "You weren't lying when you said she was a rare find."

Tomi let out a soft chuckle. "No, I wasn't. And she is."

All the anger in Kiriai fled before a wave of embarrassment. Her cheeks flooded with warmth. Definitely not maintaining the *cold* anymore. She looked away, only to lock eyes with Sento, which only made her cheeks grow even hotter. But instead of glaring at her, he gave a subtle nod that she hoped meant he would postpone their personal discussion until later. With the way Eigo was grinning at her, there was little chance he hadn't already gushed to Sento about their new relationship.

"All right. This is the socializing time that precedes the meal," said M. Shuju, his tone back to *demanding instructor* again.

Kiriai pulled on her centering skills to shelve her relationship troubles for later.

"I will leave you with a booklet of the guests for this evening's etiquette event and expect you to have all the facts memorized before it starts. Your 'ranger will be a great help in this area moving forward"—he nodded in Tomi's direction—"and he will advise you on whom to be seen with, whom to approach, whom to tolerate and whom to avoid. Tonight isn't as crucial, as they'll expect fumbling social skills from the initiates. They will make allowances for mistakes. There will be one more of these events during your initiation and after that—" His expression turned stern. "After that, they will hold you responsible for everything you say and do, whatever your intent." He paused and tipped his head toward her, waiting for her to acknowledge his words.

Kiriai took another small sip of her drink and only after swallowing did she give him a slight tip of her head. He didn't laugh, but Kiriai saw the corner of his mouth quirk up.

M. Shuju turned and grabbed Eigo and pulled him forward.

"Tonight, your sparring partner here will be a wealthy man who is scouting for a new fighter or two to add to his favorites list. If you impress him, it could mean steady income for an indefinite amount of time. Impress him. Admire his accomplishments, but don't beg. Brawlers need to project strength and confidence at all times."

He took Sento by the arm and pulled him to stand next to Kiriai. "Your trainer here will be your escort for our practice."

As M. Shuju turned to give Sento his instructions, Kiriai saw Eigo's expression. He looked torn, mouth opening, about to object. Kiriai knew whatever came out of his mouth would set M. Shuju and his short temper off again. Eigo knew this wasn't anything real, just a practice. What did it matter if Sento played the part of her escort? On the other hand, she might feel the same way if she'd just started a new relationship only to have to watch his ex step in as escort on the same day, even just in practice. These and more thoughts raced through Kiriai's mind, and she missed her chance to intervene.

"M. Shuju? I'd like to—" Eigo spoke, his voice a little harsh and not at all polite.

Kiriai could see it all playing out, crashing down. M. Shuju's opinion of her and her crew would plummet and she would lose the bit of positive ground she'd just gained. To her right, she saw 'Ranger Tomi step forward, his arm reaching toward Eigo, concern on his face. He wasn't close enough.

"Excuse me, sir."

The interruption didn't come from Tomi. Kiriai turned and surprised, she saw that Sento had spoken, drawing M. Shuju's attention. "I have spent a lot of time working social strategies to further my fighting career in the ring. I would be better suited to play the role of the businessman. Besides, Eigo will be Kiriai's escort tonight, so it will be better to practice beforehand, don't you think?"

"I don't care who does what," said M. Shuju with an irritated wave of his hand. "Just hurry up."

Eigo gave Sento a grateful look, though Kiriai detected a bit of underlying confusion in his eyes. Kiriai felt the same way. Why had Sento stepped in and helped Eigo? Had he finally accepted that he'd lost her? Kiriai swallowed, unsure of how she felt about that idea.

Meanwhile, M. Shuju moved forward at his rapid speed. "That man is a mortal enemy." M. Shuju pointed to a slightly over-weight man who was busy enjoying tasty tidbits from a plate held in one hand. "He wants to make you fail by any means necessary. Do not give him any valuable information. As you gain skills, you may offer believable misinformation to steer him in a direction more favorable to you." When M. Shuju finished, the man tipped his head at him in acknowledgement. Then his face morphed into one of haughty condescension from one second to the next.

Kiriai blinked, surprised at the transformation.

"The woman there is a possible ally waiting for a good reason to join her interests with you and yours. That man is new to his power and you need to find out what his intentions are." M. Shuju rattled off roles as he pointed at different pretend party-goers who quickly transformed following his descriptions.

Then he stopped and scanned the group, one hand rubbing his chin, while Kiriai's head spun at all the information he'd just thrown at her. "One more. That woman there has supported you since you first came to challenge the chief last year. You bring excitement to her boring life and as long as you continue to do so, she'll throw her rather hefty support behind you."

M. Shuju turned back to her and clapped his hands. "There! Did you get all that? Now you should have enough to practice for both the mingling and the meal stages." He glanced at the wallscreen one more time and made shooing motions at Eigo and Kiriai. "Go! We have fifteen minutes before we move to the meal.

Mingle. Learn what you can and avoid as many dangers as possible."

With a grin and bow, Eigo held out his arm to Kiriai, and despite how muddled her thoughts were, she couldn't help but return the smile. Who knew that the day she'd agreed to start a relationship with him, he'd be a practice partner in the afternoon and escort her to her first fancy affair that evening?

Arm in arm, they turned to face Sento. Kiriai pushed aside the flicker of worry and tried to focus on M. Shuju's instructions.

"Brawler Kiriai, it's a pleasure to meet you. I've heard a lot about your exploits in the arena and I'm looking to expand the brawlers on my company's preferred list. May I have a moment of your time?"

Kiriai stared slack-jawed at Sento, whose whole demeanor had changed to fit M. Shuju's description perfectly.

"Well, don't stand there, stupid. Say something."

Even knowing that the insulting tone was M. Shuju's version of hazing and training didn't keep Kiriai from wanting to turn and punch the man. But she sighed. M. Shuju was right. She would run into powerful elites who were a lot more irritating than he was, so she needed the practice.

Without glancing back at M. Shuju, Kiriai bowed slightly toward Sento and said, "A pleasure to meet you M. Sento . . ." Then the words just dried up. She had no idea how to make conversation with someone wealthy and powerful, unless they wanted to discuss fighting tactics in the ring.

"Ask him about his business. His interests. What type of fighters he is looking for. Get him to talk, so you don't have to. Come on!"

Everyone pretended M. Shuju wasn't behind her with berating advice, so Kiriai did the same. "M. Sento, what type of fighters are you looking for, and do you mind sharing who you currently have on your list?"

"Passable." Kiriai heard the mutter from behind her and she took it as a compliment.

As Sento waxed on about the fighters he preferred, Kiriai wondered how she would do tonight without M. Shuju standing behind her coaching every action. The thought made her stomach clench, and she forced herself to take mental notes on everything M. Shuju said. She needed all the help she could get.

CHAPTER TWENTY-THREE

"We were so busy protecting our military hardware and the people who had access to it. We should have put more effort into our firewalls and vetting the people who could get to our software and machine intelligences. Now it's too late."

—Anonymous employee. Strategic Automated Command and Control Systems

Kiriai stood with Sento in a spacious entrance hall where the other initiates, their crew members and their supporting staff milled around nervously, getting ready for the main event. At another entrance, the junior leaders were assembling, ready to act their parts in this first social practice session for the initiates. Their superiors had likely given them plenty of instructions for tonight's dinner despite the fact that its purpose was training. It was never too early to put out feelers for future alliances. At least, that was what both M. Shuju and Tomi had drummed into her all afternoon. Kiriai scanned for Tomi and the rest of her crew who must still be stuck in the registration process. Each crew member had a room off the entrance where they were signing in and receiving final instructions for the evening.

Sento had finished first and waved her over. The others all seemed delayed. Kiriai pushed up to her tiptoes and still couldn't see the rest of her crew. She did her best not to look at Sento.

"You look amazing," Sento said with quiet words that the surrounding crowd wouldn't be able to hear. Kiriai had no problem making them out and her lips moved between a smile and a grimace at the compliment. Without thinking, she rubbed one hand down the soft, stretchy material of the teal dress that hugged her curves and made her feel both beautiful and exposed at the same time.

Unsure how to respond, Kiriai pretended she hadn't heard and kept looking over the crowd. This was really not the place for a discussion with Sento. If only she'd been able to find a few free moments this afternoon, instead of having Shuju and Tomi monopolize all of her time.

"Like Eigo said on our way here," he added, and she caught a wave of his hand as he motioned at the dress she wore.

Keeping up the pretense took too much effort. With a sigh, Kiriai turned and gave Sento a half smile and shrug. "Thank you —" She paused. It was too difficult to figure out what else to say, so she just blurted out the first thing that came to mind. "I'm sorry I didn't have time to talk to you before Eigo spilled everything. I'm sure that wasn't a fun conversation for you. I know I hate being blindsided and am sorry I didn't give you a heads-up." She clamped her mouth shut and held her breath, waiting for his response.

"No. No," Sento said and raised his hands up slightly. "I'm the idiot that messed up our relationship. What you do now is your business, not mine. I just want you to be happy." He made his own resigned gesture. "I see how much he cares about you and makes you smile. You're lucky to have him."

Kiriai stared, dumbfounded. The noise of the crowd faded to the background.

Sento gave her a half smile that tugged at her insides.

"I wish I could have done that for you, but I couldn't," he said. "Now, I hope you and Eigo make a go of it."

Her expression must have been interesting, because he laughed. "Relax, Kiriai. I'm still me. I may have gone a bit crazy during the brawler tournament, but I've still got all my ambitions and smarts up here"—he tapped the side of his head—"and I'll be using everything I have to make sure we figure out a way to help save our home and that you and our crew come out ahead at the end. And this time, I'll make sure my personal ambitions take a backseat to what's best for all of us first. All right?"

"Thanks," said Kiriai and nodded with the first real smile of their exchange. "You don't know how much that means to me. And how it ended between us wasn't just you. I was just as much an idiot."

Sento looked taken aback, and something Kiriai couldn't read moved across his expression. His brows raised in question.

"I was too stubborn to compromise when I could have easily let go of my pride and lost a fight sooner." The words were hard to get out, but they'd been inside her for a while now, and Kiriai felt a weight lift after saying them.

A bit of tension seems to leave Sento's expression too.

"And I'm glad to still have you as a friend, one who is happy for Eigo and me," she hurried to say, hoping to preempt anything else he might say. "I don't want to lose either of you."

He didn't smile, just stood, examining her face while she struggled with everything spinning in her mind and heart.

"Just remember, you'll never lose me, Kiriai," he finally said, his look one that made her insides shiver. "I'll be here for you as long as you want me."

Kiriai had no idea what to say to that, part of her pushing to just fall back into his familiar arms, while the other warned her about how much hurt awaited her there, not to mention her new commitment to Eigo.

"Kiriai!"

The voice of her best friend rang out over the milling crowd and snapped her attention back to reality. Both guilt and pleasure filled her as she turned. Why did she still feel entangled with Sento when she'd just agreed to spend time with Eigo? A relationship with him was so simple, easy. She always knew where she stood with him. He'd loved her and taken care of her for most of their lives together.

"Yay! I finally found you two. I think this is all of us," Eigo said in a breathless voice as he arrived and waved behind him at the rest of the crew. Everyone was there, except for Tomi, who had stopped to speak to someone. Eigo's glance flicked to Sento before landing on Kiriai and his grin widened into one of pure pleasure. "I know you hate these kinds of events," he said as he leaned in, "but may I repeat how stunning you look decked out in the outfit from M. Shuju's crew?"

His enthusiasm was impossible to resist, and Kiriai matched his grin, flushing a bit at his enthusiasm. Eigo's smile softened. Before she could react, he moved in close, slipped an arm behind her waist and leaned in to kiss the side of her cheek before turning to face the rest of their crew with her pulled against his side. Kiriai sucked in a breath at the whole sequence, trying to figure out how she felt about it.

She must have stiffened or something, because Eigo turned to her, concern on his face. "Is this too much?" he asked, barely above a whisper. "I'm supposed to be your escort tonight, and we're dating now, so I thought"—his words stumbled to a halt like he couldn't figure out what to say—"I'm sorry. Maybe I can—"

"This is perfect," she said, suddenly deciding. She pulled him closer and patted his chest with her free hand. "You're perfect. I'm proud to have the most handsome and kind escort here tonight." She leaned into him and laid her head on his shoulder for a moment, trying to project her sincerity. It felt good to be held by him, familiar and warm. He had a strength that seemed to flow from him to her and part of her wanted to bask in it and let his confidence drive out all of her doubt.

He did a quick scan of her face and his concern vanished, replaced by her familiar jokester. "Handsome, I'll agree with, but kind?" He looked up at the rest of the crew as if for help. "I was thinking more along the lines of witty, intelligent, dashing or perhaps genius? What do you guys think?"

Aibo and Mikata were smiling at Eigo's antics, but Shisen was scanning the crowd, her expression intense. A beat later, Tomi came up behind her, his expression just as serious. Eigo quieted and everyone moved in close to hear what Tomi had to say.

"Our main goal tonight is first, for Kiriai to make a good showing as an initiate. The chief and bosses aren't here, but you can be sure their underlings will report back to them. Impressing Chief Kosui will go a long way toward a fair match for Kiriai if our crazy plan works," he said, with a slight smile at Kiriai. "Kiriai, practice everything drilled into you today. If you get a chance, your second task is to get close to Sensei Nigai, who I just found out will be here tonight. Find out where the negative attention from the trainers is coming from. Is it personal from Gebi or motivated by one of the hood leaders against Jitaku?" He scanned the rest of their group. "The rest of you, stick to the plan. We need to identify which of the three hoods is actively working against us. The first-fight challenges are at the end of next week. If we don't know who to challenge, we'll have to scrap the whole plan."

By their somber expressions, Kiriai could tell everyone was thinking of what would happen if Jitaku lost the war. The conflict would move up to the burb level and a final tournament would decide if Southern kept the hood or if Western conquered it. Worst case, Western would win and move in as conquerors, every Jitaku property and 'zen theirs to do with as they pleased. Kiriai shuddered and pushed the disturbing images out of her mind.

A gong sounded with a rich resonance. Everyone quieted as a well-dressed woman climbed onto a small dais at the back of the entrance and held up her hands for attention.

"Welcome, Initiates and crew, to your first social training exercise," she said in a droll voice familiar to Kiriai. "By now, you have all had a few days to get used to the idea that a brawler's life includes just as much maneuvering and strategy outside the ring as it does in the ring." The older woman's voice had a strong undercurrent of sarcasm.

Her mannerisms finally clicked. If she were dressed in a worn gi and brown belt instead of a dress and glittering jewels in her ears, Kiriai would have recognized her immediately. Sensei Nigai. She didn't look anywhere near as jaded and worn as she had that first day in the barracks.

"Practice the techniques your social trainers have drilled into you. The leaders tonight are also beginners in this craft, so you both have instructions to be patient with each other"—she paused and scanned the crowd in front of her—"though almost anyone in Southern Core's power structure will have more experience than you new brawlers from the hoods." Nigai laughed, but it was a caustic one, and only a few in the crowd responded in kind.

Kiriai saw emotion darken Nigai's face. "Just like your other training, our job is to strengthen you, not coddle you, tonight. Prepare to swim with sharks tonight, my baby brawlers. Try not to get eaten, and learn something. Any questions?" The condescending superiority Kiriai remembered from her previous encounter with the woman was back in full force.

A few voices murmured something in the crowd, but no one spoke loudly enough to be heard.

"All right, then. And a final surprise. Your social trainers will make the rounds, dressed identically to listen and instruct. You are to pretend they are not there unless they directly address you."

There was an increase of murmuring at the news, but Nigai ignored it and continued. "Please enter the ballroom where the socializing will start with some light dancing for those who are interested. After an hour, servants will come to seat you for dinner, after which another hour of socializing will follow."

There must have been many with expressions similar to the one of distaste on Kiriai's face, because the older sensei tipped her head back and laughed. "You lot look like you're on the way to a torture chamber instead of a social event. Go in. No one will bite. I promise."

"I still think I'd rather be tortured," Kiriai muttered under her breath as the crowd flowed toward the large entrance to the ballroom. She heard Aibo snicker to her right, and the cheerful sound helped her mood. At least she had her crew with her, even if they had plans to scatter and work the crowd throughout the evening.

When Kiriai stepped into the ballroom, she realized how small the practice event at her home had been. On the other side of the vast hall was a door that mirrored the one she'd just used. An entirely different sort of people flowed through it. The brawlers and their crews might be dressed just as well, but these people wore their wealth with practiced ease and none of the uncomfortable fidgeting on Kiriai's side of the room.

A large dance floor filled the center of the space, the polished wooden surface slightly raised to mark it from the rest of the room. Tall standing tables were scattered around the room with smaller ones and sofas clustered around beautiful rugs to create several cozy sitting areas. As the two groups intermingled, an army of servants emerged from smaller screened doors, trays full of glasses and small treats that Kiriai might have appreciated more if she hadn't just spent the whole day nibbling on similar items. On the other hand, her rapid healing needed fuel, and she had to recover as much as possible before she rejoined the initiates in the morning. Her shoulder seemed to twinge at the idea, though the rest of her was done with the boredom of convalescence, regardless of how short. She wouldn't be able to match a full brawler in the ring by the end of the month if she didn't push herself every single day she had left. *No more beatings for defiance,* she promised herself.

After taking a small plate with finger foods, Kiriai stopped and surveyed the room trying to use her fledgling social skills. Small groups formed and a soft hum of voices competed with the soft but catchy music the four-person band played on the edge of the room next to the middle of the empty dance floor. Kiriai shuddered. By the time M. Shuju had finished this afternoon, he had made it clear she should avoid dancing if at all possible . . . and she agreed. Apparently grace in the fighting ring didn't always translate to the dance floor.

Past a handful of people to her left, Kiriai saw Aibo already chatting animatedly with a small group of younger people. Tomi had a cluster of severely dressed women entranced by some funny tale, if his waving arms and their smiles were any indication. Kiriai needed to get busy. This was one of the few times free from her all-consuming training, where she could help with the information gathering crucial to Jitaku's welfare.

There!

Standing alone at one of the tall tables was Sensei Nigai with a plate of food and a foreboding expression that no one had dared brave. Yet.

Kiriai turned to hurry in her direction and failed to take into account the restriction of the beautiful but tight dress that narrowed around her lower legs. She felt the fabric stretch and the front of the delicate sandals she wore caught on the edge of the rug at her feet. Kiriai sucked in a breath and used a fast stutter step she'd have been proud of in the ring. She avoided falling, barely, and even managed to tip up her plate to keep anything from sliding off.

Until she felt a hard bump from behind and went flying.

CHAPTER TWENTY-FOUR

If she'd been wearing her gi, the bump would have been easy to shrug off. With the unfamiliar sandals and dress hampering her movement, Kiriai took a nosedive, her drink and plate of food launching into the air. Instincts took over, and she tucked her head to protect it, moving her arm to take the brunt of the fall as she flipped into a clumsy roll. She tried to harness the momentum to push to her feet on the other side of the forward roll, but landed in an ungainly flop onto her back. She hated dresses.

A shocked silence hung in the air for a moment and radiated outward from her fiasco. It only lasted a heartbeat before laughter and murmurs came back in a wave. Kiriai felt her cheeks flush, and looked behind her, determined to find the culprit.

Standing in a trio of smiling friends stood Akumu, decked out in a grey suit that flattered his figure but did nothing for the cruel smile on his face. When he saw her looking at him, his grin widened, and he gave her a shrug that made her blood boil.

She was just about to surge to her feet when movement behind Akumu caught her eye. M. Shuju! The small man tipped his head in her direction and raised one eyebrow. His silent communication was like a flush of ice water through her veins.

A game. This was all a mind game.

So instead of yelling, she smiled. As she clambered to her feet, she let the smile widen, delighted and happy. She made a complete turn, arms spread wide, so everyone could get a good look. Then, with a flourish Eigo would be proud of, she gave a cheerful bow to the spectators.

She looked directly at the crowd, seeing a mix of mockery and interest. "Thank you for holding your applause. That move works much better in my fighting uniform, believe me"—she gave her head a self-depreciating shake—" I will definitely practice it more wearing a dress before I attempt to perform for an audience again."

A laugh snorted out from someone to her left. The sound broke the tension, and Kiriai saw amusement sweep across most of the faces watching her. One or two even gave her a nod of acknowledgment and respect before turning back to their own conversations.

Kiriai brushed her nervous hands down her dress to straighten it. A slow breath escaped through the smile she kept on her face as she marveled at the save she'd pulled off.

"Your food, lass?"

Kiriai turned, startled to see M. Shuju pressing a plate into her hand, which she took reflexively. He gave her a small nod and smile, then spun on his heel and disappeared back into the crowd.

She looked down at the plate, surprised to see everything she'd had before arranged neatly by the instructor. A quick glance in the direction her plate had fallen showed the servants had already removed all evidence of a mess.

Still a little shaky about the whole thing and attempting to cover it, Kiriai picked up a small ball of flaky dough and popped it in her mouth, letting the spicy bean-and-vegetable stuffing soothe her further. It was a simple lesson M. Shuju had taught her: Keep something in your hands at all times. Pausing to eat or drink would allow an extra few seconds to think, strategize, or in this case, recover from an embarrassing fall.

You did well, despite the difficult situation, Kiriai, and you wouldn't have fallen if you'd been wearing your normal uniform and footwear.

Thanks, Yabban.

Why couldn't the shoes go out and play?

Because they were stuck attending a torturous social evening? Kiriai asked, a smile coming unbidden to her lips.

Because they were all tied up.

A laugh slipped out before she could stop it and attracted a few glances in her direction. When she glimpsed Akumu's scowl, Kiriai realized Yabban had given her the perfect finale to the embarrassing event. Her smile and laugh dismissed the whole episode as something insignificant.

Feeling much better, Kiriai scanned the room, looking for the table where Sensei Nigai had been. When she found it, she almost flinched back. Nigai was staring right at her, expression hard and eyes intense.

Knowing there was no going back now, Kiriai sucked in a breath and walked toward the older sensei.

"May I speak with you?" Kiriai asked, when she got close enough.

Nigai hesitated, as if she would refuse. Then she shrugged and motioned at the tall table for Kiriai to put her plate down. Kiriai did so and tried to examine the senior sensei without being obvious, while she waited for her to speak. Sensei Nigai didn't look sloppy as she had that first morning of training. She'd combed her light hair back and arranged it in a tidy bun with two jeweled kanzashi poking through and holding it together. The wicked points on the hair sticks made Kiriai wonder whether they could double as weapons in a pinch. The sensei wasn't wearing a dress and Kiriai was instantly jealous. Instead, she wore a pantsuit made of a loose flowing fabric that Kiriai would have loved to have been wearing moments ago.

"Are you done looking? I thought you wanted to speak to me," said Nigai, her blue eyes sharp and probing.

Caught with her thoughts wandering, it took a moment for Kiriai to compose what she wanted to say. Thankfully, Nigai seemed willing to wait. Maybe some people here tonight would be patient with the new initiates as instructed.

"I'm very interested in how you reached your senior sensei position. Would you mind sharing some of your history with me?"

A loud guffaw met her question, startling Kiriai.

"I'm guessing you're just spouting what your social trainer taught you," she said with a shake of her head. "Save that stuff for the arrogant idiots who love to talk about themselves. They'll eat it up. Don't bother with me. Just ask me straight up what you want to know?"

"And you'll answer me?" Kiriai didn't bother hiding her skepticism.

"I didn't say that, now did I?" Delight sparkled across Nigai's expression. "It depends on the question. But you handled yourself very well just now, and gave me a break from the crushing boredom I expected tonight, so I'm inclined to be generous. Go ahead. Ask your question."

Kiriai took a risk, hoping she'd gauged Nigai's mood correctly, and asked, "Question? Only one?"

"Cheeky, aren't you?" Nigai said with a chuckle. "Do you know how happy any of these beginners here would be with just one answer from me?"

"Extremely thrilled," said Kiriai quickly.

"Flattery again?" Nigai asked with a raised brow.

"The truth," said Kiriai, and she meant it.

Nigai paused and examined Kiriai, who kept herself perfectly still.

Cold, quiet arrogance, she reminded herself.

"I'm enjoying this evening much more than expected," said Nigai finally. "Go ahead, ask your questions. Be direct. I hate pretenses. We'll see which answers I feel like giving you."

"I have two questions to start," Kiriai said, feeling worry clench in her stomach. Could she risk a direct question about the information she needed? Would that reveal too much?

Nigai waved her free hand for Kiriai to go ahead.

"Who is working to prevent Jitaku from receiving reinforcements and who is willing to send them?" Kiriai blurted out the question and then winced at how blunt it was. Tomi and M. Shuju would not be impressed.

"Wow," said Nigai as she leaned back in a mock flinch. "I guess I asked you to be direct." She looked up and tapped her lips for a moment before her gaze returned to Kiriai. "You're asking who Jitaku's friends and enemies are. But it's not that simple—" She raised a hand when Kiriai opened her mouth to object, and Kiriai swallowed her explanation. "I understand why you want to know. Rumor is your hood is only a handful of losses from losing majority control of your territory. Western Burb will immediately issue a challenge for the entire hood, and then it'll be up to our brawlers to defend your home. Be honest now. A few reinforcements will not change the tide of the Jitaku–Raibaru war right now. They have too big an advantage. It's better to just let it move to the next stage, to a hood challenge tournament. Then they'll have to put up their fifty percent stake in Jitaku against the half Southern Burb still controls. If our brawlers can win the tournament, poof"—she opened all her fingers in a popping motion—"you have all of Jitaku back and life goes back to normal."

Kiriai kept quiet, though she burned to defend Jitaku's reputation. She needed Nigai to keep talking. The more information, the better.

"It could be worse, believe me," Nigai said.

She seemed to be in a good mood and really wanted to help Kiriai. But when the older woman tipped her glass back and emptied it in a few quick swallows, Kiriai wondered if there was another purpose for her reasonable mood.

"Western could just keep the half of Jitaku they've won," said Nigai. "They scrounge out anything valuable, milk it for all the profit they can until it's worthless and only then make the challenge for the rest. You're just lucky Western Chief Nishi is too greedy and impatient to wait."

The images in her mind as she visualized the scenario made Kiriai sick to her stomach. These were her friends and neighbors, their businesses, Nigai was talking about. And despite the skills of the brawlers she'd seen, what if Western's brawlers were just as good or better? No. Beating Raibaru at the scrapper level was the better choice.

"Thank you for all the information. There is plenty I didn't realize," said Kiriai. "But I'd still like an answer to my question. Even if reinforcements aren't the best solution."

When Nigai looked reluctant, Kiriai tried a different tack. "One thing I'm learning here is that knowing who your enemies are is very important," she said with a tip of her head toward the area of her mishap.

That got a smile out of Nigai. "Fine. Your 'ranger is already aware, I'm sure, that Boss Ryuin has had a decades-long feud with your boss. There's been bad blood between them so long, few remember how it started. I'm one of them, but that's a valuable piece of information I'm not just going to give away. In any case, Ryuin wouldn't spit on your boss if he were burning to death in front of her. And I'm sure if there is an active campaign to deny reinforcements to your hood, she'll have a hand in it."

"And any friends?" Kiriai asked when the older woman didn't continue.

"You're really going ahead with this plan to gain reinforcements?"

"Yes," Kiriai said, letting some of her determination shine through as she projected all the cool arrogance she could muster.

Nigai set her latest drink down on the table and leaned forward. "Well, you aren't shy about it. I like that. I deal with the arrogant sycophants all day long"—she waved at the room at large—"and your drive is refreshing, despite your hopeless goal." She stopped again and seemed lost in thought.

It was difficult, but Kiriai kept quiet. The older sensei was full of information, and anything Kiriai could get from her would be useful. Plus, if she left the encounter with even a partial ally, it would be a big win.

"The chief isn't your friend, but he respects ability, which you know already, otherwise you wouldn't even be here after challenging him. He may be actively stopping reinforcements to Jitaku, but I doubt it. There are advantages to him both keeping and losing Jitaku so my guess is that he will wait to see how it plays out naturally. Besides, he has his own troubles with the city families right now. And we may all be free of Chief Kosui if he can't figure out a way to fix whatever he did to piss them off."

Kiriai swallowed against a suddenly dry throat and reached for a drink from the tray of a servant walking by. She knew exactly how the chief had upset the families. During the brawler tournament, she and her crew had copied the list of gifted children scheduled for secret abduction and delivery to the city. Ojisan had sent the information to the gifted underground in all four burbs, and they whisked most of the children out of danger just ahead of the 'forcers sent to collect them. Kiriai had been so focused on saving the children she hadn't considered all the implications of Kosui returning to the families empty-handed.

"Do you know something about that?" Nigai's blue eyes were sharp, and Kiriai kicked herself for not controlling her expression.

"No," Kiriai said, searching for a good reason to look uncomfortable, "I'm just remembering being face-to-face with Chief

Kosui during the selection circle. I can't imagine anything
making that man worry."

Nigai let out a caustic laugh at that. "Don't you remember my
little lesson on your first day? There are always bigger, more
powerful fish above each of us. Believe me, Chief Kosui is as
afraid of the city families as you and I are of him."

"And who do the families fear?"

"Now that's a question I can't answer, but the rules of power
are universal and I would guess that the five families spend quite
a bit of their time fighting with each other and jostling for advantages," she said as her brows creased and she shook her head with
a rueful smile. "It's way above us and our concerns here, though.
As for your reinforcements, my guess is Seidai's and Rinjin's
bosses wouldn't object to supporting Jitaku if you can do one of
two things—either force Ryuin to send reinforcements or get a
public endorsement from the chief."

Kiriai felt her shoulders sag.

"Here you are," said a familiar voice next to her, as an arm
wrapped around Kiriai's waist.

"Hello, Eigo," she said with a smile. Her stress level dropped
just feeling him next to her. "Sensei Nigai, may I present one of
my sparring partners and escort for the evening, Eigo."

"Hello, young man. We were just discussing the situation your
hood finds itself in and how impossible the solutions are." The
crusty woman was back, the few moments of friendly banter
gone.

"Well, that's perfect then," he said with a smile at both women.

Nigai looked nonplussed, probably used to others flinching
from her manners. "How so?" she asked, her tone abrupt and
challenging.

"Well," Eigo said, returning the woman's ire with a smile. "My
Kiriai, here, specializes in the impossible. She doesn't really take
anything on unless it's firmly in that category." He turned to look
fondly at her. "Isn't that right, dear?"

Now Kiriai was the one to let out a startled laugh.

"I guess I can't argue that now, can I?" Nigai said, and the two friends looked back in her direction.

She seemed to have softened slightly again and answered their questioning looks.

"You made me enjoy one of these horrible affairs," said Nigai. "And that's something I would have considered impossible before coming."

Both Kiriai and Eigo smiled at that. Kiriai felt a rush of excitement, hoping she could pump the woman for more information while she was in a receptive mood.

A loud gong interrupted them and everyone else in the room.

"Dinner," said Eigo as the throng shifted and moved toward a set of large doors that had slid open on the far side of the ballroom.

Kiriai turned to Nigai, hoping to get another question in, but the woman tipped her glass in a salute to Kiriai.

"Thank you for the unexpected, youngling. Maybe one of these days I'll answer your first question about my history." And then she turned and disappeared into the crowd.

Kiriai's head spun with everything she'd learned. What would Tomi and the others think? Yes, their task was impossible, but that didn't mean they couldn't try.

As Kiriai headed into the dining room, a grinning Eigo on her arm, she felt a soft bump from behind.

"I don't approve of Akumu's actions," said a quiet voice in her ear. "You conducted yourself well. I wanted you to know some of us noticed."

Before Kiriai could respond, a stocky woman in a dark blue dress brushed past her, eyes forward and giving no sign she'd spoken to Kiriai.

"Isn't that Trainer Gebi?" Eigo whispered in her ear.

Kiriai could only nod, her brain just making the connection between the trainer's usual appearance and how she looked now.

What was she supposed to think about that comment? Didn't the woman hate her?

Perhaps she is no longer an enemy?

How is that possible? Kiriai asked.

A strong ruler, Abraham Lincoln, said, "Do I not destroy my enemies when I make them my friends?"

As she walked arm-in-arm with Eigo into dinner, Kiriai's thoughts churned with the complexity of all the plots she seemed to be in the middle of.

And tomorrow, she'd be back in training, trying to cram several months of work into a few short weeks if she had any hope of winning her first brawler fight. She sighed and decided to at least enjoy the dinner even if it felt like her last meal.

You can work out your frustration in a training session with me tonight, if you'd like.

Kiriai's smile returned at the thought. *Definitely.*

CHAPTER TWENTY-FIVE

"If strangers have enough food for two months or guide us to
that much, they get a probationary spot among us. They keep
that spot if their work is enough to feed themselves and one
other person. Put any slackers outside our walls
immediately."
　　— Journal of Yolanda Cortez. Instructions to Cortez
family leaders. First month after the Blast. Phoenix, AZ. Oath
Keepers Archive of Truth, Volume 3

"I would feel so rusty without you," Kiriai said as she
materialized in Yabban's familiar dojo and smiled. The ability
to come here and train while injured felt as if a weight lifted from
her shoulders, every time. She had too much training to cram
into the next three weeks. She couldn't afford to lose the time of
an enforced recovery period. Not to mention how crazy it made
her to do nothing, even if it was only for a few days.

　　"It is advantageous that you have a personal healer with her wand and magic to accelerate your recovery," said Yabban, as she walked in from a side door, dressed in her gi and brown belt.

"What Isha does for me is definitely magic," Kiriai said with a grin. Then she noticed Yabban's formal attire. "Full instructor mode tonight?"

"Yes," said Yabban without an answering smile. "Your time is short and while you can train here without hurting your in-game body, it still needs rest to finish recovering so you can rejoin the brawler training."

Knowing Yabban was right to be serious, Kiriai straightened and blew out a breath before nodding. "I'm ready. Principles first or intermediate moves?"

"Both," said Yabban. "As you unlock and learn the moves, I'll prompt you to focus on the individual principles so you can level them up. I also have a suggestion that might help you against an opponent with superior skills. Are you interested?"

"Are you kidding? Of course, Yabban. That's exactly what I need. Even if Tomi is successful scheming for my first-fight arrangements, they will match me against someone a step above me. I'd rather not get destroyed in my first showing as brawler. What's your suggestion?"

"As fighters advance, they fall into familiar fighting patterns called styles. If you can learn different ones and shift at will, you can startle or surprise an opponent. Winning will still rely on talent and technique, but in a close fight a small advantage at a crucial point can make the difference."

"Fighting patterns?" Kiriai asked, cocking her head as she tried to visualize what Yabban meant. "Do you mean sequences, like stringing different moves together with more variety?"

"No," Yabban answered. "I mean the overall fighting style, regardless of which moves a fighter uses."

Kiriai started to ask for more clarification when Yabban held up a hand and dropped back into a fighting stance. "Demonstrations are always more effective. Fighting stance."

Kiriai stifled a groan and readied herself. At least here, she wouldn't need two days to recover from a trouncing.

"I will demonstrate the three basic styles. As you fight me, observe and see if you can report the differences when we finish. Also, please pick one of your new principles to focus on, a simple one."

Kiriai ran through them and picked the easiest. "The clock principle?"

"As long as you realize that it isn't just the numbers. It teaches a deliberate attention to the angles and directions you are moving and from which attacks are coming. Instead of just leaping to the side, you move to 8 o'clock, which is 30 degrees below a horizontal move."

Kiriai stared and scrunched her eyes as she repeated Yabban's words in her mind until they made sense. Then she nodded, though the new awareness made her brain hurt.

"I'll try, but I don't want too much thinking to slow my reactions."

"That's a valid concern," Yabban said with a nod of approval. "Training in correct principles will make you slower at first, but by the time they become instinctual, you will exceed the skill of those who never take the time to do the work themselves."

"Clock Principle, got it. Anything else?"

"Try to use the parries you recently unlocked instead of blocks."

Kiriai shook her head. "Ugh. I get their advantage, but they feel so weak to me, as if a strong punch or kick will just blow past them."

Yabban just raised her eyebrows without disagreeing.

"Slower now, but better later. Got it," Kiriai said as she bent her knees and prepared, trying to keep her overfull mind from making her freeze all together.

Yabban bent her knees and shifted her weight to the balls of her feet. Kiriai hurried to follow suit.

"Ready for style one?"

Kiriai nodded.

Yabban's kick shot across the space between them so fast, Kiriai only kept from getting overwhelmed with an instinctive leap sideways, off the line of attack.

To 3 o'clock, she reminded herself.

It still didn't gain her much time because Yabban had already twisted to follow and attack again as soon as her foot landed from the missed kick.

But this time, Kiriai was ready, eyes sharp and focused as her instructor charged forward with a blazing combination of two long-range punches followed by a close hook and uppercut as soon as she closed the distance.

Kiriai struggled to parry the attacks, trying to redirect the movement instead of hammering into Yabban's arms as she wanted to. Kiriai spent the next half a minute feeling like a tasty morsel attacked by a starving dog as she zigzagged all over, using the entire dojo floor to keep from getting overrun by Yabban's aggressive attacks. She threw a few of her own, but didn't land anything significant.

"Break!" said Yabban and instantly followed her own command to stop by straightening out of her fighting stance and bringing her feet together before giving Kiriai a short bow.

"Ready for the second style?"

Kiriai let out a surprised huff. "I think I need a little break."

"No, you don't," Yabban said and stepped back in her stance. "Fighting stance."

Kiriai's eyes widened in surprise, but she trusted Yabban, so she complied.

"Ready?" Yabban asked.

Kiriai nodded.

Yabban moved immediately again, but this time she circled to the side.

Her 9 o'clock, Kiriai noted, as she turned to keep herself facing Yabban, poised to respond if her instructor suddenly charged again.

When time ticked by without an attack, Kiriai realized that Yabban wouldn't make the first move.

"A counter-fighter," she blurted out, fighting styles suddenly making sense.

"Fight," said Yabban, expression unyielding. "This isn't the time for discussion."

Kiriai ducked her head, acknowledging her mistake, but couldn't completely wipe the smile from her face. Times like this reminded her she truly loved fighting more than anything else she could be doing in life.

Working on her own attack speed, Kiriai launched herself at Yabban right in the middle of a sliding sideways step, hoping the abrupt change in direction would take her instructor by surprise.

No such luck.

Kiriai's lead leg lifted in a fast kick that pulled the rest of her body behind it. She launched her fists toward Yabban's face and torso while her kick was still mid air. But Yabban was faster. She even used those dratted parries to nudge Kiriai's attacks aside with almost gentle ease. When Kiriai's foot landed, her weight falling forward, pain slammed into her ribcage as Yabban's reverse punch plowed into her side.

Thankfully, Kiriai had exhaled with her attack which helped tighten her core and kept the breath from being knocked out of her. She coughed through the pain and twisted, arms up and ready to counter with a short chopping punch at Yabban, searching for anything vulnerable she could hit.

To her surprise, her instructor had already moved out of reach and waited patiently for Kiriai to make a move.

Kiriai let out a groan and straightened to try to ease the pain in her rib. "Ow, Yabban. Training, remember? This isn't a battle to the end or anything."

Yabban ignored Kiriai's attempt to lighten the mood, standing just out of reach, poised to counterattack again. Kiriai sighed. Her instructor was right. Time was short, and she had to get serious.

This time, Kiriai treated Yabban like the dangerous counter-fighter she was and used probing attacks and feints, leaping back at the slightest sign that Yabban would return an attack. Yabban landed a kick that slipped under Kiriai's guard, but Kiriai was pleased to use a parry to slide past an attack and land a hooking punch of her own, even if it glanced off Yabban's chin instead of landing squarely on her jaw.

"Break!"

The two women both stopped, and though Kiriai wasn't breathing as hard as after the first style, she hurt in more places this time.

Yabban motioned with her hand and a wave of relief washed through Kiriai, erasing the pain and restoring her back to perfect health.

Kiriai shook her head and smiled, wishing, as usual, she could use this in the real world. "Thanks!"

Yabban nodded in acknowledgment as she stepped into her fighting stance again. Kiriai sighed and followed her lead. "Third style?" Kiriai asked.

"Yes, and then we'll discuss each one before you practice them," said Yabban. "Ready?"

Kiriai put her hands up and tipped her head.

"Fight!"

Kiriai braced for an attack that never came. Wary of the previous counter-fighting tactics, she then used tentative attacks, probing Yabban's defenses. Her instructor, however, refused to engage. She kept slipping away, and even outright ran from Kiriai once when she lost patience and charged Yabban with a stream of attacks.

Kiriai was ready to give up, chest heaving even though all

she'd been doing was chasing a slippery opponent. Why didn't Yabban just call it already?

But then, just as Kiriai let her fists sag and tired legs straighten a bit, Yabban launched a blistering attack. Taken completely off guard, Kiriai desperately ducked her chin at the last moment, making the blow glance off her forehead and snap Kiriai's head back instead of landing head-on. It only took a moment for Kiriai to recover and fight back, but that hesitation left her hurting in quite a few spots by the time she disengaged from Yabban. At least the stinging knuckles on her right hand meant she'd landed a few of her own.

"Break!" Yabban said as she stood and finally unbent enough to smile.

"You enjoyed that last attack a little too much," said Kiriai with a huff as she stood and shook out her hands, waiting for Yabban to banish the aches and pains.

"I admit that the upgraded emotions and time I've spent with you makes me more able to understand why players keep coming back to the fight," she said, before her expression turned serious. "Now, tell me how you would name the three styles of fighting I demonstrated."

Kiriai stopped herself from blurting the first things that came to mind and took a moment to review the short bouts. "Obviously, the first style was continuously attacking and trying to overwhelm your opponent. The second is one I usually call counter-fighting, where you rarely initiate contact, but look for openings during an attack instead and try to capitalize on those." Kiriai hesitated before continuing. "I'm not sure what to call the third, except you ran away until I was exhausted. When I let my guard drop, you finally attacked. Are those right?" Kiriai asked, brows raised hopefully as she looked at Yabban.

"Exactly!" Yabban said with a wide smile.

With everything going on lately, Kiriai felt tempted to just bask in Yabban's approval for a while. It reminded Kiriai that despite how good the brawlers were, she was a good fighter and strategist in her own right.

"There are different ways of classifying fighting styles, but we're starting with a simplistic one that names them as Attack, Counter and Evade."

Kiriai snorted. "Sounds about right. Simplistic names, as you said. But I'd say most fighters, at least the ones I'm facing now, use a mix of the styles and fall somewhere between the extremes you demonstrated."

"True," Yabban said, "but now that you're paying attention, you will find that most fighters gravitate toward one. For example, a counter stylist may occasionally attack or run away to drain your strength, but they will prefer to lie in wait for an attack and hit what's open. Especially under pressure or when fighting tired, they will be more likely to revert to their preferred style."

Kiriai nodded as she ran through a few fights in her mind and could see the patterns Yabban was explaining. She felt a flush of excitement at the new discovery. "Sweet! This will help me anticipate my opponents better."

"Not only that, if you practice these first three, I can teach you a fourth that will help even more."

"Really? Tell me." Kiriai was more than ready for a few secrets that would boost her chances.

"The better you're able to sell a single style to your opponent at the beginning of the fight, the more they will anticipate that you'll continue fighting that way. Then, at a crucial moment, you change to a different one completely. In a close battle, it can make the difference between winning and losing. You've done something similar in the past, but not deliberately. If you practice it, you will be much more effective."

Kiriai's smile widened. "I like it. I won't ever be as big and strong as the best fighters, so I have to be the smartest. With you, Yabban, I have a chance."

Yabban nodded and moved to the center of the floor. "Ready

to practice? We'll start with the attack style, which also pairs well with the principle Back-up Mass. Focus on timing your strikes to land with your forward momentum to increase their power."

Kiriai swung her arms loosely back and forth and bounced a few times on her toes before taking her position and setting her mind into attack-and-keep-attacking mode. It shouldn't be hard, since she realized it was her preferred style. She couldn't help grinning.

A little less than an hour later, Yabban called a halt. "Time for bed. Your in-game body needs rest if you are to rejoin the brawler training in the morning."

Kiriai was breathing heavily and could feel at least five different places Yabban had landed solid blows in the last round. Her instructor was no slouch as a sparring partner.

Then from one moment to the next, her pain vanished and she let out a relieved sigh. "Please come do that for me in the game world," Kiriai said.

"The game world has different rules than our virtual training here," Yabban said with regret in her tone. Then she seemed to think of something. "You might consider acquiring a few healing spells or at least keep some potions on hand."

"Uh." Kiriai scrambled for the right thing to say.

"It wouldn't take much time or cost too much, and think how helpful it would be. You're likely to be injured more now that you're facing advanced opponents."

Yabban looked so earnest that Kiriai didn't want to put her off again. But she and Eigo had agreed it was a bad idea to force Yabban to acknowledge that the world wasn't a game. They had no idea what would happen if they forced the truth on Yabban. *Um, you can't reconnect to the main game servers because humanity destroyed itself generations ago and you're an artifact that happened to still work?*

But Eigo and Kiriai had made that decision at the beginning, long before Kiriai had upgraded Yabban's personality and autonomy. What if they fed her the truth in small doses? Gave her time to digest a little at a time?

"Actually, the world I live in isn't a game." Kiriai stopped and waited for Yabban's response.

She didn't respond, looking curious and waiting for more information.

"You know how you can't connect with any other elements of your game? How it's just you? That's because"—Kiriai stopped herself from saying none of them existed, as that seemed too abrupt—"they aren't available for you to access at the moment. What you see when we aren't in this virtual dojo is the real world."

Yabban shook her head and looked confused. "Real? Our game world is real, isn't it? We can communicate, advance, feel and experience life. Isn't that real? I don't understand."

OK, maybe *real* wasn't the best word for an AI that was created in a gaming world. "I mean, it's the world the humans come from, the one the players who used to play your game lived in when they weren't in your game world."

"Used to play?" Yabban repeated. Her eyes began flicking back and forth.

Kiriai had started this, so she continued. "By joining with my implant, you are in the players' world instead of me being in your game world."

Just as Kiriai was congratulating herself on an elegant explanation that avoided mentioning the worldwide destruction of the Blast, Yabban's eyes lost their focus. Her head jerked back and her arms and legs stiffened. Suddenly she lost all animation, her expression blank, eyes unseeing.

Worry, regret and a huge amount of anger at herself spiked

through Kiriai as she hurried up to her instructor. "Yabban? Are you all right?"

No answer.

"Yabban! Answer, me!" Kiriai grabbed her shoulder and shook the woman. Or at least tried to. Yabban was immovable, her shoulder as unyielding as stone.

What had she done?

Panicked, Kiriai waved a hand in front of Yabban's blank eyes. Nothing.

Then Yabban's lips moved. Kiriai sucked in a breath and held it, hoping.

Ancestors, help me. Kiriai wished more than anything she'd left Yabban well enough alone. She'd been happy without the truth. Why did Kiriai have to mess with everything? The truth wasn't always best.

"... parameters ... error ... unable to ... initiate reboot protocol ... failure ... initiate reboot protocol ... "

Kiriai stared, horrified as gibberish words poured out of Yabban. Her friend seemed to have transformed into an unresponsive piece of tech.

Kiriai had to do something, but what? Think! Then she remembered Yabban's main objective.

"Yabban," Kiriai said in the calmest tone she could manage. "I'd like to train now. Can you please, uh ... *initiate* your training protocol?"

The gibberish stopped, but her body remained stiff and frozen.

Was that a flicker in Yabban's eyes?

"I'd like a report of my statistics," Kiriai said, desperate for anything technical she could think of.

Yabban blinked, but still didn't speak.

Kiriai grabbed her by both shoulders and yelled in her face. "Trainer Yabban, your trainee needs your attention immediately. Display my player statistics now!"

Yabban's eyes cleared and locked onto hers.

Kiriai's hopes flared to life.

"Yabban, I need to see my player statistics now," she said in a slightly calmer voice. "I need them now. It is important. I can't wait. Please display them immediately. Stop what you're doing and do what I ask . . ." Kiriai kept up a litany of words demanding the same thing over and over, using as many words and phrases as possible.

Yabban's eyes went out of focus again, and Kiriai's worry flared back to life.

"Player service override initiated. Maintenance protocol postponed," Yabban said, her voice a dull monotone that stabbed at Kiriai's insides.

Then Yabban's face softened, the blank expression disappeared and her eyes met Kiriai's.

"You want to interrupt our training to look at your statistics?"

Kiriai sucked in a breath and her eyes stung. "Yes, Yabban." Then she couldn't help herself and flung herself forward to wrap her arms around the friend she'd almost lost. "I'm so glad you're back."

Yabban hesitated only briefly before her own arms lifted and she returned the embrace.

A moment later, Kiriai heard her soft voice say, "Me too, Kiriai. Me too."

The two friends stood for a moment in the echoing quiet of the luxurious dojo. The low sunset streamed through the wall of windows, leaving a last touch of warmth on the smooth wooden floor.

Yabban finally pushed back and smiled. "Well, let's take a look at your progress after a week of hard training."

Kiriai could only smile and nod.

Character Name: Kiriai

    Level: Error. Inaccessible.

    XP: Error. Inaccessible.

    Character Traits: Error. Inaccessible.

    Training Statistics:

    Beginning Moves: Unlocked: all. Learned: all. Proficient: all. Mastered: Stances 7/12, Strikes 5/20, Kicks 7/20, Blocks 8/10, Foot Maneuvers 6/8.

    Novice Moves: Unlocked: all. Learned: all. Proficient: Stances 4/6, Strikes 16/16, Kicks 4/20, Blocks 4/10, Foot Maneuvers 7/7. Mastered: Stances 2/6, Strikes 6/16, Kicks 1/20, Blocks 1/10, Foot Maneuvers 2/7.

    Intermediate Moves: Unlocked: Stances 1/6, Strikes 14/14, Kicks 16/16, Blocks 10/10, Foot Maneuvers 8/8. Learned: Stances 0/6, Strikes 8/14, Kicks 10/16, Blocks 10/10, Foot Maneuvers 0/8. Proficient: None. Mastered: None.

    Fighting Skills:

    Will Power Level 5 (5% progress to Level 6)

    Resilience Level 5 (5% progress to Level 6)

    Observation Level 5 (30% progress to Level 6)

    Strategy Level 2 (10% progress to Level 3)

    Injury Healing Level 5 (25% progress to Level 6)

    Evasion Level 4 (40% progress to Level 5)

    Meditation Level 3 (30% progress to Level 4)

    Centering Level 4 (30% progress to Level 5)

    Berserker Level 3 (65% progress to Level 4)

    Fighting Principles:

    Unlocked: Marriage of Gravity, Line of Attack, Moving up the Circle, Solid Foundation, Clock Principle, Back-up Mass, Environmental Awareness.

    Learned: Marriage of Gravity, Line of Attack, Moving up the Circle, Solid Foundation, Clock Principle, Back-up Mass.

    Proficient: Marriage of Gravity, Line of Attack, Moving up the Circle.

Mastered: none.

Fighting Styles: Unlocked: Attack, Counter, Evade.

Training Aids activated: Demonstration, Overlay Training, Corrective Stimulation, Surround Mirror Training, Opponent Training, Realistic Demonstration, Replay Training.

CHAPTER TWENTY-SIX

"Did you enjoy your time off, Initiate?" Trainer Akumu yelled at Kiriai as she brought up the rear of the group of runners. They sprinted across the long side of the wide, grassy field between the brawler training buildings and the orderly residences of a small, elite neighborhood.

"Yes"—Kiriai had to suck in a breath between words —"Trainer!"

"Then run faster!"

Kiriai pushed for another burst of speed but only found a trickle. Her feet were already churning as fast as she could make them move.

Jimu, ahead of her, glanced back over his shoulder. The movement caught Akumu's attention and Jimu put on a burst of speed and pulled up to the other initiate. Akumu ran with an ease that made Kiriai jealous and made her admire the man despite how mean he was.

"What are you looking at, Jimu?" Akumu yelled.

"My goal, Trainer!"

"That's right, Initiate. Don't worry your pretty little head about anyone else."

Seconds later, the initiates in front of Kiriai reached the finish line and their sandals thudded into the soft turf as they slowed their paces abruptly. Kiriai joined them a split-second later and welcomed the relief of walking even as her lungs burned and her legs wobbled with overexertion.

"Breathe, walk, focus on recovering. You have four minutes before we go again."

Kiriai heard Gebi's directions from the front of the group. Another trainer standing next to a small table placed a one-minute timing glass upright with three more waiting their turn. Kiriai began walking, doing her best to calm her heaving chest. This brawler training was a full step above anything she'd done as a scrapper. Sure, they'd done conditioning training in the dojo with heavy balls and other weights, but never anything like this all-out sprinting over and over with only short breaks—something Gebi called interval training.

However, seeing how easily the trainers kept the brutal pace, Kiriai had to admit it worked. If she could feel as fresh at the end of a match as she did at the beginning, she would do any amount of crazy training.

"Makes you respect the hard-nosed idiots a little more, doesn't it?" Jimu said under his breath as he fell in next to her.

She heard him taking long and slow breaths to recover. "Aren't you supposed to be focusing on your goal?" she whispered back, careful to keep her eyes forward.

He chuckled, but it sounded out of breath. "Making alliances with future brawlers like you is my goal, especially after last night's shenanigans, don't you think?"

Kiriai's expression soured as she remembered Akumu's dirty trick. It didn't matter how fast he could run. She'd never like or trust the guy.

"If you're fine on your own, it's no problem," said Jimu, his voice a little louder as their walking took them further from the rest of the group.

"No," said Kiriai, "It's not you. I was just remembering last night."

"Ah. Yeah. I would frown about that too, if I were you."

"Thanks." Kiriai let the sarcasm drip from her voice.

Jimu just smiled and let the quiet rest between them as they continued walking.

Kiriai took a deep breath of the crisp morning air and focused on her enjoyment of the wide-open field. They didn't have anything like this at home. They had their park, but it was usually crowded with people everywhere along the winding paths and benches, unless she went really early in the morning. All this space relaxed her.

As she counted her breaths, Kiriai engaged her centering skills to relax and pull energy back into her body. It seemed to come much easier now, and she wondered again at the impact of Yabban's game levels. Of course, Kiriai still had to remember to engage the skill instead of letting her temper take over. More moments passed, and Kiriai felt her heart slow and her breathing ease.

Jimu turned to head back and as she copied him, she came to a decision. "I'd like an ally, if the offer is still open?"

"Done," he said with a grin and a nod. "Anyone who will take a beating for her crew members is solid in my book. I'm hoping to specialize in fighting for the business sector—if you develop contacts there, I'd appreciate any recommendations or referrals."

Kiriai almost missed a step. She had given no thought to future patronage and felt stupid. Instead of making a few connections during last night's social training, she'd spent most of it scouting for information that would affect Jitaku. Even if it was just to blend in, she should have acted as if she cared about her future as a brawler.

"Of course. I'm not that great at the social scheming part. But I've got crew members who are, so I'll let them know to keep an ear out for contacts that can help you."

Jimu chuckled. "See. I knew you were a good choice."

Kiriai raised an eyebrow in question.

"Do you think any of the other initiates—or the trainers, for that matter—would admit to a lack of ability, much less that one of their crew might be better at it than they are?"

Kiriai hadn't thought of it that way, but knew it was likely true as soon as Jimu pointed it out.

"The only other one that is a halfway decent human being here is Jiseki."

"What?" Kiriai asked, surprised. "She acts like she hates my guts, and I did nothing to her."

"That's because she's a rule-follower and listens to what her superiors say. If you tell her your side of things, she'll give you a fair chance. I'm sure you know the trainers have been spreading less than flattering rumors about you since the beginning." Jimu stopped for a moment in thought. "Though I think that might be changing now that you're proving them wrong. Most of them seem fair, so it makes me wonder where the antagonism against you is coming from." He flicked a quick glance in her direction as they approached the rest of the group. "Do you have enemies with enough power to influence the brawler initiation?"

Kiriai's step faltered as Jimu's words hit her. Enemies? Powerful ones? She felt sick inside as a childish part inside her wanted to whine and ask why everyone couldn't just leave her alone.

"Yes," she said without offering further explanation.

She heard Jimu suck in a breath next to her, and a moment passed before he responded. "I'm not powerful, but count me as an ally. If there is anything I can do, tell me."

The two of them were almost back to the starting line. The trainer at the timing table flicked over the third glass and stood up the fourth. One minute before their next sprint.

"Bring me any information you hear about Jitaku and reinforcements for my home," she said under her breath.

"Nothing for yourself?" His voice had a lift of surprise to it.

Kiriai shook her head slightly. Losing Jitaku would be worse than anything they could do to her personally.

"Agreed," he said softly. "Jitaku first, but if I hear anything about this personal vendetta against you, I'll bring it to you. You'll find that I'm a good ally when I trust someone."

Kiriai gave him a slight nod of respect and acknowledgment before they both rejoined the group and lined up for another sprint.

"Your crews have a present for you. Let them in." The anticipation in Gebi's voice didn't bode well for the start of their afternoon training.

The initiates turned as doors opened on the other side of the large training hall, and familiar figures in training uniforms piled in, moving at a quick clip. The initiates weren't the only ones getting in better shape this month.

"Form up around your initiate, keeping similar distances," said Gebi.

Eigo and Mikata flashed smiles at Kiriai while Sento gave her a nod, his expression focused. Trainer Seion, a tall but mostly silent woman, joined their group, giving Kiriai an opponent positioned at each of the four corners around her. She hadn't interacted with Seion much, but she wasn't Akumu, and for that Kiriai was grateful.

A quick glance around the training floor showed that everyone was standing at attention, in position and waiting for instructions.

"I saved this lesson for the return of Initiate Kiriai," said Gebi. "Because her little challenge interrupted the exercise the first time." Gebi moved through the groups, eyes sharp and examining every detail. However, after a week of brawler training, perfect stances and posture were second nature. "If you'll recall, we were working on learning to feel and anticipate the movements of our opponents. Initiates will spend one minute with each opponent refreshing yourself with the crossed-arm drill. Begin with your crew members and end with the trainer."

Eigo stepped forward with a grin before anyone else could respond. He dropped into a surprisingly decent fighting stance. Kiriai matched him, crossed her wrist with his and waited for the command to start. But when Eigo caught her look, he waggled his eyebrows with an exaggerated excitement. "This isn't exactly what I hoped for when I imagined dating you," he whispered, "but—"

Kiriai choked on a laugh and barely kept quiet.

"Hajime!"

Eigo began circling his arm, occasionally pushing it high or low with varying speeds, but nothing like the viciousness Akumu had used.

"So what's your favorite color?" Eigo said in a voice barely audible. "Mine is green."

His arm flashed up toward her face, and Kiriai easily moved to match it as she bit the inside of her cheek to keep from smiling.

"Yame!"

"Switch!"

Kiriai turned to the right before realizing Sento was in that direction. Wow, did that feel awkward. Her half-smile from Eigo's antics dried up as Sento moved to cross arms with her. As her wrist touched his, the contrast was immediately clear. Sento had solid strength, like pushing against a tree that only a powerful wind could sway.

"Hajime!"

"This exercise is valuable," said Sento as he moved his arm, his tone one of a no-nonsense trainer. "Don't just focus on my arm.

See if you can feel all of my intentions, what the rest of me will do."

Kiriai felt silly for how lighthearted she'd been. Sento was right. She needed to learn as much, and as fast, as she could.

He pushed her hard, changing the pressure of his arm. He would push forward attacking and then pull away abruptly, forcing her to work hard to stay connected. Kiriai tried to anticipate his moves and by the time their minute was up, she'd already improved. After doing the same with Mikata and Seion, she felt even better about her new skill.

"Now, give your initiate her gift." Gebi said as everyone had stepped back to their starting position.

Sento reached inside his top, pulled out a dark blue sash and held it out to her.

A blindfold?

Combined with Gebi's gleeful voice, Kiriai knew the next exercise wasn't going to be easy. An unexpected shudder ran through her as she took the sash from Sento. A flash of memory, blindness, an ambush, powerless to fight back. Her pulse raced and her breathing came fast.

A sharp pain in her hand broke the cycle and a pull made her vision clear.

"Breathe. Focus. Feel. Count," said Sento, his tone full of sharp command that she instinctively obeyed.

It only took a moment and Kiriai was back in control, glad her skills worked so quickly but angry that the attacks hadn't disappeared completely. Her hands only shook slightly as she took the sash and wrapped it around her head. She chose this, to train, to get stronger. She was in control.

"The best fighters feel and sense an attack almost before it starts," Gebi said from the front. "This is your first step on that path. Don't expect to master the skill anytime soon. That will take years, if you ever do. For now, the blindfold will force you to use your other senses to defend yourself. We will start with a single attacker in close and the initiate touching the attacker's shoulder. Attackers will start with slow and light, tapping attacks to the head and chest. Initiates, your job is to sense the attack coming and intercept it. Understand?"

"Yes, Trainer!"

"Positions!"

Kiriai dropped into a fighting stance and held her lead hand out in front of her. A moment later, she felt someone step in close, take her hand and place it on their shoulder. Was that Mikata? The blindfold really heightened her other senses. Through the stiff fabric of the training top, she could feel a strong, solid shoulder. Probably not Eigo, and Kiriai didn't think it was tall enough to be Trainer Seion. Kiriai could hear her opponent breathing and felt a sense of heat radiating off their body. She caught a whiff of ginger and smiled. Mikata loved ginger candies and usually kept a few in her pouch at all times.

"Hajime!"

Kiriai felt a slight tension in Mikata's shoulder and was just trying to decipher it when she felt a light slap on her cheek. Her free hand jerked up in surprise to bat at her face, but only found air, much too late to do any good. Another poke into her chest, then a pat on the other side of her face. Kiriai tried to anticipate the attacks but only succeeding in flailing around, her blocks never in time to do anything. For a moment, Kiriai was glad she'd put on a blindfold and didn't have to see how horribly she was doing.

"Relax," whispered Mikata. "Focus on me and feel what I'm doing."

She is correct. You have trained your Observation skill to respond to visual cues. You must focus on your other senses now. What do you feel? What do you hear?

"Thanks," she whispered to both of her friends as she reset herself. Letting out a breath and refocusing, Kiriai lightened her grip on Mikata's shoulder and worked to focus on two things and two things only: the muscle movement under her hand, and the subtle sounds of movement in front of her. She gave a slight nod for Mikata to continue and immediately felt a small shift as her shoulder dipped and drew back just a touch. Kiriai moved her hand up to protect her face only to feel a stiff poke to her midsection. At least she had moved at the right time.

The next few minutes passed quickly and Kiriai was surprised by how much she could sense without her eyes.

"Yame!"

"Switch!"

We have to add this to our training together, Yabban.

Acknowledged. I will move it up to the schedule.

Schedule? Kiriai asked as she felt a new shoulder under her hand. Solid again, warm and strong. Sento. She just knew it.

I have a similar exercise planned to advance your Environment Awareness principle and improve your Observation skill. I had planned to begin this exercise once you had unlocked the rest of your Intermediate moves.

Oh. Yeah. Maybe we can finish those tonight. Kiriai grunted as Sento jabbed right into her solar plexus a split second before her block arrived. It made her catch her breath and cough. Kiriai hadn't realized how important it was to brace and tighten for a blow until she kept getting hit without warning, even if they were light hits.

A shift under her hand, and she went with her instinct. Kiriai smiled in triumph as her hand moved through blind space and met Sento's hand inches from her face. The next minute was a blur of attacks and blocks, some good, others swishing through empty space while Sento hit her elsewhere.

But her hand intercepted more attacks than earlier and Kiriai lost herself in the challenge of it all, lips pulled back in a fierce grin.

"Yame! And take a five-minute water break."

Kiriai straightened, pulled off the dark sash and blinked in the sudden brightness from the bank of windows across from her. She smiled and was just about to say something to her friends when she sensed an approach from behind.

"Better timing. You're getting closer. Another year or two of practice and you just might make a decent brawler."

Kiriai jerked and spun, though she knew it was Gebi. That was one voice she would have no trouble recognizing while blindfolded, or fast asleep with pillows over her head and in the middle of a nightmare. Kiriai checked her first instinct to slip back into a fighting stance and gave the trainer a slight bow acknowledging the compliment . . . though one part of it grated at her.

"Years?" Kiriai asked before she could stop herself.

Gebi didn't dismiss the question out of hand, but instead she took a moment to examine Kiriai closely, which was anything but comfortable. Inside, Kiriai kicked herself for saying anything.

"Come with me," Gebi said finally. "We need to talk."

And just like that, she spun on her heel and headed toward the fixer treatment area on the far side of the space, currently deserted as no one had been injured too badly yet today.

Her crewmates looked as surprised as she felt. With no viable alternative, Kiriai hurried to catch up with the fast-moving trainer and hoped her mouth hadn't gotten her into too much trouble again.

What runs around a soccer field but never moves?

A joke, Yabban? Now? Kiriai asked with a hint of irritation.

A fence.

Kiriai couldn't help smiling, but still . . .

Perhaps you could be more like the fence, solid and immovable in this coming confrontation, instead of letting your anger run away with you.

The words made Kiriai almost miss a step. Her trainer was

right. All the centering levels in the world wouldn't help her if she didn't use them.

Sorry. You're right, Yabban. Thanks!

Kiriai calmed her mind and breath. She wouldn't let Gebi rattle her, whatever the topic of discussion.

CHAPTER TWENTY-SEVEN

"Maybe we should have stuck with the floppy disks we used
in the Strategic Automated Command and Control Systems
for our nuclear arsenal until 2019. At least no one could hack
those."

— Ryan Holder, missile combat crew member, Air Force
Global Strike Command

As they reached one of the fixer areas, Gebi turned and
leaned back against a treatment table so she could face
Kiriai. Gebi glanced around quickly at their relative isolation and
seemed satisfied. When she met Kiriai's gaze, she just waited, as if
for Kiriai to say something.

Kiriai clenched her jaw and stayed quiet. There was no way
she would speak first.

Gebi finally nodded in what Kiriai hoped was approval.

"Perhaps you *can* learn," Gebi said. "At least that's what I told
my father this morning. Was I right?"

Kiriai waited, but Gebi didn't elaborate.

"Yes," Kiriai finally answered and left it at that. Until she had a better idea of where this was going and what Gebi's intentions were, she refused to give the trainer anything she could use against her.

A brief pause and then amusement sparkled in Gebi's eyes. "Good answer," she said. "And one that makes up my mind for me."

But instead of explaining, Gebi seemed to go back to being lost in thought.

"About what?" Kiriai finally asked.

"Oh, so you haven't completely trained away your impatience, have you?" Gebi said with a laugh. "Good, because the best fighters are driven and impatient on some level. I have two questions for you and then I'll answer a question I think you have. Deal?"

"What if I have different questions than you think?"

"You want to know why I have singled you out for negative attention and implied that you don't have the skill or even deserve to be here as a brawler, right?"

Kiriai worked hard to keep her reaction to Gebi's blunt honesty off her face and worked to come up with the best answer. It seemed obvious Gebi's opinion of her was changing, so the more essential question was slightly different.

"Almost," Kiriai said. "I don't really care what you think of me. Unless your opinion is influenced by the same people who are targeting my hood and actively working to keep reinforcements from being sent. Who they are is the real question I'd like answered. Agreed?"

"You'd give up the chance to find out who has a personal vendetta against you to get information to help your hood?" Gebi looked skeptical.

Kiriai couldn't help it. She laughed.

Gebi's eyes widened in surprise.

"Trainer Gebi," said Kiriai. "I've spent my entire short fighting career with powerful people doing their best to ruin me." Kiriai shook her head to dispel all the incidents that came to mind. Her voice went low and hard when she continued. "Once they even ambushed me, bound me and beat me unconscious while wearing masks"—Kiriai made a spitting motion to the side—"the cowards. And here I am, despite everything they've tried." Kiriai held Gebi's eyes for a moment and decided she liked what she saw there. "Despite everything they continue to try, I won't quit. I will beat them. All of them. I don't care how powerful they are, your chief included." Kiriai heard how loud she was getting and stopped, swallowed hard and took a moment to gather her control again. When she looked back up, there was interest in Gebi's eyes.

"He's your chief, too," Gebi said. "Especially if you make it through the rest of the month and become one of his brawlers. He'll expect to have your first loyalty."

Kiriai bit back a retort, though she was sure her defiance flashed in her eyes.

"If he can put aside his champion's defeat by you, you must let go of any personal animosity you have against him," Gebi said, fully back into trainer mode.

"As long as he is chief, he'll have it," Kiriai said.

Gebi's eyes narrowed. "What are you implying? Do you know anything about the chief's current troubles?"

Kiriai shook her head. When would she learn to keep her emotions from making her reckless?

"The chief's troubles started a few days after the selection circle where he chose all of you," Gebi said, a thoughtful expression on her face. "Normally, I'd dismiss you as unlikely to be involved, but the more I find out, the more . . ." Gebi's gaze bored into her and Kiriai felt as if she were trying to read her mind. "What do you know about the chief's problems with the city families?"

"Is that one of your questions?" Kiriai asked, hoping to gain a little time to think. When she saw the anger flash through Gebi's eyes, Kiriai knew it was the wrong thing to say. "Wait. I'm sorry. I didn't mean it like that," she said as she raised a hand up in apology. "I don't know anything about the city families, other than what we all see on the screens. And while I know Chief Kosui doesn't like me, I'm not privy to any details of stuff like you're talking about." Kiriai sighed and tried to explain. "I just want to stay as far away from the political maneuvering as possible. More than anyone, I know what it's like to be caught in the crossfire."

Gebi's expression had relaxed during Kiriai's explanation, and she nodded at the last. "Agreed. Too close and you get burned."

"Exactly," Kiriai said, relieved that Gebi understood.

"Well," said Gebi, "Tell me if you remember anything out of the ordinary from the selection or about the chief. Anything or anyone, all right?"

Kiriai nodded, not trusting herself to speak.

"The chief and everyone close to him is on edge, not to mention the bosses coming into town next week for your first-fight ceremony. It's supposed to be a happy milestone, exchanging bets and challenges and giving you a specific opponent to focus on for the rest of your training—" Gebi's words trailed off.

She shook her head and focused on Kiriai again. "Break is almost over. Back to my questions. If you answer them, I'll tell you what I know about your hood. Agreed?"

Relief and interest surged in Kiriai, and she nodded. She was already anticipating Tomi's reaction when she shared everything from Sensei Nigai last night and Gebi today. And here she'd been the one who wouldn't have much opportunity for information gathering.

"Why do you want to be a brawler?"

Kiriai stared for a moment in surprise. "That's your question?"

Gebi just cocked an eyebrow and waited.

"Um," said Kiriai as she waffled between the answer she thought Gebi would want to hear and something closer to the truth. Finally she let out a frustrated breath. She wasn't any good at dissembling. "First, it's something I've dreamed of doing since I could make a fist. Second, I love fighting more than almost anything else in my life. I was born to do this. Always pushing myself, challenging others, learning to do amazing things I never thought possible . . . all of it." Kiriai hesitated, thinking she could just stop there.

Gebi made an impatient gesture for her to continue.

"Third, this is the best way to make contacts in Southern Core, the only chance my crew and I have to get reinforcements for Jitaku."

"Your hood is third on your list?" asked Gebi, her expression giving nothing away.

Kiriai hadn't really held anything back and didn't figure she would start now. "Only because I'm not sure how much I trust you after how you've been treating me. Is that your second question?"

A short laugh escaped from Gebi before she said, "No, just a clarification of the first. One more. How did you get here, to the brawler initiation, only a year after you started as a junior scrapper?"

"Is that what this is all about?" Kiriai asked, eyes squinting with suspicion. Maybe she shouldn't have been so honest. Had she misjudged Gebi? "What have people been telling you about me? You keep implying I cheated to get here, but I thought it was just a part of your hazing and mind games. If someone is making accusations about me that you believe, I deserve to hear them."

"Answer the question," Gebi said, expression hard.

Kiriai frowned and was tempted to just turn and walk back to the class. A glance over her shoulder showed her the others were standing and moving back into position.

When Kiriai looked back, Gebi was still waiting. Fine.

"I'm a brawler," Kiriai purposely left out the initiate title, "by sheer stubbornness, a bit of talent, the help of friends and more luck than I deserved. Oh, and working as hard as I could, every single day." Kiriai enunciated the last three words and felt the truth of them hit her hard. As she waited for Gebi's reaction, Kiriai decided she needed a vacation. Even a few days would be amazing. Maybe when—or if—they found reinforcements?

Gebi suddenly gave an abrupt nod and took a step closer to Kiriai, making her want to flinch. The calm center she'd been holding and her own stubbornness kept her still and defiant in front of her trainer.

"Good," Gebi said in a low voice. "Maybe there is hope for you. You have the traits I require in a brawler, at least in their infant stages. In return for your honesty, I have a piece of information that might answer your question about your hood. Last month, my father told me Boss Ryuin had met with our hood boss and made a strong case for letting Jitaku solve their own problems without interference . . . or help from the rest of the hoods. That's all I know, for what it's worth."

Gebi turned to head back to the workout area as Kiriai stood, still trying to take in the implications of her revelation. "Wait," she blurted out.

Gebi turned back with a half-smile on her face. "What? Are you rethinking which question is most important to you?"

"I'd still like to know where the complaints about me came from," Kiriai admitted.

Gebi looked indecisive for a moment. When she settled and nodded, Kiriai held her breath. "Technically, you answered three of my questions. And I don't like being used, so I'll give you a second answer." Gebi paused, watching Kiriai closely. "Your hood's second, Second Jaaku. He's the one who asked my father to pay special attention to you. He claimed you manipulated and bent rules to get where you are. Since I consider it my personal duty to weed out anyone unworthy, I had no problem following his request."

"Jaaku?" The name came out dripping with disgust.

Gebi's brows shot up. "On a first name basis with your second and so much emotion? I'm guessing he's one of those powerful figures attacking you then." Gebi let out a wry chuckle and shook her head. "You haven't chosen an easy road, Initiate. May the ancestors guide you."

Without another word, Gebi turned and fell into her brisk instructor's stride back to the rest of the group.

"You have no idea," Kiriai said under her breath and hurried to follow her.

A cheery thought occurred to Kiriai, and she picked up her pace, her bare feet slapping on the smooth wooden floor. Now that she and her crew were here in Southern Core with access to powerful people and possible allies, she could take the fight to Jaaku. A cold smile emerged on her face with a hard edge to it. Second Jaaku would regret ever messing with her.

CHAPTER TWENTY-EIGHT

"Do you think we will actually pull this off tonight?" Eigo asked as he and Mikata circled Kiriai and attempted to hit her with their padded practice clubs. Sento had the three of them drilling in one of the luxurious private workout rooms supplied with every pad, weapon and training tool Kiriai could dream of and some she didn't even recognize.

Blindfolded and feeling a bruise swelling on the side of her jaw, Kiriai couldn't decide if Eigo was talking to distract her or to help her by making it easier for her to locate him. Mikata was just a soft rustle to her left.

There!

Kiriai slipped sideways and felt a fierce glee when her left arm met the edge of the padded club.

"Nice," said Mikata, her rustling already changing directions again. "And why worry about it, Eigo. We've done everything we can. Tomi has all the information we gathered. Now it's up to him and Boss Akuto. Let Kiriai focus on her training. If they arrange the fight we want, it'll come down to her fighting skills."

Kiriai heard Eigo's heavier tread to her right and shifted backward on the diagonal. *To 4:30,* she reminded herself, finding it much easier to visualize all the angles involved while blindfolded. Plus, she'd leveled up some of her principles during her practice with Yabban over the last several days. The last week had passed in a haze of long hours of training, snatched meals and healing sessions with Isha so she could keep up. There were times Kiriai had felt too tired to walk and others she'd made breakthroughs that left her smiling for hours and regaling everyone who would listen with the minute details. To her delight, Sento and both of her training partners were more than happy to pick apart the different techniques she was trying to learn. Even Eigo had helped, being privy to her late-night work with Yabban, and he helped add to the AI's suggestions.

"But the more information she has, the better, right, Sento?" asked Eigo.

Kiriai's step caught, and she almost stumbled as she heard Eigo's friendly tone and easy manner. It was a little crazy how much his relationship with Sento had changed in just over a week. Despite her misgivings, Sento had continued to stick to his role of trainer only and showed steady support for her and Eigo's new relationship. Eigo had relaxed and welcomed Sento into his circle of friends.

"True," said Sento, his deep voice behind her. "As I always say—"

"—more of the fighting happens outside the ring than in the ring," said Kiriai, her voice sounding petulant even to her own ears. "Someone is trying to train here, all right?"

A split second later, a blow smacked into her shoulder and immediately swished away and returned to jab into her chest. The club was padded, but it still hurt, especially when wielded by the relentless Mikata.

Kiriai jerked back, hands up a bit too late, her head swiveling and senses straining. She ignored the snicker from Eigo's direction. Mikata was the sneaky one.

"Together now. Flurry attack. Hajime!" said Sento.

Kiriai barely groaned before they were on her. Though her two sparring partners only had a single club each, they moved and attacked with a speed that made it feel as if she had four or five opponents. There was no more time for thinking or speaking. Blows battered into Kiriai from the front, back and both sides. She parried and blocked, spinning and dodging as best she could. They hit her as often as she deflected the blows. Time blurred into a whirlwind of movement. Breath blew through tight lips, clubs whistled through the air and fighters grunted with effort and pain. Without her eyes, Kiriai's mind scrambled to weave her other senses into a map of the movement around her. A club caught her under an elbow and even though her partners weren't hitting full-force, it still made her cough in pain and spin, hands flashing just a little too late. Another and another smacked into her. It was too much. Kiriai seemed perpetually a moment too slow and the attacks she blocked were almost by accident, making her stumble like on a missed step at the top of a staircase. Kiriai just wanted to curl up into a ball with her hands wrapped around her head and try again after a break.

Focus! Relax! she chanted to herself. She wasn't getting hit hard enough to do any real damage, so the point was to force her mind to see and defend without the help of her eyes. Kiriai let go, and just began moving without intention. *Go ahead,* she told her mind. *Figure out where they are and move to intercept the attacks.*

It didn't work immediately, but as the time ticked by, Kiriai felt her forearms connect with more blows while fewer penetrated her defenses. A few more seconds and she seemed to sense something through the blindfold. Not an image exactly, but a vague form . . . actually two of them.

What? She almost let herself get pounded on again as she squinted, trying in vain to focus, eyes covered by a dark cloth. It wasn't a visual image, but more a sense of two presences that marked where Eigo and Mikata were.

You just leveled up your Observation skill and improved your Environmental Awareness ability.

Sweet! Kiriai grinned and focused even harder. On a basic level, she could sense where her two attackers were. It seemed all the information detected by her senses coalesced into enough information that she could move and block in response to the vague images.

Well, not quite as well as seeing, she amended, as a blow hit her from the left, followed immediately by one to her upper thigh. She realized she was thinking too hard again, which interfered with the instincts she was training. Kiriai let her focus soften, like she did when trying to take in the surrounding environment instead of a single object. Then she pulled on her centering, working to calm her labored breathing and relax her muscles.

Loose and quick, she reminded herself, letting go of as much tension as possible. A savage satisfaction surged through Kiriai as her blocks moved true, her forearms and hands stinging as they slapped against the leather of the padded clubs. Her grin widened further just before a club popped her in the forehead and another hit her from behind. Was that a snicker she heard?

"Yame!" said Sento, and Kiriai pulled the blindfold up from her face and spun toward the source of the laughter.

Eigo held up his club defensively, a wide smile on his face. "Wait!" he said, backing up. "I was just doing what Sento told me to."

Kiriai snatched the club out of his hand and in one second had batted him from top to bottom on both sides, just hard enough to sting. Eigo yelped and laughed, making his attempts at blocking ineffective.

Kiriai handed the club back to him. "Now that was funny," she said with a grin.

"Fine. I deserved that," said Eigo, still smiling. "But we're even now, deal?" He held out his hand to shake.

Kiriai looked down and on impulse took his hand, pulled him into a hug and wrapped her arms around him.

His whole body froze for a second before he returned the embrace with an enthusiasm that made Kiriai smile. Eigo soothed all the rough edges inside her and made her feel loved.

"Hey, none of that," said Mikata with humor in her voice as she clapped Eigo on the back. "Save it for after we're done."

Eigo let go immediately, and Kiriai saw a red flush creeping up his neck. Without thinking, she gave his cheek a quick kiss before letting go and pulling away. He stood stock-still and looked so vulnerable standing there, eyes questioning her.

Kiriai opened her mouth, but didn't know what to say.

Mikata saved her again.

"Should we line up one more time?" Mikata aimed the question at Sento, giving Kiriai an excuse to turn and look toward him too.

Turns out that didn't help either, though.

Sento was staring at her and Eigo, his face carefully blank and not answering Mikata's question. Kiriai looked closer and saw the muscles in his jaw working. Did he have a problem with her and Eigo being together after all? Something inside her leapt at the idea, but Kiriai couldn't tell if it was anger or excitement.

"I guess we can break a little early and head to the house," Mikata drawled, her eyes moving between Sento and Kiriai.

Her words broke whatever spell had frozen them, and Kiriai smiled with relief. "Yes! That sounds like a good idea. I made a decent breakthrough right there at the end and need to give it some time to sink in."

Eigo walked up and slipped an arm around her waist. "Yes, you were blocking a lot more of our hits in the last half of that flurry round. Whatever you were doing, keep that up. Maybe you can practice it more tonight by going over it in your mind."

Kiriai smiled at Eigo's code phrase for her training sessions with Yabban.

"Sounds good," said Sento finally before he turned and walked to the counter behind him and poured glasses of water for everyone. "Drink up and then we'll head over to the house." Sento glanced quickly at the closed door of the room before continuing. "Tomi mentioned he wanted to review the plans for tonight at lunch. We'll be a little early, but we could all use the break."

Everyone walked over and grabbed a glass. Kiriai guzzled the entire thing, but held off drinking a second glass. Instead, she grabbed a towel off the rack and wiped the sweat from her face and neck.

The group grabbed their things and took a moment to put the practice room back to rights. Eigo had just finished hanging the clubs back in their places when the door slid open. Kiriai spun, suspicious. They had chosen a room at the far end of a mostly deserted hall for a reason.

Instead of an interloper, the large bulk of 'Ranger Tomi walked through the door.

"Tomi!" she said, immediately moving forward with a smile and arms wide for a hug. The man had been scarce the last few days with all of the last-minute maneuvering. The last time she'd really spent time with him was last week when she'd shared her intel from Nigai and Gebi.

Tomi returned her smile and gave her a hug, though it was shorter than usual. She understood as soon as he stood back and saw who had followed Tomi into the room.

Boss Akuto!

Kiriai sucked in a breath, and she caught a warning glance from Isha, who had come in behind the boss. The other members of her crew were there too, and Kiriai hoped that meant they had a good plan for tonight.

"Brawler Kiriai," said Akuto as he walked toward her. *Stalked* might be a better description, since all her defensive instincts flared to life. Sento would be proud of her. He'd long been warning her to be wary of the powerful figures that seemed to move in and out of her life.

"Actually, they are calling me 'Initiate Kiriai' until the end of the month," she said with a shrug before giving her boss a low bow.

Akuto snorted and waved a dismissive hand. "They have no power to stop you from becoming a brawler and they know it."

Without considering the implications, Kiriai said, "Well, now that Jaaku's plan didn't work, I should be fine."

"Jaaku's plan?" The two words were soft, but something in Akuto's tone made everyone in the room freeze. Kiriai's stomach twisted, furious with herself. Yes, she wanted revenge against Jaaku, but throwing her best piece of information away with no planning?

Kiriai wanted more than anything to rewind time a second. Where was her pre-cog gift when she needed it? Other than the fight with Akumu, she'd only been using it once or twice a day to stay in practice. Why hadn't she thought to use it for a conversation with Boss Akuto? Surely that was more dangerous than an arena fight.

She'd been quiet too long.

"Explain," Akuto said.

Kiriai searched for the right words and threw a glance toward Tomi, hoping he would step in and fix things for her.

CHAPTER TWENTY-NINE

"When artificial intelligence processes data and strategies at inhuman speeds, those who rely solely on human beings to make the final decisions risk losing everything while they dither."

— Writings of Dr. Leah Campbell, Professor in Computer Science at MIT. Cambridge, MA

"Boss," said Tomi after aiming a small head shake in Kiriai's direction. "Would you mind letting us all get comfortable first? I can secure the room, so it's safer to discuss sensitive topics, all right?" Tomi aimed a pointed glance at the open door behind them.

"Yes," Akuto said with an impatient wave of his hand. "Make sure no one is in the hall, shut the door and let's all sit down."

Kiriai took the instruction as permission to turn and start grabbing the spectator chairs arranged against the front wall. Eigo was right beside her and helped place a chair for everyone in a loose circle.

"Jaaku is in trouble," said Eigo under his breath in a delighted sing-song voice that made Kiriai grin as they moved chairs together.

"Stop it." She swatted at him with her free hand. "I wanted to save that for later, when I was ready to make a move against the man."

"What? You think he won't do more of that kind of crap? He's probably aiming minions at you as we speak. Don't worry, if you need more ammunition against him, he'll provide it. Just enjoy the chance to rat him out to the boss now."

"Hmm. I didn't think of it like that."

"Listen," Eigo said with a stern look. "You're not some junior scrapper he can ambush anymore. You're a burb brawler, and if he keeps up this nastiness, you will be able to squash him before long. Got it?"

"Please sit," said Tomi in his usual cheerful voice once he had made sure Boss Akuto had taken the most comfortable chair.

"Thanks," whispered Kiriai under her breath to Eigo as they took two seats across from the boss. She'd already planned on doing something about Jaaku, but he still loomed large and powerful in her mind. Eigo's words made her reconsider that mental image. Sento had always aspired to be a burb brawler because he'd craved power due to his harsh upbringing. Kiriai just needed to figure out how to use that power to stop Jaaku once and for all.

Eigo gave her hand a quick squeeze before he let go and turned to the boss.

"Before we continue, I'd like an explanation of your earlier words, Brawler Kiriai," Akuto said, his gaze sharp and pinning her.

Kiriai swallowed, and remembering Eigo's encouragement, she told him the truth.

" . . . and that's why Trainer Gebi had such a low opinion of me and my efforts to become a brawler," said Kiriai, finishing the story.

A snort of disgust came from her right, and Kiriai glanced over to see Shisen didn't bother to hide her loathing of Jaaku. Aibo looked even more surprised and angry, and Kiriai regretted her decision to keep Jaaku's manipulation from them.

"I'm sorry I didn't tell the rest of you, but I was still trying to decide what to do with the information," Kiriai said and made an apologetic gesture with her hands. She'd only told Tomi about Jaaku . . . well, and Eigo. But she told Eigo everything.

"Jaaku is my concern now," said Akuto, his voice flat, but still full of power. "Don't concern yourself with him anymore."

A chill shot through Kiriai.

"Don't kill him," she blurted out, and every gaze in the room turned to look at her, some amazed and others thoughtful. Kiriai did not know what Akuto had planned. But she just wanted him to remove Jaaku from power, not kill him or send him to the farms, which was often the same thing, only delayed. Jaaku was doing what he thought was best for Akuto and Jitaku, in his own misguided way.

Akuto's eyes flickered with the smallest hint of surprise. "Showing mercy for an enemy is unwise."

"And killing someone who is loyal but misguided is too," she shot back. Sento sucked in a breath to the side of her, but Kiriai held Akuto's gaze. She'd never been one to back down. He should be used to it by now.

"I'll take your opinion into consideration," he said with a sharp nod before turning back to the room at large.

Kiriai knew the subject of Jaaku was closed and pushed it to the back of her mind for later.

Akuto straightened and addressed everyone.

"I know this meeting is a surprise to most of you. But tonight's plan to save Jitaku is only possible because of your hard work and the information you spent the last two weeks gathering. I wanted to meet and acknowledge what everyone here has done for our hood. I know the 'zens here think little of us, but they're wrong. We may be the smallest hood in Southern Core, but we are one of the strongest." Akuto scanned the faces turned toward him, and Kiriai felt pride swell inside her. She followed his gaze, her emotions growing as she saw everyone she cared about here, each of them doing everything possible to save their hood. Only Ojisan was missing, still finishing out the month in Jitaku before he would come spend time with Kiriai. By the time he arrived after graduation, everything important would have already been decided. She missed him.

"Tonight is important. It's probably the only chance we have now that we've lost forty-eight percent of our territory," said Akuto. Silence and sober expressions greeted his announcement. Everyone here had already heard the bad news after this week's fights. "Our enemy, Boss Ryuin of Mabbai Hood, is behind the lack of reinforcements that has crippled us during this long war with Raibaru." A hint of consternation or shame seemed to show under Akuto's expression. "I misjudged the extent to which she would go for revenge. My victories over her were long in the past, and forgotten, I thought. For that, I apologize."

Silence greeted his words. There wasn't really a protocol for accepting an apology from your boss.

"But now that we know she is our main opponent," Akuto said, his voice hardening again, "we will take the fight right to her door and destroy her. She has crossed a boundary, letting her petty anger sabotage an ally, however distasteful she finds me."

Every member of her crew was silent, probably terrified at being included in this level of information and scheming. Only Tomi would have any experience with it.

"I am sharing this information with you because you will attend tonight's ceremony to arrange Brawler Kiriai's first-fight, and I want you to be familiar with my plans in case you find more information or a way to help. 'Ranger Tomi has given a glowing recommendation about each of you, your discretion, your abilities and your loyalty to our cause." Akuto glanced at Tomi, who smiled. "And if Tomi trusts you, then so do I."

Akuto paused to let everyone absorb his words. From the corner of her eye, Kiriai saw that Aibo looked a little shell-shocked. Kiriai knew what that felt like as she remembered her first interactions with Boss Akuto.

"After we're done here, I have an appointment with Chief Kosui," said Akuto. "His first order of business will be to berate me for failing to carry out an impossible task he gave me last month. But once he's done, I will do my best to get him on our side for tonight. Or at least not against us. We all know how important his selection of Kiriai's first-fight opponent will be to our plan."

Akuto's voice trailed off, and he looked lost in thought. Kiriai could only imagine how many convoluted schemes were running through his crafty mind.

No one spoke and even Tomi waited, not daring to interrupt without permission.

Finally Akuto's eyes cleared, and he looked up. "I think I have something that will work with the chief today. As for tonight's plan, here's how we will trick Boss Ryuin into taking the bait . . . "

Everyone listened with focused attention as Akuto laid out the details.

CHAPTER THIRTY

"Now that makes sense," said Eigo under his breath to Kiriai. She smiled at him, a bit distracted by how dashing he looked in the suit M. Shuju had picked out for him. And not only that, but the luxurious clothing didn't seem to make him uncomfortable at all. He just accepted it, without really changing from the Eigo she loved. The word made her thoughts stutter to a halt. Of course she loved Eigo. But had that grown into something more?

Kiriai finally noticed Eigo staring at her, one brow cocked in question.

"What makes sense?" she hastily asked, finally remembering what he'd said. He turned toward the front, and Kiriai followed his gaze, looking over the heads of the other crews to see where Eigo was looking. The bosses and their entourages sat in the front sections closest to the stage, chairs arranged in a deep semicircle so everyone had a decent view. The hall where they'd held their social training last week had been transformed. And this time, the chief and four bosses were in attendance and nothing tonight would be practice.

Kiriai ignored a headache that crept up the back of her neck as she saw a familiar, wiry figure making his way through one of the front rows to find his seat.

"Akumu," she said, distaste in her voice.

"Look who he's sitting with," Eigo said with a push of his chin toward Akumu's companions.

Kiriai sucked in a breath of recognition. Even from behind, the severe cut of her perfectly combed dark hair, expensive business suit and stiff posture were easily recognizable. Tomi had pointed out Boss Ryuin and her entourage during the earlier mingling time.

"No wonder he has it in for me."

"Despite all their preaching of transferring our allegiance from our hoods for the chief and the burb, huh?" Eigo's huff made it clear what he thought of the vindictive trainer and his loyalties.

"Welcome to tonight's ceremony!" boomed a voice with the characteristic power of a sensei who had years of experience projecting across a dojo floor.

Every eye in the room turned to Sensei Nigai, who stood on the raised dais up front with an uncharacteristic smile on her face. Kiriai wondered if the dour woman had had to practice that beforehand. She wore another version of the flowing suit she'd had on last week, and Kiriai made a note to ask M. Shuju if he could find something similar for her. At least tonight they had instructed the initiates to wear their best uniforms. Kiriai preferred her fighting uniform over a dress any day.

"Tonight all eight of our newest brawler initiates have reached the halfway point of their training, which is cause for celebration. And how better for future brawlers to celebrate than to arrange their first-fights after graduation?" Nigai tipped her head and held out a hand.

The crowd quickly took the cue and broke into applause and cheers, though Kiriai was sure some initiates were more excited about the graduation part than their first-fight arrangements.

When the noise died down, Nigai turned a hand toward the row of important personages seated down in the first row in front of the low stage. "Without further ado, I'd like to welcome our leader, Chief Kosui, to the front."

The room was so silent Kiriai could hear the faint clink of dishes from the kitchen facilities behind the back curtains.

Chief Kosui made his way up to the dais and gave Nigai a respectful nod, which she returned with a full bow. When the large man turned to face the group, he didn't speak right away, instead letting his eyes rove over the medium-sized crowd. Kosui was tall, with a fighter's build, but one undermined by too much good food and social fighting instead of the arena kind. His dark hair lay cropped close to his head and his eyes drew all her focus, dark, cold and powerful. Kiriai tensed, straightened her shoulders and prepared herself. When his eyes made it to the back section, they paused for the briefest moment on her. She maintained a confident expression, though she wanted to sag with relief once his gaze moved on.

As one of the newest brawlers, she'd thought she could fade into the background behind the large number of more senior fighters when she arrived in Southern Core. She hadn't known the initiates would be under this much scrutiny and was not happy about it.

"You are to be congratulated, initiates," the chief said, his voice deep and just as powerful as Nigai's. "We don't often lose new brawlers during initiation—"

"Now he tells us," said Kiriai under her breath, venting some of her emotion.

On her left, Mikata stifled a soft laugh, and Kiriai relaxed. She focused on positive thoughts. Their plan would work. With Boss Akuto and 'Ranger Tomi on the job, she didn't need to worry.

"—but that doesn't mean the initiation is unnecessary or should be less rigorous," said Kosui. "The transition from a senior hood scrapper to brawler fighting for all of us here in the burb can be a challenging one. It is significant and requires a sacrifice of both time and effort."

There were nods among the crowd, but not really from the fighters themselves, from what Kiriai could see.

Chief Kosui surveyed the crowd again, the look of a proud parent on his face. Kiriai barely kept from shaking her head at the man. He was a master at manipulating crowds.

"That is a sacrifice each of you has made during the last two weeks. And everyone here knows it hasn't been an easy one." The chief gave a commiserating chuckle and many in the audience joined him.

"What do they know?" Now it was Eigo's turn to mutter under his breath.

The chief's expression turned serious as he straightened, and the room quieted again. "Everyone here is proud of you: your crews, your previous bosses and your trainers. Tonight is a significant milestone to celebrate your achievement. Tonight is your first step into this challenging new life—the official arrangement of your first-fights as burb brawlers!"

Kiriai didn't mind joining in the clapping and cheers this time. But if they could just move straight to the fighting and skip all the social maneuvering, she'd be even more happy. Though, she reminded herself, she would need the next two weeks to prepare for her first-fight. And that would only be important if Boss Akuto's plan tonight worked.

"I'd like to invite each boss and their initiate up here, please," the chief said with a wide smile, but everyone there recognized his words were an order, not an invitation.

Kiriai's stomach clenched as she stood and did her best to appear confident as she shuffled sideways through the row. The other initiates did the same while the four bosses up front could just stand and take a few steps up onto the stage to stand next to the chief.

When Kiriai finally stood next to Boss Akuto, the eyes of the rest of the crowd felt like a physical presence pushing in on her. Why could she stand in the center of an arena without difficulty, but these people here were making the pulse throb in her throat and a cold sweat break out on the back of her neck?

What lies at the bottom of the ocean and twitches?

I don't know, Yabban. Kiriai didn't smile with everyone looking, but she was more than happy for the distraction. *The only oceans I've seen are from the pictures in my primary histories.*

A nervous wreck.

It took Kiriai a moment to understand, and then she really had to work hard to keep from smiling. The humor reminded her to breathe and center herself. By the time the rest of the initiates finished lining up on the platform, Kiriai felt calmer.

The spacious ballroom quieted again as the chief looked over the four bosses with their initiates.

"As leader of the first-ranked hood, Boss Chusei has the privilege of making the first challenge. Boss." Kosui held out a respectful hand toward Seidai's leader.

Chusei, the oldest man on the platform, gave Kosui a respectful nod before taking a step forward to address the crowd. His average height and white wispy hair reminded Kiriai of her grandfather, except there was a hint of ruthless power in his expression that she doubted she'd ever see in Ojisan. There was a reason Ojisan had chosen to be a fixer, not a fighter, as his profession.

"Thank you, Chief Kosui," said Chusei, his tone deep and cultured. "I, too, am pleased with our burb's new initiates and expect great things from them in the future." He looked over their group on the dais before turning back to the crowd. "I know this is the only time when we speak of a brawler's original hood"—Chusei pulled a small shiny figure out of his pouch and held it up to the audience—"because the outcomes of these first-fights have such significant rewards."

Soft laughter rippled through the crowd.

Chusei smiled. "I would be honored for my initiates to fight brawlers from"—he scanned the other bosses as the tension grew —"Rinjin Hood!"

Good-natured cheers greeted his declaration and Boss Yakara tipped his head in acknowledgment and stepped forward.

"I will offer a fully funded evening at Hanten Palace for the new Seidai brawlers and up to fifty guests against the warrior goddess trophy."

A murmur of approval swept through the crowd as Yakara held a hand toward Chusei, giving him the floor again to suggest the winning terms. Even Kiriai had heard of the Hanten Palace restaurant and knew, while the cost to feed fifty guests would boggle her, it was probably negligible to these hood bosses.

"What a generous offer to entertain us. I would like to suggest victory terms of . . . " Chusei paused to rub his chin, though Kiriai was sure he'd already figured out the details in plenty of time. "If my initiates can win any single round based on the judges' scoring at the end of the matches, we will enjoy your luxurious party. If not, the trophy is yours. Agreed?" He looked over at Yakara.

The much younger boss laughed. "What? Shouldn't one of them have to win a whole match, Boss Chusei?"

Chusei smiled, but Kiriai saw the muscles around his eyes tighten. "Now, Boss Yakara, don't you think we should give our newest fighters a little more time before we expect them to win against fully trained brawlers?"

"Boss Chusei is right. Let's not forget the purpose of these fights," said Chief Kosui.

The veiled banter between the two bosses stopped immediately.

"We expect the new brawlers to lose their first-fights," said the chief. "All training must start in humility and an understanding of how far one has to grow. But a small measure of victory, as suggested by Boss Chusei, is a reasonable victory term, don't you think, Boss Yakara?"

"Or course," said Boss Yakara. He bowed at the chief before turning to face Chusei. "I accept your terms for victory." Yakara held out a hand and smiled. Chusei took his hand and held up the trophy with his other as he shook. With it held aloft, Kiriai could see that it was actually a beautiful golden fighter holding out a perfectly executed high roundhouse kick. Every wrinkle in the fighter's uniform and even her hair was faithfully reproduced to suggest power and graceful movement. It might not be an expensive business holding or other significant winning, but Kiriai would have loved to own it herself.

"Challenge and terms accepted," said Chief Kosui. "I will make my choices from among the brawlers with a Rinjin hometown and post the detailed match-up at the end of the evening. Boss Yakara, as the leader of our second hood, it is your turn now."

Kiriai watched Boss Yakara and Boss Ryuin go through similar performances, while inside she wondered how something as straightforward as fighting had managed to accumulate so much useless pageantry. It was just an opportunity for the leaders to parade their power and influence in front of others. While someone like M. Shuju, and even Sento, for that matter, seemed to enjoy such matters, Kiriai would rather be kicked in the gut any day. Besides, with the final choice of the specific opponents in the hands of the chief anyway, much of this posturing had little influence on the outcome of the fights.

"Boss Akuto, our final leader, please step forward," said Chief Kosui.

Well, except for this once, thought Kiriai as she forced a calming breath in and out. Akuto left her side and stepped forward to address the audience.

"Thank you, Chief Kosui. Everyone in Jitaku Hood is loyal to you and Southern Burb. We are especially grateful for your continuous help during the long war we've been fighting." Akuto turned to squarely face the chief and gave him a full subordinate-to-leader bow.

When he stood back up, the room seemed frozen in silence, waiting.

The chief stared hard at Akuto, but he didn't flinch.

Finally, Kosui nodded. "It is our pleasure to support and reward all those who are loyal to us."

Kiriai heard a few gasps and fought against a smile herself. Whatever her boss had done in his meeting with the chief, it had paid out amazing dividends. Kiriai didn't really want to know what it had cost Akuto.

But it was worth it. The chief had just publicly acknowledged support for Jitaku. It might not be the actual fighters they needed —the chief didn't have any scrappers—but it might be enough to sway Boss Chusei with his dogged loyalty to the chief. And if others sent help, Yakara would probably follow suit.

Boss Akuto gave a respectful nod to the chief, acknowledging his support before he turned back to face the audience.

"I'm sure everyone here is excited to get back to the party and fun," he said, his voice much more companionable than usual. "Though I'm sure some of you enjoy the drama we've been happy to provide up here for you." He waved a cheerful hand at those standing behind him on the stage. A few light chuckles swept through those watching.

"Well, I wouldn't want to disappoint any of you," he said. "As my friendship with Boss Ryuin goes back to our youth, I'd like to issue my challenge to Mabbai for my initiate's first-fight."

It was only because she'd been watching the woman closely out of the side of her eye that Kiriai saw Boss Ryuin's reaction. Her whole body seemed to stiffen and one fist clenched briefly before she returned back to her calm facade.

"And the prize and terms?" Chief Kosui asked.

Boss Akuto turned to face Boss Ryuin directly before speaking, and Kiriai prepared herself for an explosion.

CHAPTER THIRTY-ONE

"The founding of Chikara City and the outskirts was a
nightmare. You'd think after seeing most of humanity wiped
out and trying to rebuild, we could all get along. Nope.
People just can't stop fighting for an advantage. I'm happy to
sit back and protect me and mine. Let the rest of them fight."
— Personal Journal of Western Burb Chief Paul Goddard.
Oath Keepers Archive of Truth, Volume 20

"I would like to put up Isan Factory as the stakes for my
challenge," said Boss Akuto in a matter-of-fact tone that gave
no hint to the fact that it was one of the top factories in all of
Southern Burb. The factory's income had explained a lot about
the boss's wealth, when Kiriai had heard the plan the night
before. Putting it up as the prize also solidified in her mind how
dedicated Akuto was to protecting his hood.

With the day almost over, Kiriai still hadn't used her pre-cog
energy for the day, and this was a sweet moment she wanted to
enjoy. Making sure she was staring directly at Boss Ryuin, Kiriai

gave the practiced mental command for the world around her to *slow*.

Her gift responded easily, and Kiriai marveled for a moment at how far she'd come from her first uncontrolled experiences. The surrounding sounds distorted into the elongated tones she'd grown used to, and Kiriai watched the next second or so of life proceed at a snail's pace.

Akuto's mouth had just closed and his words struck Boss Ryuin like a hammer-blow to the face. First, her eyes widened in surprise, followed immediately by her head flinching back in slow-motion horror as the full significance of Akuto's words penetrated. Her normally tight lips were agape with dismay, and she sucked in a shocked breath. Kiriai could see a red flush creep its way up her neck and flare across both cheeks. She looked completely incensed, and Kiriai thoroughly enjoyed it. This woman had single-handedly kept reinforcements from their hood for almost a year. And not for some big scheme to obtain power or solidify influence. No, the woman just wanted revenge. She'd lost to Akuto repeatedly via legitimate channels, so now she used sneaky subterfuge to attack an ally from the dark, with no regard for who she hurt along the way. Boss Ryuin deserved much worse than this challenge by Akuto, but Kiriai would enjoy whatever she could get.

Right at that moment, Kiriai's gift stopped and wrenched her back to the beginning of Ryuin's reaction to Akuto's challenge. Kiriai had no problem watching it a second time at full speed.

"How dare you!" Ryuin screamed, and she lunged forward toward Akuto. Just a few feet from him, she managed to stop and turned her head toward Kosui. "He has gone too far this time. I will have satisfaction for this taunting joke!"

The chief's expression flattened, and he didn't answer.

Members in the audience, all watching raptly, gasped at Ryuin's demeanor toward the chief.

The furious woman seemed to realize her mistake at the same time and some sense of self-preservation awakened.

"I apologize, Chief Kosui," she said, hastily dropping into a deep bow. "My emotion overcame me because of Akuto's taunting and mockery of what used to be my family's most treasured property." Ryuin's voice was muffled as she spoke into the floor, still holding her bow.

The entire room sat frozen as the chief took his time regarding Ryuin's figure folded double in front of him. Kiriai started counting and got to ten before he finally spoke.

"You may rise, Ryuin," he said.

Kiriai knew she wasn't the only one to notice he'd left off the honorific *Boss*.

Ryuin straightened, her hands moving with efficient motions to straighten the lines of her business suit before she stilled, holding her head erect and shoulders back.

"I don't think he is taunting or mocking you," said Chief Kosui with a tip of his head in Akuto's direction.

Ryuin jerked with surprise before turning to glare at Akuto. This time, however, she kept a lid on her emotions, though her face looked flushed enough for her to have just finished a long run.

"You are offering to return my family's factory? The one you swindled away from us over a decade ago? Why? What are you asking me to put up in exchange?"

Kiriai marveled at Akuto's ability to manipulate all the suspicion and anger of the off-balance woman in front of him. Ryuin was so distracted, it seemed she'd forgotten everyone else in the room.

"Does it matter?" Akuto asked calmly. "Wouldn't you give up anything you own for a chance to win your family's heritage back?"

Ryuin opened her mouth to object, but Akuto didn't give her a chance.

"For a chance to erase the blot on your honor." His words struck her like blows, one after another. "For the chance to put me down? To show everyone here"—he moved one hand in a sweeping motion toward the other bosses and the audience —"that you are better than me?"

"Yes!" The word broke free from Boss Ryuin, full of all her pent-up emotion. "Yes! I will match your stakes, whatever they are." She practically spat the last words.

Akuto didn't even pause. He turned back to the chief, dismissing Ryuin like a child having a fit. "I am not a greedy man to take advantage of Boss Ryuin's open-ended offering and ruin her. However, I will ask for a year-long contract of twenty of Mabbai's senior scrappers, half chosen by me and half by Boss Ryuin as the matching stake against Isan factory."

The gasp from the audience drowned out the gurgling noise that came from Ryuin, who looked completely horrified and shocked out of her tantrum.

"But the stakes for the first-fights have to be a token prize," she said, her voice pleading now.

Chief Kosui gave her a cold look that made her quail again, though she didn't bow. "You were perfectly happy to accept the stakes for one of the most valuable factories in my burb a moment ago, weren't you?"

Ryuin bowed her head.

"Do you now say that a year's service from twenty of your fighters isn't a rather inexpensive wager against something so valuable?"

"It's not the money, it's—" Ryuin clamped her mouth shut, and her face drained of color.

"It's what?" Chief Kosui's voice was even colder than before.

If the stakes hadn't been so serious, Kiriai would have laughed at the turmoil rippling across the normally calm boss's face and the way her eyes bugged out. Was the woman really going to admit here, in front of everyone, that she'd been actively campaigning against sending reinforcements to Jitaku? Kiriai held her breath and hoped.

Another silent moment passed, however, and Boss Ryuin took a breath and suddenly seemed to gain control.

Kiriai sighed, disappointed.

Ryuin's icy calm reminded Kiriai of Akuto's warning not to underestimate the woman. He'd been right that only a very personal attack would knock her off balance enough for their plan to succeed. But now that it had, she was an even more bitter and determined enemy.

"I apologize for my behavior, Chief Kosui," she said, fully back to the calm and powerful leader of earlier. "My lapse is due to the nature of the stakes. The Isan factory has been in my family for generations and its loss still cuts even me deeply. Of course the service of a mere twenty scrappers is a token amount to wager against my family's honor."

She turned back to Akuto, and Kiriai didn't like the crafty look in her eye.

"I will accept your generous wager of Isan factory against my fighters, to be decided based on victory in the first-fight."

Kiriai's heart sank as she proved Akuto's predictions correct. He'd been sure of getting one concession while Ryuin was off balance but didn't think he could get her to agree to both the scrappers and something less than a victory by his new initiate. That didn't mean he wouldn't try.

"Chief Kosui," he said, focusing on his leader and ignoring Ryuin. "It is customary to bet on something less than a complete victory. As we all know, these are first-fights against experienced brawler opponents and a victory isn't generally a possibility."

The chief took his time as he had all evening, his gaze moving between Akuto, Ryuin and the audience. At one moment, his gaze even stopped to fasten onto Kiriai. She stayed as still as possible.

"Are you asking for *customary* and *normal* when you just

wagered one of the largest prizes in my entire burb instead of a trophy or some other token prize?"

Akuto didn't flush, but he bowed his head, and Kiriai knew he'd lost this point at least.

Ryuin didn't bother to hide her smile of victory.

Chief Kosui turned to the audience. "The 'rangement for this final fight will be Initiate Kiriai against a brawler of my choice, formerly from Mabbai Hood. The victor's boss will win either Isan factory or one year of service from twenty of Mabbai Hood's senior scrappers. The loser will deliver the spoils immediately after the Brawler graduation."

There was a weighty pause before the crowd exploded into applause. Tension filled Kiriai as she realized the fate of her hood had fallen, once again, upon her shoulders. And she would have no chance at all if the chief matched her against an experienced brawler.

Ancestors, please help Chief Kosui to give me someone I have a chance of beating. Kiriai paused and felt that her plea sounded selfish. *Not for me, Ancestors, but for our hood, for the reinforcements to save our hood.*

In the midst of the audience's noisy excitement, Kiriai felt a flutter of familiar peace and reassurance wash over her. She smiled. Somehow Kiriai knew her mother was still there, watching over her from the ancestors' realm. Whether their plans succeeded or not, she would have comfort if not outright help.

The company of powerful leaders along with initiates and their crews mingled in front of the bank of screens on the far wall of the ballroom, all trying to appear calm and dignified, despite the undercurrent of excitement that pulsed through the room.

The chief, still on the dais with the other bosses, had just stepped away from his clerks, which meant he had finished his selections. The match-ups should appear on the screen any moment now. After more than an hour of socializing and nibbling delicacies that sat like rocks in Kiriai's stomach, she was beyond ready to know who she'd be fighting.

"What is taking so long?" asked Mikata in annoyance, though she kept a polite smile on her face.

"Shisen is even more impatient than you are," said Aibo with a grin that widened further when Shisen glared at her. The exchange made Kiriai smile, too. It wasn't like anyone but she would understand Aibo hinting at her ability to read a little of what Shisen was thinking. And since Shisen was being as hard on Aibo as she'd first been on Kiriai, Aibo owed her instructor more than a little teasing. Shisen had been, and still was, a harsh taskmaster when it came to training gifts. A vision of Shisen's uncle after the ravages of city-family abuse popped into her mind, and she knew Shisen had good reason for her feelings on the topic.

"Who do you think he will match you against?" Eigo asked as he walked up, his question pulling her from her thoughts. He slipped in neatly next to Kiriai, his hands full of another plate of delicacies. Kiriai leaned into Eigo as much as she dared, when she really wanted to just fall into his arms and let him tease and comfort her until her ball of stress dissipated.

"All we can hope for is the least experienced brawler possible," Sento said from her left. "It's our only chance."

Kiriai couldn't argue with him, but he could have phrased it differently. Tomi aimed a sharp look at Sento, who flushed at the implied reprimand. Kiriai aimed a quick glance around their vicinity. No one seemed close enough to overhear their group, but Tomi was right. There was no need to be careless.

A gasp rippled through the audience, and everyone's eyes looked up as the screens flickered to life.

This was it.

Scanning quickly, Kiriai found her name and picture on the

screen second from the right. The space across from it was still blank. A few others in the crowd groaned with impatience, but everyone else seemed to hold their breath in anticipation.

Then the row of screens flickered and suddenly names and ratings sprang up on all of them, one across from each of the initiates' pictures. Heads turned and eyes squinted as everyone tried to see who their favorites would fight.

Kiriai looked at the one across from her. The image of a flinty-eyed woman stared back at her, hair cropped short and face expressionless. But appearances didn't matter at all. Kiriai's eyes dropped to her ranking and just stared at the numbers, her brain stuttering and trying to take it in.

1536.

The number just stared at her, and a smile spread across Kiriai's face. As a new brawler, they would set Kiriai's ranking at 1500, so this brawler was a junior one, just as they'd hoped!

"Yes!" hissed Eigo next to her, and Kiriai felt his arm reach around her and give her an exuberant squeeze.

"She's a blank blue belt, not even a one-striper," Aibo said, as she turned to Kiriai with a huge grin on her face.

"Brawler Antei," said Mikata, her expression calm, though she had a happy glint in her eye. "I know her. She's one of last year's initiates from Mabbai and has been putting on an average performance this year. They say the transition to brawler has been difficult for her. She has decent basics and should be a solid performer once she gains more experience."

"Well, Kiriai is all about helping other fighters gain experience," said Shisen in a droll tone.

Tomi placed a hand on Kiriai's shoulder and met her gaze. "This is the best we could have hoped for. Sure, Antei has almost a year's experience as a brawler, but with her stats, very few would have hired her during that time."

The 'ranger glanced over his shoulder at the leaders still standing on the dais before turning back to her. "Boss Akuto put everything on the line and persuaded Chief Kosui to make this a fair trial of ability and determination. It won't be easy, but with two weeks to train and prepare, we have a chance, a fighting chance."

Kiriai basked in the confidence pouring off of Tomi and understood for a moment why he was so good at his job. When she glanced to see how Boss Akuto was taking it all, she found him looking directly at her. Face giving nothing away, he tipped his head in the slightest of nods.

Turning back from the boss, Kiriai couldn't resist leaning in and asking Tomi in a quiet tone, "What did the boss have to give Chief Kosui for this?"

Tomi didn't immediately respond and Kiriai could see he debated how much to say. But then he nodded and spoke. "You're in the middle of this and a trusted part of the boss's inner circle. I can't predict when or if this information might help us, so I'll share part of it with you."

Kiriai caught her breath and waited.

"Boss Akuto offered to use his resources to investigate the trouble Kosui is having with the city families. A group of valuable people went missing before the chief could deliver them to the city as ordered."

Panic flared inside Kiriai and she made a desperate grab for her centering skills, barely in time to keep her reaction from showing on her face. Thankfully, Tomi's eyes were focused over her shoulder at the boss.

"The chief is desperate and willing to do pretty much anything to save himself from the wrath of the city families." Tomi's expression was thoughtful. "I get the feeling that all this doesn't even matter to the chief at the moment. And if the city families are considering removing him for his failure, I can understand." He looked back at her, gaze sharp. "So if you hear even the smallest piece of information about this matter, make sure you bring it to me. If the chief goes down, he'll do his best to bring others down with him, including a hood boss who promised to help him."

Kiriai nodded and hoped the smile on her face didn't look as sickly as she felt. After copying the list of gifted children under the chief's nose last month, she hadn't considered the future consequences. She desperately needed to run through everything they'd done and make sure there wasn't a trail that could lead back to them. Had they been careful enough?

"Congrats!" Sento said as he slapped her back and smiled, jarring Kiriai loose from her worries. She reminded herself that she couldn't focus on the past when she had the biggest fight of her life at the end of the month. Glancing at her jubilant crew gathered around her, a half-smile returned to Kiriai's face. She was in for a brutal two weeks, but now, at least, there was a light of hope flickering ahead of them.

CHAPTER THIRTY-TWO

K iriai let her pace ease with the rest of the initiates as they finished their afternoon sprints, breath whistling in the warm air of the spring afternoon. Bright sun cast dark shadows around the lush gardens of the chief's inner landscapes. While she'd kept pace with everyone, Kiriai felt the aching reminders of this morning's pummeling that even an extra long session with Isha hadn't been able to remove. But after two weeks of her packed training schedule, she felt stronger, her breathing easier even when she pushed hard.

Both your Will Power and Resilience continue to improve. Your stubborn refusal to give up, combined with your new training, are strengthening you as a fighter.

Thanks, Yabban. I think? Kiriai responded to the backhanded compliment.

Just make sure you never try to give up on friction.

Friction? It took Kiriai a moment to dredge up what the word meant from her childhood lessons.

You won't be able to stop.

Kiriai smothered a snort and enjoyed the simple pleasure of

smiling as she ran with the group of dangerous fighters and trainers.

The whole group slowed to a jog when they reached the training hall entrance, the only sound their whistling breath and thudding feet on the stone path. Kiriai wasn't the only one to sigh in relief as they moved from the hot glare outside into the cool welcome of the hallway. As she followed her group, Kiriai noticed noises coming from the private training rooms they passed. For the first time, she wondered how many brawlers they'd displaced by using the large training hall during the month of initiation.

She didn't get much chance to linger on the thought as their trainers led them out onto the training floor. This time, however, they veered to their left and led everyone along one wall. After two weeks, their group had enough discipline to refrain from asking questions, but that didn't keep them from craning curious looks ahead to figure out where they were going.

A moment later, the lead trainer turned into a doorway that opened up into a large space Kiriai hadn't been into before. Trainer Gebi was waiting and nodded as the trainer snapped to attention and gave her a sharp bow. The initiates quickly filed in, lining up in front of Gebi with the ease of practice. Kiriai scanned the room as best she could while still keeping her eyes forward. It was a large room with one wall full of screens. Unoccupied chairs, grouped in clusters, faced each screen. Just inside the doorway sat a desk with a bored-looking clerk slouching in a chair behind it.

"Welcome to the brawler research alcove," said Gebi with a pleased smile at the initiates and their identical ready stances. "Let me emphasize this alcove is accessible to all brawlers *and their crews*. Anyone can walk by and see which fighters you are researching. However, if you use a screen in a private work-out room or your own screens at home, no one can keep tabs on what you're doing. However"—she held up one finger—"here you can take advantage of a research assistant who can help you find the exact footage you're looking for. Your aides and trainers are receiving training in how to do the basics, so for now this is your best bet if you need more."

Excitement rose in Kiriai as she realized the power of this unpretentious space. Sure, she'd been able to watch fight replays at home, but her basic home pod and screen had required the exact date, time and place to do so. To access fighting schedules of specific fighters, she'd had to wait her turn for an appointment with the few harried clerks at headquarters who helped the scrappers. Their world just had so many fights, finding one in so much footage was almost impossible.

Kiriai snuck a glance at the young lady slouched behind her wide desk sporting three pods and a clipboard. Instead of being harried by too many requests, she sat there looking bored. Kiriai couldn't wait to give her work to do. Then she remembered what else Gebi had said. Sento and Aibo would be trained to do this, too! This was almost better than the lavish training facilities. And with Yabban's Replay Training, Kiriai could practice against the specific opponent she would face after watching enough footage for the AI to get the information she needed for her simulation.

"Each initiate, choose a screen and have a seat facing me," said Gebi. Kiriai moved quickly, hoping the lecture would be short.

"Our training has entered its second and final stage," said Gebi when everyone was seated, the other trainers lined up behind her.

Kiriai wished she would just hurry.

"Now that Chief Kosui has chosen your opponents for your first-fight, our entire focus will be on how to prepare well for a specific fight."

Finally! Kiriai barely kept from saying the word out loud. Based on the smiles around her, the other initiates felt the same.

"We will work on this in the afternoons," said Gebi before

raising her voice. "Mornings will still be for conditioning and drill training!"

The smiles dimmed at that, which seemed to please Trainer Gebi. No one dared object. Even Kiriai couldn't. After only two weeks she could already feel the increase in her strength and endurance. Not to mention how much the blindfolded training and working with multiple opponents had honed her awareness.

I'm glad you are finally seeing the value in the fighting principles you are training.

Yes, Yabban. I was an idiot to wait so long to work on them with you.

Kiriai felt a flash of pleasure across her connection with Yabban that made her smile. Everyone, even a training AI, liked being right.

"Since Initiate Kiriai seems so happy, let's start with her."

Hearing Gebi say her name, Kiriai kicked herself for letting her attention wander. She tried to replay what the trainer had just been saying. Something about assigning a specific trainer to each initiate?

"Since you've already worked together, we have assigned Trainer Akumu to help you prepare for your first-fight. He will work side-by-side with you for the next two weeks to give you the best chance of doing well in your first-fight." Gebi waved at the man standing behind her. Akumu stepped forward, and his pleased smirk widened as he saw Kiriai's reaction.

A flush of outrage threatened to burst free, and it was only by the slimmest of margins that Kiriai kept from standing up and screaming at the unfairness. Instead, she aimed a betrayed, pleading look at Gebi. The head trainer looked a little sheepish, but gave Kiriai a shrug that communicated her lack of control in the matter.

Kiriai was confused. If not Gebi, then who? As soon as she asked the question, it was obvious. Boss Ryuin would do her best to ensure Kiriai lost. What better way than to assign a trainer who hated her guts and hoped she failed?

"Wait," Kiriai said and stood as something important occurred to her. "Trainer Akumu is originally from Mabbai Hood, isn't he?"

Akumu stopped halfway across the room.

Gebi nodded, but not with any encouragement in her expression. Kiriai plowed ahead anyway.

"My first-fight is against Brawler Antei, also from Mabbai Hood. Don't the rules forbid my assigned trainer being originally from the same hood I will face? It's a conflict of interest."

Kiriai was proud of remembering the term she'd learned from Shisen and how calmly she'd delivered her argument. Gebi wouldn't have any choice now but to assign a different trainer.

"Yes," Gebi said, "that is the *customary* arrangement, but it isn't actually a rule."

Gebi's expression looked resigned, and Akumu still sported his smirk as he moved toward her again.

"But—" Kiriai said.

"No." Gebi chopped a hand down. "There has been so much flouting of customs with this group of initiates that only power decides what happens next. And in this matter, Initiate Kiriai, you don't have enough power to change your trainer."

Kiriai sat back in her chair, sick anger swirling inside her. She could see that Gebi wasn't happy with the circumstances, but that didn't stop Kiriai from feeling betrayed by the woman she'd just begun to consider an ally, if not a friend.

Then the image of Sensei Nigai ordering Trainer Gebi around their barracks that first day came to mind. Kiriai would do well to remember that lesson as long as she was in Southern Core. Those with the power made the rules.

In quick order, Gebi had assigned the other trainers, and the room filled with murmuring voices as they began explaining the basics of researching.

"So my young initiate," said the hateful voice as Akumu plopped into the chair next to her. "How can I assist you with your upcoming fight?"

Stay centered, she reminded herself. With a practiced push, Kiriai shifted her perspective to look down on the two of them. From above, she saw a petty man who took pleasure in causing trouble for others.

None of it mattered, she told herself. She had her crew, resources like this research alcove and, best of all, Yabban. With the AI trainer and her tools, there was nothing Akumu could do to stop her progress. At least she hoped so.

Kiriai let out a slow breath and plastered the thinnest of smiles on her face before answering. "I'd like to see footage of Brawler Antei's fights."

To her surprise, Akumu hopped up and crossed the space to the clerk to exchange a few words. As the screen flickered to life, Kiriai realized why the odious man was smiling when he came back to sit next to her. It was footage of a very young Antei fighting. The white belt on her waist made it clear this was one of her junior scrapper fights from years ago.

"I'm sorry," Kiriai said through gritted teeth. "I'd like to see some of Brawler Antei's fights from the last year."

Akumu stood again, still grinning.

"Fights that she won, please," Kiriai called after him, and settled herself down for what she knew would be a long afternoon.

CHAPTER THIRTY-THREE

"U is for Unity. Only by working together in Unity can we all succeed and prosper."

— Chikara City Elementary Primer

"What if I don't even make it to the fight next week?" Kiriai asked as she lowered herself with a groan into the spot next to Eigo on the sofa. The rest of her crew were lounging around the informal living room at the back of her brawler quarters. The cozy room had become their impromptu gathering place, and unlike the formal living room near the entrance, they were less likely to be bothered back here. Or at least, they had ample warning of intruders.

Eigo moved an arm and pulled her in close with a sound of sympathy. She let her body sag into the fluffy cushions as she tucked her head into his shoulder with a contented sigh.

"I think I have bruises just from watching you this week," he said in a quiet voice near her ear, and she had to laugh.

"Stop," she said. "Don't make me laugh. It hurts."

His smile instantly turned to concern as he shifted to face her better. His free hand reached for her ribs and ran gentle fingers along them. When he found the tight wrap over her ribs Isha had told her she could take off before bed, Eigo paused for a moment and then set his whole palm gently over the area. The move was so tender that Kiriai set aside her worries and stress for a moment and relaxed into it. Eigo leaned over and brushed a kiss across the top of her head. He paused for a moment and then pressed another one to her temple. He pulled her closer and his hand moved up and down in a soothing stroke along her side.

Kiriai stiffened.

"Sorry," said Eigo and immediately stopped moving.

Kiriai felt him pull back slightly. "No," she said and snuggled in closer, but didn't lift her face to look at him. Relationship complications were the last thing she wanted to deal with right now. "You just surprised me, is all."

"No," Eigo said, and the hint of dejection in his voice made Kiriai's heart sink. "I promised I would take it slow and not pressure you in this relationship thing, especially with the fight only a week away."

Kiriai looked up, not sure how she was feeling, but knowing she didn't want to hurt Eigo. "It's fine, really. You just surprised me, is all," she said. "And you're right. With the fight coming up so soon, I'm jumpy. No matter how hard I train, the brawler trainers can still run circles around me. I don't know how I will have a chance against Brawler Antei."

"And here I am, giving you more things to worry about." Eigo looked away.

"No," Kiriai said and placed a hand on his chest. "You're one reason I keep trying, keep fighting. Be patient with me. I'm no good at this relationship thing either."

He still didn't look convinced.

"However awkward you're feeling right now? Double it and

that's how I feel with all of this." Kiriai said with a clumsy gesture of her free hand between the two of them.

That got a shaky chuckle out of Eigo, and while Kiriai could feel him relax, there was still some tension in his body. When she looked up at him again, he had an odd look on his face. Then he leaned forward, and Kiriai couldn't help tensing again.

He wasn't going to kiss her, was he? In front of everyone? Not that anyone was really paying attention to them.

At the last moment, he adjusted his aim and pressed a soft kiss on her forehead, reminiscent of the ones her grandfather had given her in her childhood when she was feeling sick.

Kiriai didn't know whether to feel relieved or upset. A barrage of other thoughts drove out all her worries about training and the upcoming fight.

What would kissing Eigo be like? When would he drum up the courage? She'd only ever kissed Sento and missed both the mix of heat and excitement and the closeness she'd had with him. She knew kissing Eigo would be different, but how different? Would it answer her question? Solve her quandary? Was Eigo her best friend or could he become something more? Did she even want that question answered? If it all went horribly wrong, would it ruin everything between them, even though he'd promised it wouldn't?

"Wow," said a quiet voice with a hint of laughter. "Looks like you're thinking pretty hard after a friendly peck on the forehead. Don't do that."

It was the perfect thing to say—something Eigo was always good at. The lighthearted words broke through all of her worries.

"We'll still be friends after this, won't we?" she asked. "No matter what happens. Right?"

"What?" he asked, still smiling. "Are you already planning to crush this poor heart that has been beating for you all its life?" He patted his chest, a dramatic look on his face.

But Kiriai suddenly saw Eigo with new eyes. His words rang

true, and Kiriai saw how much her best friend truly loved her . . . and always had. Worry stabbed at her, and she suddenly wondered if agreeing to this experiment was fair to him when she was so unsure of how she felt.

Eigo's face fell when she didn't respond to his joking as usual.

"Eigo, I don't know if this is a good idea," she said before he could speak. "You have to know the last thing I want to do is hurt you."

"No. Give us time. You agreed," Eigo said with a note of panic in his voice. "Just because I'm sure of what I feel doesn't mean I can't be patient while you figure out what you feel."

Kiriai debated letting the topic drop. This was painful. All she had to do was lean back into Eigo and move on to something else.

But like everything in her life, sometimes you had to keep fighting, no matter how hard it was.

"And if it doesn't turn out how you hope?" There. She'd said it . . . into his chest, instead of looking up at him, but still, she'd said it.

He didn't answer for a long time. Kiriai snuck a glance around the room, relieved that their conversation hadn't attracted any attention. Mikata sat at a small table across from Aibo, playing a card game where they both alternated between laughing and frowning. Tomi and Shisen held a quiet debate, something about types of government systems if that's what the words drifting from them meant. And somehow Isha had cornered Sento into a straight-backed wooden chair and made him pull up his pant leg. Kiriai had ratted him out to the fixer. He couldn't completely hide the limp he'd developed after the new melee exercises Trainer Gebi had introduced. Good thing they still got Ancestor's Day off to recover and regroup, though Kiriai was sure the others would be busy again soon enough. Keeping a close eye on Ryuin and her possible schemes was hard work.

Eigo had taken so long to answer that Kiriai thought maybe

he'd be the one to let the difficult subject drop. Then he shifted, and Kiriai braced herself.

"I can't promise how I will feel about it, however our relationship turns out . . ." he said with a rare, serious tone to it.

Kiriai couldn't keep herself from looking up at him. He paused and seemed to search inside himself for a way to explain.

"—of course I won't be happy if this between us falls apart. I want it to work, almost more than anything. I said almost, because the one thing I want most of all is for you to be happy. And if that means we go back to being friends, then"—Eigo shrugged and let a corner of his mouth turn up in a smile tinged with something Kiriai couldn't identify—"then I'll count myself lucky to have you, Kiriai, as my best friend forever."

Kiriai just stared at him, her own emotions a jumble of confusion. This was the most vulnerable and open she'd ever seen Eigo, and she wanted to be careful with what he'd entrusted to her. But how could she ever refuse him now? When he'd made it clear how much their relationship meant to him?

"No," he said, and now his usual chiding smile was back. "Don't take my burden like you do everyone else's. I let you see how I feel because I want us to be honest with each other. When you're ready, I want you to know you can be just as open with me, understand?"

Kiriai let out a slow breath and nodded.

"And if you never feel the same for me, we'll figure out how to move on from that . . . as friends. All right?"

Before she could respond this time, he grinned and pulled her in close again. "For now, I will be the best blasted training partner you've ever had . . . who might occasionally kiss you." He took a short breath and his smile was back. "Hey, did I tell you what I figured out about the pods they've given us here? They can access a lot more information through the screens than our normal ones back home."

Kiriai took the proffered distraction eagerly and leaned back to look at him with interest. "Did you figure out how to get me better footage of Brawler Antei?"

"Oh, way better than that drivel Akumu has been feeding us this week," said Eigo, his eyes sparkling. "Tomi got permission for me to *help* Shisen with some of her clerk training, and now I've got our pod sifting through every fight Antei has fought in the last year and even some recorded training sessions."

"Help?" Kiriai was having a hard time imagining Eigo and his bouncing energy being much help at all among a group of clerks and their officious training.

"He carried my books for me," Shisen said with a laugh from across the room.

Shisen's interjection startled Kiriai. Maybe she and Eigo had spoken louder about the training matters? Kiriai really hoped the others hadn't overheard their earlier conversation. At the thought, her eyes darted over to Sento, only to find him staring at her. Her breath caught for a moment, but his gaze jumped back to Isha and she heard him thanking the fixer for her treatment.

"It's no shame for a clerk to need a big, strong training partner to help her get all her supplies to a class on using the pods to research records." Sento started out with a teasing voice, but Kiriai could hear excitement too. She forced herself to stop trying to guess what his earlier look had meant. She couldn't afford to let personal matters distract her. There would be time enough after her fight next week.

And if Eigo had succeeded . . . well, getting proper footage had been a struggle all week. The chance to focus her training made a thrill run through her.

"I take it we're done relaxing and ready to get back to planning?" Tomi asked, his eyes scanning their group.

Kiriai expected a groan. They were all operating on little sleep as everyone did their part to gain every advantage for Kiriai's upcoming fight. They might not all be taking the same physical battering she was, but their work was just as exhausting. Kiriai shuddered when the thought made her remember the social maneuvering she'd already had to endure.

Bring on the training and fights any day, she thought.

Instead of groaning, however, her crew nodded, eyes alight with interest as they glanced between Tomi and Eigo. Just like Kiriai, they recognized how important his breakthrough could be.

"Eigo, if you could explain what you've learned about researching the fighting footage? Then the others can share any further information they've gleaned. I know both Sento and Mikata have made contacts that run in the same circles with Antei. After that, Fixer Isha will report on Kiriai's health and her recommendations."

Kiriai swallowed, not looking forward to that part. Isha always wanted her to get more sleep and avoid injuries. At least she didn't know about the late hour of training with Yabban, or she would have surely done her best to put a stop to it. Kiriai figured she could sleep after the fight.

"At the end, I'll give you a report on the news among the leadership. As you know, Boss Ryuin is pulling out all the stops to sabotage Kiriai as much as possible before next week's fight. We have to all be on guard for underhanded tactics." Tomi's face was grim for a moment before he waved to Eigo to speak.

The gravity of Tomi's words couldn't smother Eigo's excitement, which fairly burst from him. He hopped to his feet and faced the group, hands already moving as he prepared to explain. "First, here in Southern Core, the brawler's advanced pods can access footage through all the hoods in the entire burb, not just here."

Kiriai smiled, enjoying her boyfriend's enthusiasm.

"The final breakthrough was a discovery that these pods can recognize people in recording archives, not just the names the judges register for each fight. I don't know if they are tracking the fighter implants or if it is actually the faces, but the upgraded pods Kiriai has here, with the right tweaking, can find me every piece of footage in the entire archives where Brawler Antei was present since she first became a scrapper!"

Eigo's excitement increased as he explained how he'd sorted and grouped the footage into chunks that he expected all of them to help go through. Mikata groaned, but Kiriai shook her head and smiled. Sitting in a comfortable chair watching fights of her opponent would be a nice break from her training. And it was even a legitimate exercise Gebi would have to approve. It might actually be nice if it took hours.

And when Kiriai thought of what Yabban could do with the information, she smiled even wider.

CHAPTER THIRTY-FOUR

"What is the point of this stance?" Kiriai asked in a petulant voice. She maneuvered her body into a twist stance, or at least attempted to. It involved rotating her body while keeping her feet in place until both her knees touched together, and she came up on the ball of one foot.

"It's a transition stance, like I explained earlier," Yabban responded, ignoring Kiriai's cranky mood. "Just like the front twist and rear twist stances, but instead of stepping into this one, you rotate in place."

Kiriai moved a little too far, lost her balance and stumbled out of the stance with a growl.

"Perhaps you'd like to practice the intermediate kicks you've unlocked for a few minutes," Yabban said. "You seemed to enjoy those, and once you're in a better mood, we can finish these stances."

Kiriai bit back her retort. She'd spent Ancestor's Day alternating between Isha's ministrations and watching footage of Antei's fights late into the night. Now, after a full day of brawler training where Gebi kept ratcheting things to ever higher levels, Kiriai just wanted to crash into her bed. But it was already

Monday. The big fight was in five days. She had to squeeze in some training against the virtual Antei before she was too tired to function.

But Yabban had insisted that she take the first part of her training to unlock the handful of intermediate stances she had left.

"This upgrade you keep hinting at better be worth it," Kiriai groused as she contorted herself into the rotating twist stance again.

"I believe it is," said Yabban, her eyes sharp and watching Kiriai's every move. "It's a sub-skill of autonomy that will allow me to better aid you during in-game training and focus your skills on defeating Brawler Antei." Yabban stopped and met Kiriai's gaze. "I know how important this fight is to your hood, Kiriai. This is the path that is best calculated to bring you success."

Kiriai was suddenly struck by how much Yabban, and for that matter her entire crew, was doing to help.

Shame crept in, and Kiriai ducked her head. "I'm sorry, Yabban. I know you're doing your best. I'll try to be less grouchy about it."

Kiriai twisted and bent, sure she finally had it right. When she looked up, Yabban had cracked a smile.

"I have to admit the rotating twist stance has very few practical applications in an arena fight," she said. "But you look quite skilled all twisted up like that. It reminds me of a joke."

Kiriai stared at Yabban for a minute, torn between humor and outrage.

"Congratulations, Trainee Kiriai," Yabban said. "You have unlocked all the intermediate skills, which gives you one attribute point you can use to give me a new skill or upgrade an existing one."

Kiriai relaxed her limbs and stood with a sigh. "You said something about a joke. Maybe you should tell me and I can decide if your humor attribute needs an upgrade."

Yabban frowned. "That would be a waste when an autonomy sub-skill upgrade would unlock new training aids and allow me to offer valuable information out in the game world."

Kiriai just raised her eyebrows and waited, doing her best to keep her expression stern.

Yabban narrowed her gaze for a moment, then shrugged. "A rope walks into a diner. The man inside says, 'Sir, we don't serve food to ropes here.' So the rope goes outside, twists himself up, much like you just did. He messes up his hair and walks back in minutes later. The owner shouts at him, 'Hey aren't you the rope that I told to leave earlier?'"

Kiriai waited

Yabban didn't say anything.

"And?" Kiriai finally asked.

"I'm pausing for comedic timing, Kiriai," said Yabban with a satisfied smile.

Kiriai snorted but kept quiet, letting Yabban have her fun.

She finally gave a slight shrug before delivering the punch line. "The rope looks at the owner and says, 'No sir, I'm a frayed knot.'"

A sputtering laugh erupted from Kiriai and with it, the last bit of her tension. "All right, Yabban. You're right, your humor is perfectly fine the way it is," she said. "But before I do the upgrade, give me a rundown of your stats, please. Not that I will disagree with your recommendation," she hurried to add. "I just want to make sure we're not missing anything. We don't have any room for mistakes."

Yabban nodded, her expression serious again. "You have unlocked the first level of personality as well as the two sub-skills humor and wise sayings. Your last attribute point unlocked my first level of autonomy."

"What about fighting skills? Do you have any upgrades that would let you teach me more advanced fighting moves?"

"No. I have the full library of martial arts moves and skills.

Teaching them depends on what you've unlocked and which prerequisites you've completed. My attributes points affect how you and I interact and how helpful I can be with my suggestions."

"So this sub-skill you're talking about, it will let you help me in the"—Kiriai caught herself and made sure to use Yabban's term —"game world? How is that different from what you already do when you give me advice?"

"The only real way to understand is to unlock it and find out," Yabban said. "It's difficult to explain with words alone, much like all martial art skills."

Kiriai stared at her trainer. But instead of seeing sarcasm, she saw an earnest desire to help in Yabban's eyes.

Curiosity still tugged at Kiriai. This was the most she'd been able to pull out of Yabban and how the AI trainer worked. Learning about the possibilities was too much to ignore.

"Try," Kiriai said.

An almost human expression of exasperation accompanied Yabban's sigh. "I am restricted from doing anything that will give you an advantage during fights in the game world, but the more autonomy attributes you unlock, the more I can assist you as you train in the game world, not just here in the virtual dojo."

Kiriai gave Yabban's words some thought, trying to imagine how Yabban's abilities to do things like simulate opponents would be any more useful in the real world than they were here where she could actually feel and touch them. When they'd first been experimenting, Yabban had presented Kiriai with opponents in the real world that looked and sounded real, but were insubstantial as ghosts. Only once they'd moved to her virtual dojo could Kiriai interact with them as if they were real. It made sense, once Kiriai had figured out that Yabban could only affect Kiriai's senses in the real world, not reality itself. The *error* had disconcerted Yabban and she'd blamed it on a problem *integrating with the main game servers* . . . whatever that meant. In any case, the virtual dojo solved the problem.

"Do I have other choices besides the one you've picked out?"

"Yes, many of them, though some also have prerequisites you haven't met yet."

"Can you give me the list?"

"Are you sure you want to take the time for this? The list is extensive."

"Fine," Kiriai said with a huff. "I just want an idea. Give me five that I could do right now if I didn't take your wise advice."

Yabban's eyes narrowed for a moment before she nodded. "The autonomy sub-skill I recommend you unlock is called Coaching, specifically Mental Coaching, which is different from its partner skill called Physical Coaching. The choices under Personality are as varied as you can imagine and new ones can actually be added to if you come up with a variation and submit it for approval. Also, there is an entirely new attribute tree called Analytics which includes various statistical sub-skills like Predictability and Attack Frequency—"

Kiriai held up her hand and Yabban stopped speaking. The different terms were making Kiriai's head spin. "Fine," she said. "You're right. We don't have time for this, but when this week is over, I want you to explain all those to me, including some personality ones. All right?"

"Agreed," Yabban said with a smile and tip of her head. "Now, would you like to spend your attribute point to unlock Mental Coaching?"

Kiriai blew out a breath and said, "Yes."

"Congratulations," said Yabban with a smile. "Time to get to work."

A moment later, a stocky woman appeared in front of Kiriai, already in a fighting stance, hands up and one eyebrow raised in challenge. She was only slightly taller than Kiriai but definitely outweighed her, with broad shoulders and muscular arms under the black gi top she wore.

Kiriai recognized Brawler Antei immediately. The fighter

made her think of a stocky tree, full of solid strength that would take strenuous chopping to affect.

With a quick breath, Kiriai shook out her arms, loosened her neck and dropped back into her own stance. At least she felt full of energy and pain-free. Here in Yabban's virtual studio, she could leave her tired and injured body behind for a few blissful minutes.

"Wait," said Yabban. "Before we get started, let's review my recommendation for the time you have left before the fight."

Kiriai let out a groan as she looked at Yabban, but didn't object.

"First, you will spend as much time as possible practicing against Antei's favorite attacks and defenses. There isn't any substitute for repetition and hard work. Second, you will drill the two fighting styles you rarely use, Counter and Evade, until you are as familiar with them as your usual Attack style. Then we'll incorporate it against my simulation of Antei. And finally comes Mental Coaching. I will teach you the most effective time to use your pre-cog during a fight and we will use your new training aid, Targeting."

Kiriai stared at Yabban, her mouth agape. She struggled to process everything Yabban had just said, but one thing stuck out to her. "My pre-cog?"

"Yes," Yabban said with emphasis. "It is an unusual skill with great potential that you have been neglecting."

"Hey," Kiriai said with a frown. "I use it twice a day, every day morning and night to keep the energy from building up too much. And I used it in that fight with Akumu, if you can call that a fight. Plus, my control is improving a lot. I can make it manifest on command now, almost every time. That's loads better than in the past. Even Shisen thinks I'm doing well." Nothing Kiriai said seemed to affect Yabban, which made her stop and think. "What do you have to do with my pre-cog gift, anyway? You said you had no *game data* on it. Shisen is my trainer for it, since she's the one with the experience."

"I may not have your pre-cog skill in my basic database, but it isn't unheard of for players to gain unique skills from quests or other gameplay. I have been monitoring how you use it and have enough data now to know that you are wasting a very valuable fighting tool."

"Wasting? But I've used it in fights before. It's made a huge difference."

"And lately?" Yabban asked with a raised brow.

Kiriai flushed. "Well, with everything else going on—training all day, healing, watching hours of Antei's fight footage, the political nastiness. Blast"—she let out a frustrated breath—"even everything you've got me working on: the Clock Principle, Environmental Awareness and finishing all these mostly useless Intermediate moves." Kiriai's words trailed off. Sometimes it seemed like everything was too much.

Instead of arguing back, Yabban just smiled. "Exactly why you needed to unlock mental coaching. From now on, I will cue you to activate your pre-cog twice at the perfect times during practice, instead of wasting it the way you are now. Sound good?"

Kiriai felt relieved at the idea. As long as she didn't have to calculate when to use her pre-cog along with everything else she was trying to perfect, she was fine.

"What would you like to use as a command?" Yabban asked. "It needs to be a word that neither of us will commonly use, so there is no misunderstanding in the middle of a fight."

"I'm assuming you don't want to use the word *slow*, which I use to activate the gift?"

"No," said Yabban. "Too easy to misunderstand."

Kiriai thought for a minute and the answer was simple. "Just use *pre-cog*. It isn't a term you use with me, and during a fight, it will be very clear what you want me to do."

Yabban gave a brisk nod before waving at the figure of Brawler Antei, who hadn't moved.

"Activate Targeting training aid."

Kiriai watched, fascinated, as a fine reddish hue fell over the brawler, like a transparent paint. But instead of being a uniform color, it was very light in some areas and darker in others.

"Observe," said Yabban with a grin.

Antei suddenly began shadow boxing, moving at the medium pace of a warm-up.

At first, Kiriai wasn't sure what Yabban meant, but she kept watching. Antei's fists and feet were only the faintest of reds as she moved, so that wasn't it. Then Kiriai's eye was drawn to a pulse of dark red that flashed on Antei's torso, only to jump from one spot to another, under a rib, to her solar plexus, up to her jaw?

Was that—?

"Those are where she's open!" Kiriai said, almost yelling in her excitement.

Yabban's smile widened as she nodded. "I can only do this during training, not during a fight, but with enough practice, it should hone your ability to spot openings as soon as they appear and even to anticipate them."

"Sweet! Let's get started. I still need to get some sleep at some point."

"And since you haven't used your pre-cog for a second time today, I will call out the command during one of the rounds tonight, so be prepared. Agreed?"

Kiriai nodded.

Yabban's expression turned serious, and she took the sensei's usual position between Kiriai and the virtual Antei. "Ready?"

Kiriai let her knees bend and toes grip the floor before she nodded.

"Hajime!"

CHAPTER THIRTY-FIVE

"Can we please send out more scouts to round up survivors?
The farms desperately need more workers and we both don't
want our people out there pulling weeds so we can eat."

— Memo from Founding Matriarch Yolanda Cortez to
Founding Matriarch Nancy Reynolds. Oath Keepers Archive
of Truth, Volume 18

"You agreed to provide reinforcements to Jitaku?" The
cloaked man enunciated every word of the sentence with
care and underlying incredulity.

"It isn't what it looks like," Boss Ryuin said in an even tone she
hoped masked the nervous twist of emotions inside her.

"Please explain how offering Jitaku exactly what they need to
win this blasted war is somehow a good thing."

"That isn't what's happening, and you know it. It is the girl's
first-fight. Every brawler loses their first-fight!" Ryuin clamped
her mouth shut and cast a look toward the closed door keeping
their conversation private. This area of her hood's offices was

deserted once the dinner hour came, but there was no need to be careless. Members of the evening cleaning crew might come early. She turned back to Raibaru's spy and was more than glad there was a table between the two of them. Neither of them had taken a seat. The atmosphere felt as tense as an arena even though they were fighters in the game of intelligence and information, instead of punches and kicks. Ryuin aimed a stoic look at the spy and waited for him to make the next move. They both knew how this game was played.

"My boss isn't pleased that you've offered Boss Akuto exactly what he needs to ruin everything we've worked so hard for." His dark eyes amid hooded features glinted with warning. "Not pleased at all."

Ryuin's iron will and years of practice came to her rescue and helped her keep quiet and project a confident demeanor. He hadn't asked a question or made a demand.

Moments ticked by, and through the closed window on the far wall, Ryuin could hear the faint sounds of cheerful voices from the restaurant across the street. Someone laughed and, if she wasn't mistaken, a woman with a rich voice had broken out into a song.

Was that a glint of respect she saw from her opponent? Ryuin wanted to insist that the man pull back his hood and let the dim lantern from the door light his face so she would memorize his features. Fat chance of that.

"He wants an answer," the man finally said, voice cold and demanding.

It still wasn't a question, but Ryuin knew playing word games at the moment wouldn't go over well.

"Tell your boss he has nothing to worry about. If the huge odds against Akuto's newest pet aren't enough, I have my own plans in place to ensure that Brawler Kiriai has no chance at all of winning. None."

"And those plans?"

"We both know what happens to a shared secret," she countered. No way was she going to share operational details with a temporary ally.

He shook his head, his whole body radiating unhappiness. "We are discussing the same fighter that came here last year and beat your chief's champion, aren't we?"

Ryuin's jaw tightened, making her teeth hurt as she nodded.

"And what odds did the bet takers give for her to win that fight? How similar are those odds to the ones for a new brawler to win her first-fight?"

Ryuin didn't answer, hating that his point was a valid one.

"If I'm not mistaken, the chance for a backwater scrapper to beat the chief's champion who, I might add, was deceptively ranked lower than his ability, was extremely small, correct?" The man's voice was harsh, his facts coming hard and fast like punches. "Perhaps even worse odds than this girl's current ones of winning on Saturday?"

"She was lucky and had a lot of help," Ryuin said through gritted teeth, but even she knew it was a weak excuse.

"Her crew is bigger and more experienced now. And in this fight, she's matched against one of the most inexperienced brawlers the chief could have chosen?"

Ryuin nodded, unable to refute the facts.

"And normally, she'd fight someone more experienced, a brawler who could easily teach her the lesson of initiations, that she is starting at the bottom of the brawler ranks, right?"

"Yes," Ryuin said, almost spitting the word. "There's no need to go through everything we both already know."

"Like how you stand to win the title to your family's fortune again that you lost years ago?"

Ryuin froze, an icy wash of caution cutting through her emotions.

"To my boss," the man continued, "this looks like you are risking everything important to him to satisfy your own greed.

And he would like me to remind you that when he loses, so does everyone else around him."

"Is that a threat?" she asked, unable to keep the outrage out of her voice.

"Yes."

His word slammed into the room like a knock-out punch, and Ryuin stared at him, speechless for the first time in years.

"How dare you? You can't—"

"Be quiet," he said with a chopping motion of his hand that made Ryuin flinch back even as she reached for her hidden knife.

"You are a boss of a hood. So is my boss, but we both know my chief holds the reins. You entered an agreement. We have kept our side of it. You have put your side at risk to satisfy your greed. It is only fair that we hold you accountable for your decisions. That is the message my boss and chief sent me to deliver." He stopped to look her up and down.

Ryuin ground her teeth, hating the feeling of impotence.

"Your plans to prevent this initiate from winning on Saturday had better be effective. If she wins reinforcements for Jitaku, my boss and chief will hold you personally responsible. You have their oaths."

Ryuin sucked in a breath at the spy's final words, but maintained her stiff posture while the man strode from the room. He didn't bother to slide the door closed behind him. Only after she heard his footsteps fade and disappear did she let her shoulders sag and lower herself onto one of the clerk's uncomfortable stools. She rubbed one hand over her face and groaned as her mind flew through everything that had happened. How had her perfect plan fallen apart so unexpectedly?

Akuto! Everything that man touched ruined her life. *Well, not this time.*

She stood up again, straightened her shoulders and blew out a breath, attempting to release her worries and troubles. She was the boss of Mabbai Hood. One inexperienced fool of a fighter wouldn't stop her from getting her revenge on Akuto and winning her family's honor back. She left the room, brushing past her guards who had been standing uselessly at the front of the hallway the whole time. Her fists clenched as she reviewed her plans. By the time she made it out to the street, she had a grim smile on her face.

CHAPTER THIRTY-SIX

Kiriai desperately wanted to rub at her temples or neck to ease the headache that had been building during the brawlers' morning training. The training hall was noisy with everyone split into groups led by their assigned trainers. That meant Akumu for her group, and he was up to his same tricks. Kiriai leaped to the right, with the same front-hand parry followed by a reverse punch she'd been repeating over and over. Her punch landed with a dull thud into Eigo's padded chest protector. Kiriai didn't respond to his grin before she spun and repeated the same maneuver against Mikata, who was attacking from 6 o'clock. Mikata's frown showed what she thought of this most recent exercise dictated by Akumu. He had announced that the simplistic single lunging punch was a favorite attack of Brawler Antei's and instructed Kiriai to practice the same parry-punch counter to the attack until she satisfied him. At least he'd had Sento, Mikata and Eigo put on chest protectors so she could land her punches without worrying about injuring them.

Sento lunged in from her 9 o'clock, and Kiriai's body moved quickly, on autopilot, not needing the dark red color pulsing from his ribcage to know it was the open target. True to her promise, Yabban had activated Targeting during her real-life practicing. Learning to respond to rapidly moving markers of red color wasn't helping her headache any. Though that might be one positive to the drudgery of the exercise Akumu had assigned: The targeting was appearing in the same place and with the same timing over and over, training her eye to its significance.

A sharp pain hit her right shoulder blade, and Kiriai winced before spinning and repeating the same counter. The smirk on Mikata's face reminded Kiriai not to let her thoughts drift too much, even in the middle of such a simple drill. Kiriai worked to pull in more energy with a deep breath. Good thing her resilience continued to improve. Handling her brutal training regimen wasn't easy, but was doable, even if just barely.

Parry, counterpunch. Spin. Parry, counterpunch. Dodge.

Determined not to waste valuable training time, even with such a basic drill, Kiriai let her focus soften and tried to take in the world around her. She listened for sounds and worked to sense movement, especially from the opponents she couldn't see. She also tried to see the red Targeting overlay as a whole, instead of each individual marking.

Instead of letting Akumu waste her time, Kiriai would level up her Environmental Awareness. The movements in this exercise were perfect practice.

As she breathed and relaxed, Kiriai felt some of her stress melt away. Her Centering skill kicked in and her movements smoothed out, becoming more natural.

Sento noticed right away.

"Nice! Whatever you're doing, keep that up," he said after shooting a glance at a bored-looking Akumu, who was staring at a neighboring group led by an attractive trainer. "We have to follow Akumu's directions, but he didn't say how fast to attack, did he?"

Kiriai saw a smile bloom on Mikata's face and groaned, though the spark of challenge excited her.

"Faster," Sento said.

Her three attackers did just that and for a moment, Kiriai lost her grasp on the calm awareness around her and stumbled as she responded to each attacker individually.

"Hold," said Sento only a few attacks later and caught her eye. "Focus and get back to the state of mind you just had."

She closed her eyes for the briefest of moments, relaxed and sent her senses out with a breath. When she opened her eyes and nodded, he attacked.

This time, she could sense the other two attackers and was already moving to intercept them as soon as her fist landed on Sento's ribs. The scuff of a foot, the huff of breath and even the vague push of their presence in the surrounding air warned her of attacks. Soon she anticipated their moves, already facing them before they were halfway through their attacks.

"Shift and move. Try to catch her off guard," said Sento.

Her attackers sped up again and changed positions continuously around her, using the whole space to come at her from every angle, some close, others from just out of her peripheral vision.

Kiriai's breath whistled through her lips. Her muscles burned. Lips pulled back into a grin, she reveled in the rare moment of perfection. Her senses warned her. Yabban's red targeting flashed, and her body responded almost without command.

Parry. Punch. Dodge and spin. Again and again.

Eigo jogged behind and to her left as Kiriai parried Mikata's attack and she suddenly couldn't sense Sento . . . had he quit?

Her fist sank into Eigo's pad when a presence pushed from behind her boyfriend.

Sento was behind Eigo!

It was so unexpected that it jarred the relaxed, hyper-aware state she'd reached just enough for Sento to land his punch into her upper chest a fraction ahead of her parry. It barely landed before she'd pulled that side back and slipped the follow-up punch into Sento's ribcage with a satisfying thud.

He let out a grunt before straightening with a delighted laugh. That was the cue to end the burst of energy they'd spent and the other two followed suit. Kiriai took another moment to convince her mind that no more attacks were coming before she also relaxed and let her hands drop.

It was only when she noticed her three friends looking behind her, that she spun and saw Akumu striding in their direction. He didn't look happy. They weren't supposed to be having fun and improving.

Thankfully, Gebi's voice broke through the sounds of practice. "Yame! Circle around me. Move!"

Everyone stopped, including Akumu, before hurrying to follow her instructions. In moments, the initiates, crew members and other trainers were arrayed in a large circle around Gebi, standing in ready stances and waiting to hear what she had planned next. The smile on her face wasn't very reassuring.

"I think that is enough drilling for the morning. In less than a week, you will be brawlers, unless any of you feel like grabbing the 'forcer sash?" Her eyes flicked over to the stand holding the sash that had been a tempting presence with them all month. Kiriai had long ago stopped paying attention to it.

"No?" she asked when everyone was silent. "Then I think we need to start fighting. How else are you going to be ready for your first-fights this Saturday?"

No one said anything, but the uptick in energy and excitement was palpable. Kiriai knew she wasn't the only one who was tired of the endless conditioning and drilling. If she hadn't been able to spar in Yabban's virtual dojo, she would be going crazy by now.

"Grab headgear, hand-wraps and mouthguards, and then have a seat," Gebi said before holding a hand out toward one of her trainers. Everyone ran to the supplies against a far wall, murmuring excitedly under their breath. Kiriai knew exactly which size of the padded canvas helmet to grab, having paid attention back at the beginning orientation, even though they'd yet to use the training gear. She grabbed the small box labeled with her name from the mouthpiece cubby and shoved the precious device in her mouth before sitting down to wrap her hands with practiced motions. Fighters had to rely on the scrounger clans to venture into the wastelands to get the material to make mouthpieces. Without one, a fighter risked cutting up their mouth or losing teeth. Clenching her teeth on the soft, but perfect fit, Kiriai shook her head at how, once again, the brawlers got the best.

She wasn't the first one back and seated in the large circle, but it was close. She couldn't keep the wide grin off her face. She wasn't the only one. Trainer Gebi stood in the middle, a red ribbon dangling from one hand and a blue from the other. She stared at the initiates, and Kiriai mentally urged them to hurry.

When the final two dropped into place, they kept their eyes averted from the glaring trainer, and Kiriai didn't blame them.

"Initiates Kiriai and Jiseki. Places!"

Kiriai was startled to hear her name, but Jiseki had no such trouble. The taller fighter was already up and moving before Kiriai jolted into action. Jiseki snapped into her ready stance, eyes straight ahead as Gebi moved behind her and tucked the red sash into the back of her blue belt. Kiriai followed suit, mind running through what she knew of Jiseki's fighting style. After over three weeks crammed together for hours every day, Kiriai should know more about her opponent than she did. But she'd been so focused on her future fight, that she had given little consideration to her colleagues.

Pick a fighting style and stick to it for as much of the fight as possible. And not Attack, since that is your favorite style. Evade or Counter.

I thought you couldn't help me during in-game fights? Kiriai asked while she tried to decide which of the two styles to choose.

Gebi was behind her now, and Kiriai felt the tug on her belt as the trainer attached the blue sash.

This is still training. I will engage the targeting aid and also prompt you to use your pre-cog once during the fight if an appropriate time comes.

"Positions!" Gebi said with a nod to the trainers, who had taken spots in the four corners, red and blue scoring flags held down and crossed in front of them.

Kiriai stepped back into her stance and grinned at the judges. This bout would be live-scored as they went, instead of everything being tallied at the end. It could be distracting to see flags popping up in your peripheral vision with no pause in the fight, but the instant feedback was valuable when learning. Besides, if you got distracted by a flashing flag or two, how would you handle everything an exuberant crowd did during a real battle?

Your choice of style? Yabban prompted her.

Counter. I'll fight the Counter style.

Good choice. That will mesh well with the targeting aid.

"Ready?" Gebi stepped forward into a fighting stance, her front hand held out between the two fighters.

"Hajime!" Gebi's hand chopped down, and Kiriai shuffled back with two quick steps. One key to fighting with the Counter style was to keep enough distance to have time to predict her opponent's moves.

Jiseki didn't give her time to do that. With a quick skip of her long legs, she moved forward, her lead foot flicking out with a probing kick that had a much longer reach than Kiriai expected. Kiriai skipped to the side as she flung up her lead hand in a quick slapping parry that kept the foot from landing into her jaw and ending the bout before it got started.

Counter style, right? Not Evade?

Be quiet, Yabban, Kiriai thought with a sputtered laugh.

Jiseki's eyes narrowed, and she moved to attack again.

Oops. She probably thought Kiriai was laughing at her.

With no way to reassure her otherwise, Kiriai shifted sideways, and narrowed her focus. She needed to learn and then predict Jiseki's moves to be effective at countering. Still moving, Kiriai kept a medium distance from Jiseki as the woman moved on the balls of her feet, darting in and out to throw quick probes, testing Kiriai's defenses.

Kiriai used the minimal movement and energy required to stay just out of reach, not even responding to some of the feints. Instead, she let her vision relax so she could see the all pulsing reds and let them guide her to the best targets for countering. At this level of fighting, she had to train her instincts to react. If she took the time to think about something, it would be too late.

Jiseki was too good to let her frustration become obvious, but Kiriai saw her jaw clench. Jiseki launched forward with another flurry that Kiriai barely avoided, but she smiled with the valuable information it gave her. Jiseki left the front of her torso open just after her kick and a spot under her left ribs when she threw her roundhouse punch.

Kiriai saw the flicker of motion at the bottom of her vision just before the sidekick hit and pain blossomed in her side. Operating on instinct, Kiriai ignored the pain and twisted to pull her injured side back. She brought up both hands to cover her face just in time to take two sharp punches that had been heading toward her face. Jiseki was on top of her, her grunts and hot breath inches from Kiriai as the other fighter pushed to finish the fight in a single brutal attack.

Kiriai had to attack. Now. Otherwise, Jiseki would overwhelm her in seconds. A brief pulse of despair pushed into her mind. Destructive thoughts pressed in on her with every blow she felt landing into her arms and shoulders. If she went down so easily to one of her fellow initiates, how would she have any chance against Antei on Saturday?

CHAPTER THIRTY-SEVEN

"I think we're all agreed that democracy is out. We didn't fight and build what we have out of the ashes just to give our power to those weaker than us."

— Founding Father Elliot Tucker in the Chikara City Organization meetings. Oath Keepers Archive of Truth, Volume 15

"Quit taking it so easy on her, Kiriai!"

Eigo's cheerful voice cut through the destructive thoughts with ease. Her best friend's indomitable spirit made her smile inside and swept away her brief paralysis. Another punch clipped the top of her head in a tooth-rattling blow, further jarring her to take action.

All thoughts of Saturday, Antei, fighting styles, principles or targeting fled. Kiriai gathered her power, hunched down for a moment until she felt a break between the thuds of Jiseki's blows. Then she exploded with a burst of tight, hooking punches and uppercuts, driving with all the power she could summon from her legs and hips. The sting of contact pulsed through her right fist. Her left sank into Jiseki's helmet. More. Faster. Harder.

And just like that she could breathe again. Jiseki backed off, and they faced each other, both breathing heavily with the sharp ache of exchanged blows. Their eyes bored into each other, legs bent and ready to respond in an instant. Kiriai tipped her head side-to-side, silently urging the slight dizziness she felt to stabilize. She took the stolen moment to fill her lungs and pull on her Centering skill. She'd almost activated her Berserker skill, and that was the last thing she wanted in a practice bout.

Wait, she mentally asked Yabban. *Why didn't you prompt me to use my pre-cog before she blindsided me?*

You have to save that skill not only for a moment it can help but also one in which you could lose the whole match. I trusted you to find your bearings this early in the fight and be able to recover.

Kiriai suppressed her inclination to grumble. Yabban was right.

Jiseki was on the move again, and Kiriai snapped her attention back to the fight.

Without meaning to, Kiriai let a smile slip out, unrestrained. It was refreshing to set everything aside and enjoy being back in the ring, sparring, pushing herself to her limits with a real opponent!

No disrespect to your training dojo, Yabban. But no matter how real you make it feel, I still know it's different.

Of course you do. All fighters do. That is why skills level up faster in the game world.

Kiriai sent a mental nod of acknowledgment to her trainer just as Jiseki hesitated.

To Kiriai's surprise, the woman's expression flickered for a moment, and she flashed Kiriai an answering smile, hers full of the same fierce challenge.

This would be fun.

Right on the heels of that thought, Jiseki's fists flashed

forward in a direct line for Kiriai's face. This time they didn't catch Kiriai off-guard, and she easily pivoted and moved to evade. Remembering the state she'd achieved during the earlier practice exercise, Kiriai diffused her focus, letting her other senses work for her. The others watching were quiet enough that Kiriai could hear the slide of Jiseki's feet and the rustle of her gi as she circled with a sharp eye, looking for an opening. Kiriai's vision relaxed, taking in her opponent's movement and Yabban's targeting markers that undulated in lighter and darker reds with Jiseki's movement.

Counter, Kiriai reminded herself. *Stay close, slip just past her attack and counter.* She would not lose control again.

The fight picked up, faster and more intense with every passing second. Jiseki attacked again and again. Kiriai engaged without letting Jiseki overwhelm her, doing her best to slip in only a few counters before retreating to a safe distance, despite her instinct to keep attacking. Satisfaction flushed through Kiriai as she landed another solid punch after slipping just an inch inside a front kick that had enough power to crumple her.

As the round continued on, Kiriai's muscles burned and her lungs worked overtime. Her mind became less sharp as the constant vigilance and calculations took their toll. Meanwhile, Jiseki was adapting to Kiriai's countering style, leaving fewer openings and working to trap Kiriai in when she closed for a counterstrike.

Kiriai had just landed two sharp punches, one to Jiseki's upper arm while the other slipped into her ribs with a satisfying thud. This time the taller woman swung a short chopping hook, but when Kiriai blocked, it flew past its mark, wrapping around one of Kiriai's shoulders instead. With a quick jerk, Jiseki kept Kiriai from retreating.

Pre-cog.

Slow! Kiriai forced out a breath as she gave the command to her gift, just like she'd practiced with Yabban last night. For a moment, her gift stuttered, not quite willing, but then succumbed, flowing from the center of her mind and flooding out through her arm and hand to impose its will on the world.

Jiseki's fist hung a few inches to the left of Kiriai's face. The pre-cog caught her opponent's face in a very unflattering mix of a sideways snarl and one eye half squinted.

With an internal chuckle, Kiriai let go of her mental focus with relief. She needed the break to analyze the fight as her gift gave her the relief of time passing at a crawl. Frozen in a dangerous clasp with Jiseki, it was immediately obvious why Yabban had given her the command to activate her gift.

While Kiriai had focused on Jiseki's outstretched right arm, her other arm, blocked from view by Kiriai's own, had already crossed half of the distance in what would be a brutal uppercut to Kiriai's solar plexus or chin. Kiriai winced internally, knowing exactly how badly that punch would hurt, even through the padding of the helmet.

She only had moments before time returned to its normal flow. Kiriai scanned for an opening from her own slow-moving position as she watched Jiseki's punch move with inevitable power toward her . . . obviously the target was her chin, not her torso. At least the red targeting markers were also stationary for once, making it much easier to choose where to aim her counter-strike.

There!

Just under Jiseki's elbow. If Kiriai could deflect the stealthy punch up and out, Jiseki's side would be open for a split second. Kiriai finished her plan just as her gift expired, and a sickening lurch dragged everyone backward a full second or two in time. With the help of much practice, Kiriai was ready to act as soon as time returned to normal speed. With a twist, she brought one hand up under Jiseki's uppercut and slapped it up and out, just enough to deflect it safely. Kiriai used her body's motion to power her other punch, so it landed with a solid thud directly in Jiseki's newly exposed ribcage.

Her opponent let out a yell, the explosive breath and tightening of her core muscle doing a lot to mitigate the damage of the punch. But not the ones that followed. Knowing a chance like this was rare in a match, Kiriai tucked her head and did her best to rain down blows, instinctively targeted toward the darkest reds she could spot on a fast-retreating Jiseki.

Stop! Counter! Don't attack!

Yabban's command broke into Kiriai's concentration just enough for Jiseki to break away to a safe distance, and Kiriai felt like a starving hound who'd had a meal ripped from its mouth.

Why did you do that? I was going to win!

Kiriai stood, chest heaving, fists clenched as Jiseki moved out of reach, eyes vigilant for another attack.

This is practice. You are being observed. If you show how well you can switch styles now, during practice, what use will it be on Saturday when it really counts?

The words snuffed out Kiriai's heated battle emotions with a rush of cold logic. Her trainer was right. Again. She'd spent the entire sparring match convincing Jiseki and those watching that she was a counter fighter. She had to hope that someone here, maybe a crew member or other observer, would communicate that back to Antei. She needed any piece of an advantage she could get for Saturday and couldn't afford to reveal any of her tactics early.

Without warning, Jiseki attacked again.

How? She had to be hurting after that last exchange.

There was no time for thought as Kiriai gave herself fully over to her role as a counter fighter. The next seconds passed in a blur, a ferocious dance between two opponents, Jiseki pushing to overwhelm Kiriai while she did her best to slip past the worst of the attacks and land blows whenever an opportunity presented itself. Just as earlier, Kiriai fell into a trance, her senses extended to their furthest reach, vision relaxed to take in everything all at once and her muscles twitching from one movement to the next almost without direction.

"Yame! Yame!"

A figure jumped into her battle, a stiff hand slammed into Kiriai's chest and some part of her barely kept her from responding with a counterattack against Trainer Gebi. Her gaze locked onto Kiriai's, searching for something.

Kiriai blinked, dragging herself back to the present. Everything she'd been ignoring suddenly clamored for attention. Her lungs heaved, her legs burned and her arms felt so heavy, it was a relief to let them drop.

Gebi nodded briskly before turning toward Jiseki. Kiriai saw that her opponent had also dropped out of her fighting stance. Her eyes caught Kiriai's, and the other fighter hesitated for a moment, expression inscrutable.

Then with a deliberate motion, Jiseki straightened, clapped both hands to her legs and slowly bowed to Kiriai, respect in her eyes. A stab of emotion burned at the gesture. Kiriai hadn't realized how much the lack of respect from her fellow initiates had been bothering her. And Jiseki's gesture really touched her. Their match had been a good one between two women who loved the art of battle with equal intensity. With matching care, Kiriai held Jiseki's gaze as she returned an identical bow. One corner of Jiseki's mouth pulled up.

It was only as Kiriai straightened from her bow that she noticed how quiet the training space had become. Just as she looked past Jiseki to scan the group, a single clap started to her left. A moment later, another followed, and another, until the rest of the room joined in.

Kiriai struggled to keep her expression controlled, the approval of this small group more overwhelming than that of an entire stadium. She saw a huge grin on Eigo's face as he clapped with enthusiasm. Mikata and Sento were more restrained, but she could see the pride on both their faces. As she glanced around the circle, she saw Akumu's nasty scowling face, his hands unmoving on his knees, the only one not clapping. Of course. He was one person she would be glad to never see again after Saturday. However, Jimu's wide smile next to him made up for it. He returned Kiriai's nod with enthusiasm.

"Well, enough of that," said Gebi, her stern voice cutting through the noise and silencing everyone instantly. Both Kiriai and Jiseki snapped back to attention, expressions carefully blank. Gebi took a moment to shift her gaze between the two of them before she turned back to those circled around. "These two initiates just demonstrated the skill and fighting spirit that is expected from every Southern Core brawler. Let's see what the rest of you have."

The compliment shocked Kiriai, and she saw a similar reaction from Jiseki.

Kiriai hardly noticed as Gebi circled behind each of them and pulled the sashes free from the backs of their belts before saying, "Have a seat."

The command jolted Kiriai to move and, feeling stunned, she sat in the empty spot where Eigo had scooted over for her. To her surprise, Jiseki was right behind her. Instead of sitting with her own crew members, she wedged herself into the spot next to Kiriai, forcing Mikata to shift closer to Sento to make room.

The limber woman crossed her legs into a sitting position and stared straight ahead at the center of the ring, back straight and hands loose on her knees.

Kiriai snuck a questioning glance at Eigo on her other side, but he just shrugged.

"Initiates Jimu and Kontan. You're next," said Trainer Gebi from the center of the ring.

The two fighters scrambled up to their places. Normally, Kiriai would have been drooling with anticipation to watch them spar, but she couldn't stop thinking about the public acknowl-

edgment Gebi had just made and its implications. Not to
mention she hurt . . . everywhere. Jiseki could really hit. And why
had she sat next to her?

"Hajime!"

The command startled Kiriai out of her distracted thoughts.
At Gebi's order, Jimu didn't hesitate, immediately moving to put
distance between himself and Kontan, who didn't look happy
about that fact. Kontan charged, and the match turned quickly
into a fast-moving chase scene, with Jimu obviously using the
Evade style of fighting. It wasn't a popular one, based on the
grumbling noises from the observers and the frustrated grunts
from the larger and slower Kontan, who was having a difficult
time pinning down his slippery opponent.

"Watch yourself."

For a moment, Kiriai wasn't sure she'd heard anything, the
words having come simultaneously with a yell from Kontan as he
attacked again.

"Akumu is planning something against you."

Kiriai barely stopped herself from turning to look at Jiseki in
shock. This time she'd heard barely audible words coming from
Jiseki, but some sense of self-preservation warned her not to give
anyone watching a clue to the whispered warning. With her
peripheral vision, Kiriai could see that Jiseki was staring directly
at the match as if it consumed all of her attention.

Opening her mouth slightly and doing her best not to move
her lips, Kiriai whispered, "What? Details?"

"Don't know. Something to hurt you so you have no chance
on Saturday. Be careful."

A sick feeling curled inside Kiriai, ruining the high she'd just
been enjoying. Then again, had she expected anything different?
Saturday's fight wasn't a simple affair. Boss Ryuin's family legacy
and the fate of Jitaku Hood were at stake.

A flicker of movement from the other side of the circle caught
her attention, but Kiriai was careful not to respond visibly,

instead relying on her peripheral vision. Through Jimu's and Kontan's moving bodies, Kiriai caught glimpses of Akumu. His eyes bored into her, making him look as if he would leap across the ring and attack her at any moment. Kiriai congratulated herself on being careful during the whispered words she'd just exchanged with Jiseki, while resolving to squeeze in another strategy session with her crew as soon as possible. All the training wouldn't matter if their enemies got to her before Saturday.

CHAPTER THIRTY-EIGHT

"I recall that I was clear what would happen next time you went against my wishes and moved against Brawler Kiriai, wasn't I?"

Jaaku stood frozen at attention, his mind scrambling for an answer, anything that would fix this.

Boss Akuto sat at the desk in the well-appointed study of the suite assigned to him by Chief Kosui's staff for his current visit to Southern Core, a few days before the brawler first-fights and graduation. The ornate surroundings and blatant display of wealth were a stark contrast to the boss's office back home. Akuto still surrounded himself with quality items, but didn't care whether it was obvious at first glance. The dark leather-bound chair he sat in now shone with hand-stitched leather and shiny gold buttons riveted along the edge to emphasize its beauty and cost.

None of that really mattered at the moment.

What mattered was that the man he'd chosen to dedicate his life to so long ago was on the brink of severing that connection. Whether that severing also included his life wasn't important. If

Jaaku lost his link to Akuto after decades of following him, he might as well be dead.

"'Forcers!" Akuto's command caught Jaaku by surprise. The desperation of the moment had frayed his control enough that he visibly flinched as the door behind him slid open and bounced against the doorstops with a soft thud.

A quick glance over his shoulder made Jaaku's mouth go dry, and it took everything he had to keep an impassive expression on his face as he turned back to Akuto. Was his boss really going to do this? To his oldest . . . if not friend, then acquaintance?

Jaaku felt hands take him by both shoulders and grab both of his wrists. The 'forcers jerked them up and behind his back with sharp tugs that stabbed pain through his shoulders. Jaaku kept his eyes locked on Boss Akuto's, keeping a firm lid on his emotions. He refused to beg or even let the hint of a plea show on his face. If this was the end, then he would not shame himself. His only regret was he hadn't been able to finish destroying the girl who had caused all this trouble in the first place.

The 'forcers weren't gentle as they wrenched him around toward the door. Jaaku barely kept a wince from showing on his expression. It had been quite some time since he'd experienced pain like this, and even longer since he'd let anyone lay hands on him without retaliating.

The ominous silence for such a monumental experience was disconcerting as the lush carpeting of the suite muffled everyone's steps, and Akuto sat unmoving in his chair, watching it all play out.

The two bruisers pulled him to the doorway, and Jaaku tried his best not to visualize how his end would come, a quick death or the brutal life of the farms, a delayed death.

"Stop. Turn him back around."

The two 'forcers halted, one of their hands digging into his left shoulder with casual cruelty as they obeyed the boss's order with alacrity.

A sting in the back of Jaaku's throat surprised him, and he blinked his eyes rapidly to keep his stoic expression from crumbling as he faced his boss again across the spacious suite.

After long moments that seemed to take an eternity to pass, Akuto pursed his lips and addressed the 'forcers. "Let him go, and return to your posts outside the door. I will call you back when I need you."

The same man who had jerked him around painfully took an extra moment to squeeze Jaaku's wrist hard enough that he felt the bones grind together. Jaaku made a mental note to find out the man's name and return the favor soon . . . if he made it out of this alive.

When the door slid shut behind him with a soft hiss, Jaaku ran a quick hand over his clothing before standing straight and waiting. Anything, anything at all would be better than where the 'forcers had been taking him.

The boss let the silence drag on, and Jaaku tolerated it with the aplomb of one who had a lifetime's experience with power games like this.

Akuto finally relented and spoke, his voice icy enough to send another chill through Jaaku. "I don't normally give an underling the chance to explain a mistake, but I find myself swayed by our history together."

Jaaku let a small breath escape.

"But only by the smallest of amounts," Akuto said as he raised one finger in warning, his eyes hardening further. "You have one minute."

Jaaku's first instinct was to slant the facts to show his actions in the best light, but one glance at Akuto and his years with the man advised him otherwise. Akuto was a hard boss, but also a fair one who preferred the facts even if he disagreed. Jaaku only had one choice left. He told the truth.

"I'm sure it's obvious I never liked Kiriai, right from the

beginning. And, as you've always known, my first loyalty is to you."

Jaaku paused for a moment and was gratified when Akuto gave him the barest of nods in acknowledgment.

"Which means I spend all of my efforts furthering what I know is most important to you. When we were here in Southern Core, that was to climb the power structure. When you took the reins of Jitaku Hood and made them your people, the hood and its people became my focus, too." Jaaku blew out a breath and steeled himself for the next part. He needed to sound matter-of-fact and quash any anger or other emotions when talking about Kiriai. His actions had to come across as professional if he were to have any chance of saving himself.

"I saw Kiriai as a disrupting influence right from the beginning, during a time when we were especially vulnerable to the attacks from Raibaru. I believed and still believe that she is harming the stability and success of our scrappers, and through them Jitaku Hood as a whole, which I am sworn to protect on your behalf. However, I knew you had taken a special interest in her and admired her fighting spirit. Therefore, I did my best to help minimize her destabilizing influence on the tradition and training that makes Jitaku's scrappers the best in the burb. When she attempted to bypass fighters with more experience and skill than her and jump to the front of the line, I advised her to follow our traditions, but she wouldn't listen. I had the other scrappers discipline her to give her a clear message to fall in line. Even that didn't work. She had the temerity to challenge the chief himself, bringing his angry attention directly against us during a time when we desperately needed his support and help."

Jaaku paused and took another breath. He had to stay calm to sway his boss. "I firmly believe that without her antagonism against him, the chief would have already ordered the other bosses to send us the reinforcements we need. And now, not only is she attempting to bypass all those senior to her and become a burb brawler with scarcely a year of experience, but she is destroying another long-held tradition of the brawler first-fights. It should be the climax of the initiation experience and teach the new brawlers their place in the organization, at the bottom with a lot to learn. Instead, she's twisting it into another political maneuver, alienating other leaders and putting your most valuable property at risk."

Jaaku knew his time was up, so he hurried to add his last bit of argument.

"I know you had a lot to do with the planning, but without Kiriai's willingness to defy all our traditions and interfere where she isn't wanted, we would not be in the desperate straits we are in now. And as for my most recent actions with my acquaintance in Rinjin, I merely asked that he ensure the trainers stringently test Kiriai to ensure that she met the requirements of being a burb brawler. I was clear that I didn't want any sabotage or other trickery to take place, merely that her character and skills be truly tested. I don't like this fighter and how disruptive she is. But if she is to be a brawler from Jitaku Hood, I wanted to ensure she was as strong as possible. I only did what I thought would be in your best interest."

Jaaku stopped talking. He'd done his best.

Akuto stared at him before he finally spoke, his voice still cold. "Even if it went against my specific instructions to not interfere with Brawler Kiriai?"

Jaaku bowed his head, eyes downcast. "I've always respected your willingness to consider opinions that differ from your own. I have and always will live to serve you and you alone, Boss Akuto." Jaaku stopped speaking, gaze still down, and standing absolutely still. There wasn't anything else he could say.

The warmth of the afternoon sun shone in through the large windows, filling the room with a light at odds with the tension. It was so quiet, Jaaku could almost hear his heartbeat. Sparkles of dust motes swam lazily in just in front of his sandaled feet, and Jaaku forced his breathing to stay calm even as sweat dripped down the back of his neck.

"I am torn, Jaaku."

Relief flooded Jaaku, but he remained still and quiet, head bowed. Anything that wasn't a call for the 'forcers again was a very good thing.

"Stand up," said Akuto, irritation in his voice.

Jaaku straightened, and it took all his control to keep his expression impassive at the reprieve he received from his boss.

"Might as well try to wrench a bone from a starving dog, as get you to give up one of your prejudices," Akuto muttered under his breath. Jaaku pretended he didn't hear.

"I will make it completely clear right now." The cold tone of Akuto's breath made Jaaku stop breathing. "Regardless of how you think it helps or hurts me and Jitaku Hood, you are not to have anything to do with Brawler Kiriai. If you feel strongly that she presents an imminent danger, you will bring it to me first. Me! You will not act on your own against her again. Am I clear?"

"Yes, Boss! Absolutely clear!" Jaaku put as much emphasis into the response as he could, trying his best to convince the boss of his compliance.

Akuto looked at him with consideration on his face and no small amount of conflict. "I never do this," he said, lifting a finger and pointing it at Jaaku, "and you know it."

Jaaku nodded quickly in agreement.

"We both know that consequences should be swift and harsh. Mercy is just an invitation for the next underling to defy me even more."

Another nod.

Akuto sat back in his chair and glanced out the window for a moment before returning his gaze to Jaaku. "However, I find

myself feeling nostalgic today. You really are my last connection
to my roots. Not only that, I have a problem here in Southern
Core." Akuto's gaze bored into Jaaku's. "A problem that your skill
set is ideally suited to solve, better than anyone else I have."

"Tell me and I will take care of it for you, Boss," Jaaku said,
unable to resist speaking without being asked.

Akuto's gaze narrowed, but he didn't rebuke Jaaku. "As you
know, the chief has angered the city families. What you might
not know is why."

A familiar thrill grew in Jaaku, and part of him was amazed at
how much his prospects had shifted in just a few short moments.
On his way to death or the farms one moment and being given a
juicy political puzzle to solve the next. The adrenaline coursing
through him in that moment reminded him of years gone by, and
he welcomed it like an old friend.

"At the end of the brawler tournament, Chief Kosui had a
meeting with just him and the four bosses. Yes," Akuto said with
a nod, "with no seconds or assistants, we all knew it was something serious. It didn't take long. With little fanfare, he handed
each of us a list of names with instructions to round up the
people on the list and deliver them to his 'forcers in Southern
Core within the week. He even gave us instructions on which
night we were to pick up the rebels so none of them could warn
the others. Rebels." Akuto paused and let out a derisive huff.
"They were just children."

"The ones we couldn't find? Those names were from the
chief?" Jaaku's eyes widened as he made the connection. As usual,
he had asked no questions when helping Akuto plan the collec-
tions weeks ago. If the boss wanted him to know the details, he
would have told him. When every 'forcer had returned empty-
handed, Jaaku had been furious and felt no small amount of fear
reporting back to the boss. Thankfully, Akuto wasn't one to
punish the messenger, and the situation had been so unusual that
both of them had known some other variable was at work. Akuto

had said he'd handle it himself. No wonder, if the chief and the city families were involved.

Akuto nodded, expression grim. "Not only did we have problems finding any of the child rebels on our list, the other hoods found empty beds as well."

"All of them?" Jaaku asked, incredulous.

"Almost. I think they caught three who couldn't get away in time," said Akuto with a dismissive wave of his hand. "If I had been the only one to turn up empty-handed, I know there'd be a new boss in Jitaku right now, but with all of us failing at such a simple task, the chief couldn't punish everyone."

"And when he told the city families?"

Akuto shook his head and leaned back. "His days are numbered if he doesn't produce these children or those responsible for spiriting them away from under his nose."

"What is so important about these children? Are they truly rebels? Or merely related to rebels and being used to coerce cooperation?" Jaaku's mind was already jumping to all the possibilities.

"Chief Kosui told me as much about that as I told you when I gave you the orders," Akuto said bluntly.

"And your guesses?" Jaaku knew, more than anyone, how good Akuto's sources in the core were. His boss wouldn't sit idle, following orders, without trying to find out as much information on the subject as possible.

Instead of answering, Akuto looked at Jaaku, eyes probing.

Suddenly, Jaaku remembered he had been in the hands of the 'forcers only moments earlier. He ducked his head again. "I'm sorry, Boss Akuto. Forgive me for being presumptuous."

"No, Jaaku. Your clever political mind is a main reason I am considering offering you a reprieve from the consequences of defying me, even as obliquely as you did."

Jaaku lifted his eyes again and waited this time, knowing Akuto would share his information when he was ready.

"Despite your weaknesses for holding onto a useless vendetta, I don't think you have ever revealed a secret I have entrusted you with, in all the years we've been together."

"Never!" Jaaku said, recoiling in horror. Then he modulated his voice to something calmer before repeating, "Boss Akuto, I would never."

"I know, Jaaku," said Akuto.

Relief filled Jaaku, though he couldn't help noticing that the boss was consistently leaving out his title of *Second*.

"If this will help you in your mission, I want you to know the clues I have gathered over the years," said Akuto. "These aren't the first child rebels the chief has tasked us with abducting so he can send them to the city. Only in the past, they've been scattered, mixed in with our other arrests and not so noticeable."

Jaaku nodded. It wasn't unusual to arrest a teen occasionally, and he never asked questions.

"However," said Akuto, "someone is actively working to save these specific children. That's the reason I think we had a large list this time and the chief ordered everyone to move simultaneously . . . to foil the opposition."

"It didn't work," said Jaaku, eyes thoughtful as he considered everything Akuto was telling him.

"Someone warned them," said Akuto.

"Obviously."

"But not by natural means."

Jaaku stopped and stared, unsure what Akuto was getting at.

"In all your experience, have you ever known or met someone who seemed able to do or know things, impossible things?" Akuto asked the question, his eyes sharp on Jaaku, waited for his response.

Jaaku thought before answering. "I've been bested, sure. And not always known exactly how it was done." He gave a shrug. "Take how we met, for example. There's a reason I immediately swore loyalty to you. I have always looked to ally with those who have knowledge and talents that I don't."

A half-smile emerged on Akuto's face at the mention of their beginnings. Then his eyes focused back on Jaaku. "Talents?"

"Well, yes. There are others smarter, with more charisma . . . maybe connections or innate ability to influence the people around them."

"What if there were talents that went beyond the ability to choose the right words or expressions? Abilities up here." Akuto tapped the side of his head with one finger.

It took Jaaku a long moment to parse what Akuto was saying. Did he mean—? The idea was ludicrous and Jaaku smiled, wanting to show Akuto that he got the joke. But Akuto wasn't smiling. A cold ball of dread formed inside Jaaku.

"Are you saying there are people with mental talents, like what—?" He could hear his voice was out of control, but didn't care at the moment. "—can they read my mind or make me do stuff? Are you saying these children could fight with their minds? Wait. If they can do that, how could we ever capture them? And how could something like that be kept secret for long? They'd have to kill anyone they used their mind powers against, to keep word from getting out. And if that were happening, we would know, wouldn't we?" Jaaku's voice trailed off as he remembered where he was and under what circumstances. "I apologize, Boss. It's just such an outrageous idea that I lost control for a moment."

"No need to apologize, Jaaku," said Akuto with a soothing wave of his hand. "I had much the same reaction, and you recovered more quickly than I did, asking relevant questions even before the shock wore off. And have a seat. If you take on this job for me, you can at least sit down, so I don't have to crane my neck up at you anymore."

Jaaku sat in the stiff wooden chair in front of Akuto's desk and kept his erect posture, not daring to lean back and relax.

"Most of the information I have is from our agents in

Southern Core. Visiting city 'forcers often have loose lips when they're relaxed or say, having expensive drinks gifted to them."

Akuto gave him a wolfish grin that Jaaku returned. They both knew how the game was best played.

"These children have mental powers that allow them to read surface thoughts, emotions and sometimes actually move things with their minds. At least those are the abilities that have been mentioned. The city 'forcers have alluded to other rarer powers, but not in enough detail to be sure of anything."

"And none of our people have these abilities?" Jaaku's mind was already whirling with the potential of such people.

"Not that we know. And we don't know how they are identifying these children. Keeping one for ourselves would defy the chief and the city families. Not a good choice. Though if I'd had any warning this time, I would have grabbed one or two, knowing I could hide their loss in the loss of all the others. Believe me, when I heard of the three found in the other hoods, I was extremely jealous. I would have never turned them in."

"And it's not something you can just tell our 'forcers to keep an eye out for. Spreading the knowledge of powers like that would ruin the advantage they would give us."

"Yes," Akuto said with a nod of approval that made Jaaku's heart swell with pride.

"This is the mission I'm giving you in consideration for our history as well as the urgency of our need. To get Chief Kosui's public support and his agreement to choose an opponent Kiriai had a chance of beating, I promised to bring him those responsible for spiriting away these children before the family's deadline. So now your welfare joins the chief's. Find out who did this, and depending on how successful you are, you may keep your rank with me or at least your life and freedom. Understand?"

Jaaku popped up to his feet and said, "Yes, Boss," before giving Akuto a sharp bow.

"Dismissed," said Akuto.

Jaaku turned for the door and made a mental note to get the name of the 'forcer with the harsh grip. He smiled as he slid the door open.

For the moment, he still had his power and freedom. It was time to hunt.

CHAPTER THIRTY-NINE

"Every citizen can rise as high in society as their hard work
and talent takes them. Anyone can become a warrior, boss or
chief if they work hard enough."
    — Chikara City Elementary Social Studies Text, 2nd
edition

The door to their cozy living room slid open, and the
tension spiked as everyone went quiet and turned to see
who it was.

It was early Friday evening, and a handful of Kiriai's crew had
just enjoyed a small dinner together. Isha and Aibo were still out
in late classes. Kiriai would meet them both in a treatment room
Isha had reserved after their classes finished. And 'Ranger Tomi
was out too, scheming until the last moment.

Kiriai couldn't believe time had almost run out already. With
the whirlwind of brawler training during the day and Yabban's
ruthless pushing in the evenings, the last few days had blended
together into what felt like both forever and no time at all.

Earlier today, Trainer Gebi had looked almost friendly as she'd dismissed the initiates early, wished them luck and encouraged them to get some good food and rest for the next day. Kiriai hoped her final session with Isha would relax her enough to help her sleep despite the tension jittering through her body.

A large figure stepped into the room, and a relieved grin tugged at Kiriai's mouth when she recognized Tomi's big figure. It quickly faded when she saw his expression. His usual smile was missing, and Kiriai saw his brow creased in concern as he moved toward the only empty chair in the room.

This couldn't be good.

He didn't speak. Instead, he sat down and scanned the faces staring at him, waiting for his news.

"I don't suppose I can pretend I have good news," he said with a sigh.

"We haven't had any all week," muttered Shisen from her chair to Kiriai's left.

Tomi grimaced in response.

Kiriai swallowed hard and bit down on her desire to ask Tomi to just hurry. Eigo's hand reached over and squeezed hers. She shifted a little closer to him on the couch. At least one thing was going smoothly in her life at the moment. Well, the comfort and caring part. She was still waiting for some kind of zing of excitement in her relationship with Eigo. Maybe if he would kiss her already?

Tomi started speaking again and Kiriai pushed the distractions away. Lately, she'd found her mind sliding to smaller issues to avoid facing the bigger ones. She was out of time now. Tomorrow evening, she'd be in the chief's private arena facing Brawler Antei with Jitaku Hood's survival on the line. Her stomach clenched, and Kiriai reminded herself to breathe. It took only a moment's concentration to feel the familiar relaxation of her centering take hold.

"We've been avoiding Boss Ryuin's schemes all week, and she

isn't stopping," said Tomi. "My sources, as well as Representative Kiyo's, confirm that Boss Ryuin is throwing even more resources at supporting Brawler Antei tomorrow and doing everything she can to ruin Kiriai's chances," Tomi said with a tip of his head in her direction.

"Well, it's a good thing we don't let Kiriai go anywhere by herself," said Mikata with a pointed glance at Kiriai, who flushed. Mikata had caught a server in the cafeteria switching out a roll on Kiriai's tray when she'd been distracted. Kiriai shuddered to think what it might have been laced with. She still had a perfect memory of Boss Akuto falling and writhing on the ground after being poisoned during the chaos of her first junior scrapper battle.

"At least Gebi and the other initiates have been helping run interference when Kiriai's at the dojo," said Eigo, and he turned to Kiriai and smiled. "Good job winning them over this week. Jimu and Jiseki are as good as official bodyguards."

Kiriai returned his smile, but all the harassment of the last few days kept it halfhearted. It was amazing how annoying it was to have random people cause her trouble, from the servant who'd handed her a sopping, cold towel with a smirk to whoever had tripped her in the crowded hallway yesterday. She'd avoided a bad fall only because Jiseki had grabbed her in time.

"We know Boss Ryuin won't do anything to cause permanent harm to Kiriai. She'd risk forfeiting." Tomi caught and held Kiriai's gaze. "But we know she *will* do everything she can to hurt you in ways that aren't detectable. She's a very skilled and manipulative boss who knows how to make things go her way. Your actual fight in the ring will be the least of what happens between now and the final outcome."

Kiriai shot a glance toward Sento, sitting to Tomi's right, and he shrugged in an *I told you so* gesture. A brief flash of nostalgia made Kiriai long for the days, not so long ago, when she was so sure her fighting ability was all that mattered.

"I know you'll weather the mental games easily; we just need to make sure Ryuin doesn't succeed in anything major against you between now and the fight, because—" Tomi hesitated, and a brief silence followed.

Kiriai could tell she wasn't the only one who really didn't want to ask him to explain further.

Tomi sighed and rubbed a hand across his neck. "Despite all Boss Akuto, Second Jaaku and I could do, Ryuin got two of her lackeys into judge positions for tomorrow's fight."

"What?" Both Mikata and Sento demanded simultaneously.

"How did that happen?" Sento asked, a flush of anger on his cheeks.

"It isn't 'Ranger Tomi's fault," Kiriai said in a quiet voice.

Sento's flush deepened, and after a glance at Kiriai, he turned back to the 'Ranger with an apologetic expression. "I'm sorry, 'Ranger. And I'm the last one to complain about underhanded tactics, but the judges should be above reproach or at least pretend to be, or it ruins the whole system."

"Can we get to any of the other judges?" Shisen asked, her face hard. Kiriai could almost hear her rifling through strategies to get things to benefit them.

"And how strong are Ryuin's ties to the two judges?" asked Mikata. "Is it anything we can counter?"

"What if they suddenly got sick?" Eigo said with a crafty glint in his eyes.

Tomi looked nonplussed for a moment before he tipped his head back and let out a booming laugh of delight. Kiriai looked at the others and smiles and grins emerged, replacing the mercenary looks of moments ago.

When Tomi quieted, he caught Kiriai's gaze and gave her a nod of respect. "You have accomplished what few have in life, surrounding yourself with people who love you and will fight on your behalf."

Kiriai looked around the room. Appreciation for everyone

there pushed aside the anxiety that had been swirling through her.

She smiled and asked Tomi, "Can you work out a way for them to join me in the ring tomorrow?"

That got another laugh from everyone.

"No. But I think I speak for everyone when I promise we'll do everything we can for you outside the ring."

Nods all around helped the mood finish morphing into something positive, something confident. Despite all of Boss Ryuin's manipulations, she didn't have a crew like this.

"If you want to head out for your last treatment from Isha, I'll finish briefing everyone here and see what we can do about the judge situation."

"I'll take her," said Eigo as he stood and held out a hand for Kiriai. "You'll need Mikata and her contacts for whatever plan you come up with."

Kiriai briefly thought about insisting on staying, but Tomi's intent was clear. There wasn't much she could do about what happened outside the ring. It was up to her to get in the best condition for the fight, or none of their work would make a difference.

Kiriai took Eigo's hand and stood with only the slightest of winces.

OK, maybe a final session and dose of herbs with Isha was a good idea. Kiriai needed to be in top shape and moving easily by tomorrow evening. And Isha was the one who could make that happen.

At the door, Kiriai stopped and turned for a minute to look at the people who were committing everything they had to support her. A deep gratitude filled her and without a word, she bent forward into a bow of thanks before she turned and followed Eigo out, leaving silence in her wake.

"That was good of you," Eigo said as they slid the front door of her villa shut behind her. "You know how we all feel about you, don't you?"

Kiriai stopped in the cool night air and turned to look at Eigo, not sure how to respond.

His smile was soft and without another word he pulled her into a hug that soothed all the rough edges inside her. She wrapped her arms around his waist, tucked her face into his chest and felt his chin rest on top of her head. One of his hands moved across the back of her shoulder and neck before stopping. She felt him finger the soft cord around her neck.

"You're still wearing it?"

She paused and glanced up briefly. "The medallion you made me? Of course. I never take it off."

He smiled and his arms tightened around her.

For a moment, she wondered what it would be like if she and Eigo just left all this and never came back.

"Your people are good at making someone disappear, aren't they?" she asked.

She felt the rumble of laughter against her cheek and smiled in response.

"Depends on what you mean by *disappear*," he said before his voice turned pragmatic. "The 'forcers are better at the bad kind of disappearing, but yes, the scroungers have been known to provide a new life for one of their own, on occasion."

He pushed her back and looked down at her.

"But you don't need to disappear, you know." His expression was intense, and Kiriai didn't know how he could believe in her more than she believed in herself. "That's what I was trying to say. We all know you can win tomorrow. Let us handle the stuff outside the ring, and you work your magic inside it."

Now that they were alone, Kiriai felt like she could be honest. "Eigo, I don't know if I can do it."

"Tell me what's going on in your head then."

Kiriai leaned forward into the comfort of his hold, finding it easier to open up if she didn't have to look at him. She tried to order her thoughts to explain what was bothering her the most. "It's just that I've been training non-stop with the other initiates for almost a month now. And they are good fighters. Really good fighters. But even with all that, none of us compares at all to the trainers." She paused and shook her head. Eigo was the one person she'd always been honest with. If she could be open about her doubts with anyone, it was him. "Eigo, they are just so much better than we are that at times I feel like a child trying to compete with an adult."

A low chuckle wasn't the response she'd expected after sharing her biggest doubts.

"It's not funny," she said, leaning back and smacking him hard in the chest. "These are the brawlers we've watched on the screen for years. They fight burb battles, not just for disputes between neighbors. These are the brawlers who win the City Warrior Tournament and are inducted into the city . . . as *warriors*, Eigo."

He only smiled wider.

"Sorry," he said, while not sounding apologetic at all. "First of all, you have the talent to make warrior yourself someday. But for now, you're an initiate, just getting started. Why are you comparing yourself to the most elite brawlers in all of Southern Core?"

She stared at him, not understanding.

"Kiriai. Who do you think the chief picks to run the initiation and test the incoming brawlers?"

Eigo turned and looped an arm through hers, pulling her toward the training complex as she processed his words.

"I'm an idiot," she finally said.

"Of course you are," said Eigo, which earned him another hit, this time a solid fist into the shoulder.

"Hey," he said in protest, but smiling. "Isn't your boyfriend supposed to agree with you?"

"I think you need to go back to boyfriend school for more training," she shot back.

"Seriously though, Kiriai. While you've been devouring everything you can about Brawler Antei, you didn't realize how her skill level compared to Trainer Gebi and her people?"

"I focused on training to counter her, not compare her to other fighters," she said, trying to keep her tone from sounding too defensive.

"All right. Do it now. Run through what you know about Antei and all the information you know about the trainers' fighting abilities. How do they stack up against each other?"

Arm in arm with Eigo, Kiriai let her mind contemplate the question. The cool night air soothed her as they strolled along the cobbled walkways, the occasional whiff of flowers and fresh grass reminding her that spring had truly arrived. It didn't take long before she knew he was right. It had been in front of her face the whole time, and she'd been too close to see it. By selecting Brawler Antei as her opponent, Chief Kosui had truly given her a realistic shot at winning.

As the couple entered the training hall and moved through the quiet hallways toward the fixer rooms, Kiriai shook her head and smiled, trying to decide how best to admit that Eigo was right, and she'd been wrong.

She stopped in front of the door to the room Isha was using and squeezed his hand before turning back to face him. "Thank you," she said, a bit of wonder in her voice. "How do you always know exactly what to say to make me feel better?"

Eigo was smiling, but there was an intensity in his light blue eyes that made her want to step back and lean forward at the same moment.

Would he finally kiss her? Did she want him to? Kiriai held her breath as Eigo looked down at her as if he could see her innermost thoughts.

Just as he leaned forward, the door behind them slid open to reveal Isha. She wore a harried expression, and her mouth hung half open to say something when she saw them and froze.

"Oh," she said as the three of them stared at each other, no one moving.

Kiriai tried, unsuccessfully, to keep from blushing.

"I am *so* sorry," said Isha awkwardly. "I'll just—" She fluttered a hand back toward the fixer suite behind her as her cheeks flushed a pretty pink. "I thought you were Aibo. Let me just close this—" Isha stepped back and reached for the door handle.

Eigo turned back to Kiriai with a wry grin, who returned his smile and shrugged, knowing that the moment had passed. Then Isha's words sank in, and Kiriai shot out a hand to stop Isha from closing the door. A twist of worry clenched inside her that had nothing to do with Eigo or Isha.

"Aibo isn't with you?" she asked.

No one moved, the implication of Kiriai's question sparking worried expressions from each of them.

"No," Isha said slowly, her eyes searching the hall behind the two of them. "She just ran over to the house to check in with all of you and grab some food." Her voice sped up and rose in pitch. "And since there is a fixer working late next door, she thought I'd be safe on my own. You haven't seen her?"

Eigo shook his head, and then suddenly winced in pain.

Kiriai realized she'd clamped her hand down on his arm. Hard. She let go, and then without another word pushed past Isha into the suite. After a quick scan of the space, she dashed back out and ran for all she was worth back to the villa.

"Kiriai!"

"Wait!"

She heard both Isha and Eigo calling after her, but didn't slow.

All she could see was the cold promise of vengeance in Boss Ryuin's eyes as Boss Akuto had manipulated her to do what he wanted.

Kiriai might be off limits for permanent damage before the fight. But did that apply to her crew?

Her breath came faster as her feet pounded across the path she'd just strolled along moments ago, and she prayed with all the energy she had.

Ancestors, please let Aibo be at the villa. Please let her be safe. Please!

CHAPTER FORTY

Kiriai barreled around a dark corner of the tree-lined path, and her heart slammed in her chest for an entirely different reason. Four masked figures stood silently on the shadowed path, blocking her way. She skidded to a stop and just stared. They were dressed in dark clothing with masks and hoods disguising everything but their gleaming eyes. Their lack of surprise at her appearance could only mean one thing. They had been waiting for her. Anger mixed with fear and urgency made it hard for Kiriai to think straight.

For a moment, she contemplated just charging forward and hoping to break through. She had to get to the villa!

The two center figures must have sensed her intention, because they stepped closer and braced their large bulks against each other, blocking most of the path. Kiriai knew she didn't have a chance of breaking through.

That didn't mean she had to stop. The masks, the ambush, Aibo missing, all of it rushed through Kiriai. And there weren't any 'forcers around as help or witnesses. With a cry of rage, she charged, using her momentum to kick directly at the brute on the right. The inner storm raging inside her gave it the power of a battering ram.

They'd obviously thought their numbers would intimidate her, because her attack caught them flatfooted. Kiriai felt the tip of her sandal sink into the heavily muscled center of the taller man, and his breath burst out in a pained whoosh. But she didn't slow to celebrate, her body and fists spinning to her left with a speed and power that overwhelmed the hastily raised hands of the second bruiser. There was nothing like the advantage given by a surprise attack.

It couldn't last.

Even as her third punch slammed into the man's jaw and snapped his head around, Kiriai knew she had to keep moving, and fast. Four on one would be over as soon as she stopped. She landed a quick chop to the man's collarbone at the same time as she pushed past him and spun, anchoring her elbows to wrench the man around to use as a shield.

Just in time. The third man behind her couldn't stop his own kick in time. Kiriai felt the body in front of her jerk in pain, and he spit out a curse. With a shove, Kiriai pushed the man toward the two attackers who were trying to get to her. If she could get just a bit of space, she could break free and sprint to safety.

A hiss of movement behind her was her only warning. It wasn't enough. Even as she twisted, forearm tight and ready to block, pain exploded in her lower back. At the same time, the two men in front of her caught their companion and threw his body back at her. His mass was impossible to ignore as he crashed into her. Kiriai fell backward, doing her best to curl her body for a proper fall to save herself from injury. The man's dead-weight smashed down on top of her and knocked all the air out of her lungs. The gravel from the path dug with sharp edges into her skin as she kicked and struggled with all her strength. On the ground, she would be in trouble against this many opponents.

"Get him off of her," a quiet voice said with the snap of

command that let her know who was in charge. It was the fourth man, the one who'd sucker-punched her from behind.

Kiriai stilled and did her best to force air into her lungs as the two men grabbed fistfuls of fabric and levered their companion off of her. She sucked in a full drought of sweet air as soon as his weight lifted. Ignoring her spinning head and aching back, Kiriai scrambled to her feet. Still woozy, she held her fighting stance and tried to keep all of her opponents in view. It was fruitless as the men had spread out to surround her in a practiced maneuver that made her think they did this kind of thing often.

"What do you want?" she finally asked, aiming her question at the man with the slender build who had given the order earlier. He was dressed in dark, form-fitting clothing and the cap, combined with the cloth tied over his face, only left his eyes exposed. They were staring at her, so cold and emotionless that Kiriai suppressed a shiver.

"Funny you should ask that," he said. "Because we're here to deliver a simple message and if you stop resisting, I promise we'll finish and leave."

Instead of reassuring her, his words made Kiriai tense further, her eyes scanning for any chance to break away.

"I've heard you care deeply about your crew members."

Kiriai froze, all thoughts of escape gone in an instant. "Do you have Aibo?"

The man tipped his head, gave the slightest of shrugs and chuckled.

Rage ignited in Kiriai and she lunged at the man, fists already in motion.

She had to give his crew credit for learning from their mistakes, because this time, the other three were on top of her before she could reach their leader. Two more shots landed into her kidneys and one of them bore her down to the ground. She heaved, frantic as a heavy hand pushed her head down, grinding her cheek into the gravel of the path.

"Don't leave any marks." The sharp order made them let go of her face, but heavy hands kept hold of her arms with vice-like strength.

"Pick her up."

Kiriai stopped struggling as they hauled her to her feet and forced herself to take a calming breath. The threat to her young protege had thrown her off balance. But she needed to keep her wits about her if she wanted to get out of this and help Aibo. That didn't keep her from glaring at the leader and mentally running through the things she'd like to do to him. Two of his goons held her immobile, keeping hard grips on her arms and pulling her up so her feet barely touched the ground.

The leader moved close to her, invading her space, his face just above hers and close enough she could hear his breathing. "I don't have time for this. We are here to give you a message, so quit fighting and listen closely."

Kiriai clenched her jaw, but kept quiet. If they really had Aibo, then this was her only chance to get information. Her insides quailed as images of Aibo captured by ruthless people flashed through her mind. What if they were hurting her? Another breath, and Kiriai pushed her worries aside. There would be time for that later. Now she needed to stay calm. What would Tomi or Shisen do in this situation?

"During the fight tomorrow, *after* putting on a good show, you are to give up and let your opponent beat you. Do you understand?"

She'd been expecting something like this, but hearing it stated so baldly made her heart sink. She would have to choose between her hood and her friend tomorrow. How could she?

Mouth dry, Kiriai said, "And if I don't?"

She couldn't see the man's mouth, but his eyes crinkled, evidence of his cruel smile under the mask.

"Then you won't see your little aide ever again."

Her worst fears confirmed, Kiriai couldn't help asking, "Why?"

He didn't answer.

"Take me instead," she said, desperate now. "I'll go with you right now if you let her go."

The man let out a bark of laughter and turned to his followers. "See? She's exactly as described, ready to do anything for one of her underlings." He shook his head before turning back to her. "We can't touch you . . . at least in a way that leaves any evidence. It should be obvious to a smart girl like you that my employer doesn't want you. They want you to *lose* tomorrow. If you can do that, you'll get your little aide back, safe and sound."

"How do I know you'll do what you say? Boss Ryuin isn't known for being merciful."

The flinch from one of the hands wrapped around her left arm was all the confirmation Kiriai needed. As if there was any question of who was behind this.

"Nice try," said the leader. "You'll just have to trust our *employer* to do what they say, because one thing you can trust is that your aide will disappear if you don't follow orders. Understand?"

The cold eyes were back. Kiriai knew she wouldn't be getting anything more from the man, so she just nodded. The leader gave her a considering look as she moved her arms to pull them free from the mens' grips.

"One last thing," the leader said. Kiriai looked back at his face and instinct had her tightening her core just in time. The man drove a fist into her gut, then the other, and then back again, a rapid-fire pummeling that stabbed at her and left her torso in a blaze of pain. Kiriai coughed out a breath and gasped for air as he straightened and brushed his hands against each other.

"My employer asked me to add a little something to make sure you had a taste of what will happen to your friend before she permanently disappears if you don't come through for us. Understand?"

This time the man didn't wait for a response from her. He jerked his head toward his followers, who let her drop to the path and followed their leader to disappear silently into the trees. Kiriai, doubled over and trying to manage the pain, groaned and lowered herself carefully to a seated position. She felt like throwing up. Her back radiated a dull ache, but she could tell the attackers had done no permanent damage, just caused a lot of pain to make their point. And Aibo . . . Kiriai shook her head, not wanting to imagine them doing the same to the younger girl. Instead, Kiriai forced herself to breathe slowly through the pain and try to clear the chaotic mess of thoughts spinning through her mind. One thought emerged above them all. Her crew. She had to get back to the villa. Her crew would know what to do.

With a wince, Kiriai ignored the pain and levered herself up to her feet. She stood for a few long moments as her body swayed and her head took a moment to adjust to her new position. From behind her, voices drifted down the path. Kiriai flinched, worried for a moment that her attackers were coming back, before she realized that they wouldn't be yelling loudly and advertising their position. A weary smile broke across her face as Kiriai realized who would do that.

Sure enough, a moment later, she heard the familiar voice of Shisen yelling her name just before the woman spotted her and started running.

"Kiriai! Is that you?" Shisen's excited expression quickly morphed to one of concern when she got close enough to see Kiriai's hunched posture and the arm she kept wrapped tightly around her middle. "What happened to you? We've all been out looking for you. Eigo and Isha got back and said you'd left before them."

Kiriai made an impatient brushing motion at all the questions. There was really only one important thing at the moment. "Aibo?"

Shisen's eyes dropped briefly, and she shook her head. A heavy weight sank inside Kiriai. After the ambush, it had been obvious Aibo's disappearance was deliberate, but Kiriai had hoped that the girl had escaped or somehow made her way back to the villa.

As Shisen's mouth opened, Kiriai forestalled further questions with a small shake of her head. "Help me back and I'll explain it all to everyone at once, all right?"

Shisen nodded and moved to Kiriai's side. "Here. Let me give you a hand."

Kiriai didn't object as her friend slipped an arm around her waist and pulled one of Kiriai's arms across her shoulders for support.

As the two of them hobbled through the cool night, Kiriai felt her anger growing. An undercurrent of determination helped her ignore her body's insistence that she stop and rest.

She would get Aibo back, no matter the cost.

CHAPTER FORTY-ONE

"Didn't Nietzsche say, 'The best weapon against an enemy is another enemy'? If we set up the burbs to be in competition against each other, we can keep them from ever looking our way."

— Founding Matriarch Miya Tagami during the Chikara City Organization meetings. Oath Keepers Archive of Truth, Volume 14

"But the Chief has to do something!" Kiriai leapt to her feet, almost yelling. She tried not to wince as pain reminded her of the evening's events.

Silence greeted her. Even worse was the sympathy she saw underlying anger in the expressions of some of her crew.

"Come, Kiriai-chan. Drink this and move to my table," said Isha, her tone a mix of concern and command as she placed a warm mug, sharp with a medicinal odor, in her hands. "Whatever we work out, you are still fighting tomorrow evening and your injuries won't heal themselves."

Kiriai sighed and gave in. Anger wouldn't generate solutions. Too tired to object, Kiriai gulped the tea down in large swallows, doing her best to ignore the bitter undertones that the liberal sweetening couldn't mask.

"Let Isha tend to you, Kiriai," said Tomi. "To be clear, I'm not implying we do nothing, only stating the facts, regardless of how distasteful I . . . and all of us here find them." He paused and shook his head. The naked concern for Aibo in his expression, more than anything, convinced Kiriai to obey. She followed Isha over to a long, padded bench set up against the far wall so Kiriai could still take part in the discussion while being tended to.

After Kiriai painfully situated herself on the table, it felt heavenly to lie still on the padded surface.

"The sad fact is we have no proof to bring to the chief," said Tomi. "By leaving this to the last minute, any investigation into the matter will take much longer than the day we have left. Boss Ryuin is obsessive about leaving no evidence of her activities. Even tonight's threat—she sent her goons to deliver a verbal message to Kiriai, so we wouldn't have anything tangible to bring to the chief." Frustration grew in Tomi's voice as he met Kiriai's eyes from across the room. "Even the injuries can be explained as normal for brawler training."

Lying on her stomach with her head turned to the rest of the room, Kiriai tried to relax as Isha ran her fixing wand over her back. She pushed aside her emotions and forced herself to think strategically. There had to be a way to force Ryuin to give Aibo back.

"You can't tell me this is the first time an opponent has used blackmail to influence a fight," said Shisen, her voice just as full of outrage as Kiriai's had been. Pain tugged inside Kiriai as she remembered how much time Shisen had been spending with Aibo, guiding her through the emergence and training of her 'path gift. Kiriai swallowed a lump in her throat. Everyone here loved Aibo. They needed to get her back safe and sound. There had to be a way.

"No," said Tomi with a weary shake of his head. "If there is a way to cheat or bully to get a victory in the rings, I can guarantee it has been tried before. And Boss Ryuin is an expert, which is why we've been so cautious lately. It's no coincidence that both Aibo's abduction and the attack on Kiriai happened when both of them were alone and isolated. Blast—" Tomi stopped and looked down. The rest of her crew fell silent as the normally cheerful man ran a hand through his hair, his expression a mask of worry and pain. When he looked back up, his eyes were cold. "I would strangle that woman with my bare hands if I could get away with it."

His words expressed exactly how they were all feeling, and instead of flaring up their emotions, they brought a firm sense of purpose to the room.

After a moment, Sento broke the silence. "So what are our options?"

Tomi gave him a grateful look and cleared his throat. "First thing in the morning, Boss Akuto will ask for a grievance audience with Chief Kosui and the judges. They're required to hold it before the fight, but there's no telling how long before."

"And the Chief can force Boss Ryuin to give Aibo back?" Eigo said, excitement written on his face.

"It's not that easy," said Tomi with a shake of his head. "Yes, the chief can demand she return the girl, but only if Boss Akuto can make a convincing case that first, Boss Ryuin had a hand in the abduction, or if not, then that she stands to gain the most from it, which would mean one of her allies could be responsible."

Shisen let out a derisive snort. "Who else stands to benefit from holding one of Kiriai's crew hostage?"

Tomi shrugged one shoulder. "And if she argues that Aibo is a young girl and just took a few days off to party with friends?"

"The day before the biggest fight for her brawler and when the future of her home hood is at stake?" Shisen's tone showed what she thought of someone who would accept that excuse.

"Or that she's overwhelmed by the stress of it all, couldn't take the pressure and is hiding out until it was all over?" Tomi said.

That stopped Shisen, and Kiriai could see how reasonable the explanation would sound to anyone who didn't know Aibo personally.

"So we have tonight and early tomorrow to find evidence to help Boss Akuto make his case?" Mikata asked.

"Exactly," said Tomi with a nod in her direction. "If we don't find some concrete evidence or someone willing to testify, the Chief will have to base his decision on the arguments the two bosses make. And—" He stopped and made a helpless gesture with one hand.

"—that won't turn out in our favor," said Sento, finishing the thought for the 'ranger. "Especially with everything on the line for this fight. The chief and all the other bosses want the fight to happen. No one but us will be happy if the chief calls for Boss Ryuin to forfeit."

"You're right," said Tomi with a shake of his head. "We have to find something proving Boss Ryuin's role in Aibo's disappearance. It's our only hope."

"It's not all we can do . . . or not all I can do," said Kiriai as she sat up and paused before turning over so Isha could work on the front of her.

Every eye in the room turned in her direction and Kiriai swallowed, the words she was about to say sticking in her throat. But she had to speak up, especially if it was Aibo's only chance.

"I could throw the fight."

There. She'd said it.

Her blunt words hung in the room like a storm threatening to lash out on those below. Everyone knew exactly what a horrible choice she was contemplating, her hood or her young friend and charge.

"You can't."

"You might have to."

Shisen and Tomi spoke, opposite sentiments clashing, making everyone look between the two of them.

"Go ahead. One at a time," Kiriai said, forcing herself to ignore the sick feeling in her stomach. "I value both of your opinions and need them to help me make my decision, if it comes down to it."

"Technically, the decision is up to Boss Akuto, and what he tells you to do . . ." Tomi's words trailed off as a wry smile appeared on his face. "But we all know you'll do what you think is right, regardless of orders or consequences." He shook his head. "Boss Ryuin couldn't have picked a better fighter to blackmail by snatching one of her friends." He caught Kiriai's eyes. "You know, this would be much easier with a normal brawler who followed orders. But then again, if you were a normal fighter, we wouldn't be here in the first place, with a chance to save our hood."

Kiriai flushed at the respect she saw in the man's gaze and he continued.

"I will keep you updated on what we know right up to the time you step into the ring tomorrow evening. You'll have as much information as possible to make your decision."

At a loss for words, Kiriai could only nod as Tomi turned back to the others in the room. "It's up to us to do as much as we can between now and the grievance audience to make sure Kiriai doesn't have to choose between Aibo and our hood."

"It's late," said Mikata as she stood, a determined expression on her face. "But I know where training partners will still be hanging out. Coming with me?" she asked, glancing between Eigo and Sento.

As he stood with Sento, Eigo held up a hand in Mikata's

direction before he strode over to where Kiriai sat on the bench, her feet swinging in the air and trying not to let worry overwhelm her.

He stepped between her knees and pulled her in close, his hands careful not to squeeze too tight.

The random thought that her boyfriend had a bit too much experience with injuries made her wonder if she'd ever have a normal life.

"Don't worry about us. I'll make sure we don't let each other out of sight tonight," he said in a quiet voice next to her ear.

Kiriai felt a knot of tension loosen inside her, only then realizing how much her crew going out tonight bothered her.

"I can come—"

"No," he said, quickly shushing her as he pushed back enough to see her face. He reached up, his palm warm against her cheek, and she couldn't resist leaning into it. "You have one job tonight: Let Isha fix you up and then get enough rest for tomorrow. Understand?"

She nodded wordlessly, a sudden wave of tiredness washing over her. "Be careful," she said. "Promise."

He nodded, his confident smile back. "Of course. I'm too likable to get into any serious trouble."

Kiriai gave him a half-smile that faded as she watched the three of them leave together.

Tomi also rose and gave Shisen a nod. "If you come with me, we'll try and find a few of the more official gatherings tonight before it gets too late."

Shisen stood and followed him, but stopped at the open doorway and turned back to Kiriai. "Don't worry, little sister. We'll figure out how to get her back. No matter what it takes."

Shisen's promise hung in the air behind her as Kiriai turned to look at Isha, the only one left now.

"Child, trust them to do everything that can be done."

"But she's so young and who knows what they are doing to her?" Kiriai's voice cracked, and she blinked back tears.

"Stop that," said Isha, her tone stern. "Aibo is a lot stronger than you give her credit for. She isn't the young girl you picked out of the youth arena months ago. She practically runs all this." Isha waved a hand at their surroundings.

Kiriai glanced around and sucked in a calming breath before looking back at Isha. "She is, isn't she?" It came out as more of a question than a statement.

"Yes, she is," Isha said. "And what do you think she'd be telling you to do if she were here right now?"

That startled a laugh out of Kiriai. "She'd tell me to let you finish fixing me, drink all your concoctions, and get enough sleep for tomorrow."

Isha gave her shoulder a gentle squeeze. "Then let's do what Aibo says, all right?"

Kiriai lay back on the table and tried not to think about the choice she faced tomorrow.

You will make the right decision when the time comes. The thought from Yabban came as Kiriai gave herself over to Isha's ministrations.

You really think so, Yabban?

Abraham Lincoln, a strong leader in history, said, "Be sure you put your feet in the right place, then stand firm."

Kiriai gave the words some thought and decided that for tonight, she'd do her best to follow Abraham's advice.

CHAPTER FORTY-TWO

Kiriai's heart sank when she saw Boss Akuto walk back into the room that a clerk had set aside for the crew and witnesses during the grievance audience. Despite the luxurious surroundings, soft sofas and deep chairs, a few of the occupants were standing. Shisen paced back and forth in front of the large window that spanned the far wall. Kiriai was following Tomi's example and sat on a sofa next to Eigo and tried to keep up a relaxed facade.

Every eye in the room was on the boss as he turned to shut the door behind him and then strode across the room to sit in the high-backed chair at the front of the room. He sat there, silent, and waited as the rest of the crew hurried to find a place to sit.

When everyone was seated, he spoke. "I could not persuade Chief Kosui to rule against Boss Ryuin for tonight's fight."

There was a collective gasp and distressed murmurs at the news.

"Aides Onjun and Benri, I'd like to thank you for coming in and giving statements about Aibo's state of mind even though it wasn't enough. My second and a clerk are just outside and they will compensate you for your efforts. You have friends in Jitaku Hood if we can ever be of service."

The young man and older woman who had been in classes with Aibo stood and bowed before heading toward the door. The woman slid it open and Kiriai caught a glimpse of Second Jaaku outside the door. When would Akuto get rid of the snake? Thank the ancestors, she didn't have to deal with him in the room with everyone else.

The other aide hesitated before leaving and stopped to look at the rest of the crew. "I almost feel like I know you from how much Aibo talked about you," he said. "I hope you find her and bring her back. She doesn't deserve to be caught up in all this." He dropped his gaze and followed his companion out the door.

Only when it slid shut did Boss Akuto turn back to the rest of them.

Kiriai wanted to demand an accounting of the audience from him. Why hadn't the chief seen the obvious and ordered Boss Ryuin to return Aibo? But Eigo's hand squeezed hers in warning, and she clamped her mouth shut.

Thankfully, Tomi asked for her, after a quelling glance in her direction. He gave the boss a respectful nod before asking, "Would you mind sharing how the audience went? How was Boss Ryuin able to convince the chief she wasn't involved in Aibo's abduction?"

Boss Akuto looked out the window for a moment, lost in thought before he turned back to the room and let out an uncharacteristic sigh. That small loss of control, more than anything, drove home to Kiriai how dire the circumstances were for her home.

"Chief Kosui agreed that Mabbai stood the most to gain by any interference with Kiriai's crew the night before the big fight, but didn't feel I made a good enough case that Aibo hadn't just left for her own reasons."

"Alone?" said Shisen, jumping up. "Without saying anything to anyone? The night before Kiriai's fight? The fight that could save her hood? How does that make any sense?" Shisen stood, fists clenched and face flush with anger. She belatedly seemed to realize that everyone was staring at her. Kiriai saw Sento trying to give her a discrete head shake in warning, and Mikata's glance flicked between the angry woman and the boss.

Kiriai could see the moment Shisen realized that she had just yelled at the boss and insulted the chief, the two most powerful men in her world. She swallowed hard, but instead of wilting, she straightened and kept her gaze direct under the calm scrutiny of the boss. His look made Kiriai think of a cat contemplating a tasty morsel.

But instead of chastising Shisen, Boss Akuto turned to look at Kiriai.

Following her friend's example, Kiriai held his gaze, just as unflinching as Shisen.

After a tense moment, Akuto shook his head slightly and the ghost of a smile flickered across his face. "It appears that your attitude of defiance together with loyalty is contagious."

Kiriai didn't know what to say. She heard a muffled snort from Eigo next to her. Or was it from Tomi on his other side?

"Have a seat, child," said Akuto with a dismissive wave at Shisen, who quickly took her seat, a chastened expression on her face. "You're only saying the same things I've been thinking throughout this whole mess. If there were any other way—" He stopped and looked over the group of friends in the room, obviously united in their desire to rescue Aibo. "Boss Ryuin produced two young aides from Aibo's training class who testified that she'd been under a lot of stress and mentioned needing to get away for a break."

Only Eigo's hand on her knee kept Kiriai from objecting out loud.

"Obviously, we all know that isn't true, but it gave Chief Kosui enough reason to decide in favor of the fight tonight. Not that I don't understand," said Akuto. "The chief is under extreme pressure at the moment from the city, and I haven't been able to deliver on my promise to help him track down the culprits. At least not yet," he said, flicking his glance toward the closed door.

Kiriai couldn't help but follow his gaze. The only person of significance out there was Jaaku. Was the second helping Akuto investigate what had happened to the chief's list? Kiriai's gut clenched at the thought. Her breathing picked up pace before she forced it under control, reassuring herself there was no evidence leading back to the involvement of her and her friends.

". . . the last thing he needs is discontent among his bosses by canceling the fight tonight," Akuto continued. "I can only imagine the bets that they've placed on it, not counting the stakes we and Mabbai have riding on it."

As the boss looked back at her, his brow creased in concern. "Relax, Kiriai," said Akuto, "We all know how slim your chances of winning are tonight. But we all agree that a small chance to gain reinforcements is better than none. I expect the best you can give us tonight, but win or lose, I won't forget your loyalty and willingness to risk everything for our hood." He paused and looked toward the closed door. "Others could learn a lesson or two from you," he said under his breath, so softly, Kiriai wasn't sure she'd heard him right.

Was it Jaaku he kept referencing out in the hall? A small bit of cheer lifted her spirits at the idea that the vindictive man might finally fall out of favor with the boss. It couldn't have come at a better time, especially if the man was looking into the list on behalf of the chief.

"So how do we find Aibo?" Isha asked, her tone much more respectful than Shisen's had been.

From the boss's expression, Kiriai knew she wouldn't like what he said even before he spoke.

"We will do everything in our power to find the girl," he said with a tip of his head in Tomi's direction, "but it is unlikely we'll be successful in the few hours before the fight."

He focused on Kiriai, and she could feel the attention of everyone in the room on her.

"Brawler Kiriai, you find yourself in a very difficult position, but not one unknown to me," he said and then paused. "And to every leader at some time or another. You have to choose between the welfare of one and the welfare of many. With the recent wins by Raibaru, they are only a handful of victories away from a majority control of Jitaku territory. And we all know Western Burb will immediately challenge for the entire hood when that happens."

His words hung in the air, and Kiriai felt tension pressing down on her.

"If it helps any, while I am not directly your superior any more in brawler matters, in this matter, I still have authority over you as my chosen fighter." Akuto's compelling gaze locked onto hers as if he could impose his will on her with thoughts alone. "My orders are to win at all costs tonight."

A sound of objection slipped past her lips, but Akuto held up one imperious hand to silence her. "Leave it to us to find your young friend and protect her from harm. You hold the welfare of our entire hood in your hands tonight and must do everything you can to save us."

"You promise you'll save her?" Kiriai asked, desperate for some kind of reassurance if she had to make a decision that would abandon her friend to her enemies.

The slight shake of his head and flicker of regret in his eyes made a sharp pain stab inside her. "You know as well as everyone in this room that there are no guarantees in life, especially when powerful men and women are involved. I can promise to use all the resources available to me to save your friend, but that is all I can do. Just as you can't guarantee you'll win tonight, even if you do everything in your power." He held her gaze, challenging her to object.

But she couldn't. He was right. There were no guarantees.

"So are you agreed? We will both do our best in our separate endeavors?"

Kiriai couldn't help it. Her eyes flicked away from his. Only briefly, but it was enough.

He let out a harsh chuckle. "I don't know why I thought a direct order would have any influence on you."

Kiriai swallowed, but didn't look away this time. She hoped her expression communicated her intent, because her mouth was too dry, at the moment, to speak.

"I guess I can't ask you to change the loyalty that I value so much, can I?" said the boss with a shake of his head. "Without it, we wouldn't even have this chance at victory, regardless of how slight it is." He looked at the others arrayed around the room. "And without it, you wouldn't have all these fine people bound to you as close as family. I will leave you with this," he said with a look at her crew members. "Please help Kiriai see how much her actions can help everyone in the entire hood, instead of a single young girl, regardless of how close your ties are."

Boss Akuto stood and strode toward the door. For the first time, Kiriai noticed a hitch in his step and movement that suggested encroaching pain that came with age. The thought startled her. She'd never considered that the powerful man might be subject to the same ravages of time as everyone else. And if she didn't win tonight and Western Burb challenged for ownership of Jitaku as a result? What would become of Akuto then?

The rest of her crew followed Boss Akuto out of the room, looking as despondent as Kiriai felt. Instead of following, she stayed seated and stared out the window. All her possible actions and their repercussions spun and twisted through her thoughts.

She felt the sofa sag a moment later and looked over in

surprise to see that Eigo had sat back down next to her. Behind him, she saw that everyone else had left, and he'd closed the door.

He put an arm around her shoulders and pulled her into him. With a relieved sigh, she turned and tucked herself into his chest, wishing she could disappear for a bit and everything would be solved when she came back.

Instead, a feeling of gloom settled inside her as she once again imagined where Aibo was and what was happening to her while Kiriai sat on an expensive couch with her boyfriend in sun-warmed luxury.

"I'm not going to fight tonight," she blurted out, the words surprising herself . . . and Eigo too, since she felt him flinch slightly.

But instead of immediately objecting, his arm tightened around her and she felt his hand stroke her back. She was still too tense to relax into him completely. How had everything become such a mess?

CHAPTER FORTY-THREE

"The politicians and their hangers on can lock themselves up
in the city with their toys and comforts for now. Out here,
we'll be fighting and growing stronger. Once I take over the
other burbs, we'll come knocking."
— Personal Journal of Southern Burb Chief Makara
Foster. Oath Keepers Archive of Truth, Volume 20

Kiriai wasn't sure how long she and Eigo sat there. At one
point, someone slid the door open a fraction, only to shut
it quickly when they saw them sitting there.

In the slow moments of comfort, Kiriai's breathing evened
out and the tension that seemed to accompany her everywhere
lately finally seeped out of her muscles. For the first time in days,
she truly relaxed.

"Well, that took you long enough," said Eigo with a smile in
his tone. "I thought you were some big-shot fighter with all kinds
of meditation and focusing skills, but you took forever to relax."

"Hey," Kiriai said and pinched his chest in retaliation.

Eigo twitched and one of his hands snatched at her attacking one and held it tightly so she couldn't pinch him again. "No fair," he said. "I was all ready to block a punch, but didn't expect an elite brawler would stoop to pinching."

Kiriai grinned, but didn't sit up. It felt too good snuggled right where she was, even though she knew all her troubles were still waiting for her.

"So you're not fighting tonight?"

"No," she said without thinking, but even to her own ears, she sounded petulant, like a child told to go clean her room.

She felt a quiet chuckle rumble in Eigo's chest, and it helped her relax.

"You know I support you first, right? Before the hood, before Boss Akuto and his schemes, before the whole burb and everyone in it." He spoke in such a matter-of-fact tone that Kiriai knew they were simple facts to him, regardless of how they hit her heart and filled her with strength.

"Yes," she said, struggling to come up with the right words. "I don't know what to say. It's just—"

"Shh," he said in a quiet voice, his hand moving across her back again.

"No," she said, her voice stronger. "You've always been there for me, and I want you to know how much it means to me. I wouldn't be able to do any of the things I've done without you. I know that. And it means the world to me."

Eigo didn't answer, but a moment later, Kiriai felt him press a soft kiss to the top of her head. For a moment, Kiriai wondered what he would do if she turned to face him. But part of her wasn't sure she wanted to find out. Could she risk his friendship?

Still unsure how she felt, she didn't resist when he reached for her chin and tilted her face up toward his.

She saw exactly what he wanted as soon as their eyes met. But instead of pressing like Sento would have, he waited, so close she could feel the heat from his skin and feel his breath moving, quick but soft.

She'd never been good about thinking before acting. Why start now? And she wanted to know. What would kissing Eigo feel like?

Kiriai reached up and slid one hand to Eigo's neck as she leaned in slightly. His eyes widened and then he wasn't hesitating anymore. Both of his hands moved up to cup her face with gentle care. His eyes, full of love and appreciation, held her gaze for just a split second.

"So beautiful," he whispered just before he leaned in and his lips met hers.

The wild spark that swept aside control was missing. Her world didn't explode or force her to push for more.

Instead, Eigo's lips held hers captive with a love and warmth that enveloped her, wrapped her in arms that promised to protect and shield her from everything and everyone in the world. She pushed forward, diving in, wanting more, but the intensity didn't change. His love and strength was constant, soothing her rough edges, a steady rock that would always support her.

She quit trying to change the kiss, change him, and let herself simply relax, lower her walls and enjoy what he offered. At that moment, it was exactly what she needed. With a sigh, she let her best friend take her burdens, her stress, her anguish, all of it, for just a small moment of time, for just this kiss.

Time slowed and she felt his hands move through her hair, to her neck, and one stroked her cheek. He enfolded her completely in a warm cocoon of love and care. His lips pressed soft kisses to her cheeks, forehead and back to her lips . . . even to her closed eyes, damp with unwilling tears. Part of her never wanted to leave, hoping she could hide here, safe, forever.

She found herself pressed up against his chest, his heart

beating at a much faster pace than hers as his hand stroked down her hair in slow, careful movements.

But was this what she wanted? His soothing and supportive love or the kind that made her heart pick up in excitement, that always pushed into her thoughts?

And despite how much she wanted to, she couldn't stay here forever and ignore all the turmoil in her world right now. As if summoned by her thoughts, the urgent concerns of the day pressed back into Kiriai's mind.

"Shh," he said. "No need for that. I'll take care of everything, all right?"

"But—"

He leaned in for another kiss and Kiriai flinched back, not sure what she wanted.

"I'm sorry, Eigo. Can we just pretend this didn't happen? Just for a little while?" What had she been thinking? She couldn't do this right now. Adding a new relationship to everything already going on had been stupid.

Hurt flickered across Eigo's expression, but was quickly replaced with controlled calm, a forced patience. "Kiriai, take all the time you need. I won't push you. I just want to take care of you."

"And if you can't?" she asked, not sure if she was talking about their new relationship or their friendship.

"I can still do my best. I know you said you won't fight tonight, but we both know you will. Just let me help with that part at least."

Kiriai didn't answer, her thoughts a mess.

"Your muscles are tensing again," Eigo said. "I can almost feel your mind churning. You only do that when you're in fighting mode, calculating and strategizing." He paused and moved further back to get a good look at her. "Yep, you're fighting tonight."

Kiriai shook her head, glad he wasn't going to discuss the kiss.

She already felt unbalanced enough with the upcoming fight and all its implications. "I can't. If I fight, then what happens to Aibo? To our hood? How am I supposed to choose between a friend and our home? That's no choice." Her expression turned pleading. "Come on, Eigo. How about we just leave? Let the bosses fight it out amongst themselves instead of making us do their dirty work."

"And where would we go?" he asked as he tapped a finger on his lips, almost as if he were considering the outlandish proposition. "First, we'd have to break into Mabbai Hood's headquarters to free Aibo, then the three of us sneak past the core checkpoints to make it back to Jitaku on foot, since we can't use the transports. And I'm sure some of my interfering family wouldn't mind donating a few rad suits and supplies so we could head out into the wastelands and set up a cozy home in a small building. Surely there is a decent one still standing." He grinned at her, his expression chipper. Something inside Kiriai loosened to see his familiar teasing glint. "Sounds easy, doesn't it?"

"Knock it off," Kiriai said, and hit him in the chest with a lackluster punch.

"Ow," he said, rubbing the sore spot with an exaggerated motion. "First pinching, then kissing and now punching? Is this how you treat your boyfriend? Weren't you just saying how much I mean to you?"

She immediately felt a flash of regret. "Sorry. You've always been a better friend. You know it's not you I'm angry at. It's this whole mess."

"Hah!" A huge grin bloomed across Eigo's face, and he let out a gleeful whoop.

Surprised, she just stared at him.

"I just beat you for the first time," he said, still grinning. "You admitted I'm a better friend than you, so that means I won. I beat you!"

Kiriai couldn't help smiling too. "Yes. You win. You beat me."

She tipped her head in a respectful bow. "I, Brawler Dento Kiriai, concede victory to the much better friend Scrounger Nakama Eigo."

When she looked back up, his eyes were soft and understanding.

"And you'll fight tonight? Let us all help you? Let *me* help you?"

His words almost punctured the ease of the previous moment, but their relationship was more resilient than that.

Finally, she nodded. "Of course I am. But you knew that already, didn't you?"

He gave her a slight shrug with a wry smile. "Best friends know these things."

Looking at him, she wanted to tuck herself back into his chest and pretend the outside world would just fix itself. But would he take that as an invitation? Did she want to offer one?

As if he could read her mind, he pulled her close. But instead of another kiss, he wrapped her in close and simply held her.

Kiriai tried to decide if she felt disappointed or relieved.

"Now, you really need a plan for tonight. Once you have a plan, a lot of your stress and worry will disappear. You're feeling all of that because you still don't know what you will do."

"Eigo, I can't choose between Aibo and our hood."

"You might not have to. I can guarantee that at this very minute, 'Ranger Tomi is unleashing hordes of his best people to find where Aibo is being held. If anyone can find her before tonight, it's him."

A sliver of hope soothed the storm inside her. "If he finds Aibo, then the plan is simple. I'll just have to beat Brawler Antei." An unbidden scoff slipped out from Kiriai after she said that. "As if that were a simple task."

"That's your plan, then. You focus on how to beat Antei, got it? Leave all the other stuff to us." He gave her a comforting squeeze. "That's why you have us, right?"

She nodded, wanting to believe that the plan could be so simple, and it would all work out.

"We're here to do all the hard stuff, while you play tag in the ring."

She almost pinched him again, but stopped herself and just laughed instead.

Eigo extricated himself from their embrace, stood and reached out a hand for her. When she took it, he pulled her to her feet.

"Then let's get busy. You have a lot to do before tonight."

"You know I can't do any training this close to the fight."

"Not in the *game world* you can't, but our friend can run you through all kinds of practice in the time we have left."

Kiriai tried not to groan, knowing Eigo was right.

When they reached the door, Kiriai felt better, more focused and ready for the fight.

"Oh, and one quick thing," Eigo said as he stopped, his hand on the door. He suddenly looked unsure, and Kiriai groaned internally, ready to tell Eigo that he had to wait until after tonight to talk any more about that stuff.

"No, not about us. I just—" He hesitated and then blurted out the rest of the words in a quick rush. "I bet on you winning tonight."

She stared at him. The words took a moment to penetrate, since she hadn't been expecting anything of the kind. "You bet on me? With credits?"

"Just a few," he said.

A sick suspicion bloomed inside Kiriai. "You placed your bets with the official wager office, right? Not with one of your shady bookies, right?"

Eigo shrugged with a sheepish smile. "I hate using the wager office. You know they take a huge cut, whether you win or lose. And I know these people."

Kiriai frowned.

"It's not a big deal, Kiriai. It's just harmless fun. With the small wagers I've been making, my little nest egg is growing into something decent."

"Eigo, if this is about the credits, you know I have more than I can use."

"No," Eigo said, voice and demeanor suddenly stubborn. "You worked hard, fighting and bleeding for those credits. I won't take your charity. I've learned from you and am decent now at predicting who will win a fight. Why shouldn't I earn some money with my own skills?"

"Bet through official channels then," Kiriai said. "If you get caught, they'll take everything you own and maybe even arrest you."

"What?" Eigo asked, as he spread his hands and pasted on his characteristic smile. "Little ol' me? I'm too small for them to worry about. Besides, I have powerful friends." He tipped his head toward her.

"So you won't take my credits, which I wouldn't have earned without your help, but you'll use me to get out of trouble."

He shrugged. "I have my standards. I don't expect you to understand them. I disagree with a lot of things you do, but if they're important to you, I support you."

Ouch. Kiriai knew he was right. Hadn't he just been doing that a moment ago? She was just about to drop the subject when something he'd said earlier made her suspicious.

"Wait. You said you're good at predicting the winners? These wouldn't be the fighters that you and I have been watching lately? The ones we've been analyzing strengths and weaknesses in case I have to face them?"

Eigo's flush was all the answer she needed. By his mulish expression, however, she knew she needed to stop pushing.

"Fine. Just don't get into any trouble I can't get you out of, all right?"

"Yes, Brawler Kiriai," he said, followed by a sarcastic bow that made her laugh.

She saw the tension leave him at her concession and tried not to feel bad for harassing him on the topic. But by the ancestors, it was dangerous. She resolved to bring it up another time, when things weren't so crazy. There had to be something else that Eigo could earn credits doing besides illegal betting.

"So Isha first," said Eigo as they left the room and moved through the hall of the chief's headquarters. "She wants to treat you now, and then once more right before the fight. I'm pretty sure she's been brewing concoctions for you all morning. I hear the fixers on either side of her have complained about the smell."

Kiriai smiled, glad for the change of subject and the return of their easy camaraderie. "Maybe they should drink some or wear the poultices before they complain."

"Shh," he said. "The smells are the best defense we have to keep Isha's herbs as our secret weapon."

Kiriai nodded. She could still feel the stiffness from last night's encounter and knew that, however bitter, Isha's creations would do wonders. With them and the judicious use of her fixing wand, Kiriai would be in top shape for tonight.

Now, if only the others could find Aibo. Kiriai swallowed and let out a slow breath. She reached out and took Eigo's hand. The look he gave her eased her worry. He squeezed her hand back.

They would find her.

They had to.

CHAPTER FORTY-FOUR

"How is she?" Isha asked Eigo as soon as he and Kiriai stepped into her fixer room and slid the door shut behind them.

"Feeling much more stable," said Eigo. "She's worried about Aibo, but we came up with a plan and now she's focused on winning tonight."

"*She* is right here," Kiriai said, a touch of irritation in her voice.

Isha waved a dismissive hand at her. "No one really knows how they're doing. The opinion of loved ones around them is much more accurate."

Kiriai didn't have a ready answer for that and suspected it might be more true than she liked. The mention of loved ones made her suddenly miss Ojisan. She couldn't wait to see him next week. How would he react if they didn't get Aibo back?

"Now out of your clothes and on the table please," Isha said, breaking into her thoughts.

Kiriai's eyes flicked to Eigo, and she flushed. She felt a little less embarrassed when she saw that his face had also reddened.

"Ach, young people," said Isha as she hurried across the room and manhandled a screen over toward the table. With a few practiced movements, she had it set up to divide her treatment area from the small sitting area with its couch and two chairs.

"Um, I'm going to go see what the rest of the crew wants me to help with," Eigo said as he ran an awkward hand through his hair, making it stick out in even more directions than usual.

"I'll just—" Kiriai aimed a finger toward Isha.

"Make sure you—" Eigo tapped a finger to his temple and then mimed a few shadow boxing moves.

Kiriai laughed at his crude sign language and gave him a reassuring nod. She just needed to find a creative way to explain to Isha why she would be mostly unconscious during her treatment. Normally, Kiriai wouldn't try to combine the virtual training with a fixing session, but there just wasn't much time left. She needed every minute.

"I don't care if you want to stay or go, Eigo, but I need Kiriai up on the table," said Isha in her brisk voice of command.

"Oh, I'm going," he said and then without warning, he reached out and pulled Kiriai into a hug. "Do everything Isha and Yabban tell you," he said in a quiet voice next to her ear.

She started to answer when he whispered, "I love you," into her ear, and then kissed her, a soft peck on the lips that startled her with how easy and familiar it was. Without giving her a chance to answer, he let go of her and was out of the door. She stared at the closed door, still unsure of how to respond.

It wasn't as if they hadn't said those words to each other since their childhood, but now they meant so much more. Or did they? Did he mean them differently now that they were a couple?

If she were to say them, what would they mean? Yes, she loved Eigo and always had. But could she love him with the wild abandon she'd felt with Sento? Did she want that again? Or was the stable comfort Eigo offered better?

"Don't bother trying to figure them out, child," said Isha as she took Kiriai by the hand and pulled her toward the table. "Men have just as hard a time understanding us. He's a good man, though, and has always wanted the best for you. That is a strong foundation to build on."

"You think I should commit to Eigo?" Kiriai asked as she slipped out of her loose workout clothes and climbed onto the table with only a slight wince at the lingering soreness.

"I'm not saying that," said Isha as she draped a warm blanket over Kiriai that made her sigh in pleasure. "Only you and he can answer that. The magic that pulls two people to love and cherish the other more than themselves is rare and precious. Many look for it their whole lives and often settle for a pale imitation of it. Who's to say what the best choice is?"

Kiriai felt the bone-deep thrum of the fixer wand as Isha started at her feet, taking the time to cover every muscle, giving each a boost in healing and recovery time.

"Trust your instincts, Kiriai-chan. You have a good heart and it hasn't steered you wrong yet."

Suddenly Kiriai wondered if they were talking about men anymore. "And tonight?"

Isha chuckled softly, her hands moving over Kiriai's legs with sure strokes. "My advice is the same, child. Follow your heart. You can't choose the outcomes, only your actions as life challenges you. Try your best to look back at your choices without regret."

Kiriai wondered how she should apply that advice tonight, especially if her crew didn't find Aibo. Surely whichever choice she made, she'd regret the damage done to either Aibo or her hood.

"Enough of that, though," said Isha with a sharp clap to Kiriai's back, indicating she should turn over. "You need to focus on the fight. I hear that your mental state is important at the level you're fighting, right?"

Looking up at her mentor and friend, Kiriai nodded with a smile, realizing Isha had just fed her the perfect excuse.

"Speaking of mental state, I need to do some deep meditation to solidify my strategy for tonight," Kiriai said. "Are you going to need me to move anytime soon?"

Isha stopped to consider before shaking her head. "If you'll drink two cups of tea first and then lie back down, you should be good for the next half-hour to an hour. I had planned to tuck poultices around you, followed by warm blankets, and see how long I could get you to lie here and let them penetrate. Having you do some deep meditation is perfect. It'll give the poultices more time to work. Are you sure you have enough time?"

"Yes." Kiriai hurried to reassure her. "I can't do any training right before the fight and I'm too wired to take a nap, so meditating here and soaking in your *lovely*-smelling herbs is probably the best thing I can do right now."

Isha swatted Kiriai's shoulder at the sarcasm before moving over to her bench and getting busy with her supplies.

"I'll start meditating now and probably won't respond if you ask me something, all right?" Kiriai said.

"Relax away," said Isha in a distracted tone. "I'll just move you around if I need to."

Yabban, can you wake me if Isha seems to need my attention?

Yes, Kiriai. I'm glad you can finally train. I don't know if we have enough time to do everything you need, but I will start with the most crucial items, and we will see how much we can fit the time we have.

I'll need to take a break to eat about two hours before the fight and to get cleaned up from all the poultices, but then we can go for another final round of practice, all right?

Yes. Are you ready?

Kiriai smiled at the impatience she felt from Yabban and once again realized how lucky she was to have so many people devoted to helping her succeed.

Yes, Yabban. Let's focus on beating Brawler Antei.

The transition to Yabban's virtual dojo hardly fazed her. Kiriai mentally ran through all the skills and principles she'd been leveling up lately as she appeared in the peaceful dojo. Yabban stood in front of her, dressed in her sensei uniform with a worn brown belt tied loosely around her waist. Kiriai nodded with approval. Today was for training, not friendly banter.

"Trainee Kiriai," Yabban said, using her serious instructor voice, "let's see how much you've learned after almost a month of my training, shall we?"

Kiriai laughed. "Are you going to ignore all the brawler training? Trainer Gebi would be so offended."

Yabban unbent enough to offer a small smile. "I'm sure a few of her exercises helped reinforce what I've taught you. We both know how important it is to practice and repeat skills to advance them."

"Is that sarcasm?" Kiriai asked in surprise. "And I didn't have to spend an attribute point on it?"

"No. I am combining truth with my sense of humor. If you are smiling, then I have succeeded." Yabban then swiped at the air and the familiar chart of Kiriai's skills popped into existence, translucent letters and numbers floating just in front of her view. "Look these over, and then I'll explain exactly what we will focus on in the short time we have left."

Character Name: Kiriai

    Level: Error. Inaccessible.

    XP: Error. Inaccessible.

    Character Traits: Error. Inaccessible.

    Training Statistics:

    Beginning Moves: Unlocked: all. Learned: all. Proficient: all. Mastered: Stances 7/12, Strikes 5/20, Kicks 7/20, Blocks 8/10, Foot Maneuvers 6/8.

    Novice Moves: Unlocked: all. Learned: all. Proficient: Stances 4/6, Strikes 16/16, Kicks 4/20, Blocks 4/10, Foot Maneuvers 7/7.

Mastered: Stances 2/6, Strikes 6/16, Kicks 1/20, Blocks 1/10, Foot Maneuvers 2/7.

Intermediate Moves: Unlocked: all. Learned: Stances 2/6, Strikes 12/14, Kicks 14/16, Blocks 10/10, Foot Maneuvers 4/8. Proficient: None. Mastered: None.

Fighting Skills:

Will Power Level 5 (10% progress to Level 6)

Resilience Level 5 (15% progress to Level 6)

Observation Level 6 (5% progress to Level 7)

Strategy Level 3 (50% progress to Level 4)

Injury Healing Level 5 (45% progress to Level 6)

Evasion Level 4 (45% progress to Level 5)

Meditation Level 3 (50% progress to Level 4)

Centering Level 4 (40% progress to Level 5)

Berserker Level 3 (75% progress to Level 4)

Fighting Principles:

Unlocked: Marriage of Gravity, Line of Attack, Moving up the Circle, Solid Foundation, Clock Principle, Back-up Mass, Environmental Awareness.

Learned: Marriage of Gravity, Line of Attack, Moving up the Circle, Solid Foundation, Clock Principle, Back-up Mass, Environmental Awareness.

Proficient: Marriage of Gravity, Line of Attack, Moving up the Circle, Clock Principle.

Mastered: none.

Fighting Styles:

Unlocked: Attack, Counter, Evade.

Learned: Attack, Counter.

Training Aids activated: Demonstration, Overlay Training, Corrective Stimulation, Surround Mirror Training, Opponent Training, Realistic Demonstration, Replay Training, Targeting.

A grin spread across Kiriai's face. "It's nice to see all my intermediate moves unlocked and a big chunk of them are even up to learned."

"Yes, you worked hard for those, even though you rarely use the moves in your fights," said Yabban. "Well, except for the parries. Learning all of them will be valuable, especially when you become proficient enough to replace blocking entirely."

Kiriai looked over at Yabban, interest piqued.

"No," said Yabban hastily as she held up one hand. "That is for another time. It would take much longer to achieve than we have today."

Kiriai sighed and looked back to examine the rest of her stats. She scanned the numbers and rifled through her memories. It was difficult to tell how they compared to the last time she'd looked at them, which had been only a week into the initiation month. "So my skills have all bumped up a little, but not by very much. And I've got the three new principles up to learned?" The last came out more as a question.

"Yes, after level 5 in a skill, it takes much more work to improve it further," said Yabban. "Any other questions?"

"Just what secret you will teach me so I can win tonight," Kiriai said with a grin.

Instead of smiling, Yabban gave Kiriai a serious look. "There isn't any secret, Kiriai. You've spent the last month training long and hard as possible, while listening and following the guidance of your trainers. That is and always has been your secret to winning."

The respect in Yabban's demeanor and the unexpected compliment caught Kiriai by surprise. A flush of embarrassment made her look away briefly.

"I'm not really anything special," she said when she looked back up at Yabban. "Fighting is something I have a talent for, and I love it enough to be happy spending every waking minute training to improve."

Yabban stared at her for a moment before giving a small shake of her head. "I disagree. I, or versions of me, have trained many players and you are exceptional—not the perfect trainee, but one who will work harder, with more dedication and loyalty than any other."

Kiriai stopped herself from immediately disagreeing. Yabban wouldn't say something like this lightly, and Kiriai felt obligated to give it the consideration it deserved. She held Yabban's gaze before doing the only thing she could to express herself. She pulled her shoulders back, bent her hands in front of her and slowly, deliberately gave Yabban a deep bow of respect. She held the bow for a long moment as her heart filled with gratitude for the friendship she'd found from this construct that shared her mind with her.

Once she straightened again, Yabban's gaze was intent on her. "Thank you, Trainee Kiriai. You honor me. I didn't anticipate this when we first met."

Kiriai smiled at the memories Yabban's comment sparked. "You left out stubborn in your little list of my amazing qualities. That's probably one of the main reasons we got to this point."

"That is true," Yabban said with an answering smile. "Another competitor, in a game called baseball, Babe Ruth said, 'You just can't beat the person who won't give up.'"

Kiriai stopped and considered the words for a moment. "I really like that, Yabban. Your wise sayings are growing on me."

"I'm glad they are helping," said Yabban. "Are you ready to continue not giving up?"

Kiriai laughed and tipped her head at her trainer and friend. "Let's go. Show me how I will beat Brawler Antei."

CHAPTER FORTY-FIVE

"We don't need any blasted rules to know how to take down an enemy gang. My crew and me have been doing this kind of stuff since before the blast. We'll teach Hokori Hood not to mess with us. We don't need the city founders and their fancy arenas."

— Last known statement by Tiny (Esteban Lopez), scrapper for Baka Hood, Northern Burb. Oath Keepers Archive of Truth, Volume 22

"Yame!" said Yabban.

Kiriai stopped gratefully, letting her hands simply drop as she forced herself to stay upright and suck in deep lungfuls of breath instead of falling forward as she wanted. In front of her, the figure of Brawler Antei returned to an attention stance, calmly waiting for further orders. Kiriai glared at the woman, even knowing she was just a virtual construct.

The requisite seconds after the bout passed, and Kiriai groaned in relief as her tiredness and injuries magically disappeared, Yabban having removed them as she did at the end of every match.

"I think I've done enough practice against her with the Counter and Evade fighting styles now," said Kiriai as Yabban strode across the dojo floor to discuss her progress.

Yabban nodded. "Yes, I think you can finally suppress your instincts to just attack when under pressure."

"Hey," Kiriai objected, but stopped when she saw Yabban's raised brows. "Fine. Maybe I do attack when I'm under pressure, but it's better than running away."

"Not necessarily," said Yabban with a significant look at the dojo floor where Kiriai had just spent the last hours practicing just that.

Kiriai flushed. "Yes. Evade. Counter. Got it."

"Actually, with all your practice between the two just now, you've unlocked the fourth style I hinted at weeks ago."

Kiriai perked up at the proud smile she saw on Yabban's face.

"It's nothing very complicated," she continued. "It's called the Switch style. It just means that you are adept at changing seamlessly between all three styles, as if each one were your preferred way of fighting."

"You mean I've finally practiced enough at Evade and Counter to be convincing?" Kiriai couldn't keep the excitement out of her voice.

"Yes," said Yabban. "And my recommendation is to rely on those two styles through as much of the fight as possible. Save your aggressive attacks for one, maybe two, crucial moments in the fight. This is how the Switch style is used to win a close battle."

Kiriai nodded, doing her best to impress the concept into her mind, into her instincts. There wouldn't be any time to think things through during the fight. Everything had to come without thought, operating on trained reflexes and instincts.

"You and your virtual dojo are priceless, you know that?"

Kiriai said. "You're the only reason I have a chance at winning tonight."

It almost looked as if Yabban flushed slightly as she bowed her head. "Thank you, Trainee. It is truly my pleasure." Then she straightened, eyes serious again. "Now, we need to practice the timing of your pre-cog skill and if possible, level up your principle Back-up Mass to proficient."

"What?" Kiriai said, almost whining. "I thought we were done."

"Training is never done," said Yabban.

"Is that another of your wise sayings?" Kiriai snapped. Her gratitude of moments ago fled at the idea of more training.

"No. It is my saying."

Kiriai stopped and just stared at Yabban. The moment balanced for a pause and then tipped.

A grin spread across Kiriai's face. A giggle escaped, followed by a burst of laughter that eventually brought tears to her eyes. Yabban smiled in response, though there was a touch of confusion in her expression.

"I'm sorry," said Kiriai when she could speak again. "It's an excellent saying and just perfect for you."

"I'm glad I could combine wisdom with humor," said Yabban with a nod. "I would much rather see you laughing than angry. And perhaps a break right now would be advisable. Sometimes I forget how biological beings need time to recuperate to perform at their peak."

"Yes," said Kiriai eagerly. "I'll take a break for lunch and then figure out a way to come back here for at least an hour before the fight. Will that work?"

Yabban nodded slowly. "More time is always better, but I will help you as much as I can in the time you're able to find. Agreed?"

"Yes," said Kiriai. "Send me back. If I'm lucky, Isha already cleaned up the poultices and I can get something to eat."

The brief feeling of disorientation hardly fazed Kiriai as her surroundings spun and blended into flashes of lights and images. Moments later, she found herself lying on Isha's table, comfortably ensconced in a heavy cocoon of warm blankets. It felt wonderful, and her muscles tingled with the aftereffects of the spicy herbs and what was probably multiple applications of the healing wand.

"Ah, welcome back," said Isha in a soft voice. "I'm glad you've improved your meditation skill so much. With everything going on, it is important that you have tools to help you handle the stress."

Kiriai winced at the reminder of her problems. How had she forgotten about Aibo? What if she was being hurt right now?

"Ach, I'm an idiot," said Isha as she moved closer and began unbundling Kiriai from the coverings. "Here you were all calm after meditating and I had to ruin it by reminding you."

"No," said Kiriai with a shiver as cool air hit her skin. "It's all right. Ignoring troubles doesn't help either." She sat up, taking the fluffy warmed towel from Isha with a grateful nod before rubbing herself dry.

"No, but a constant focus on the negative helps no one either," said Isha as she picked up the neatly folded stack of Kiriai's clothes and brought them over.

Kiriai took them and moved with deliberate care to dress herself, still feeling slow from the long session with Yabban.

"Have faith in our crew," said Isha as she helped Kiriai with her tunic. "We all love Aibo, and we will figure out how to get her back. Your job is to focus on the fight, understand? Even I know that your chances drop if you fight distracted."

Kiriai nodded, doing her best to follow Isha's advice. Tomi would find Aibo, and Kiriai needed to win her fight. It was as simple as that.

"Now, I've got to run," said Isha. "I have a few contacts among the fixers that might have information to help us. Get some lunch. Eat a lot of healthy foods, a mix of everything and as much as you want. We'll limit you to something light when it's closer to fight time. Got it?" Isha had moved to the door, her hand on the handle as she looked back at Kiriai, brows raised.

"By myself?"

"No," Isha flinched back, horrified, before she held up a stern hand in Kiriai's direction. "Of course not. You aren't to go anywhere by yourself, at all, ever! Do you understand?"

"But—" Kiriai looked around the empty room.

A look of comprehension flashed across Isha's face as she waved a hand at the sitting area on the other side of the screen. "He is taking you to lunch." Without waiting for a response, Isha slipped out of the door, sliding it shut behind her.

Kiriai stood frozen for a moment.

A rustling sound came from the other side of the screen and someone cleared their throat before asking. "Are you decent?"

Kiriai sucked in a breath. Sento! Seeing him suddenly felt awkward again after she'd kissed Eigo.

"Kiriai?"

She winced, but forced herself to move. "Yes," she said as she came around the screen and faced Sento who stood, his expression concerned as he waited for her.

"Oh, good," he said with relief as his trained eyes scanned her from top to bottom. "You're moving a lot easier. How do you feel?"

A familiar spark flared to life inside her as his eyes roamed over her. She'd just been comparing that spark to how she felt when Eigo kissed her. With an impatient shove, she pushed it aside. She was with Eigo now, and Sento was her trainer. That's all he was.

"Kiriai?" he asked for a second time.

"Sorry," she said, chastising herself for not paying attention. "Just a little slow after the treatment session and meditation."

"Nothing else is bothering you?" he asked as he stepped forward, examining her more closely.

"No," she said with a quick step back. "Isha worked her miracles as usual. Everything is feeling good and in working order."

"If you're sure—"

"Yes," she said as she turned toward the door. "Let's get some lunch."

"You're in that much of a hurry to get away from me?"

There was a note of sadness under the question that stopped Kiriai in her tracks. She turned back around to look at Sento, her first love, her mentor and now her trainer. He stood there, tall and strong, broad muscles that held a power she knew intimately. But under it was something fragile, something that made her want to reassure him.

"No," she said, but then couldn't come up with words to follow.

The silence stretched as neither spoke.

Finally, Sento let out a harsh laugh. "Look at the two of us. When it comes to discussing how we feel, the most we can come up with is a handful of words."

Some tension drained from Kiriai, and she ventured a half smile. "True," she said, purposely saying nothing more.

There was a pause, and when she said nothing more, Sento let out a chuckle. Kiriai joined him.

Standing alone together in the treatment room, for just a moment, all their past closeness, their friendship, their love seemed to echo inside Kiriai, treasured memories that she'd banished to a dusty closet, coming out for attention.

When the shared humor wound down, Sento looked at her intently again, but not with a trainer's eye this time. No, definitely not.

He took a step toward her.

Kiriai panicked. "Eigo and I are doing well together," she said with a stutter.

He stopped moving, and he seemed to back up, even though he didn't move.

"In case you were wondering," she added with a helpless wave of her hands.

A half smile returned to his face and whatever had been there just moments before disappeared. "He has always loved you and put you first." Sento paused and gave a small shrug that might have been aimed at his inability to do the same. "I'm glad to hear that you are happy together."

Kiriai looked at him, eyes narrowed. "Really?"

Sento's expression turned serious. "Regardless of how I messed things up between us, that is something I've always wanted: you to be happy." He stopped and took a small breath before continuing. "And if your best friend who has loved you all his life makes you happy . . . really, Kiriai, I'm glad for you."

He stopped and held her gaze, waiting for her.

She looked at him, the intensity and obvious sincerity in his gaze, and relaxed. "Thank you, Sento. I just—" She looked away, surprised at the sudden emotion that overwhelmed her, unsure of its cause.

Sento didn't move, giving her time to recover.

When she felt more in control, she looked back at him. "That means a lot to me. Thank you."

He tipped his head and gave her the rare smile she'd always loved.

"Then, Brawler Kiriai, would you like to go to lunch so you can stock up enough energy to trounce Brawler Antei tonight?" He gave a half bow with one hand held out toward the door.

Kiriai laughed, happy to feel that perhaps a friendship with Sento was still a possibility. It was one thing for a relationship to fail, but to lose a friendship, too? That was worse.

CHAPTER FORTY-SIX

The rush of pre-fight nerves twisted through Kiriai with the familiar storm of swirling anticipation and dread. It didn't make any difference that they were holding the brawler event in a much smaller arena than she was used to. This was where the powerful came for satisfaction. Intimate sections of seats filled with influential people and their followers surrounded a single arena floor glistening under the focused 'lectric spotlights.

Below, workers and judges moved with efficient haste. Three people in tidy servant attire pushed dry mops across the burnished wood floor, cleaning up after the last fight and preparing for the next. A judge at the timing table inspected and set up the set of timing hourglasses.

One more fight and it would be Kiriai's turn. She had tried to enjoy the unusual treat of being able to sit up in the stands instead of her normal place in the prep areas below the arena. For a few moments during the earlier fights, the spectacle had sucked her in. She'd been busy analyzing the brawlers and predicting their moves and successes. It had been rather fun to be up high and among friends as waves of excited chatter swept through the stands . . . until she looked at the people in the stands with her. Their expensive clothing and powerful bearings were obvious and only reminded Kiriai of how much was at stake on the fighting floor—now and for her and her hood's future.

Aibo.

Her heart twisted at the name, never far from her thoughts.

"We'll find her," said Eigo as he grabbed her hand and squeezed it.

"Will we?" Kiriai kept her eyes glued to the arena, not bothering to keep the hopeless note out of her voice.

"Tomi has leads," said Eigo in a low voice. "And Shisen collected a list of locations Mabbai likes to use for her illicit activities. We just need more time and we'll find her."

Movement in the stands caught her eye. In her peripheral vision, Kiriai watched as two more brawlers in different sections stood and, amid well wishes from their people, made their way through the crowd toward the arena floor entrances. With their crew and equipment following them, the next pair of fighters moved toward the arena floor.

It wouldn't be long now.

Kiriai turned to look at him, and when Eigo saw her face, his features sagged. "Fine," he said, able to speak a little louder now that the crowds' noise was louder. The new fighters ran through their warm-up routines and played to the crowd. "We both know Aibo's chances drop considerably once the fight starts. But Boss Ryuin will have no use for her after the fight. It would be easier for her to just let Aibo go, wouldn't it?"

More than anything, Kiriai wanted to agree with the plea she saw on Eigo's face, but she was sure he knew how unlikely his scenario was. "And keep around someone who can prove that Boss Ryuin gave false witness at a grievance audience? For a brawler's first-fight?" she asked.

Eigo swallowed and looked away.

"Don't give up hope, Kiriai," said Isha. She had been a quiet and reassuring presence through all the earlier fights. Kiriai felt her hand reach from behind and squeeze her shoulder. "Never give up hope," she continued. "We have people out searching everywhere for her, right now. We're doing everything we can."

"But am I?" Kiriai couldn't keep back the bitter words. "If I don't throw this fight? What happens to Aibo then? I can give Jitaku a last chance in the war, but the trade-off is condemning my friend, a kid who has absolutely nothing to do with all these people and their games." Kiriai almost spat the last words as she scanned the crowd arrayed around her. Maybe it would have been better downstairs in a prep area where she didn't have to see all the schemers who cared so little about how their actions affected those beneath them.

"Enough of that," said a stern voice behind her.

Kiriai turned around, surprised to see Mikata and Sento had threaded their way through the crowd to join them. The two moved to take seats in front of her, but sat backward in them so they could face her. Neither looked happy.

Kiriai was afraid to ask the question that pushed inside her, and just looked at Mikata, pleading for good news.

Mikata's gaze flicked away briefly before she gave a quick shake of her head, and Kiriai's heart sank.

"You have to let her go—" Sento started.

"Let her go?" Kiriai demanded, the flush of outrage so strong she barely stayed in her seat.

"Shh, Kiriai-chan," said Isha with a firm grip on her arm and a quick look at those seated nearby.

Kiriai flushed and waited until the curious glances turned back to watching the fight preparations below. The head judge stood poised to start it, and Kiriai hardly cared.

"Obviously, I'm not saying you need to forget about Aibo," said Sento as he leaned even closer, a look of distress on his face. "I care about her just as much as you do. But you have only a few minutes before you'll be down there in the fight of your life." He tipped his head and Kiriai saw the brawlers had already started.

"You know if you're pulled in different directions, you'll lose the battle before you even start."

Kiriai held his gaze, knowing he was right. Then she spoke before she could stop herself. "And if I want to lose?"

Mikata sputtered, but Sento put a hand out to quiet her. With a wry grin and one cocked eyebrow, he looked back at Kiriai. "We both know that isn't you, don't we?"

She couldn't answer and looked away, wanting more than anything to not have to make this choice.

"Kiriai, look at me," said Sento, his tone both strong and reassuring at the same time.

She looked back.

"If there is one thing I know about you, more than anything, is that you fight with everything you have and never give up, no matter the consequences. Right?"

Kiriai gave him a small nod. He had more reason than anyone to know how true his words were.

"And what would Aibo tell you to do, if she were here right now?"

Kiriai let out a sound that was half laugh and half sob. "She'd tell me to beat Brawler Antei and show her what kind of fighters come from Jitaku Hood."

"Then that's what you'll do, what you're good at. You'll win this fight. For Aibo." Sento's voice was low, but demanded a response.

Kiriai nodded before closing her eyes. With a slow and deep breath, she pulled on her determination, her training, and began centering herself. She could still change her mind, but if she didn't clear thoughts right now, that would make the choice for her. As her emotions calmed, she ran through everything she'd practiced over the last month as well as everything Yabban had helped her cram in at the last minute.

Kiriai might have been unimpressed with the initiation month at first, but she couldn't argue with the results. Her conditioning had exploded and being attacked over and over by multiple opponents had done wonders for her awareness and response times. Together with the new principles Yabban had helped teach her, she could beat Brawler Antei. Just an hour ago, Yabban had helped her level up her Back-up Mass to proficient, and Kiriai could still feel the perfection of that moment when her entire body landed simultaneously with a strike.

Don't forget to trigger your pre-cog at the right moments.

Kiriai smiled, eyes still closed, as Yabban's reminder triggered another flood of training memories—the command to trigger her pre-cog, the red flashes of the Targeting training aid teaching her to pick out her opponent's most vulnerable targets by instinct.

You can still coach me during the break, right? Kiriai asked hopefully. Mikata and Sento would provide valuable help, but Yabban knew everything and could pull it all together into the best strategy.

Of course, Kiriai. But based on the information I have, you are more than able to win this fight.

It was exactly what Kiriai needed to hear. With so much out of her control, her trainer still believed she could do this one thing.

Don't forget, a battle does not determine who is right—only who is left.

A reluctant smile crossed Kiriai's face as the words penetrated. *Is that a joke or a wise saying, Yabban?*

Her trainer sent a pulse of humor back at her before answering. *I find it a challenge to combine both. Did it help?*

Yes, Yabban. Thank you.

"That's more like it," said Mikata.

Kiriai opened her eyes and saw that all her people were looking at her. Only Tomi and Shisen were missing. Kiriai took a last moment to send a prayer to her ancestors for their success before she blew out a breath and looked at Mikata and Sento. "I'm ready to win."

CHAPTER FORTY-SEVEN

"The Romans knew how to keep the masses happy. I vote we take a page out of their book. We don't need to bring back the colosseum, but we have the fabricator blueprint for screens, energy beaming components and solar collectors. How hard would it be to televise these dispute fights we've been talking about and kill two birds with one stone: siphon off discontent and entertain at the same time?"

— Founding Matriarch Nancy Reynolds during the Chikara City Organization meetings. Oath Keepers Archive of Truth, Volume 16

"All right," said Mikata, her expression all business. "See the slender judge down there? The bald guy?"

Kiriai looked over Mikata's shoulder, picked out the man and nodded.

"And the dark woman who is scarcely paying attention to the fight?"

Kiriai glanced at the other corner judges. Sure enough, the

woman in the far corner had a bored expression on her face, and her body language radiated a desire to be anywhere else but judging the fight.

"Those are Boss Ryuin's judges," said Mikata when Kiriai focused back on her. "The man is a true ally, but Tomi thinks Ryuin is using some kind of dirt to blackmail the woman. Too bad we couldn't find proof in time to influence her."

"Wow," said Kiriai with a sarcastic half-smile. "So much good news. How can I possibly lose this fight with so much going my way?"

Sento whacked her arm with a backhand. "Stop that. It's not all bad news. Boss Akuto pulled some strings and got both of Ryuin's judges positioned next to each other."

Kiriai's eyes widened at the implication. That would help.

"Yes," said Mikata. "That leaves the three impartial judges positioned together, so if you can make sure they see your best hits, you have a reasonable chance of getting points from them."

"If I position Antei's forward side to face them as much as possible—" Kiriai's words trailed off, her mind already running through the implications and trying to find tactics that would work best.

"Exactly," said Sento. "Just keep switching and moving until Antei's openings face the neutral judges. Plus, there is always the head judge who can weigh in on your side. She will move around through the whole fight and isn't one of Ryuin's plants."

Kiriai didn't bother complaining about adding one more thing to her already overloaded strategy plans. There wasn't time for it. Without a word, she closed her eyes and began visualizing exactly how she wanted the fight to proceed. Her mental vision blurred at high speed as she and an imaginary Antei flashed around the ring, Kiriai maneuvering her opponent to always face the correct judges. Faster than would ever be possible in reality, Kiriai layered on all her other tactics and abilities onto the mental imagery. It wasn't the same as practicing with Yabban in her virtual dojo. Instead, it felt like a high speed puzzle that Kiriai added piece after piece until she was using everything she hoped would give her the advantage she needed to win.

"And it's time for our final fight of the evening, esteemed guests."

The cultured voice filled the arena space, its words penetrating Kiriai's concentration. Well, that, and the sudden squeeze of her hand by Eigo.

"Ouch," she said.

"Oh," he said, looking startled and immediately loosening his grip. "Sorry, I'm just—" He floundered for words, looking so lost for a moment that Kiriai felt bad for not realizing she wasn't the only one having a hard time. Eigo always reassured her, yet she'd barely given his feelings a thought.

She leaned close to him and squeezed his hand almost as hard as he had hers. "We both know I can't promise how this will turn out," she said in a quiet voice, for his ears only. "But I will do everything I can to save both Aibo and our hood, all right?"

Instead of looking reassured by her words, Eigo frowned and clenched his jaw before replying. "How about saving yourself?"

"What? Me?" she asked in surprise, a frown forming as she considered his words.

A bitter laugh escaped, and he shook his head. "Why am I not surprised?" He turned in his seat, his whole body facing her now. "Listen, Kiriai. I care about Aibo and our hood, but there is one thing, one person, I care about more than either of those, and apparently more than she even cares about herself." He lifted a hand up to her cheek. "You. In all of this, will you do me a favor and take care of my best friend, my girlfriend, Kiriai, for me?"

Kiriai stared at him, nonplussed, his words shifting things in her mind. Did he really care that much for her? For just a moment, the arena surroundings faded. Images and memories of their lifetime of friendship and love flashed through her thoughts. Years of taking care of each other scrolled past. Ever since their first meeting as children when she'd driven off his bullies, he'd had a single-minded focus on protecting her in return. It only took a moment, and she blinked before giving him a shaky nod. "Yes, Eigo. I'll do the best I can to come out of this in one piece."

His answering smile was infectious. "Perfect! That's all I need." He pulled her into an exuberant hug that Kiriai couldn't help returning. He leaned back with a grin and then without any warning, he kissed her, a kiss that started soft, but changed enough to distract her.

When he pulled back, she just stared at him, emotions and thoughts spinning.

His smile wobbled at her reaction, looking a little unsure. "For luck," he said. "To help you win your fight."

Kiriai opened her mouth, with no idea what to say, but knowing she had to say something. Why did she have such a hard time with the relationship stuff?

"Brawler Onwa Antei, originally from Mabbai Hood, and Brawler Initiate Dento Kiriai, originally from Jitaku Hood. Will you and your trainers make your way to the ring, please?"

Kiriai had never been more happy to hear an announcer's voice in her life. She might not have the right words, but she could at least reassure Eigo. He was the one taking all the risks in their new relationship. She leaned forward and kissed him back, a quick one that left him staring back at her, a slow grin emerging on his face when she pulled away.

"Thank you," she said softly before she stood and with a conscious effort swept all the emotional stuff away to handle later.

It was time to fight.

The chatter over the previous fight subsided, and eyes everywhere turned to her and Antei as they rose to their feet on opposite sides of the arena. Kiriai didn't hesitate and strode out to the aisle with all the confidence she could muster. Behind her, she heard the noises of her crew members right on her heels. Head high, Kiriai made her way down to the gate and gave the attendant holding it a nod of acknowledgment as she stepped onto the arena floor. Just inside the gate, Kiriai leaned over, pulled off her sandals and handed them back to Mikata. The feel of the cool wood against bare feet triggered a burst of adrenaline and made a fierce smile break across her face. Kiriai snapped her blue belt and tugged her gi top to straighten it before moving toward the judges waiting at the center of the ring.

It was time to see if her training and plans would be enough.

Even after Kiriai reached her mark and took her place, it still took long moments for the fight preparations to finish. It was the calm before the storm, allowing Kiriai a few extra moments to prepare. To her left, her crew was settling in on their stools, and Isha crouched down next to a low table, setting out her supplies. Despite the restriction against healing wands during a fight, Isha could, and had, worked wonders with her tonics, ointments and herbs.

Kiriai held her position, a ready stance with fists held low and forward. Across from her, Antei did the same, her eyes a hard stare focused on something in the distance. It was strange for Kiriai to see her in person. After all the hours spent analyzing past fights and sparring against Yabban's simulation of the brawler, Kiriai felt as if she knew the woman even though they'd never met in person.

That she was in league with Boss Ryuin made Kiriai's blood boil. She expected that kind of plotting from a boss, but from another fighter? How could she live with herself? Kiriai knew that many underhanded tactics went into winning fights, especially important ones, but there had to be some lines a fighter wouldn't cross, didn't there?

A pair of judges finished inspecting the crew fixers and their equipment. The timing judge straightened after positioning the six timers that would regulate the fight—two rounds, three minutes each.

With a wrench, Kiriai pushed all thoughts of intrigue and plotting out of her mind and focused her breathing, in and out slowly to the count of six. A familiar calm swept through her, and she used her visualization technique to imagine the scene from above, herself across from Antei as the judges took their places. The mental image flickered and then combined with the environmental awareness she'd been training so heavily. Her attention broadened, marking and noticing the shuffle of Antei's crew shifting, the rustle of a judge's gi behind her, and the way Antei's jaw muscles tightened on and off as the last moments ticked by.

If only her newly trained awareness were all it took to win the fight. Sadly, at this level, it would take every skill she'd been honing, plus a little luck from the ancestors, to win.

I'm a counter-fighter. I've always been a counter-fighter. That's my default when pushed. I might also occasionally evade. Kiriai chanted the words mentally to cement them in her mind as the head judge walked to stand between the two of them. Neither fighter moved a muscle. After glancing at both fighters, she held out a hand and said, "Bow and shake hands."

Startled for a moment by the tradition few judges still adhered to, Kiriai moved a beat slower than Antei, who bowed and stepped forward with a hand held out. Kiriai took her opponent's grip and felt the strength in her hand. Instead of squeezing hard in some kind of dominance test, Antei gave her hand a firm shake.

They moved back to their positions and Kiriai wondered how much Antei knew.

"Stances," ordered the head judge.

The low rumble of noise in the stands quieted, and a hush fell over the entire space. Spectators leaned forward in anticipation.

With mirrored movements, Kiriai and Antei stepped back into fighting stances, knees bent, poised like two rival predators.

Now in a stance herself, the head judge held one arm up, midway between the two fighters and hesitated, letting the tension build.

Kiriai's attention flicked to the targets on Antei's body, comparing them to where Ryuin's judges stood and what they could see. It was a bad starting position. Antei's forward side faced the wrong way. Not that it mattered. This would be a long fight, with plenty of time for repositioning, especially since Kiriai was playing the role of a counter-fighter for the moment.

Kiriai blew out a sharp breath and focused. With all the stakes hanging on the outcome of this fight, she could hardly believe it was finally time.

"Hajime!"

CHAPTER FORTY-EIGHT

Antei pushed forward with a fast lunge, front hand darting forward and testing Kiriai's defenses. Without bothering to engage, Kiriai danced back and circled to the right, doing her best to switch positions with Antei before a serious exchange happened. A counter-fighter rarely scored, so when Kiriai did, she wanted to make sure the right judges saw it.

To her chagrin, Antei refused to let her dictate positioning and moved with a burst of in-and-out attacking, forcing Kiriai to backpedal and shift to the left so she wouldn't be overrun. Giving up on the position of the judges for the moment, Kiriai focused on what openings Antei revealed with her probing. Staying loose and ready to move at the slightest warning, Kiriai was ready when Antei skipped forward with a low-angled kick designed to stay hidden from view beneath Kiriai's guarding hand. Too bad it was one of Antei's signature moves. Yabban had forced Kiriai to practice countering the sneaky kick until she could do it reflexively, without thinking. And just as in practice, a small area opened up on Antei's torso as her lead hand followed the kick into action. A memory of red color highlighting the target guided Kiriai as she dropped her rear hand to intercept the kick, her front hand high to meet the punch all at the same time as she pushed forward at an angle. Toward 2:30, her thoughts whispered. Both hands tied up with her defense, Kiriai let her weight shift back a fraction so her lead foot could launch off the floor and drive a front kick right into the small opening Antei had left.

Though she'd lost momentum shifting her weight and missed out on engaging her Back-up Mass, Kiriai felt the impact rock back through her leg and hip. Her lips pulled back in a fierce grin.

A pained grunt burst from Antei, and the crowd cheered with surprise. However, Antei, a skilled fighter, pulled her hands in close and skipped back to keep Kiriai from capitalizing on the blow.

Adrenaline surged through Kiriai, urging her to follow. Now! Almost.

Kiriai almost charged after her opponent, knowing that regardless of how well Antei handled the hit, she had to be unsettled, vulnerable.

But that wasn't the plan, and Kiriai wasn't about to ruin a good strategy, at least this early in the fight.

I'm a counter-fighter, Kiriai reminded herself as she forced her fighting blood down and did what every self-respecting counter-fighter would do: back off and wait for the next opening to appear. *One hit at a time. That's how I'll win the first part of this fight. Later. There'll be time for attacking later.*

With a hint of caution and maybe respect in her eyes, Antei circled away, light on her feet and seemingly unfazed by the kick. As Kiriai moved to keep a good angle against Antei, a flicker of movement from outside the ring caught her eye. Sento motioned at her, expression urgent. When he saw her attention, he flicked a hand low, his finger pointing to the judge standing just in front of him.

Kiriai's stomach clenched as she realized she'd failed to keep track of Ryuin's stooges. She replayed the recent exchange in her mind. A sinking feeling filled her as she realized that only the head judge and Ryuin's two judges would have been at the right angle to see it land. Antei's back had been facing the other two, who couldn't see well enough to score the kick.

Kiriai's hands jerked up by instinct, her feet pushing her body to the side faster than she could think.

Antei had capitalized on her small moment of distraction and closed the distance with blinding speed. Unable to completely dodge the attack, Kiriai tried not to stagger as she took a hooking punch with a painful thud into her shoulder. At least it hadn't been her jaw.

Her forearms sparked with pain as they clashed with Antei's. And Kiriai was too off-balance to throw a solid counter. An uppercut flashed. Kiriai jerked her head to the side at the last minute as Antei's fist slipped under her guard. The punch glanced off the underside of her cheekbone, creating an instant flash of pain and dizziness, but much less than it would have been if it had landed on her chin.

Pain was an old friend of Kiriai's. Her long experience with it and maybe her new centering level allowed her to ignore the bulk of it and keep fighting. Still in motion, Kiriai blinked and shook her head to clear it. Her arms and hands still moved as she did her best to parry and counterattack. She refused to give Antei the advantage in the exchange.

Antei kept the pressure on, while Kiriai did her best to dodge and slip through the attacks by the slimmest of margins so she was still close enough to land her own.

A glimpse of Antei's ribs.

Instinct sent Kiriai's hook punch to slam into that perfect pocket.

And she coughed in pain when a knee from Antei barreled into her center.

Back and forth the fight moved. Both fighters spent their energy freely in an amazing display of skill and instinct that drove their lightning-fast actions and reactions. The judges leaned in, intent on following the action, while the crowd was glued to the scene playing out in front of them.

All too soon, when Kiriai dodged back, Antei didn't follow, letting Kiriai disengage and end the long exchange.

Kiriai clenched her teeth, fighting the instinct to charge the woman again. She had to be hurting after all that. How did counter-fighters do this all the time? It was almost as infuriating to play the role as it was to fight one. Kiriai would much rather hedge her bets and throw hundreds of overwhelming attacks than hang the whole fight on one or two well-placed counter strikes. But she did it, facing Antei, whose chest was also heaving. Kiriai's muscles burned and various spots throbbed from taking a well-thrown attack. She wondered who had come out ahead.

The surrounding noise finally penetrated Kiriai's focus, and she realized the crowd was screaming. Many were on their feet, fists pumping in the air. Antei's gaze flicked to the crowds too, and when she looked back at Kiriai with a small smile, Kiriai realized many of them were chanting Antei's name.

Antei?

Kiriai blew out a breath and forced her frustration back where it wouldn't interfere with her concentration. That was another part of the counter-fighter's role. It wasn't much of a crowd pleaser to hang back and pick only the choicest targets to attack piecemeal. Plus, it had been impossible to keep track of the judges' positions during the heated exchange. How many of her points had the impartial judges seen?

Kiriai shook her head and focused on recovering and breathing. These natural breaks in a fight never lasted long. Still moving in a slow circle but keeping their distance from each other, Antei caught Kiriai's gaze. To Kiriai's surprise, Antei gave her the slightest of nods. It was a nod Kiriai recognized, an acknowledgment from one professional to another, one given to a worthy opponent.

While it was flattering, Kiriai hesitated. Sure, she respected Antei's fighting—her cheek's insistent throb underscored that fact—but she couldn't respect a fighter involved in kidnapping Aibo.

But what if Antei wasn't in on the plot? Ryuin definitely had the arrogance to leave others out of planning. If that were true—

Making a snap decision, Kiriai returned Antei's nod. The edge of the woman's mouth tipped up for a moment, and a flicker of hope sparked inside Kiriai.

Then Antei's lazy movements sharpened, her knees bent a little further, and Kiriai knew the short break was over. The fight was on again.

Reversing her movement, Kiriai worked to keep Antei facing the correct direction this time. When Antei willingly moved, seeming to have no concern about the position of the judges, Kiriai's hope that she wasn't involved grew further.

A flashing sidekick started them off again. Kiriai caught it with her elbow, barely keeping it from slipping into her ribs as she pivoted away and focused back on the fighting.

She and Antei were once again engaged in their dangerous dance, Antei attacking and Kiriai evading as she searched for the hint of an opening she could exploit. Antei threw kicks that darted out almost as fast as punches. Pulling on all her speed, Kiriai did her best to keep them from landing, her own punches lashing out at every chance she saw, while her feet pushed her body to move back and forth as fast as possible.

In the middle of another exchange, Kiriai jolted forward, slightly off the line of attack, her instincts reacting faster than her thoughts. A tug at the side of her uniform let her know how close Antei's kick had come to drilling into her torso. Antei's eyes widened as she saw Kiriai suddenly in close, but she couldn't respond fast enough, one leg still off the ground completing her kick.

With a fierce glee, Kiriai threw her lead punch straight at

Antei's face, the decoy doing its job and pulling both of Antei's hands high and tight, leaving just the sliver of an opening front and center between her elbows. Kiriai whipped her reverse punch forward with as much speed as she could muster.

It was a beautiful punch. The full weight of Kiriai's momentum landed with the punch as it smashed dead center into Antei's solar plexus—Back-up Mass at its finest.

An explosive gasp of pain from Antei blew past Kiriai, and though every instinct insisted she rush forward with a flurry of attacks, Kiriai pushed away, darting to a safe distance.

And it was a good thing she did.

Kiriai's eyes widened in surprise, and she leaped further back.

Somehow, despite Kiriai's punch, Antei had summoned enough energy to ignore the pain and bring up a basic but powerful front kick, punching straight out where Kiriai would have impaled herself if she'd attacked further.

Disappointment flickered across Antei's expression as her foot whipped through empty air. The kick seemed to have drained Antei's reserves, and she moved out of reach herself, hands raised defensively and breath ragged.

Kiriai kept her distance and reminded herself to thank Yabban for the training in the countering style. Perhaps it had some advantages after all.

Just as she thought Antei had gathered enough energy to engage again, the head judge's voice rang out with finality.

"Yame!"

CHAPTER FORTY-NINE

"I've always been a good lieutenant to Boss Makara, and she gave me my own little town to rule and even let me name it as long as I picked some Asian-sounding name. I knew being loyal to a strong leader would keep me safe after the blast. Who knows what the future will bring?"

— Personal Journal of Seidai Hood Boss Sparky (Darren Sparks). Oath Keepers Archive of Truth, Volume 19

K iriai flinched at the command to end the round, surprised again.

She hurried over to her mark across from Antei and copied her, both straightening and coming to attention.

"Bow," said the judge with a wave of her hands at the two fighters.

Still a little stunned, Kiriai bowed at Antei before turning to go back to her crew. On her way, a quick glance at the timing table verified that, yes, the last timer was empty, and the judge had tipped the first two on their sides. Kiriai shook her head, disgusted. With everything else she'd been focusing on, she'd failed to keep track of the time. She couldn't afford to make a mistake like that in the final round. It should have been second nature for her to pay attention to how much time had elapsed in a fight.

"Drink this and sit," said Isha, her voice urging haste. Kiriai sat, gulped down the mix of spicy and bitter tonic and held the mug out to Eigo. She refocused her breathing as she felt Mikata reach around from behind, untie her belt and pull open her gi top. Isha's fingers gently explored her face, pausing at her cheek and then pinching a painful spot above her left eye where Kiriai didn't even remember getting hit.

"Listen to me while Isha works on you," said Sento as he crouched down just to her side. "You're holding your own and the counter-fighting is working well. If the judges were fair, I'd say you both came out even this round."

Kiriai frowned.

"Hey, even is amazing. Why do you think the crowd is going crazy?"

"But—"

"Yes, I know we need a win, but holding your own for the first round makes a win still doable, got it?"

Kiriai didn't nod, because Isha was smearing a cool ointment across her eyebrows and forehead with one hand, while another pressed a warm poultice gently against her cheekbone.

"OK, big things first," said Sento. "Stick with your fighting style strategy. Keep up the counter-fighting and even add in some evading style for the beginning of the final round. Do your best to keep Antei facing the right judges. Since she isn't fighting you on that, I don't think she knows about the ones under Ryuin's control."

"Agreed," Kiriai mumbled, trying not to interfere with Isha. The fixer reached out, took Kiriai's right hand and moved it up so she could hold the poultice in place herself. Behind her,

Mikata rubbed a cool cloth over the back and sides of Kiriai's neck, which felt amazing.

Isha pushed up Kiriai's sleeve and began rubbing ointment into her battered forearms with firm strokes. Kiriai sighed in relief as soon as the pain-numbing properties set in. In moments, Isha turned her attention to Kiriai's torso, her skilled hands probing ribs and muscle, working her way down.

Realizing Sento was waiting for her attention, Kiriai focused and nodded for him to continue.

"Then somewhere after the start of the round and definitely once the halfway mark has passed, look for the best opportunity to surprise her with a switch to your attack style. That will decide the fight. She's used to your counter-fighting style now, regardless of what she's seen of your previous footage. That one moment when you charge her with everything, instead of backing off as usual, she'll hesitate, however briefly. That'll be your one chance to land as many points as possible. You've seen how much pain she can handle, so a knock-out isn't likely, but if you can position her correctly and land a lot of points all at once, well . . ." He gave her a tight smile and shrugged. They both knew how small Kiriai's chances were, but she'd been fighting the odds her whole career.

"Got it," Kiriai said, her mind visualizing the end exactly as described by Sento. Sure, they'd both gone over the strategy multiple times before this, but a fast summary between rounds helped with visualizing. And if she could use her two shots at pre-cog correctly, she might just be able to pick the perfect moment.

Kiriai felt cool air on her side as Isha lifted her undershirt. An impatient wave at Eigo, and he was holding it clear while she applied a tacky tincture that gave off a sharp disinfectant smell. Eigo caught her gaze and winked at her while mouthing, *You're doing great.* She smiled back and tried not to wince as Isha attached strips of a stretching bandage to the adhesive tincture in a pattern that supported her sore rib.

The relief was almost instant when she finished and pulled her shirt back down. Kiriai hadn't even realized how much the dull, aching pain in that side had been nagging at her.

As Isha's ministrations moved to her legs, Kiriai gave Sento her attention again.

"And the little things?" she asked.

"Pay attention to her feet," said Mikata from behind her in a soft voice. "If you can see them in your peripheral vision. She turns her front foot just a tad before she kicks off the back leg. With that much warning, she shouldn't be able to land that again."

"And that brings me back to a big thing," said Sento, his expression intense. "You've got so many things you're trying to focus on, you're missing the big picture a bit. Relax your focus and your training will pick up on things like her feet without you really noticing. Remember the attacks by all of us at once? When you didn't have time to think?" He stopped for a moment, organizing his words. "Kiriai. You've trained for this. You have the skills in this body"—he patted her leg—"to beat her. Just let your training work for you. Pay attention to the big picture, but let your training dictate the details, which blocks you use, how and where you attack. Let your instincts and inner mind keep track of the specifics. Does that make sense?"

Kiriai nodded. Without realizing it, Sento had summarized how her environmental awareness skill worked. She resolved to engage it better during the next round.

"Your legs are in decent shape," Isha said as she pulled her pant legs down after treating Kiriai's legs and feet with the same ointment she'd used on her forearms. A quick swipe of a towel made sure that the bottoms of her feet were dry and not slippery.

"Here," said Isha as she took a mug from Eigo and passed it to Kiriai. "One more dose."

Kiriai didn't let the taste linger as she chugged it quickly and held her hand out for a refill of water this time. Eigo took care of that without being asked, and after a last month-cleansing swish, Kiriai stood. With gentle movements, she bounced on her feet and swung her arms loosely back and forth. It wouldn't do to get stiff before the final round. She paced a bit in her space, mind turned inward to her plans for the final round. A sharp whistle from the crowd caught her attention. Without thinking, she looked for the source and her heart skipped a beat when she recognized the man standing among the crowd milling around during the break—the leader of the group who had ambushed her.

She froze, trying to process what she was seeing and the fact that the man had appeared so close to her, only a few rows into the stands.

He brought one fist up and then with a slow motion drew a line under it with his other hand.

Kiriai frowned. What was happening?

He repeated the motion before drawing the same line across his throat, and Kiriai suddenly realized what he was trying to communicate. The image of him pulling Aibo's head back with one hand and cutting her throat with the other was suddenly all too real.

"Isha, Sento," she said, spinning toward her crew, panic in her voice. "That's him. He's right there." All eyes were on her and she turned, arm outstretched, finger pointed, only to find the man gone. In his place, a row of happy fans waved back at her, delighted to have caught her attention.

She turned back to her crew, shoulders sagging. "He was right there."

Instead of disbelief, she saw her fury mirrored on the expressions of her crew. Sento made a quick motion at Mikata, and with a quick nod at Kiriai, the woman jogged toward a tunnel that led to the complex under the stadium.

"Don't worry," said Eigo as he reached out and squeezed her hand. "Tomi and Akuto have people scattered all around here, just waiting for something like this. If anyone can find him and trace him back to Aibo, they can. This is a good thing."

"Really?" Kiriai didn't mean the plea to come out so lacking in hope, but it did.

Sento reached for her but hesitated and looked at Eigo, waiting for something from him.

When he got a short nod from Eigo, Sento turned back and grabbed both of Kiriai's shoulders. "Look at me, Kiriai. Our best people are finding Aibo. That's their job. The one they've trained for. You can't do their job and they can't do yours. Your job right now is to beat Brawler Antei. Our home needs Boss Ryuin's reinforcements, and you're the only one who can get them for us. Right?"

Kiriai looked into his eyes, the strength she'd always admired shining back at her. She sucked in a breath and drew on that strength, that sure knowledge that his way was the right way. It was what she needed at that moment.

Her first nod was shaky. She blew out a long, slow breath and stood up straighter before giving him a much more confident nod. "Right," she said as she pushed everything else aside and let her inner fighter to the front. It had always been the one thing she'd excelled at. Sento was right. This was what she'd trained for, what she was meant to do.

"Positions!"

The judges had moved into their places, the head judge in her center position as she waited for both fighters. The ambient noise of the audience quieted as people took their seats again, and anticipation built.

Kiriai took her time moving into the ring, mentally triggering her centering techniques and sending a delicate touch to that part inside her mind where her gift lived. It moved with familiar strength, built up energy pushing for release. Perfect.

She took her position, and Antei stepped into a matching ready stance. The judge looked up at the crowd and then back to the two of them before nodding.

"Bow and shake hands," she said, following her custom from the start of the fight.

After a quick bow, eyes locked on Antei's, Kiriai stepped forward and returned Antei's firm shake. Then before she could think better of it, she leaned in close and whispered, "You had nothing to do with blackmailing me to throw this fight, did you? With kidnapping my friend?"

Antei flinched back, her face a picture of surprise, followed immediately by suspicion. But before she could say anything, the head judge stepped forward, voice snapping with command.

"Positions!"

Kiriai stepped back to her line and watched Antei's face go blank with the ease of an experienced fighter. Sento wasn't the only one to use mental tactics to give him an edge in a fight, and Kiriai figured Antei had already decided her words were a ruse. It didn't matter, though. Kiriai had her answer in Antei's first reaction. She didn't know.

"Stances."

Unsure how to use the information or if it could be useful, Kiriai took a moment to savor the knowledge that she faced a worthy opponent, not one involved in despicable tactics. Then just as quickly, she pushed the distracting thoughts aside as her body moved into its familiar position, legs bent and fists clenched.

"Hajime!"

CHAPTER FIFTY

Antei lunged forward immediately with a sharp kiai and a lead-hand jab. She almost caught Kiriai flat-footed. Despite Kiriai's earlier question, or maybe because of it, Antei started the round aggressively. Her kicks and punches moved with power and speed, forcing Kiriai to use all her skills just to keep from being overwhelmed. It was a common tactic used against counter-fighters and prevented them from retreating to a safe distance between strikes.

Following Sento's encouragement to let her instincts guide her, Kiriai pivoted on her front foot, her back leg moving up the circle and helping her entire body shift sideways instead of moving straight back. Her front hand whipped out and brushed Antei's punch with the briefest of touches, knocking it off path enough to just miss. But Antei moved so fast that the openings left by her reaching attacks disappeared before Kiriai could take advantage of them.

Even with her misses, Antei didn't stop. She whipped around and came again, though this time she used a few feints, obviously doing her best to provoke and then anticipate Kiriai's responses.

Letting her training guide her movements, Kiriai focused on

the big picture and reminded herself to change up her movements and be unpredictable.

The two moved through more exchanges, neither landing anything of significance. The crowd was making impatient noises, but Kiriai ignored them. Impatience was a quick way to lose focus and possibly the whole fight.

An opening flashed as Kiriai skipped to her left, bobbing through and beneath a wicked combination of three punches. Without conscious thought, Kiriai's lead leg launched a sidekick at the vulnerable spot. Moving even faster, Antei slammed a blocking forearm down just above Kiriai's ankle. Pain sparked and Kiriai jerked her leg back and dodged Antei's follow-up attack, doing her best to ignore the pain when her weight landed on the leg.

A flicker of motion from the timing table caught her eye, and she knew a third of the final round had already elapsed with little change from the first one. Desperation grew, and Kiriai pushed it back down. Eyes narrowed, she searched for another opening, anything. She moved back and forth, dodging and evading. Her feet launched her from one angle to another, avoiding Antei's attacks as she searched for any advantage she could exploit with a clever counter strike.

Crack!

Kiriai's head snapped back. The last hook in Antei's flurry of punches had come in from an unexpected angle and caught her square on the jaw.

Pain made sharp lights shoot through her vision. Kiriai felt her knees almost buckle, the strength sapped from them in an instant, as a perfect chin shot had a way of doing. Suddenly desperate, she sucked in a breath, staggering backward with hands raised, hoping to gain a little distance.

No such luck.

In true attacking fashion, reminiscent of Kiriai's usual style of fighting, Antei was all over her in an instant. Her fists landed into arms, ribs and any part of Kiriai's head she left unprotected. Her body jolted side-to-side under the blows. Kiriai couldn't get away. She had to do something. Fast.

Her thoughts turned sluggish, as slow to respond as her body. And before she could consciously trigger it, her pre-cog came to her rescue. The world slowed around her into a movement that switched from frantic to stately in a heartbeat.

Relief washed over Kiriai, even as she watched two of Antei's punches creeping directly at her face and jaw. She had a moment to think, to regain her bearings, and as an experienced fighter, that was all she needed.

Kiriai's recently trained counter-fighting instincts made her attention snap to the openings on Antei's torso. Antei's eagerness to overwhelm Kiriai had made her just a touch careless. Held under the same spell as the rest of the world around her, Kiriai couldn't do anything to stop Antei's punches as they finally reached her, one plowing in slow motion into her cheek while the other followed into her temple. She forced herself to ignore the ringing in her head. If she wanted to keep from losing the fight in the next few seconds, Kiriai would have to execute her new plan perfectly.

When the slow plodding of time expired and the world around her shifted back in time by seconds, Kiriai prepared herself to move immediately once time restarted. It would be close.

The pitch of the crowd's yelling switched back to normal.

That was her cue.

Instead of moving back, Kiriai dove her head forward on a diagonal, hands raised to deflect the incoming punches moving at full speed this time. She drove her leg forward with all the strength she could muster. Kiriai's blazing roundhouse kick slammed full force into Antei's forward thigh, the one holding all her weight. Antei couldn't move her leg out of the way in time, forcing the limb to absorb all the power of Kiriai's kick. Having been hit by similar kicks plenty of times herself, Kiriai knew how much it hurt. But she didn't stay close enough to find out how Antei would respond. Her opponent's resilience had already surprised her, and she certainly didn't need another surprise. As soon as her foot touched the ground after the kick, Kiriai scrambled away and only stopped when she had reached the far edge of the ring.

There, Kiriai forced her breathing under control.

Antei didn't follow her. In the center of the ring, Antei tipped her head toward Kiriai in acknowledgment as she bounced tentatively on her leg. She shifted her weight back and forth, and shook her leg to loosen the injured muscle. A muscle spasm after a blow like that could easily end a match.

Kiriai returned the nod, wondering what her opponent would think if she learned the facts about the conspiracy. Was there a way to let her know?

Watching closely for another attack, Kiriai pushed as much pain to the background as possible and mentally gathered her energy for a last push. Time was running out. She had to play her last card and switch to a full-out attack the next chance she got. Thoughts whirling, Kiriai rolled her shoulders before she stepped cautiously back toward the center of the ring, tacitly agreeing to engage again.

The crowd roared its approval and for a moment, their enjoyment of the match caused a sour feeling in Kiriai's center. Would they be cheering like this if they knew a young girl's welfare was on the line? That one of their bosses had threatened a fighter if she didn't throw the fight?

She scoffed, the bitter sound drowned out by the surrounding cacophony. It would probably make little difference to them. It was the way of the world they lived in. The strong and powerful got what they wanted. Simple as that.

Antei circled, throwing out feints that were only a tad slower than the ones at the beginning of the battle. It was more proof of how important Trainer Gebi's brutal conditioning regimen was. Without it, Kiriai wouldn't have the energy to put up a last effort to win the fight. Her lips pulled back into a fierce grimace as she sucked in a fast breath and moved, forcing her body to respond as fast as Antei's probes.

Her muscles burned, her arms insisted she lower them, and the dull throbbing in the back of her head made sure she knew how much everything would hurt when this was finally over. She ignored it all, pulling on her Resilience and Centering skills. A pained flicker in Antei's eyes said she was doing the same.

On the defensive, Kiriai moved in her familiar role, slipping under and around attacks, attempting to counter, doing her best to land blows that would score points the right judges could see. Time passed, and as her energy waned, Kiriai knew she needed to predict one of Antei's moves and go with a preemptive counter. And if she was wrong?

Perhaps she could use a ruse to bait Antei into doing something expected? Physical fatigue was something they were both fighting equally, but the mental fatigue was just as severe.

A memory from the first round came to her, and Kiriai immediately worked to set up the half-formed plan. She circled quickly when Antei flicked a probing kick toward her head. She stayed just close enough that Antei would follow. Once Kiriai had her facing the right judges, she pushed back, putting a little distance between them, but not quite enough to be safe.

Kiriai blew out a breath. This was it. She didn't have to work too hard to force a worried expression to flit across her face. Immediately afterward, Kiriai turned her head just enough to glance at the timing table, as if concerned that there wasn't much left.

That was all Antei needed. Like waving a piece of raw meat in front of a starving dog, Kiriai's brief inattention provoked a similar response. Antei lunged forward, the front kick from her rear leg closing the distance in a flash. But Kiriai had been hoping to provoke just this response and was already moving.

Luckily Antei was using the same attack she'd used in the first round, leading with a front kick followed by a flurry of straight jabs and reverse punches. Exactly what Kiriai had gambled on as she lunged just off the line of attack, letting Antei's kick graze by. Kiriai hammered a block into the back of Antei's punch. The block moved Antei's lead arm just enough to expose her ribs with her back hand not close enough to help.

Kiriai tucked her right elbow in tight against herself and let her training guide the blow. The inward elbow slammed into Antei's ribs with a sickening crunch, as Kiriai twisted her hips in perfect time with her body's momentum to increase the power of the blow.

Again, Antei wasn't out of commission. Obviously in pain, she still looked poised to use her speed to disengage and recover.

Now.

Kiriai knew this was the chance she'd been waiting for.

Slow! She gave the mental command as she reached for her gift, holding onto the sense of calm and confidence that would give her the best odds of activating her gift.

For the briefest of moments, Kiriai thought it wouldn't work.

And then for the second time in minutes, the world around her slowed to a crawl, and she felt a vacant hole, empty of energy, where her gift resided.

She had more important things to focus on, though. With attentive eyes, Kiriai watched Antei's glacial retreat, where she placed her feet, how her hands moved, and most importantly, the small targets that revealed themselves. Kiriai marked every vulnerability in her memory. With frantic speed, she pieced together a plan of attack that would exploit the openings. She didn't bother with defense.

If Kiriai could have smiled in the slowed time, she would have. She was finally going on the attack, free to charge after

Antei and do what she did best. All too soon, the crawling movement slowed and reversed, everyone returning to their starting
positions like actors in a play that needed a do-over.

Kiriai strained against the controls of her gift as it forced her
body back into position, her elbow returning to the spot buried
deep in Antei's ribs. Any second now, she'd have her final chance
to win this.

CHAPTER FIFTY-ONE

"An aristocratic government has a lot going for it, and it's
pretty close to what we're doing in our own groups at the
moment. With a few tweaks to prevent unrest and allow for
talent to rise, I think it's our best choice."
— Founding Father Elliot Tucker in the Chikara City
Organization meetings. Oath Keepers Archive of Truth,
Volume 16

Taking her cue again from the pitch change in the
surrounding sounds, Kiriai exploded forward as soon as
her pre-cog let her loose. Her left hand shot up in a tight hooking
punch that came from Antei's blind side while her right quickly
checked against Antei's shoulder. Antei tried to block the
incoming punch, one desperate hand interfering enough to
knock it slightly off course. Kiriai felt the burn as her knuckles
glanced off Antei's temple.

And then, instead of retreating as she'd done every other time
in the fight, Kiriai pressed her advantage.

It could have been the shot to Antei's ribs, the accumulated weariness and pain, or falling into the trap of expecting Kiriai to stick to a script. In that critical moment, Antei's vigilance failed her.

Kiriai took full advantage of it. It was her turn now to drive a fully powered front kick at a retreating opponent.

Antei's eyes widened in surprise, and she hesitated for just a beat. When her instincts finally kicked in, she lurched back, her block moving just a little slower than usual.

It didn't matter, because Kiriai finally let her true nature break free. Her lips pulled back in a fierce battle grin as she charged full-force at her opponent, the carefully planned sequence of attacks flowing out without a thought, her instincts in full control and out for blood. Kiriai's kicks flew, driving Antei back and corralling her when she tried to slip to the side. Kiriai's fists weren't idle either. She hammered a relentless mix of jabs, hooks and driving punches that shot between high and low targets so fast Antei couldn't block them all, especially not after the hard blow she'd taken to the ribs. Kiriai didn't bother blocking Antei's attempts to counterattack. She just accepted the blows, letting out explosive kiais as she tightened her core against the pain and continued to batter forward.

Attacking. Always attacking.

Berserker mode activated.

And there it was. Her whole body filled with a primeval energy that made her attacks escalate even further. And while she had a touch more control than the mindless rage of the earlier stages of the skill, Kiriai gave her inner berserker free rein.

An ax kick chopped into Antei's forward hand, letting the following roundhouse punch catch her on the cheekbone.

Kiriai coughed when Antei slipped a stiff sidekick into her ribs, but pushed forward anyway, the pain a distant sensation that could be addressed later.

With the surreal feeling of trying to keep the Berserker mode under control, Kiriai watched her strikes land, one after another. Even if Antei fought her way free, there was no way she could make up the loss in points that had just flooded to Kiriai's score regardless of where the judges were standing.

Kiriai grunted in pain as one of Antei's signature front kicks caught her just on the edge of her hip and stopped her forward momentum. With surprising speed, Antei launched herself to the side, and Kiriai's burning muscles yelled that she needed a break as much as her opponent did.

The rage inside insisted she continue attacking. Kiriai sucked in a deep breath and forced the fury to acknowledge her control. Like a wave whose power was spent, her Berserker mode subsided leaving her back in full control.

Berserker mode deactivated.

Kiriai's normal fighting skills were plenty to sew up the end of the fight. She still drove Antei back, but worked to pick the best targets so she could conserve the remnants of her energy and avoid receiving any more damage.

Antei backpedaled faster, doing her best to try to escape to either side, but Kiriai's heightened state of awareness seemed to almost predict her opponent's moves and intercept them. In moments, Kiriai had Antei pressed close to the out-of-bounds line. She landed another hard punch. This one hit Antei's arm and slammed it into her chest with a solid thud.

That was the moment Kiriai knew she'd won.

There was a look in an opponent's eyes when they know they've lost. Antei's breathing was ragged as she stood slightly hunched, arm cradled against her chest, eyes still fierce but with an underlying resignation. Kiriai knew Antei wouldn't quit, but she couldn't stop Kiriai's next attack.

A direct front kick would land for points and knock Antei out of the ring, which accrued additional penalties. Kiriai had won.

Just as her feet tightened on the floor and her knees bent, an anomaly in the screaming, waving crowd tugged at her sense of danger. Kiriai flicked her gaze up. There, standing completely still among the chaos raging around them, were her three attackers from the night before.

But it wasn't their figures that made her motion stutter and mouth go dry. No, it was what the center man held in his hands. Dangling from his outstretched fingers was a chain. Even though it was too far away to make out details, the familiar shape of the pointed crystal charm hanging from the chain was easy to recognize. Aibo's necklace!

The moment he saw he had her attention, his meaty hands holding it pulled apart in a sudden powerful movement, snapping the chain, the beloved charm flung violently out of sight.

Kiriai's eyes snapped up to the man's, and she felt a chill even from this distance. His head shook side-to-side in two slow, measured motions.

Even though the interruption had been brief, it was noticed. The crowd screamed for her to finish the fight with a few calls from Antei's fans for her to retaliate. When Kiriai met Antei's eyes, she found them narrowed and suspicious. She shifted, looking for an escape route.

But all Kiriai could think about was Aibo. How could she have forgotten her friend? She'd let everyone convince her to do her job, to win the fight, but that hadn't been her decision.

This. Right now. This was her decision. She stood at a tipping point, able to choose either. The churning emotions surrounding both choices made it impossible. Frozen, her advantage slipping away, she still couldn't decide.

Ancestors! Please! Help me!

With all the desire to do the right thing when both choices promised doom, Kiriai sent a desperate prayer heavenward.

Shh, child.

Mother? Her heart tugged in a completely different way, the soothing presence soaking into her soul like water into parched ground.

You already know what choice to make. Do as you always do, my child. Follow your heart.

But—

You have the answer to this, Kiriai-chan.

Kiriai almost smiled at the touch of frustration in her mother's voice. It resonated with an old memory of a similar tone used when Kiriai had been a toddler.

Look inside and make the decision that will let your heart rest easy, so you won't look back on the past with anguish, child.

Her mother was right. Kiriai knew exactly what she had to do.

In that moment, she felt her mother's presence fade.

No. Stay. Please?

A warm blanket of emotion enveloped her, the feeling of a child wrapped in a mother's arms, safe from everything in the world.

Love you, Kiri-chan.

In a sensation oddly reminiscent of the end of a pre-cog episode, Kiriai blinked and everything around her came crashing back to her awareness. *Maybe the gifts really do come from the ancestors,* Kiriai thought as she backed up to the center of the ring, a feeling of unreality suffusing everything around her.

Antei's eyes followed her, filled with disbelief.

But Kiriai had decided and wouldn't change her mind now.

Antei's stance changed. Her defeat fell away as resolve beat back the pain and exhaustion in a manner familiar to all good fighters.

Kiriai looked into the stands and locked eyes with her enemy. She let all her rage fill her eyes before she tipped her head in a slow nod at the man. Hopefully, he understood her message. If they didn't return Aibo . . .

He gave her an abrupt nod, turned and disappeared from view.

Resigned, Kiriai turned toward Antei and then let her hands sag until they were barely at chest level. Sounds of confusion sparked from different directions in the crowd. Antei moved forward, hands up and face back to her fighter's mask.

She feinted forward, a quick test with a kick and punch.

Kiriai stood still and didn't respond. This would hurt, but she was used to pain.

"What are you doing?" Antei hissed under her breath, just out of range. "Is this a trick?"

Kiriai shook her head, wishing the woman would just take the gift already.

Antei's eyes narrowed. And then she attacked.

It was surprising how fast Antei could still move after all the punishment she'd traded with Kiriai.

The jab rocked Kiriai's head back. She staggered a half step, and both eyes watered. It was hard to keep her hands lowered as she shook her head and met Antei's eyes again. Something Kiriai couldn't identify had replaced the suspicion.

Then Kiriai experienced what the full force of Antei's front kick felt like. Despite tensing her core in anticipation, it was definitely not enough. A nauseating explosion of pain forced the remaining breath from her lungs, and Kiriai had to clench her jaw to keep her cry of pain to a harsh grunt as she flew backward, barely managing to keep her feet.

But Antei didn't follow up. Instead she moved back, just out of reach, and then stopped. Kiriai met her gaze as the other fighter studied her.

"They really kidnapped your friend so you would throw this fight, didn't they?"

The screaming crowd was loud enough that Kiriai didn't think anyone else could hear Antei's words. The final minute of the battle going completely off script had thrown the whole arena into an uproar.

Surprised by the question, Kiriai settled for a quick nod in answer.

Antei glanced around the stands before her eyes found the

timing table where a single glass still stood, almost empty. When she looked back at Kiriai, she seemed to have decided.

Kiriai wasn't sure how to react as she watched Antei mimic her pose, hands dropped to a loose guard position, weight back on her heels, a position that severely limited her response time.

"No," Kiriai whispered harshly as she realized what was happening. "You can't do this. You have to fight. If you don't, my friend—" Kiriai's voice broke before she could finish.

Antei's look wasn't without sympathy, but she shrugged as she shook her head. "I'm sorry. I really hope your friend comes safely out of all this, but you and I are fighters. We don't have a lot of power in all this, but here, now"—she tipped her head at the surrounding arena—"we have to stand against this or we lose everything we are. Understand?"

Anguish warred with agreement at the other fighter's words, and Kiriai didn't know what to do. Her grand sacrifice to save Aibo was being refused. She doubted that Boss Ryuin would care that she'd done her best to throw the fight, and Antei had refused to take the gift. Ryuin would only care about the final results.

"Please," Kiriai tried again. "Just a couple more good shots and you'll win."

Antei shook her head. "I might use deception in a fight and take every advantage I get, but I won't let you hand me a win, especially if someone is holding a friend of yours to force the matter."

The noise in the arena escalated with demands that the fighters do something, anything. Kiriai knew the timing glass had to be almost empty.

Short of running and slamming her face into Antei's fist, there wasn't anything else she could do.

"It's in the hands of the ancestors now," said Antei, circling slowly, hands in a loose guard. "We both landed good shots. I might still win on points."

A small hope grew in Kiriai, and she perked up. "Especially with your two judges help."

Antei frowned, her eyes flicking to the corner judges before coming back to rest on Kiriai. "The judges, too?"

"Just two of the corner ones," said Kiriai with an apologetic shrug. "The stakes are important."

Antei let out a disgusted huff. "They're always important."

The truth of the comment startled a laugh out of Kiriai. After a brief look of surprise, the edges of Antei's lips turned up.

With chaos exploding around them, the two fighters stood like that, smiling as the last seconds of their brutal battle trickled away in a shared moment of camaraderie. When the command came, signaling the decision was no longer under their control, neither of them flinched.

"Yame!"

They straightened before returning to their marks. This time when the judge signaled they should shake hands, a look of true respect and understanding passed between the two women.

The judges moved to surround the timing table to tally the points. From their body language, it was obvious the discussion was heated. They continued to argue and the atmosphere in the arena shifted its anger toward the judges, individual voices calling out, demanding results.

Kiriai shivered with a chill as the heat of battle fell away, and her soaked undershirt cooled. She and Antei stood, identical statues of fighters who had finished their roles and waited for others to complete theirs.

From the corner of her eye, Kiriai could see her entire crew standing, staring at the tableau playing out in front of them with the same intensity of everyone else crammed into the arena. What were they thinking right now about what she'd done? Kiriai deliberately didn't meet their eyes, keeping her gaze up and straight ahead, waiting with stoic silence for the decision.

Finally, the judges finished and broke ranks, the head judge striding toward the two fighters. Neither of the corner judges looked happy, and Kiriai didn't know what to think.

The crowd cheered in excitement, while Kiriai wished the judges could go back to their huddle. She wasn't ready for the decision. If she'd had another charge of pre-cog, she might have triggered it, just to delay the decision for another moment or two. Because right now, before the decision, both Aibo and Jitaku Hood were still safe. She hadn't yet condemned either one of them with her actions.

But time didn't stop. In moments, Kiriai stood in the position that always made her heart beat fast with anticipation. The head judge stood between her and Antei, gripping the wrist of each fighter. Lined up together, the three of them faced the crowd. The noise had quieted to an anticipatory hush.

The announcer's voice prattled on and on, the crowd full of excited whispers.

Kiriai didn't notice any of it. Her entire being focused on the feel of the strong hand wrapped around her wrist and tried to predict its actions. Was the judge's grip loose or tight? For the first time in her life, Kiriai hoped and even prayed that the hand would stay lax while the other lifted her opponent's high in victory.

"And our winner is—" The announcer drew out the last word in a long hiss while the head judge delayed another second longer.

The grip tightened around Kiriai's wrist and, before she could object, jerked her hand high in victory.

"—Initiate Brawler Dento Kiriai!"

Pandemonium erupted in the arena, but Kiriai stood frozen, numb.

She'd won? After everything? All she could see was Aibo's face in her mind's eye and wondered . . . would she ever see her again?

Trust, Kiriai. Trust in your crew. Trust in Aibo.

A desperate hope flared to life at Yabban words.

Did I miss something? Did they find her?

No. Yabban's answer was tinged with regret. *But your crew is as accomplished at their skills as you are at yours. Don't give up. There's still hope.*

Kiriai swallowed and did her best to pretend it was enough.

CHAPTER FIFTY-TWO

"Ancestors curse her!" Boss Ryuin leapt to her feet and hurled the mug of wine across her private viewing box. It shattered in a splash of bloodred liquid and sharp fragments. "Curse Akuto! Curse them all!" Ryuin spun to glare down at the arena floor. Nothing had changed. The horrible image of Akuto's fighting brat with her hand held high in victory mocked her and stoked her rage further until she felt as if she'd explode. She scanned the seats around her, looking for a target, something, anything to relieve the fury that boiled inside her.

None of her people met her eyes, all of them trying to look busy as they packed up supplies in the viewing box. The curtain fluttered as a short man slipped out, his hands full with a basket of food that he'd cleared in record time. Another woman was already sweeping up the shattered mug pieces, a wine-stained rag on the floor next to her.

Even her two guards stood in stoic silence by the curtain, eyes trained straight ahead and refusing to meet her gaze as they focused off in the distance.

Ryuin's mind raced, generating and discarding idea after idea as she searched for some solution to this disaster. There had to be a way to fix this. She couldn't lose her family's factory after coming so close to getting it back after all these years.

And the reinforcements—

Her thoughts stuttered as she almost choked on the magnitude of the disaster. Western Core! Her agreement. Before she could stop herself, she looked around and out into the crowd below for anything or anyone that looked suspicious. Would they be coming for her now? What if they sent their masked man after her? She had to contact them, fix this.

Seeing no immediate danger, Ryuin forced herself to take a steadying breath. What she needed was time. With a little time, she could come up with a new plan, one that still helped Raibaru beat Jitaku as Western wanted.

Maybe she could delay the reinforcements? Send incompetent ones? Something would work. Her clever strategies had always saved her in the past. There was no reason to think she couldn't do it again. But she had to get a message to Western Core. Right now—before they moved against her.

Ryuin's eyes fell on an assistant clerk who was diligently gathering his writing supplies, placing the pens and ink bottles carefully in a wooden case.

"Clerk Toko!"

The man's eyes snapped to hers with an appropriate level of fear that immediately soothed the rough edges of her anger. She still had power. She still had control.

"Yes, Boss Ryuin!" Toko said, looking ready to bolt at the first opportunity.

"Come here and take a message for me," she said, looking around for another clerk. "You," she barked at a younger woman whose name she'd forgotten. "Find our fastest distance messenger and bring them back here."

The slender woman froze and stared.

"Now!"

She jolted and without a word, turned and disappeared through the curtains.

Ryuin smiled. The woman might be new, but she caught on fast.

"Write this down," she said as she turned back to Toko, who sat with a portable desk in his lap, pen poised. A quick glare at the others in the box had most of them moving out of earshot as quickly as possible. Two more servants darted out through the curtains, arms full. Ryuin glanced out of the front of the box. The thousands of spectators attempting to cram themselves through too few exits generated plenty of background noise to cover Ryuin's voice.

Leaning close, she dictated a message filled with doublespeak and codes that should only make sense to her intended recipient, and if she were lucky, reassure her Western Core allies that she could still fulfill her part of the agreement.

By the time she finished, only her guards and the cleaning lady were left. The clerk applied a generic mottled-colored wax to seal the message instead of Mabbai's official orange. Ryuin fished a special seal out of her pouch and pressed it to the message, making sure the clerk didn't get a good look at it. She needn't have bothered, because the man had his head tucked down, busy putting all his supplies away as quickly as possible.

Then another idea occurred to Boss Ryuin, and she held out a hand for the man to stop. The smile on her face was one that everyone close to her had learned to fear. "I need one more message written. This one is to Master Kancho."

Without hesitating, her clerk dug around for fresh supplies. Ryuin watched his complete obedience, and her smile widened. She was still the boss.

"Boss Ryuin?"

It was the small woman who had been quick to clean up the broken mug of wine. She stood just out of reach, head bowed and with a subservient posture that appealed to Ryuin. She held a fresh mug of wine in her hands.

"Yes?" Ryuin asked, though it was obvious what the woman was offering.

"Would you enjoy a new cup before I finish packing the rest away, Boss?"

Ryuin took the mug and then looked for her taster. The idiot had fled with the others, but that didn't mean she needed to be careless. She held it back to the woman. "Take a sip," she ordered, keeping a close eye on the woman's reaction.

She didn't blanch or hesitate at all. In fact, a spark of pleasure lit up her face as she reached for the glass, took a sip and let a quiet sigh of enjoyment escape after swallowing.

"Give that back and clean up," said Ryuin, snatching the mug from the woman's hand before she could drink any more of it. That was expensive wine.

When Ryuin turned back to the clerk, he sat poised to take another message.

Envisioning exactly what would happen to a young girl once Kancho received the note, Ryuin smiled and sipped slowly at her wine, enjoying the exquisite satisfaction in both activities.

Power and wealth together were heady pleasures.

CHAPTER FIFTY-THREE

"K is for Kado Tagami. Founding Father KadoTagami gave us the laws that keep us safe."
— Chikara City Elementary Primer

K iriai kept quiet as she and her crew hurried off the arena floor and through the underground hallways. She had no idea what her crew members were thinking and didn't want to guess. The thought made her miss Aibo even more, remembering the girl's enthusiasm and congratulations for every one of Kiriai's victories. What would she do without her?

No! Kiriai stopped her thoughts from going in that direction. They would find Aibo before Ryuin's goons could do anything to her, and next time Kiriai won, Aibo would be there, exuberant hug and all. Kiriai picked up her pace. They had to hurry. Next to her, Eigo matched her speed.

Perhaps a review of your progress would help distract you.

Not now, Yabban.

Worry is counterproductive. The statistics will help order your thoughts and a review of your advancements may be helpful for any upcoming confrontations as you fight to find your friend.

Running through the halls, her insides roiling with nerves, Kiriai couldn't really argue. Fine. *Pull them up, but make sure I can see through them enough to keep running.*

Acknowledged.

Kiriai blinked and powered through the slight disorientation as words and numbers appeared just to the left of her vision in an overlay that left the center of the hallway clear.

Character Name: Kiriai

Level: Error. Inaccessible.

XP: Error. Inaccessible.

Character Traits: Error. Inaccessible.

Training Statistics:

Beginning Moves: Unlocked: all. Learned: all. Proficient: all. Mastered: Stances **10/12**, Strikes **11/20**, Kicks **16/20**, Blocks **9/10**, Foot Maneuvers **8/8**.

Novice Moves: Unlocked: all. Learned: all. Proficient: Stances **6/6**, Strikes 16/16, Kicks **8/20**, Blocks 4/10, Foot Maneuvers 7/7. Mastered: Stances 2/6, Strikes **9/16**, Kicks **2/20**, Blocks **2/10**, Foot Maneuvers **4/7**.

Intermediate Moves: Unlocked: all. Learned: Stances 2/6, Strikes 12/14, Kicks 14/16, Blocks 10/10, Foot Maneuvers 4/8. Proficient: Blocks **4/10**. Mastered: None.

Fighting Skills:

Will Power Level 5 (**25%** progress to Level 6)

Resilience Level 5 (**20%** progress to Level 6)

Observation Level 6 (**8%** progress to Level 7)

Strategy Level 3 (**75%** progress to Level 4)

Injury Healing Level 5 (**75%** progress to Level 6)

Evasion Level 5 (**15%** progress to Level 6)

Meditation Level 3 (**60%** progress to Level 4)

Centering Level 4 (**45%** progress to Level 5)

Berserker Level 4 (**15%** progress to Level 5)

Fighting Principles:

Unlocked: Marriage of Gravity, Line of Attack, Moving up the Circle, Solid Foundation, Clock Principle, Back-up Mass, Environmental Awareness.

Learned: Marriage of Gravity, Line of Attack, Moving up the Circle, Solid Foundation, Clock Principle, Back-up Mass, Environmental Awareness.

Proficient: Marriage of Gravity, Line of Attack, Moving up the Circle, Clock Principle, **Back-up Mass**, **Environmental Awareness**.

Mastered: none.

Fighting Styles:

Unlocked: Attack, Counter, Evade, **Switch**.

Learned: Attack, Counter, **Evade**, **Switch**.

Training Aids activated: Demonstration, Overlay Training, Corrective Stimulation, Surround Mirror Training, Opponent Training, Realistic Demonstration, Replay Training, Targeting.

For a moment, Kiriai scanned the statistics, her sandals slapping against the stone floors as they navigated the hallways in a rush. Her eye was drawn to some of the figures displayed in darker, heavier letters and numbers.

What?

She looked closer and when she saw both her Berserker and Evasion skills were different, it came to her.

Yabban. Did you do something to mark the skills and moves that have improved since the last time you showed me my stats?

Yes, Yabban projected, her thoughts pleased and a little smug. *Do you like it?*

A half-smile emerged on Kiriai's face. Yabban had been right. Her gaming statistics had pulled her analytical mind to the fore, helping her push her emotional side back. Not only that, her improvements marked all the high points of her recent fight: Evasion and Berserker skills, an improved Environmental Awareness, and levels up in the Evade and Switch fighting styles. Maybe she wasn't that far behind the regular brawlers in skill. Or at least she wouldn't be for long.

I do. The list was getting too long and confusing. Now it's much easier to see my improvements. Thank you for helping me feel a little better, Yabban.

You're welcome. That's what friends are for, Kiriai.

"This is it," said Eigo, jarring her out of her mental conversation. He jogged a quick step in front of her and reached for a door handle.

Kiriai skidded to a stop, her mind fully back on the current problem. They had to find Aibo before Ryuin could whisk her away or hurt her.

Kiriai hurried into the room, just behind Eigo, into a large preparation suite that would have stunned Kiriai with its luxury not that long ago. Now, however, she scanned the room and almost cheered in excitement when she saw Tomi and Shisen already there. Before she could blast them with questions, she noticed Boss Akuto sitting in the largest chair positioned in the corner of the room where he could easily see everyone. Kiriai held her tongue until the last of her crew had entered and secured the door behind them. She couldn't sit down, though, and her feet paced as she flashed a desperate look at Tomi.

But it was the boss who spoke first. "Brawler Kiriai," he said, and then waited until she looked at him. His expression was as inscrutable as always. "Congratulations on your win. Once again, you've done the impossible. I know how much credit you'll give to everyone here for helping. But it was your battle prowess, your punches and kicks, and your pain that earned our hood a fighting chance to keep Raibaru from claiming a territory majority. Without your win, Western Burb would be challenging for Jitaku as we speak."

Kiriai didn't know how to respond. Yes, she was glad that Ryuin would cough up the reinforcements that Jitaku needed, but none of that mattered right now. They . . . she had to find Aibo. Now.

Her distress must have been obvious, because Akuto shook his head and allowed a touch of sadness to show. "It's obvious to all of us what happened at the end of your fight. As Jitaku's boss, I can only condemn your attempt to sacrifice all of us for one girl. But as the sometime beneficiary of your fierce loyalty, I can't argue when you do exactly what you've always done."

Impatience surged in Kiriai, a moment away from overriding her common sense, which tried to keep her from antagonizing those more powerful than her.

"Besides, it's the results that matter, not your intentions at the end of the fight. I'll keep Ryuin's family factory, and she is now obligated to provide scrappers for an entire year. Plus"—he held up a hand as others stirred, obviously having concerns —"the chief and I have plans in place to forestall any attempts Ryuin makes to wiggle out of the deal. The other bosses are sending a sensei each to verify the abilities of the scrappers Ryuin provides. The chief will have transports and 'forcers on her doorstep as soon as graduation is over on Monday to ensure the new scrappers all arrive in Jitaku before Tuesday's battles."

Kiriai heard a few relieved noises from others and had to admit that Akuto, or probably 'Ranger Tomi on his behalf, had set up effective strategies to ensure Jitaku had a fighting chance. But Akuto's words about the results crushed what little hope she'd had that her attempt to throw the fight at the end might sway Ryuin to have mercy on Aibo.

"But—" The word slipped out before she could stop it, and

even though she clamped her mouth shut, everyone in the room had to know exactly what she meant.

Tomi lifted a hand toward the boss, and when Akuto nodded, he turned to Kiriai. "Kiriai, none of us have forgotten Aibo." He shook his head, his expression so fiercely protective that it boosted Kiriai's hope regardless of how slim Aibo's chances had to be now. "Not for a second. Every moment you've been training, every punch and kick you've thrown, we've been using our skills to find that girl and bring her home safe. Understand?"

Kiriai blinked back tears and nodded, her voice suddenly too choked to answer.

"Want to hear some details, now that you've done your job and won the fight?" Tomi's smile was contagious as always, despite the grim situation.

Kiriai sniffed and returned his smile, finally feeling calm enough to stop pacing and sit down. "Yes. Tell me what to do." Kiriai forced herself to tamp down the fighter's rage that tried to flare back to life. She wanted to just start wading through enemies with her fists until she got to Aibo and saved her.

"All of our contacts are watching Ryuin, her headquarters, her people and everyone associated with her." Tomi stopped and indicated the other crew members. "Mikata has trainers in Ryuin's dojo who are watching for any sign of Aibo or suspicious activity. Shisen has informants, both paid and not, who are watching for signs of messengers being sent to or from the boss herself. Eigo has a slew of children who think it's a game to keep track of the *bad lady* and her people."

Kiriai's eyes shot to Eigo, alarmed at the idea of children spying on Ryuin.

"Hey," he said, hands raised defensively. "They have strict instructions to only report information back to me, no active spying."

"And you pay them? Kids who suddenly have money can come under just as much suspicion," Kiriai said.

"No. Of course not," Eigo said, his expression so serious, Kiriai instantly regretted her accusations. "I would never put children in danger like that. I share sweets with them at a story time during my lunch hour in the park. It's open to all children and is a regular occurrence that everyone is used to now."

Tomi cleared his throat, and Kiriai mouthed the word *sorry* to Eigo before turning back to the 'ranger.

"Isha is friends with one of Ryuin's assistant fixers who is happy to complain about his employer. And I have been able to plant a few well-placed people in her organization. She makes it easy with the way she treats her underlings. There is enough turnover and discontent to glean a lot of information."

"Including where she's holding Aibo?" Kiriai couldn't keep the hope out of her voice.

"Not yet," said Tomi, his tone making it clear how unhappy he was about the fact. "She is keeping Aibo and her location known only to herself and her most loyal followers. But with your win, Ryuin's entire organization will be in as much chaos as a kicked bee's nest. One of the first messages she will send will be—" Tomi stopped speaking and his jaw clenched.

"—orders to get rid of Aibo," Kiriai finished for him, her words ringing into a deathly silence in the room full of determined people all itching to turn their abilities on their enemy.

"And that messenger will lead us right to Aibo," said Shisen as she stood and, with an impatient glance at the door, paced in similar fashion to Kiriai only moments earlier.

"And my 'forcers will be seconds behind the messenger," said Boss Akuto, his icy tone promising repercussions against Mabbai.

No one spoke the question they all had to be thinking.

Would they be in time?

CHAPTER FIFTY-FOUR

Aibo had always been afraid of Boss Akuto, and though she hadn't said anything, she felt a touch of awe at how brazenly Kiriai interacted with the powerful man. She even argued with the boss when she felt it necessary.

Now, however, after being confined in such proximity to Boss Ryuin, Aibo had a new appreciation for Boss Akuto. His pragmatic power was better, by far, than the caprice, cruelty and just plain evil of Ryuin. Her true nature was obvious by how she treated everyone around her, but Aibo saw an even worse view of the woman. When Ryuin was close by or her thoughts were particularly strong, Aibo had to suffer the woman's horrible thoughts popping into her mind.

Aibo shuddered. Even if she got out of this, she'd never forget how that woman made her feel. Aibo clenched her jaw as she glanced around the small space that had become so familiar to her. It wasn't much, a simple room crowded with just a lumpy bed, chair and table holding a small washbowl. They'd pushed a narrow wardrobe against the back of the room. A tiny window sat above it, high and out of reach even if she'd been able to squeeze through it. But still, she looked up at the window, letting the narrow beam of light nourish her hope. The window might just help her escape. Aibo had a plan. It wasn't a grand and amazing plan like the ones Kiriai came up with. But if she were lucky and the ancestors smiled down on her, she might just be able to stay alive when Ryuin's people came to get rid of her.

The thought made her heart pound, and Aibo's breath sped up. Was this how Kiriai felt all the time fighting in the arena? How did she stay calm?

Just thinking of Kiriai helped, and Shisen. Sitting in the hard wooden chair, Aibo focused on her mentors and the things they had taught her. Concentrating on calming down, Aibo forced herself to take a few long, slow breaths. It helped. At least some.

The problem was that time had run out. Today was the fight. Ryuin's gleeful thoughts had been right up front where Aibo couldn't avoid them as the boss had come in to gloat one more time. The hateful woman hadn't even bothered to lie when she'd told Aibo her fate whether or not Kiriai threw the fight. That more than anything made Aibo sick to her stomach. What if Kiriai threw the fight, condemning Jitaku, only to have Ryuin refuse to honor her side of the bargain? Knowing Kiriai, that outcome would haunt her forever.

A sense of determination swelled inside Aibo. She took another calming breath before standing and moving to the door. With all the stealth of a mouse, Aibo stood and listened as the minutes ticked by. She would stay until she could identify everything happening in the room beyond hers. Now was not the time to rush and risk ruining her only chance.

Her bare little room sat right off Ryuin's own bedroom suite, the door between them barred and guarded night and day. In the normal course of events, Ryuin's personal maid lived here, always available at her boss's beck and call. Before she brought Aibo there, Ryuin had fired her maid and pretended to deliberate about a new one, even interviewing a few prospects for appearance's sake.

Listening for sounds from the suite, Aibo only heard silence for the longest time. Finally, just to the left of the door, she heard a familiar shuffling noise right where she expected it. 'Forcer Shikko was diligent and never left his post, even when no one was around to watch him. It was probably a good survival tactic when working for Ryuin, who was quick to punish even the slightest error.

Another few breaths, and when Aibo was sure there was no one else in Ryuin's suite on the other side of the door, she turned back to do a final check and make sure she had everything she needed in place and ready. As she moved quickly through the small room, part of Aibo hoped she wouldn't have to implement her plans. Her practical side had forced her to plan an escape, however low the chances of success. And that same pragmatism told her no one would rescue her.

Aibo was sure Kiriai and the crew were doing their best to find her. But only three people had seen Aibo during her entire captivity, which made it practically impossible for her friends to figure out where she was being held. And even if they did, how would they ever be able to penetrate Ryuin's inner sanctum, much less before Ryuin got rid of Aibo?

No. Aibo needed to act as if no one was coming. If she wanted to make it out of this alive, she needed to save herself.

A muffled sound through the door made Aibo flinch and then hurry to put everything back in place.

M. Sukuna was early with her meal!

Aibo pursed her lips and forced herself to breathe slowly as she finished up, her hands shaking with nerves. She scrambled across the room and made it into her chair, just as the door to her room slid open and the matronly figure of Sukuna bustled in.

"Ach, honey. I'm so sorry," she said, a kindly look of concern on her face as she walked into the room. "Try not to worry so much. I'm sure your brawler will get you out of here soon enough."

Aibo gave her a wan smile, though she wanted to object to what they both knew was a lie. The older woman moved into the room with more agility than her bulk would suggest. She wore a dress of simple lines made of an expensive fabric that hinted at her position in Ryuin's household.

"Now, I brought you a surprise today," she said as she moved the washbowl to the side and set the meal tray down. With a little flourish, Sukuna pulled the dome away, revealing a plate piled with colorful food that gave off a delectable aroma. There was even a small dessert plate with four bite-sized selections of pastries.

Aibo stared at the tray. Even as her mouth watered, her heart sank. There was only one reason for Sukuna to be early and with such a feast.

"What?" Sukuna said, disappointment filling her face. "I thought you'd like it."

Aibo looked up at the woman, unable to hide her feelings. "How can you work for that woman? How can you do this? You know exactly what they have planned for me, don't you?" Aibo's voice rose and her control slipped. "That's why you brought me all these treats!" In a surge, Aibo hit the tray and flung all the carefully prepared food into the wall. Vegetables, rice and sauce stuck to the wall while the tray and plate banged to the floor with a loud clatter.

"What's going on?" The door to the room slammed open and 'Forcer Shikko charged in, a metal rod poised in his hand, eyes searching for danger.

"It's all right, 'Forcer Shikko," Sukuna said with a smile as she stepped forward, both hands out and making soothing motions. "The girl is just feeling a tad upset. You understand, don't you?"

Shikko didn't back up, his gaze taking in Aibo, the mess of food, and Sukuna's expression. Finally he gave a gruff nod, and Aibo thought she saw a touch of sympathy in his eyes. "See that you get this cleaned up before the boss gets back, all right?"

"Of course," said Sukuna with quick agreement. "No one will be able to tell we spilled anything."

Shikko grunted and then spun on his heel, sliding the door closed behind him with a lot more care than he'd opened it with.

M. Sukuna gave Aibo a disappointed look before turning to clean up the food without a word.

Aibo felt a surge of guilt that she immediately tried to push aside. She was the one being held prisoner here to blackmail one of the best fighters and best people in all of Southern Burb.

"She wasn't always this bad, you know."

Aibo looked at Sukuna in surprise. She still had her head down, cleaning.

"It was my first job as an adult. They hired me to help take care of her when she was young." Sukuna looked up now, a soft smile on her face as she reminisced. "She had such fire in her, determined to take on the world and make a place for herself in it." With a small shake of her head, Sukuna turned back to her cleaning. "I don't know when she took the wrong path to become what she is now."

Sukuna's words gave Aibo a different view of the woman. Of course it would be hard to turn on someone you'd cared for as a child. But still.

"And now? How can you support what she is doing now? To others and to me—" Aibo's words choked in her throat as her own very real danger crashed down on her again.

The woman didn't answer or even look up. Aibo wanted to yell at her, demand answers, force her to help. But the 'forcer just outside the thin door made her keep her voice calm. If she could persuade the woman to help her, she'd have a much better chance at escape than the shaky plan she'd come up with.

Keeping her voice as calm as possible, Aibo said, "Sukuna, it's not too late. You could help me. Boss Ryuin and all her most powerful people are at the arena right now. If I could get free before they get back—"

"No," Sukuna interrupted her, one hand making an abrupt chopping motion.

"But—" Aibo couldn't help herself. She thought she'd been close to convincing the woman.

Sukuna stood, the tray and all the spilled contents piled in a mess on top of it. Whatever kindness had been in her expression had fled. Now, she just looked cold and resigned. She started to speak, but then stopped, clamping her mouth shut again.

Aibo kept quiet as she watched the woman struggle with something. Maybe she would change her mind?

"I don't just obey Ryuin because of an old fondness, you know," Sukuna finally said. Now there was a bleakness in her eyes. "Both my son and daughter work for the boss, too. In different places. Far from me."

It didn't take a genius to realize how Ryuin kept control over the woman.

"She lets us visit twice a year though," Sukuna said, and Aibo watched the woman gather up the remnants of her control and put herself back together. The kind smile and even the sympathy was back. "I'm sorry you didn't get to enjoy the nice meal. It's truly all I could do to help you." Sukuna gave Aibo a helpless shrug. "This is the world we live in, and there's only so much we can do."

With that lame excuse, Sukuna turned and left. The door slid shut behind her with a depressing finality.

The aroma of wonderful food still hung in the air, and Aibo had a pang of regret that she hadn't eaten. Regardless of how things turned out, Sukuna wasn't wrong. A nice meal might have soothed her nerves.

CHAPTER FIFTY-FIVE

"Have you given our idea of a voting block some thought?
Our goals for Chikara City seem to be compatible."
    — Memo from the Tagami siblings to Elliot Tucker. Oath
Keepers Archive of Truth, Volume 17

"What in the world is happening?" Kiriai whispered from behind Tomi, doing her best to stay back when everything inside her demanded she rush forward and find Aibo. Honestly, the only thing keeping her back was that she didn't know where to find her friend in the extravagant building in front of them. The Mabbai Hood Embassy towered over the nearby buildings, surrounded by a high wrought-iron fence and sharp-eyed 'forcers guarding the gates.

Kiriai and her group stood a half block away from the gates, watching and giving Akuto's 'forcers a chance to get in first. They weren't having much luck as frantic people exited the building and hurried out of the gates. And the 'forcers were refusing entrance to everyone, some waving tokens and papers to be allowed to pass. The line in front of the gates grew, people impatiently shifting in place, heads craning for a view past the gate. Too bad there were so many Mabbai 'forcers at the gate. Otherwise, Akuto's 'forcers would have already forced their way inside. As it stood, the Mabbai 'forcers were holding their ground, expressions grim and unyielding.

"I don't know." Tomi finally answered her question as his eyes scanned the scene in front of him, taking in every detail. "Something big just changed, and it can't have anything to do with your arena win. That was almost an hour ago."

Kiriai's heart pounded like it did just before a big fight, but the sick worry wasn't something she was used to. Others usually worried about her, not the other way around. It was horrible. She stepped forward. If something bad was happening inside the embassy, she needed to get in there now. Even a minute could make the difference. It didn't take much to imagine Ryuin's people with instructions to dispose of anything or anyone incriminating in an emergency.

"No," Eigo said, grabbing her hand. "The boss's 'forcers need to clear the way first. They've got the messenger we caught and the chief's writ of permission to secure and protect Jitaku's winnings."

"Just another few moments," Tomi said as he reached out and patted Kiriai's shoulder. "Take a look. The Mabbai 'forcers are wavering. They know ours have the power of the chief behind them. They just need to make an objection for show."

"We will find her," said Eigo. He paused and added in a low voice, almost as if he were talking to himself, "We have to."

"Now. Follow me," said Tomi as he straightened and strode forward with that confident air that seemed to make doors just open up in front of him. Kiriai sucked in a breath, scrubbed the back of her hand across her eyes and followed him, doing her best to mimic his confidence. It was just the three of them. The others had scattered to follow other leads. Some were chasing

down other messengers, searching different locations including
Boss Ryuin's home. Isha's fixer friend had been more than willing
to sneak her in as an assistant to search for Aibo once he'd heard
the whole story.

But this was where she was most likely to be. At least that's
what Kiriai kept chanting inside her head. This was Ryuin's
center of power in Southern Burb and where she had the most
protection against intrusion, even by the chief.

"'Forcer Heta will accompany you to our barracks so you can
monitor the scrappers that belong to you now," a grim faced
'forcer was saying to Akuto's men. "You don't have permission to
be in any other part of the embassy, understand?"

"Once we deliver this messenger to his destination, we will
head to the barracks as instructed," said the leader of Akuto's
men before he started forward, his grip still wrapped around the
tunic of the unfortunate boy he'd caught darting away from Boss
Ryuin's entourage at the arena. It hadn't taken much to get his
destination from him.

"No!" said the Mabbai man. "We'll take the messenger, and
you can go straight to the barracks."

Both groups of 'forcers stopped moving, and the tension
between them ratcheted up, hands reaching for the butts of
weapons. Kiriai's fighting instincts flared to life and without
thinking, she began scanning for strengths, weaknesses and
angles of attacks.

Tomi ignored it all and walked right into the mess, his bulk
and big smile working equally to part the way in front of him.

"Why, thank you and your fine men for doing such a good job
of securing your embassy," he said with a tip of his head toward
the Mabbai men in their orange-accented uniforms. "As Jitaku's
head 'ranger, it isn't every day I get to see such professionalism.
What do you think, 'Forcer Hageshi?" Tomi looked at the man at
the head of his own 'forcers, eyebrows raised. "Top-notch 'forcers
Mabbai has here, don't you think?"

The scowl on 'Forcer Hageshi's face had relaxed as soon as he saw Tomi walk up. Kiriai wasn't surprised that Tomi knew the man's name. The jovial red-headed man was well known at home for soothing tempers and resolving disputes.

'Forcer Hageshi tipped his head with respect. "Yes, 'Ranger. Boss Ryuin should be proud of these 'forcers," he said with a wave at the men and women arrayed to block his entrance.

"And who is this young man?" said Tomi with a touch of surprise on his face as he looked down at the small waif. The messenger in his worn tunic looked as if he'd rather be anywhere else in the world than right in the middle of two opposing groups of 'forcers.

"Um, Denrei's me name, 'Ranger, sir," the boy stuttered out.

"I'm sure you have a very important message there in your pouch," said Tomi, pointing at the thin leather item strapped across the boy's chest.

Denrei's hands moved in a protective gesture over the pouch. "I'm a Mabbai messenger. No one can touch my pouch. It's the law."

Tomi straightened with a soft chuckle and reached out to place a gentle pat on the boy's shoulder. "Of course you are. And none of us would dream of interfering with your message, would we?"

Kiriai stared in fascination as almost every head around Tomi bobbed as if on cue.

"In fact, young Denrei, I am on my way to visit the esteemed Boss Ryuin myself, so I'll tag along with you while you deliver your message."

"But my message is for Master Kancho, not the boss, sir."

Tomi didn't even bat an eye at the crucial information, merely placing an arm around the boy's shoulders and turning back to the guards.

"I understand your reluctance to let strangers inside with whatever situation has disrupted your embassy, so I'll send my 'forcers directly to your barracks. They won't make a single detour, and I would ask that you send one of your 'forcers with them as a guide so they don't get lost. Would that be acceptable?"

The Mabbai 'forcer looked surprised as Tomi gave him exactly what he wanted, including a *guide* to ensure none of the Akuto group did any snooping.

"But the boss isn't here and now we don't know—" The man clamped his mouth shut as if he just remembered that he was speaking to the head 'ranger of his boss's enemy. "She isn't in residence, sir, and I can't say when to expect her."

Tomi pursed his lips and seemed to consider the situation. "I don't think my errand from the chief can wait. If it is suitable to you, I and my two assistants here will accompany this young man to deliver his important message to"—he rubbed his chin as if searching his memory—"Master Kanchee, wasn't it?"

"Master Kancho, sir," said the boy, correcting Tomi's pronunciation.

"Ah, of course. What I wouldn't do for the memory of my youth," he said with a smiling look that invited both groups of 'forcers to chuckle at his expense. The relaxed stances and half-smiles were quite a contrast to the bristling confrontation of only moments before.

"After helping young Denrei here, we'll go straight to Boss Ryuin's reception area and wait for her arrival. Please let her know that we're waiting." Tomi reached into his pouch and pulled out an official-looking document, the pure white wax of the Chief's seal drawing every eye close enough to catch a glimpse. "I'm sure she'll want to see this note from Chief Kosui as soon as she arrives."

Whatever objection the Mabbai 'forcer had been considering seemed to disappear, and his head bobbed in respect as he stepped aside, motioning for his underlings to do the same.

And just like that, 'Ranger Tomi, Kiriai and Eigo walked into the Mabbai Embassy, accompanying the messenger they hoped carried Ryuin's message with her plans for Aibo.

The trio entered through two ornate doors twice the height of a man, flanked by two 'forcers who ignored their presence, eyes fixed straight ahead. The luxurious entrance and vaulted ceiling barely fazed Kiriai as her eyes scanned the lavish staircase and the various hallways leading away from the foyer.

"I know my way from here, sir," said the boy as he moved off to their left.

Thankfully, Tomi seemed to have been expecting something of the sort and grabbed the boy's tunic to pull him up short.

"No, young Denrei. My word is my bond. When I say I will do something, I follow through. Who would ever believe a 'ranger that didn't?"

The boy considered the words for a second before nodding with resignation. He was probably thinking of how much slower Tomi and his assistants would make him.

"Let's go then, my young friend," urged Tomi, and this time the boy's eyes widened in surprise as the large man took off at a fast walk that left everyone flatfooted. Denrei grinned, and in no time the four of them were winding through hallways until they came to a back staircase. A quick climb without seeing anyone, and they came to a halt in front of an unpretentious door somewhere in the dusty back rooms of the embassy.

Tomi grabbed the boy's hand just before he knocked. "Let's surprise Master Kancho, why don't we?"

The boy's face blanched at the idea, and his obvious fear made Kiriai hope that this was the man Ryuin used for her darker deeds.

Kiriai held a hand up as she looked up and down the hallway to ensure they were alone. When she saw no one, she nodded at Tomi.

With a swift movement, he slid the door open and walked in,

his voice already booming. "Master Kancho, we are here with an important message from your boss—"

Tomi stopped talking mid-sentence, and Kiriai's heart jumped into her throat. She lunged around the large man, ready to face whatever threat the office held.

Instead of a dangerous master, Kiriai saw a matronly figure smiling at them from behind a receptionist desk. Behind her, the door to a luxurious but empty office stood open for everyone to see. A lump of dread sank inside Kiriai. They were too late. How would they find Aibo now?

"I'm sorry, but you just missed Master Kancho," said the woman, her eyes moving to the messenger boy, who was dancing from foot to foot with impatience. They probably paid him by the job, and the faster he completed them, the more he earned. "Young man, if you'd like to leave your message here for him, I can sign your log."

"Yes, ma'am," he said, and then snuck around Tomi without an apologetic look at the large 'ranger.

"I'm sad to have missed him. I'm on my way to visit Boss Ryuin next, but she hasn't arrived yet. Is Master Kancho somewhere close by so that I could visit him on my way?" Tomi gave the woman one of his wide smiles, and she visibly softened.

"You're in luck, sir. Master Kancho is heading to the boss's personal quarters himself. You should be able to speak to him there."

"The boss is back already and asked for him?" Tomi's voice had just the right amount of surprise.

"I don't think so," said the receptionist, her words slow and brows drawn together in puzzlement. "The message he just received wasn't an internal one." Her brows relaxed, and she smiled. "Maybe she instructed him to wait for her return, just as you're doing."

Without another word, Tomi spun on his heel and darted into

the hall to snatch the sleeve of the messenger boy before he could disappear.

"Thank you," said Eigo over his shoulder as he followed Kiriai out in a rush not to lose Tomi.

"You can keep it all if you get us to your boss's personal quarters in the next five minutes," Tomi was saying to the boy, his tone urgent.

The boy's face lit up at however many credits Tomi had pressed into his hand, followed immediately by concern.

"You just have to get us there and point out the room. Then you can disappear and we'll do the rest, all right?"

The boy nodded and spun away. "This way." He waved at them to hurry before he turned and loped back toward the front part of the embassy.

Kiriai ran after the boy, Eigo right on her heels. Tomi waved her on, no match for the speed of youth. "I'll be right behind you. Do what you can for her and delay until I get there."

Kiriai waved a hand in acknowledgment, her focus already on not letting the boy out of her sight. Her breath whistled through her teeth when the boy bounded up three floors on the gaudy staircase with a wide grin and hardly any effort. The final hallway this time was much nicer. A patterned wood floor inlaid with intricate designs slid smoothly under her sandals while small tables holding vases, statues and other artistic pieces shouted to visitors that this was the residence of someone with wealth and power.

Halfway down the hallway, the boy slid to a stop. "I don't know where the guards are that are usually posted here, but this door is the boss's office and that one is her entertaining suite." Denrei pointed at two large doors on either side of the hall framed with decorative molding. "Those two big doors at the end of the hall are to her private rooms here at the embassy. She doesn't let anyone back there." When he finished speaking,

Denrei looked back at Kiriai, eyes hopeful. Kiriai was already hurrying toward the end of the hall.

"You did well, Denrei. Just find 'Ranger Tomi and point him in the right direction and you can keep the credits he gave you, all right?" Eigo said before hurrying to catch up to Kiriai.

"We can't just burst in on her, Kiriai. This is a boss we're talking about. What do you think Boss Akuto would do to someone who barged into his private rooms without permission?"

Kiriai ignored him, only stopping when she came to the doors. She glanced back and saw the hallway was still deserted despite marks on the floor indicating Ryuin usually had guards posted here. Where were they all?

She held Eigo's gaze for a moment. "If Aibo is behind this door, I will get her out. That's all I care about right now. Understand?"

Eigo examined her for just a second before he shrugged and gave her a wry smile. "And I'll be right behind you. You can count on me. Always."

She smiled back, but it was a sad one. Both of them knew how little chance they had of finding Aibo in one piece. But that didn't mean they wouldn't try.

With a curt nod at Eigo, Kiriai grabbed the handle of a door and jerked it open as fast as possible. Maybe surprise would help even the odds.

CHAPTER FIFTY-SIX

K iriai burst into the richest bedroom suite she'd ever seen. The space was large enough to fit an entire home, with enormous rugs and curtained walls adding to the wealthy feel of the space. A lavish sitting area with fancy cushioned furniture lay directly ahead while an alcove farther into the suite split off to the right with the foot of an enormous bed just visible.

And it was completely empty.

Eigo bumped into Kiriai from behind as she stopped and stared, eyes searching for Aibo, someone . . . anyone.

But Boss Ryuin's suite was deserted.

Hopes sinking, Kiriai turned to Eigo, at a loss. He gave her a hopeless shrug and turned to look back into the hallway.

Still empty.

"Where is she?" The bellow made Kiriai spin and search for the source in the empty suite. How could they have missed someone? Was the voice coming in through a window? And *she*? Did that mean Aibo?

The booming voice had come from somewhere on the other side of the sitting area. Holding one finger to her lips, Kiriai motioned for Eigo to follow her as she crept forward, eyes searching.

"You had one job! ONE! And you couldn't do it?" roared the voice.

Kiriai waved Eigo over and pointed at a small door neither of them had seen earlier. It was hidden in a nook along a wall hung with floor-to-ceiling draperies. Besides hiding the door, the rich fabric added color to the room and softened any sounds. Now, however, someone had pulled a section of curtain back and tucked it into a hook, leaving an open doorway where the raging voice emanated from.

Waving at Eigo to take one side, Kiriai moved to the other wall so they approached the doorway from both sides. When they got close, both did their best to peer inside the small room without alerting the obviously angry occupants.

"—the window, sir—" Kiriai heard an apologetic voice say as she finally got a look into a room that looked extremely homely, especially compared to the luxury of the huge outer suite.

Window? Kiriai's mind latched onto the word and at once decided it was the most beautiful word she ever heard . . . if it meant what she hoped it did.

"That window is too small for a person to fit through," said the first voice in a tone that demanded the world conform to what he knew of it. Kiriai shifted for a better view. The yelling man was of medium height, his hair a modest brown, and his expensive robe the most noteworthy thing about him. Well, that and the bellowing that meant he was the one in charge. The 'forcer he screamed at was taller and looked to outweigh him by half. And yet the second man was obviously the underling, his gaze down and body slumped in as subservient a posture as possible with his height advantage.

"She was in the room at mealtime a few hours ago. I never left my post in front of the door. She isn't here now. The chair is pushed up against the wardrobe. The window is broken, and there is a thin rope made of torn bedding tied off up there. So—I don't know what happened." The underling ended his report with a shrug, his eyes trained on the floor during the entire recitation.

"I don't know?" The first man imitated the report in a sing-song voice that had an edge of panic underlying it. He slammed a palm holding a note into the chest of the bigger man, who just took it, head bowed the whole time. "And when I don't follow the boss's orders in this message? Do you think she will accept *I don't know* as an answer about what happened to the girl?"

The taller man shook his head, looking like someone weathering a storm and hoping it ended soon.

"Argh!" The first man picked up a washbowl from a small table, spun and hurled it against the wall, where it cracked into pieces.

Kiriai didn't have time to duck out of the way and froze as the furious man's eyes locked onto her with surprise. His gaze flicked to the side and spotted Eigo, too. He responded instantly and charged in their direction. "Who in ancestors' name are you two? How did you get in here? Come here. Do you know where the little brat went?"

Kiriai couldn't help it. She dropped back into a fighting stance, hands raised and ready to defend herself and Eigo from the man barreling toward them. She was not letting them take another of her friends.

Her response must have surprised the man, because he skidded to a halt at her defiance, just out of reach. Kiriai hadn't thought it was possible, but his face turned even angrier. A dark red flush moved into his cheeks and a vein in his temple visibly throbbed. His mouth moved soundlessly, as if he couldn't believe how the world continued to defy his wishes.

"You're raising your fists to me?" he finally managed to sputter. "Do you have any idea who I am?"

"Master Kancho?"

The man stopped mid-rant, Eigo's calm answer not what he was expecting.

"Brawler Kiriai and I are here," said Eigo, speaking quickly before the man exploded again, "with the Jitaku contingent to ensure nothing goes wrong with the delivery of the scrapper reinforcements. We were hoping to speak to Boss Ryuin, if that is possible."

"Kiriai?" Kancho's eyes snapped to her. "I thought you looked familiar."

For a moment, Kiriai thought they would have a rational discussion with the man—until his gaze scanned the empty suite behind the two of them. Kiriai could see the moment he realized the two of them were alone. The smile that spread across his face a moment later made her heart beat faster. She closed her fists, and prayed Tomi was close.

His arrogant rage was back in full force as he waved a hand behind him. "Shikko, grab them both. We'll take them to the basement and get some real answers. I'm sure *Brawler* Kiriai will know exactly where her little crew member has disappeared to."

Regardless of the reluctance in every line of his body, 'Forcer Shikko moved forward to follow his orders.

"Get behind me," Kiriai said with a snap to her voice, glad when Eigo obeyed and stayed close as she moved to put a sofa between herself and the approaching 'forcer. The delicate wood barely looked barely strong enough to support a seated guest, but Kiriai wasn't about to quibble. A barrier was a barrier.

"So you let my aide escape, did you?" she said, hoping for more information.

Kancho just growled as he and Shikko split to come around the couch from both sides.

"Couldn't keep a teenage girl safe, could you? I wonder what Boss Ryuin will think about that," said Kiriai, hoping the man's anger and pride would force him to give her the information she needed.

"If you're stupid enough to come here after getting your friend loose, I'm sure you'll be fine taking her place. Boss Ryuin will probably reward me for this."

Kiriai and Eigo scrambled back toward the entrance, but that small room pulled at Kiriai, making her reluctant to leave. Even though the men's words made it obvious Aibo had somehow escaped, Kiriai still wanted to see for herself.

"You wouldn't dare kidnap a burb brawler," said Eigo as he leapt back from a lunging grab by Shikko and made it to the doorway. "The chief would come after you with everything for doing that."

Kancho scoffed, reached into his pouch and pulled out a device Kiriai had never seen before. "What the chief doesn't know, he can't punish, now can he? Besides, my boss doesn't really care what the chief thinks." He pointed the small rod-shaped piece of metal toward Kiriai. She knew immediately that she didn't want to be on the receiving end of whatever it did. Looking around frantically, she saw Eigo had made it to the doorway because Shikko had stopped pursuing him and was instead attempting to flank her, his familiar 'forcer stick hanging loose in one hand. As her eyes came back to Kancho, the flicker of malice and the slight forward lean of his body was just enough warning. Something flickered on the end of the rod.

Acting on pure instinct, Kiriai dove into the sleeping alcove, toward the edge of the huge bed. She tucked into a tight roll that moved her across the soft carpet and put the bulk of the bed between her and the two men. She heard a quiet zapping noise. A smell like the middle of a lightning storm made her very relieved that Kancho's device hadn't caught her. She rushed to peek back around the bed.

"Hold! Drop it!" The loud voice was so full of anger and command that everyone in the room froze, except for the 'forcers that came piling in behind 'Ranger Tomi, weapons drawn. Kiriai stared in disbelief as 'forcers in the chief's colors charged into the room side-by-side with 'Forcer Hageshi and his men.

And her congenial friend 'Ranger Tomi had transformed into a force for vengeance who looked ready to tear Kancho apart by hand if there hadn't been witnesses to stop him.

"I think Chief Kosui will be interested in hearing how one of Boss Ryuin's masters thinks he can kidnap one of his newest brawlers without repercussions."

A woman walked in to stand next to 'Ranger Tomi, her smile friendly but her eyes cold enough to make Kiriai shiver. Maybe sitting here on the floor out of sight next to the bed wasn't such a bad place to be right now.

"Master Tatari," Kancho stuttered as he dropped his weapon and raised both hands in an appeasing motion. "This is all a horrible misunderstanding."

Tatari's brows rose. "Did you not just fire an illegal weapon at Brawler Kiriai? Did you say Boss Ryuin doesn't care about the chief's law as long as he doesn't find out about her illegal activities?"

The spymaster swallowed, and it was obvious Kancho was trying and failing to salvage the situation. His mouth opened and closed without saying anything.

"Unless this was all your idea, and your boss had nothing to do with kidnapping a brawler crew member to put pressure on the outcome of a fight?"

"That's not what—" The words were out of Kiriai's mouth before she could stop them. Tomi's abrupt motion toward her made her choke down the rest of her objection as every eye in the room turned toward her.

Kiriai got to her feet and glared defiantly at all of them. If they thought she would sit by while Ryuin's underling took the fall for everything she'd orchestrated . . .

"Your description of the brawler is quite accurate," said Tatari with a touch of amusement in her tone before she turned back to Kancho.

Tomi aimed a reassuring look at Kiriai, which asked her to both be quiet and trust him. Knowing his skill in this arena far surpassed hers, Kiriai forced herself to keep quiet.

The small break from scrutiny seemed to have breathed new life into Master Kancho, who had an appeasing look plastered on his face now.

"I'd like to apologize, Master Tatari, for my words. They were simple trickery, an attempt to get these two intruders to confess their purpose. Same for the weapon. I'm sure you can sympathize that I might resort to extreme measures when forced to defend the innermost sanctum of my boss's embassy." The oily man waved a hand around as if everyone there didn't know this was Boss Ryuin's personal suite.

Kiriai clenched her jaw and began slowly edging around the bed. She needed to get a look in that room while she still had a chance. She knew all too well that Aibo's fate was unimportant to most of the powerful people in the room.

"And the kidnapping and blackmail?" Tatari asked.

"The only non-Mabbai people here are these two intruders," Kancho said, and aimed a glare in Kiriai and Eigo's direction.

Of all the nerve.

"I'm sure you won't mind if my 'forcers verify that?" Tatari said, and it wasn't really a question.

"By all means," said Kancho with a quick look at his underling, indicating he should step aside. Shikko looked more than happy to move to a corner and stand in the shadows there.

This was the moment Kiriai had been waiting for, and without asking permission, she bolted for the room before anyone could stop her.

The first thing that struck Kiriai was a familiar smell that reminded her of smiles and exuberance. Emotion rushed through her as she knew immediately that this was where Ryuin had held Aibo since the night her people had snatched her.

But where was she now? Did Kancho really not know, or had Ryuin's people done something to her friend?

Kiriai looked around the room, eyes missing nothing. The scene stood just as Shikko had described it. Aibo had pushed a chair up against the wardrobe, above which a small window let in a breeze through the broken pieces of expensive glass. Kiriai hopped up onto the chair and saw the rope made of shredded linen tied off around a decorative wooden post at the top of the wardrobe. With a heave, Kiriai pulled herself up onto the wardrobe, hunched down in the small space between it and the ceiling. Leaning forward, she looked out the window to the rope that fluttered below, nowhere near long enough to reach the ground. She squinted, scanning the area below for any sign of Aibo's broken body, and let out a relieved breath when she saw the grounds below were empty.

"Anything?"

Kiriai scrambled backward, careful of the glass, and lowered herself to the chair.

"No," she said to Tomi and Eigo. "And the drop looks impossible to survive, though there's no sign of her."

The three stood as 'forcers moved through the room, checking the few hiding places for signs of Aibo, inside the wardrobe and under the bed.

In just a few minutes, they finished and left the small room to search every part of Ryuin's large suite.

Kiriai looked at Eigo, as her weariness and loss came crashing down. He opened his arms, and Kiriai sank gratefully into his embrace. She felt Tomi's large hand patting her shoulder in commiseration.

When she felt steadier, Kiriai pushed back and cleared her throat. She moved across the room and sat down on the bed, her whole body aching and unwilling to support her much longer.

"We have to think like Aibo. She's clever and if we can figure out her plan, we can find her."

Eigo's eyes relaxed, and Tomi looked around the room, all three of them searching for any idea about the location of their friend.

"Kiriai?"

Someone whispered her name.

Kiriai turned to the two men in the room, only to find them looking back at her in question.

Adrenaline surged through Kiriai as she leapt from the bed. "Aibo?" She kept her voice quiet, the same volume as the whisper.

"Is it safe?"

Tears sprang to Kiriai eyes, and her throat clenched so tight she had a hard time squeezing out her reply.

"Yes, Aibo. It's safe."

Was this happening? They'd thoroughly searched the room. Where could she be hiding? Kiriai looked up at the ceiling and then down at the floor.

Nothing.

A small movement from the bed caught her eye. The mattress was squirming like a kitten trapped under a blanket. Kiriai hurried to the edge of the mattress against the wall, searching for an opening.

As she pulled the mattress back from the wall, a portion of the covering split apart. Kiriai sucked in a surprised breath as a dark head of hair pushed its way free. When the head turned to reveal Aibo's worried face, a cry of joy escaped Kiriai's lips. She leaped forward to pull her friend free, hardly noticing when Eigo's and Tomi's hands joined her.

"It's really you?" Aibo asked, her eyes both scared and happy, tears threatening to fall.

Kiriai pulled Aibo tight against her, lifting her feet off the ground, determined to never let her go again. "Yes, it's me. You know we would never stop looking for you. All of us. We've been trying to find you every second of every day since they took you. You know that, right?"

Aibo's smaller body shook with tremors, and she sucked in a shaky breath. "I know," she got out with a choked sob that made Kiriai hold her even tighter.

When some of the tremors had died down, Kiriai set Aibo down and pushed back to look at her face again. She still couldn't believe it was really her.

"How?" Kiriai asked, before glancing back at the mattress. "I can't believe you were in there the whole time."

A sheepish expression came across Aibo's face as she followed Kiriai's gaze toward the mattress and shrugged. "I pulled out enough of the stuffing rags to make the rope up there." She waved a hand up toward the small window. "I figured if I could give them something obvious to pursue, they wouldn't look so hard in here."

Kiriai pulled her friend back in, the flesh-and-blood feel of her slight frame going a long way to soothe the part of her that insisted Aibo's presence here, safe and sound, was impossible. Kiriai barely noticed when Tomi stepped out. Angry words filtered back into the small room. Something about *kidnapping*, *evidence* and *the girl*. But this time, Kiriai had no problem trusting Tomi to win the fight.

She was happy to just enjoy the time holding the friend she'd risked everything for and finally found unharmed.

Aibo finally let out a long breath and moved back. Once Kiriai was sure she was steady, she let her go.

A fierce expression had replaced Aibo's earlier one, surprising Kiriai. Her mouth worked, and Kiriai stayed quiet, giving the younger woman room to say what was on her mind.

"I always knew you would come for me—"

When Aibo hesitated, Kiriai nodded with encouragement.

"—but I didn't just wait for you to rescue me. I did what I knew you would do."

When Aibo looked away, suddenly shy, Kiriai asked, "And what's that?"

"I made a crazy plan and saved myself."

That startled a delighted laugh out of Kiriai, and she pulled Aibo back into a hug, a congratulatory one this time instead of a soothing one.

"That you did, my young fighter," Kiriai said, clapping her on the back. "You saved yourself!"

A wide grin split Aibo's face, and Kiriai knew her own pride was beaming just as brightly.

"Wait, I have something for you," Kiriai said and dug into her pouch. Where was it? Her fingers found the crinkled scrap of paper she'd used to wrap it in. She held it out to Aibo, who reached for it, a question in her eyes.

"Just open it," said Kiriai, her voice still giddy. Part of her still couldn't believe they'd found Aibo unharmed.

Aibo peeled open the paper, let out a soft gasp and froze when she saw what was inside. Threaded through a new chain, Aibo's amber crystal sat nestled in the soft fabric.

"I gave credits to a handful of messenger kids and told them which section in the stands to search. I was going to have another one made if they didn't find it, but—" Kiriai shrugged, suddenly uncomfortable when she saw the tear trace it's way down Aibo's cheek.

Aibo launched herself back at Kiriai in a hug that made her stagger.

"Thank you, Kiriai. I couldn't stop them from taking it. Thank you," said Aibo in a muffled chant, her face pressed into Kiriai's chest.

"You're strong, just like this crystal we gave you," said Kiriai as her arms held Aibo tightly. "You didn't break, and you saved yourself so you were alive when we found you. Thank *you*, Aibo. Thank you."

For a moment, all the other troubles didn't matter. Boss

Ryuin's machinations and the reinforcements critical to Jitaku faded in importance compared to having a friend back, one she'd thought she'd lost forever.

Ancestors, Mama, thank you for helping get Aibo back, safe and sound.

Whether it was her own joy over finding Aibo or a touch of comfort from the heavens, Kiriai let herself sink into the peaceful happiness that fell over her.

Even the noises in the other room had quieted as Master Tatari, her 'forcers and 'Ranger Tomi wrapped up the questioning and apprehending of Ryuin's people.

For a handful of moments, it seemed Kiriai's world would finally settle down.

Then a shrill scream shattered it into a million pieces.

"Help! Master Kancho! Help!"

A sick feeling stabbed Kiriai, and she pulled Aibo with her as she hurried out to see what the problem was.

A flustered woman in servant clothing stood in the doorway looking from face to face, searching. When her gaze landed on Kancho, her face lit up, not seeming to notice the two 'forcers holding him captive.

She blurted out her message, looking desperate to transfer the burden to someone else. "The fixers you sent didn't help. Boss Ryuin isn't just feeling poorly, she'd been poisoned!"

CHAPTER FIFTY-SEVEN

"We need to divide the fabricator blueprints evenly based on both industry and percentage of control of our future economy. None of us wants a single family to outstrip the rest of us, agreed? . . . And I'll take healthcare if no one else wants it."

— Founding Matriarch Jasmyn Stark during the Chikara City Organization meetings. Oath Keepers Archive of Truth, Volume 14

It was the worst graduation ever.

Kiriai's crew sat with her in their section of the arena, all dressed sharply in clothes picked out for them by M. Shuju to project strength and unity at the same time. Thankfully, graduation required that Kiriai wear her uniform and belt for the ceremony. At least her plan to avoid M. Shuju and his dresses was working.

Surviving Trainer Gebi and her minions, being the first in ages to win her first brawler fight and having Aibo back should have filled Monday evening's events with exhilaration and happiness.

Instead, Kiriai sat with a grim and tense Jitaku contingent. Around her sat powerful people forced by rules to sit and wait for an outcome, except for one of her crew: 'Ranger Tomi.

More than anything, Kiriai wished he would walk in bringing good news so they could all relax and enjoy the festivities. Instead, the powerful 'ranger and his underlings were fighting tooth and nail to hurry along the inquiry into Ryuin's poisoning.

Kiriai shook her head to clear the familiar anger that tried to surge up again.

Eigo's hand reached for hers, and the soft squeeze reminded Kiriai to breathe and relax her shoulders.

"I wish she had died," Kiriai said under her breath and heard a few murmurs of agreement from those who'd heard her words despite the noisy political posturing that was happening on center stage. Kiriai ignored it. She'd had more than enough of that this month.

"It would have surely been much easier," said Isha from her other side, "but death is permanent and such desires have a tendency to stain the soul who entertains them, child."

Kiriai frowned, not wanting to admit Isha was probably right.

"Trust the ancestors to sort it all out in the next life, Kiriai," said Isha as she reached over to pat Kiriai's leg. "You carry enough on your shoulders as it is."

Kiriai stared at the stage floor as another pompous person walked up to drone on in self-importance about nothing. Why couldn't she just fast forward to the end and find out what would happen? The waiting was driving her crazy.

"They would still have had an inquiry if she'd died," Sento said as he turned to look back from the row in front of Kiriai. "And an inquiry always stops the prize distribution until they reach their conclusion."

"But if she weren't giving orders to delay as much as possible from her sickbed, the inquiry might be done," Shisen said from her place next to Sento. "And the reinforcements Kiriai won for us would already be on their way. If they don't get to Jitaku in time—" Shisen stopped and shook her head.

No one responded, all of them likely visualizing tomorrow's outcome if the reinforcements weren't sent in time. Jitaku had a full battle schedule against Raibaru, plenty to lose them the majority ownership of the hood.

"There's still time," said Aibo from behind Kiriai, her optimism sounding a little flatter than usual. "Tomi has been working day and night to push the delivery through. If anyone can do it, he can."

Kiriai still felt a flush of relief seeing her young friend back and whole. But her confidence that Tomi could work another miracle—? She wanted to believe it would happen, but her experience with politics didn't bode well for a speedy result.

The mood of the crowd changed as voices rose, and a charge of anticipation filled the arena.

"That's you," hissed Eigo from next to her. He nudged her with his elbow.

Jarred from her moody thoughts, Kiriai looked around. Sure enough, her fellow initiates stood in their various sections amidst congratulations and back-slaps as they made their way down to the arena floor.

Kiriai stood and made her way down in a path that was oddly reminiscent of Saturday's first-fights. Only this time, politics might have stolen the rewards from Saturday's hard-fought victory, and with it, the only real chance her hood stood at fending off its enemy.

The noise from the spectators grew as the eight new brawlers made it to center stage. Kiriai heard the occasional name yelled out amidst the noise and had to smile a little when a woman shrieked Jimu's name in a voice high-pitched enough to pierce through it all. The man's neck turned red, but he kept his eyes focused straight ahead and expression calm.

At least this was a celebration for someone. The man deserved it for weathering all the abuse during initiation without taking part in the nastier parts of it.

Kiriai felt strange stepping up onto the stage, assembled for the occasion, to face Chief Kosui in a line with the other new brawlers. It hadn't been that long since she'd stood in the selection circle that had put her on this path. For a moment, her childhood dream of a brawler's life clashed with reality. The two visions were so different that Kiriai wondered if she'd have taken a different path in life if she'd known the truth. How naïve she'd been when Sento had first told her how much *fighting* took place outside the ring. Here at the burb level, it was even more true than it had been at home as a scrapper.

But when Kiriai thought about her fellow Jitaku scrappers fighting with the last of their strength to hold on to their territory, she knew she would do it all again. Some things you just had to fight for, and your home was one of them.

"Ladies and gentlemen," said Chief Kosui as he held an amp up to his mouth so his voice filled the arena space with a deceptively friendly tone. "Please join me in giving a warm welcome and congratulations to Southern Core's newest brawlers!"

The chief waved a hand at them and Kiriai joined the others in turning a full circle, waving in all directions. She hoped the smile plastered on her face looked somewhat convincing, at least from a distance.

"These eight fighters in front of you have fought for you and for their homes so that each of us can live in peace. They have sacrificed everything to be the best and qualify as part of the most elite fighters in our burb. Not only that, they survived a month of the most brutal training we could design and have been forged into true brawlers, fighters who will not back down from any challenge thrown at them."

Another roar of approval sounded as soon as Chief Kosui paused for a breath. The chief took a moment to let the sound crescendo as he smiled at the brawlers facing him in identical ready stances. With perfect timing, Chief Kosui waved a clerk over just as the cheers slowed, but hadn't died out completely.

The woman, dressed in a shimmering silk dress, carried an ornate wooden tray and moved into a position just behind the Chief. Without a backward glance, Chief Kosui strode to the first brawler at the end of the row. He gave the new brawler an appropriate bow from chief to subordinate and received a much deeper one in return. Then, with a swift movement, the chief grabbed the edge of the man's yellow-and-white Rinjin Hood patch and ripped it off in a single jerk. The man didn't flinch, and Kiriai worked to keep herself calm as the chief made his way toward her.

She kept her eyes raised even as she executed a properly deep bow to the chief. His eyes narrowed, but he didn't comment. When he reached for her Jitaku patch, part of Kiriai wanted to pull away and slap both hands up protectively over the symbol of her home. She'd never chosen to become a brawler, to leave her first loyalty and transfer it to someone as distasteful as Chief Kosui and his people. They had forced her into this position, and at this moment, she hated it. But common sense prevailed. She stood frozen as the chief ripped her identity from the front of her uniform, the green and white pattern one she'd loved since the day she'd sewn it on the new uniform Ojisan and Isha had gifted her.

Kiriai clenched her jaw and blinked back her emotions.

Finally, the chief had finished and stood before the fighters whose black uniforms were now empty of color except for the blue belts they wore around their waists. He stood, silent and expectant. The crowd stilled as the anticipation grew.

When it was quiet enough for the chief, he lifted the amp back to his lips. "Raise your right hands and repeat after me."

Kiriai's hand might have lagged a touch behind the others, but she followed the command.

"I, Brawler—state your name—"

The chief waited until everyone had said their full name before continuing. "—promise, by my ancestors, that I will support and defend Southern Burb against all enemies, and that I will obey the orders of the burb chief as well as all duly appointed superiors above me."

The other brawlers' words rang out with a strength and purpose Kiriai wished she had. Instead, she felt a tug of remorse as the simple words severed her ties to her hood and placed her firmly under the control of Chief Kosui.

The crowd roared as the last words finished, and the brawlers dropped their hands, many of them unable to contain their smiles.

Amidst the sounds of celebration, Chief Kosui moved back to the first brawler, took a new patch from the tray held behind him and stuck it to the man's chest. The hawk embroidered in swirling white thread shimmered when the brawler moved, a trick of the light making the bird's wings seem to move.

Kiriai held stock-still until it was her turn. Her expression carefully controlled, she felt like a stone standing still as the river rushed past her with all its chaotic energy.

"What? No triumphant grin this time?" the chief asked in a low tone as he shook her hand, his smile for the crowd firmly in place.

Her sense of caution was too slow to stop the words. "Maybe if you'd helped the reinforcements I won get to Jitaku in time to be of any use—"

A scoff slipped past the chief's careful control and his eyes narrowed, making Kiriai clamp her mouth shut.

"How nice it must be to have such petty things to worry about," he said.

She couldn't help bristling, but he ignored her.

"Yes, Raibaru will probably win a majority today, but Western still has to issue a burb challenge and win the tournament before they can actually take your home. A lot can happen before then."

"But I won the fight and the reinforcements—"

"And someone poisoned one of the plaintiffs, which requires an inquiry before distributing the winnings. It's all in the rules, my young fighter." He waved a hand dismissively. "Talk to your boss about why I didn't help hurry the inquiry along."

He was already turning to the next brawler, but Kiriai couldn't stop herself. "My boss?"

The chief stopped, and the smile on his face chilled her. He stepped back in her direction and leaned in, his voice low and threatening. "Maybe if he had come through on his promise to help me with my city family problems, I could have helped him with the inquiry. But—" The chief stepped back, a smile back on his face. He shrugged as if the fate of her home was of no significance.

He moved to Brawler Jiseki, the next in line, already dismissing her. His clerk placed another patch in his hand, and Chief Kosui glanced at the crowd with a proud smile before he placed it on Jiseki's chest. She grinned broadly, fairly vibrating with excitement.

Feeling even more isolated, Kiriai fought between anger and fear—anger at the chief's refusal to help Jitaku and fear at being discovered for her role in helping the gifted teens escape. How could she warn Boss Akuto not to pursue the matter without giving herself and the others away? What would she do if the truth came out? Kiriai couldn't shake a sick feeling of dread that this problem wouldn't just disappear.

The chief's voice interrupted her anxious thoughts.

"Attention!" said Chief Kosui over the noise after he had finished with the last brawler and returned to center stage.

The eight new brawlers snapped to attention, but that wasn't what stopped the crowd mid-sound. The rows of seats closest to the stage emptied as what looked like at least a hundred brawlers leapt to their feet and snapped to attention at the same time.

Kiriai sucked in a breath at the surprising display of force. The event planners hadn't warned them this would happen. As Kiriai scanned the faces of the fierce fighters, something inside ignited and the first sense that she might actually be able to make a home here flickered to life. Every man and woman in the group had trained hard to be the best at the fighting art she loved.

"My Southern Core brawlers," said Chief Kosui with a roar as he flung both hands at the veteran fighters, "please welcome your newest brother and sisters!"

"Oda!" The whole group encircling the stage roared out the battle cry in unison, sending an unexpected thrill through Kiriai.

"You're part of them, now. Brawlers, again!" the chief said as he jabbed a hand in their direction.

The eight of them knew immediately what he expected and this time, when the chorus of brawlers yelled out the battle cry, they joined in.

"Oda!"

"And there you have it, my people, the Southern Core brawlers, new and old!" Kosui timed his words perfectly. The arena seemed to explode in response, and the newest brawlers grabbed their old patches, throwing them into a delighted crowd where children scrambled to grab one of the prizes. Kiriai was tempted for a heartbeat to hold on to hers. But knew she needed to step fully into her new life, and this was one way to do it.

With a sharp exhale, Kiriai forced a smile onto her face. Then, with only the slightest hesitation, she threw the green-and-white Jitaku patch out into the jubilant crowd.

Staring out at the sea of people, all celebrating what she and her fellows had achieved, Kiriai hesitated and wished she could put everything else aside and just enjoy the moment.

But her eyes drifted up into the stands, and she saw her crew with the rest of the Jitaku contingent, their celebration definitely more muted than those around them. With good reason, she knew.

Kiriai forced herself to move off the stage and through the crowd. Smiles, congratulations and back slaps made it hard to move quickly, and Kiriai discovered that parries had practical uses outside of a fight. It was only when she got within a few rows of her crew that she saw Tomi's distinctive red hair a few rows farther up, his head bent in conversation with Boss Akuto.

He was back.

Her feet missed a step before she picked up her pace. Had Tomi done it? Would the reinforcements be sent tonight in time for tomorrow's battles?

Kiriai stepped into the Jitaku section, heart full of both dread and hope.

CHAPTER FIFTY-EIGHT

The next evening, every eye was glued to the screen as a brawny man wearing Jitaku's green-and-white patch faced off against a lanky woman wearing Raibaru's red and black insignia. Anyone just looking at the two scrappers would likely have chosen the Jitaku man to win until they watched him move.

He favored his left leg and his kicks were slow and hands a little sluggish when blocking. Compared to his opponent, he was in big trouble.

"He can still land a lucky blow," said Eigo. "Maybe he's acting, trying to draw Scrapper Yanagi in so she'll let her guard down."

The rest of Kiriai's crew, arrayed in their burb living room, didn't respond, their bodies tense despite the lush surroundings and tasty array of finger foods that sat untouched on the low table between the couches.

Kiriai couldn't be the only one who knew Eigo's prediction wasn't likely, but she didn't want to be the one to say so.

"You're right, Eigo," said Isha, her tone calm and reassuring as usual. "As long as the fight isn't over, there is a chance."

"If Scrapper Suji weren't on his second battle today and hadn't fought multiple times last week too," said Shisen, voice full of anger and derision. "He's the least injured scrapper we have and Yanagi hasn't fought a battle in two weeks."

Shisen's words stoked the anger simmering inside Kiriai at the injustice of it all.

"The reinforcements are loading up as we speak," said Tomi from his seat against a far wall. "They'll arrive in Jitaku in time for the second set of fights this week, but not for—" He swallowed and lifted a hand toward the screen, looking more defeated than Kiriai had ever seen him. "I did my best."

"Everyone knows you did," Kiriai said. "It's not your fault. It's a stupid policy, paperwork and a chief who doesn't care. Together they ruined everything we've worked for." Kiriai stood and paced, her eyes glued to the action on the screen. "It had to be obvious to anyone with half a brain that we wouldn't attack Boss Ryuin after we'd already won. How stupid would we be to trigger an inquiry that left us fighting today without the new scrappers we won?" Kiriai waved at the screen. "And even with all the evidence that Ryuin was colluding with Western Burb, she's still the boss? How is any of that fair?"

Kiriai stopped and realized that her rant had increased in volume, and everyone stared at her.

"It isn't." Tomi was the one to answer her. "Most likely, she found something extremely valuable to trade with Chief Kosui for his mercy. And she didn't come out unscathed. Kosui stripped away her top people and knocked her hood to fourth place. Plus, I'm sure, he hit her with significant fines and extracted promises for future favors and obedience."

"But she'll have a hood at the end of it all?" Aibo asked, both disappointment and a touch of fear in her voice. It couldn't be helping her confidence to have her kidnapper hold on to power, even diminished.

"Yes," Sento said with a nod. "And if Scrapper Suji doesn't win this fight, we'll be the ones a step closer to losing ours."

"Who knew a simple clothing shop would become so important?" said Mikata in a glum voice.

Kiriai stared back at the screen, feeling the same sense of disbelief Mikata expressed. The prize for this fight, a small clothing shop, was of no great significance, except that the percentage of land it sat on would finally give Raibaru majority ownership of Jitaku territory. With a victory here, Western Core could finally issue a hood challenge, a week-long tournament for ownership of the entire hood. How could it all come down to this one fight between a worn and broken fighter with twice the spirit of his opponent?

It wasn't fair.

Aibo, looking worried, glanced at everyone in the room and didn't seem to find the reassurance she was looking for. Kiriai exchanged a look with Mikata and Sento. Their expressions said it all. It didn't take much experience in the ring to predict the outcome of the final battle tonight.

The crowd on the screen, made up of mostly Jitaku fans, watched with grim faces, looking just as pessimistic. Only the occasional cluster of Raibaru fans had ecstatic smiles on their faces.

Kiriai had to give Scrapper Suji credit. He kept fighting, hard. As the image on the screen zoomed in close, everyone could see his jaw tight with pain as he refused to go down. His punches lashed out even as his body rocked with blows from Yanagi.

Somehow, he held his own and even landed a few blows . . . until Yanagi slipped an agile ax kick past his defenses. It cracked into his cheekbone, snapping his head down and to the side. The kick was so devastating, Yanagi didn't bother following through. With a triumphant expression on her face, she leaped back as if expecting the heavier man to topple.

A hush fell over the Jitaku arena on the screen, mirrored by an identical quiet in the living room of Kiriai's brawler quarters.

Suji staggered, his legs buckling slightly. But he didn't go down. Instead, he drew on some inner strength, shook his head and pulled his hands back up. Amazed he was still standing, Kiriai held onto the small fragments of hope inside her.

Suji sucked in a few breaths, visibly struggling to recover. Instead of toppling, the man bent his knees and gripped the wooden floor with his bare feet.

Then he surprised everyone watching.

With a roar, Suji launched himself at the Yanagi.

A short distance away, Yanagi had let her cheering supporters in the crowd distract her.

A collective gasp broke the silence, and everyone leaned forward. Would Suji catch her unawares? Maybe Eigo would be right after all.

Yanagi's expression of shock and surprise was beautiful. Suji had caught her with her weight back on her heels. She had no way to evade his powerful front kick. It slammed full speed into her stomach, practically lifting her off her feet.

"Yes!" both Eigo and Aibo yelled, leaping to their feet, hands pumping in the air.

Scrapper Suji's charge and kick, however, seemed to have taken all of his reserves. When Yanagi's quick footwork created some distance, Suji wasn't fast enough to follow and capitalize on his advantage. The two opponents glared across the ring at each other, one drained of everything but his will and the other hurting when she thought she should be celebrating.

None of her crew seemed to breathe as they watched the stand-off.

A split second later, Yanagi made her own charge at Suji, fists a blur.

Both fighters had to know exactly what was at stake. Ancestors, the whole stadium did. The two slammed together with a crash that made everyone watching wince. Punches, elbows and tight hooks flew back and forth, with more bobbing and weaving than outright blocking.

Every Jitaku fan in the stadium was on their feet, screaming, desperate for a win, one more reprieve in the war. Yanagi's supporters were just as loud, probably already salivating about the possibility of taking over and looting an entire hood.

Kiriai felt her eyes sting as she watched Yanagi slam blow after blow into Suji. The beleaguered fighter did his best to return the same. His body rocked even as he pushed himself past his limits, giving everything he had to try to save his home.

And then, just like that, it was over.

"Yame! Yame!" the head judge screamed, his hands pushing between the two fighters as the corner judges came to help pull the frenzied combatants apart.

Once again a hush fell outward from the center as the two scrappers moved back to their marks to stand, swaying and bloody, to wait for the outcome. Scrapper Suji didn't make it. As his foot touched his mark, his eyes rolled back into his head, and he fell in a boneless heap to the floor. Everyone in the arena that wasn't already on their feet stood, a chorus of gasps and cries of distress audible through the screen. Kiriai heard her friends echo the same.

Two Jitaku fixers raced across the floor toward the downed fighter.

The screen zoomed in on him, and Kiriai felt sick at the sight. When the bodies of the fixers obscured the view, the screen panned out to move across the spectators. Instead of the normal cheering and impatience, they stood in silence, respect on their faces for Scrapper Suji and his sacrifice. Even the Raibaru 'zens held their tongues.

But there was still the matter of the fight to decide.

Once the head judge had spoken quietly to the fixers, he gathered the rest of the judges and they moved aside to deliberate.

Along with an arena full of people, everyone in the room with Kiriai waited in silence for the results.

"Was it enough?" Aibo was the first one to whisper the question they all had.

No one answered her. When Kiriai looked at Sento and Mikata, she saw a confirmation of her pessimistic thoughts. Suji's only real hope had been a knock-out. Now that it had come down to points . . . well, it didn't look good.

Kiriai swallowed and sat back on the couch, her stomach in knots. How had it come to this? In just a few days, she'd been whipped back and forth on an emotional seesaw, both Jitaku Hood and Aibo at risk, then saved, and then at risk again. Had it been just Saturday that they'd found Aibo and Boss Akuto had made ironclad plans for the new reinforcements? Couldn't things in her life go according to plan, just once?

"They're done," Mikata said, breaking the silence and pulling Kiriai's thoughts out of their downward spiral for a moment.

On screen, the huddle of judges had broken up, and the head judge moved back to the center of the ring. Once there, he took the hands of Yanagi and a young man, a Jitaku scrapper who stood as a proxy for Suji. Fixers still tended to the downed scrapper. The announcer prattled on as tensions rose, making Kiriai want to throttle the woman. She finally wound down and said the words everyone was waiting for: ". . . and the winner is . . ."

The two fighters, judge standing between them, faced the crowd and screen, frozen for just a moment. It was a point in time where the future had yet to be decided, a moment Kiriai wished didn't have to pass.

And then he jerked Scrapper Yanagi's hand high into the air. The isolated pockets of Raibaru supporters went wild, standing amid a sea of shock and disbelief.

Kiriai stared at the screen along with her friends, feeling much the same as those in the crowd. Sure, logically, she knew Suji hadn't had a great chance, but somewhere inside her, she'd still hoped he would win. As the last fight of the night, his win would have given the reinforcements time to arrive, a whole cadre of fresh fighters ready to step in and win back their territory from Raibaru.

But now, that would all be impossible. Jitaku's role in its own defense was over. Western Burb clerks were probably already filing the hood challenge.

Kiriai scoffed. Even the heroic fighting spirit of Scrapper Suji was powerless against corruption and intrigue. Kiriai hated the dirty truth of her world. Western Burb and Raibaru Hood had to be behind the attack on Boss Ryuin, a last gambit to delay the reinforcements one more day. And it had worked. Raibaru now owned a majority of Jitaku territory.

Suddenly, it was all too much. Kiriai turned on her heel and stormed down the dim hallway that led to the bedrooms. She stormed into her room and slid the door shut behind her, not even wincing when it thudded hard against the stopper. She didn't bother with a light. Even the spring of the expensive mattress bothered her. She wanted the solid bulk of the rag-stuffed mattress she'd grown up with and the itchy weight of her heavy wool comforter at home.

Alone.

In the dark.

She indulged herself and let her thoughts rail at the injustice of it all, like a child, wishing she could fix everything in the world and change it back to the way she wanted it.

CHAPTER FIFTY-NINE

"The founding families divided responsibilities evenly to meet every need in our new society, with no single group having all the power. We are lucky they stepped up to rebuild after the Blast."

— Chikara City Elementary Social Studies Text, 1st edition

The quiet, peaceful scene out of her window seemed to mock Kiriai as she stared with an unfocused gaze into the night. She sat in a dark room full of things that probably cost more than her entire home back in Jitaku. Outside, the street lamps flickered like stars in their random patterns scattered out across the core. As she sat there, alone at last, Kiriai finally let down the rigid control she'd been holding tightly for so long.

Her eyes burned. Her breathing hitched and then with hardly a sound, tears flowed down her cheeks in hot trails. She didn't bother wiping them away. Crying made her eyes burn and nose flow, but she couldn't stop. She hated crying, but an overwhelming sense of sadness insisted she let it out somehow. The undercurrent of anger pushed her to smash something, preferably Boss Ryuin's face or whoever from Western Burb was behind everything.

The tears continued to fall, but instead of lancing the emotions, they seemed to swell, filling her head, heart and mind.

Why?

Kiriai sucked in a choked breath.

Why? Why? WHY?

She wanted to stand, kick out the window and scream the question at the entire world. Instead, she sat on her bed, fists clenched as sobbing shudders racked her frame, and tears continued to fall. She leaned forward and dug angry palms into her hot eyes and quit trying to fight.

After everything she'd done, everything they'd all sacrificed—Ancestors, after everything Aibo had gone through—somehow those in power had ripped victory out from under them, anyway.

Why did she even bother? What was the point of fighting if the powerful could still just take it all away?

Kiriai's bitter thoughts twisted and swelled in a downward spiral that fed the anguish and turned her breathing even more ragged as her tears tried their best to relieve the pressure.

Time passed, but Kiriai didn't pay any attention as she let herself sink into a dark place she wasn't sure she ever wanted to leave. What was the point?

"Shhh."

"It's all right."

"I'm here."

The quiet murmurs finally penetrated, and Kiriai realized that she'd been hearing them for a while now. As her awareness returned, she felt arms holding her. Her cheek pressed against a warm chest that rumbled with soothing sounds and a string of words repeating over and over in a reassuring loop. She opened her eyes.

Eigo was on her bed, back against the headboard and holding her curled up against him in a tight ball as she rocked in small movements side-to-side. When had he come in?

"Hi."

That's all he said. No questions. No pressure.

"Hi," she replied. The dull note of her voice would have bothered her if she'd cared.

"How are you feeling?"

Kiriai bit down on her first angry answer of, *How the ancestors do you think I'm feeling?*

"OK, stupid question," he said as he tightened his arms around her. She was glad she'd held her tongue. He had to be just as upset as she was and didn't deserve to be yelled at.

Slow moments passed in the quiet and dark, and Kiriai felt herself calm in slow, small steps. Being held by someone who loved you went a long way toward fixing what was wrong with the world.

"The others are discussing the hood challenge Western will make," he said after more time had passed. "Now that you're officially a brawler, there's a good chance you could be part of the tournament. You know, another chance to save Jitaku?"

Kiriai flinched, wanting nothing more than to disappear and never think about any of it again.

Eigo's voice changed to something deep, but lighthearted. "How will the hero Brawler Kiriai swoop in this time to save her hood from being claimed by the evil minions of the enemy, Western Burb? Come back to next week's story time to find out."

Eigo's antics pulled a reluctant smile out of Kiriai.

It was a weak smile, a watery one, but the important part was that one corner of Kiriai's mouth moved up.

"They know I'm officially retired from the hero business, right?" Kiriai finally said, not looking up at Eigo.

A soft chuckle rumbled through his chest. "Um, I don't think they allow heroes to retire."

And Kiriai finally gave in, joining her boyfriend in a blubbering mix somewhere between crying and laughing.

Some time later, he grabbed an edge of her expensive bed cover and reached up to wipe her face.

"Wait," she said, pulling back. "I'm a mess. Don't ruin my covers."

"What else is a bed cover good for then?" he asked with all the aplomb of someone who didn't wash his own laundry.

"The whole thing will have to be washed," she said, fending off his hand.

Eigo laughed.

"What?"

"You still don't get it, do you?"

Kiriai looked at him, trying to figure out what he meant.

"Kiriai. You're a burb brawler now. You will have more credits than either of us could ever dream of. You don't even have to wash this if you don't want to. You could just buy a new one whenever you want."

The abrupt change in topic threw Kiriai for a loop. She looked down at the cover and tried to imagine living like that, so careless of costs. She shook her head.

"You can take me out of the hood, but you can't take the hood out of me," she said. On impulse, she grabbed Eigo's sleeve and with a quick tug, used it to scrub at her face before he could stop her.

"Hey," he said. But he had an indulgent smile on his face and didn't pull away.

"There," she said with no small amount of satisfaction. "Washing a tunic is much easier than cleaning an entire bedspread. And if I'm rich, then you are too, and can afford to get that cleaned or buy a new one."

Something flickered in Eigo's expression at her last words.

"What?" she asked, instantly on alert.

"Nothing," he said, grin back in place. "You know how much I hate to do laundry, right?"

She smiled in agreement and turned to lean back into him, feeling better, even though nothing had really changed.

"Ready to go back in there?" he finally asked.

Part of her really didn't want to. But another part knew they were her family, her crew, and regardless of the difficulties life threw at her, she needed them by her side, not to fix everything, but to buoy each other up . . . just as Eigo had done for her. Life was too much to navigate alone.

"Did I mention there's a surprise waiting for you?"

"A surprise?" Kiriai tried to drum up some enthusiasm for whatever gift her friends had found to cheer her up.

"Oh, don't be like that," he said as he pushed up from the bed and held out a hand. "You're going to love it. I promise."

She nodded, took his hand and followed him. Eigo opened the door and motioned she should go through first. She forced herself to step out into the hallway. Part of her insisted she go back and hide in the darkest corner of the bedroom.

Soft voices drifted from the living room. Tomi's deep rumble. Isha's soothing counterpoint. A spark of enthusiasm that had to be from Aibo. They were all there, figuring out the next steps together.

Kiriai stopped just before stepping out of the shadows and looked over her family. Sento and Mikata argued different strategies. Isha interjected ideas to shape their plans, adding something here and there, her words soothing tensions before they spiraled out of control. Shisen mentioned possible conspiracies. Kiriai was impressed with how much she'd become a part of the group despite her isolationist tendencies.

And then there was Aibo. Her usual enthusiasm seemed muted after everything, but it wasn't gone. Boss Ryuin hadn't been able to snuff the younger girl's spirit, and for a moment, Kiriai was ashamed at her own weakness just moments ago. How could she focus only on the losses when there, in front of her, stood a dear friend everyone had thought lost? And while Western Burb had won a significant victory toward owning Jitaku Hood, the Southern Burb brawlers still had a chance, one chance, to save her home.

"Going in?" Eigo asked in a soft whisper as he stepped up behind her and wrapped his arms around her. She felt his lips, soft against the side of her neck.

She leaned back, taking strength from her oldest friend, still not sure where their relationship would end up, but happy, for the moment, to let him support her. She didn't move or answer for a few moments, enjoying the view and his support.

Then, knowing if she delayed much longer, she might never go in, she stepped into the room.

Everyone looked up. A smile spread across Aibo's face, but the others glanced over toward the opening that led to the kitchen. She followed their gaze and froze at the sight that greeted her.

"Surprise," said Eigo in a soft voice behind her as he nudged her forward.

His touch broke through her shock.

"Ojisan," she said, her voice breaking, a storm of emotion making her shake as she hurried across the room.

He opened his arms, his expression letting some of his usual control slip.

She had to reach down to hug him now, but his arms still carried all the strength and comfort that had shielded her all her life.

"Ach, Kiri-chan," he said. "I'm so sorry I couldn't be here for everything you went through. I didn't know. It was supposed to just be a month of training." He pushed her back and ran a hand across her cheek, pushing her hair back and examining her closely. "How are you, child?"

She closed her eyes, let out a slow breath and tried to calm herself before she looked back at him.

He waited.

"I'm a bit shaken, but recovering, Grandfather. Everyone here is helping, and especially now that you're here . . . I'll be fine," she said. As she met his gaze, she found herself believing it. She had survived. They had found Aibo. And there was still one last chance to save their hood. She had her family here and there was still hope.

A moment passed as Kiriai let the love and concern in her grandfather's hands and gaze pour into her. She soaked it up, feeling like a neglected plant stretching and standing in the first full sun, the best she'd felt in a while.

Just as she felt steadier, Ojisan let out a harsh laugh and shook his head in exasperation. "I guess we better sit down, so you can tell me how you went from a simple training regimen to the middle of a battle between warring hood bosses and burbs. How do you always do that?"

Kiriai gave him a wry smile, shook her head. She wasn't sure she could explain it herself. But she tried anyway.

"I just try to do the right thing, Ojisan," she said, meeting his eyes, old ones full of love and knowledge. "That's all."

He squeezed her hand with a small nod of approval before they both turned to join the rest of her family.

As Kiriai's steps moved soundlessly on the lush carpet, she felt an echo of approval that just might have been from her mother. At least, she hoped it was.

A very wise mother named Theresa once counseled, "Yesterday is gone. Tomorrow has not yet come. We have only today. Let us begin."

Yabban's words helped feed the flicker of hope growing inside Kiriai once again. She sent a pulse of gratitude to her friend. *Yes, let's.*

EPILOGUE

"Thank you for coming in to give me your version of events, 'Forcer Mazeru," said Second Jaaku as he stood from the lush leather chair and gave the younger man a slight bow. The serious 'forcer wearing the chief's colors rose and returned the bow with precision, deeper than Jaaku's by the perfect amount.

"It was my pleasure, Second Jaaku. And I appreciate the—" He stopped and seemed to have trouble finding the right words.

"Oh no," said Jaaku with a smile and wave of his hand. "The package sent to your family is the standard one we give everyone who is helping us in this matter. Consider it a small token of appreciation from both Boss Akuto and Chief Kosui."

"Thank you," Mazeru said with a respectful tip of the head. "Might I ask the significance of a party weeks ago?"

With the practice of long experience, Jaaku kept his face pleasant while he inwardly wished for less clever 'forcers to interview. "Oh, nothing much at all," he said with a dismissive wave of his hand. "The chief asked Boss Akuto to look at how our current best practices are working. An analysis of the most recent events seemed like a good place to start. If we can improve things to prevent incidents like the brawl that broke out at the party in the chief's house—" Jaaku gave a small shrug as he walked toward the door, one hand held out toward the 'forcer.

When a flush crept up Mazeru's face, Jaaku smiled internally. There was nothing like reminding someone of a failure to divert their attention.

"Well, I hope you are successful, Second Jaaku," the 'forcer said with a last tip of his head before he turned and left the luxurious office.

As the door slid shut, Jaaku let his mask drop with a sigh and walked over to his desk. He sat in the finely stitched leather chair and took a moment to run his hand across the beautiful mahogany desktop. The well-appointed surroundings soothed his rough edges. The tasteful and elegant luxuries were his due, and for a moment he hoped his investigation took a while so he could stay and enjoy the royal treatment a little longer.

With a shake of his head, he forced himself to move on from the short break. With a small key, he opened a low desk drawer and pulled out stacks of files. When the drawer was empty, he felt along the back and pulled on a small tab of fabric tucked in like a forgotten scrap. The drawer bottom lifted and revealed a small space that made Jaaku smile. There was something about having a stash of valuables and weapons no one knew about that just made him feel happy. It probably went back to growing up in a large family with more children than food. He'd learned early to hide his valuables if he didn't want to lose them. In fact, he had stashes like this scattered both here and at home in Jitaku. As he well knew, disaster often struck unannounced and an emergency exit plan could make the difference between life and death.

After running a soft touch over his favorite items, Jaaku lifted the small stack of papers out. After carefully rearranging the drawer, he took each paper from the stack and laid it out in a tidy row in front of him, the top edges lined up almost perfectly.

Quiet filled the office suite as Jaaku read through all the information he'd collected so far. It hadn't taken a genius to figure out that the brawler tournament this year was the event to focus on. The chief hadn't even had the city's list before the tournament. And since the targets went missing in all four burbs just ahead of the 'forcers, that meant someone had copied the chief's master list, instead of one of the individual ones given to each boss.

His methodical sifting through every disturbance during that week and free rein to interview whoever he wanted to had filled up several pages with information. The problem was, he still couldn't see a pattern that pointed to a single culprit.

There were two scrappers, one from Jitaku and one from Rinjin, who had siblings on the abduction list. He'd been able to find a family member of one of them here in Southern Core. The aunt, convincing in her distress, was pathetically grateful to hear someone was investigating her nephew's disappearance. Jaaku planned to interview more family members as soon as he arrived back home, but didn't hold out high hopes for significant answers. It was too much to imagine a hood family having influence that stretched to the other hoods as well.

He scanned the incident reports he'd thought were noteworthy. A 'forcer patrol had dissuaded a few visitors from snooping around the core headquarters with a warning and a few well-placed blows to make sure they understood.

The chief had assured Akuto that he'd kept the list in his personal pouch at all times, except for when he had his personal clerk copy out the names for each hood boss. Jaaku had tried to speak to the clerk, but he found her too traumatized after the attention she'd received from the chief's men.

With a shake of his head, Jaaku lamented the lack of skill in his counterparts working for the chief. Intimidation and physical punishment had their place, but there were better ways to get information out of a loyal clerk.

A follow-up notation mentioned that her assistant had disappeared. Jaaku didn't blame the man for running after what happened to his boss. But was the man part of the plot or simply being prudent so he could avoid a brutal questioning?

On another sheet, Jaaku had noted the multiple dust-ups reported at local restaurants and bars. These were to be expected during a tournament week when the chief relaxed his rules and the core filled up with out-of-town fighters. And while they likely had nothing to do with the theft of the names on the list, Jaaku was thorough.

The next sheet made his blood boil. He could understand ambition and the need to remove competitors to succeed. In fact, he'd even admired Boss Ryuin . . . from a purely tactical stand-point. She had always climbed the ranks with a single-minded ferocity that made him wish at times he'd attached himself to her instead of Akuto.

Not now, though.

It was one thing to take out competitors for a position. It was another thing entirely to betray them to an enemy burb. Jaaku wanted to spit in the woman's face for such a betrayal. He scanned all the information he'd been able to gather about the despicable woman, including information Aibo, the young aide, had overheard during her capture that confirmed other accounts of Ryuin's dealings with Western Burb.

How could the chief allow her to keep her position as boss, even with harsh punishment? Might as well invite a venomous snake into your bed at night. Perhaps some of this information would be new to the chief, and when Akuto submitted it, Ryuin would finally get what was coming to her. The grin on Jaaku's face was predatory. After all, Boss Akuto had almost sent him to the farms for interfering with a single fighter. Ryuin deserved far worse for directly conspiring with Southern Burb's enemies.

Now, if only Jaaku could find evidence that she'd been the one to whisk away the names on the list. He would need a good motive for Boss Ryuin to do that. The only one that made any sense was if she were making a bid for chief. Provoking the city families against Chief Kosui would be a good first step to weaken him. If she'd been behind it, her next step would be to contact the families directly and deliver the youth on the list. She'd have to spin it in a way to disparage Chief Kosui and emphasize her own loyalty to the families, but that should be child's play to the woman.

But then why risk so much by interfering with the recent brawler first-fights? And she definitely didn't poison herself. According to his informants, the poison had been a very dangerous one that left her survival doubtful the first day. There had to be another powerful entity in play. It made the most sense for Western Burb to be involved, especially since the inquiry delayed the delivery of the reinforcements just long enough for them to win a crucial battle.

Jaaku let out a breath and ran a hand through his dark hair, careful to pat it back into place afterward.

It was all so convoluted, like a snarled ball of string that took hours to untangle into a semblance of order. Instead of frowning, he grinned. He loved the challenge, and this was exactly what he was good at. Boss Akuto knew he would continue at the task, doggedly digging out connections and information until he got to the truth.

The truth. He refused to stop until he found it.

His gaze moved to the last page to his right, and his jaw clenched.

The letters on the page were bolder, showing more pressure and anger.

Kiriai. The girl who had wormed her way into Boss Akuto's good graces and climbed her way into the powerful position of burb brawler.

Jaaku stared at everything he'd written and felt a sense of disbelief, the stunned emotion of someone hit by an unexpectedly powerful blow. How had she done this in just over a year? How? It made no sense.

Someone like Ryuin making a brutal climb to the top made perfect sense to him. But a child who insisted she was only doing her best for her hood? Yet somehow she beat everyone thrown against her and achieved a position other fighters spent their lives working for.

His anger at how she'd upset his entire world left no room for admiration. Without her ruining the system that had protected Jitaku Hood for generations, they wouldn't be in this precarious position, one tournament away from becoming the property of their enemy.

Jaaku forced his fists to relax, and he ran a finger down the page of information he'd collected on the girl. He knew he couldn't bring any of this to Akuto yet. Right now, it was full of suspicions and conjectures. He'd seen her and one of her friends sneaking around the chief's house during a party, but that proved nothing. And like the family members of the abducted, it was hard to imagine a single hood fighter having the influence to be behind all of this, regardless of how well she fought in the ring.

Plus, Boss Akuto already thought he was too obsessed over the girl to think straight. Blaming her for the theft of the list and ferreting the targeted youth away in all four hoods? Even in his own mind, it sounded crazy.

But Jaaku also had an instinct that rarely led him astray. As he tapped a finger on the paper listing everything he knew about Kiriai, he resolved to dig even deeper for as long as he had to, until he found proof, real proof. And then he would bring it to Boss Akuto and show him how he'd been right all along.

A short knock at the door made his gaze lift.

"Yes?" he asked.

The door slid open a crack, revealing the mouse of a man assigned as his temporary clerk.

"Second Jaaku, your next appointment has arrived."

Jaaku leaned back in his chair, a smile of anticipation on his face. "Send him in."

A familiar figure moved past the clerk with a predator's grace. The clerk bowed, stepped back out and slid the door shut behind him.

"Please have a seat," Jaaku said with a polite motion toward one of the chairs facing his desk.

"Tell me why I'm here first."

Jaaku gave the young man a considering look before nodding. "I have a proposition for you, Trainer Sento."

Dying to read more?
Download the FREE PREQUEL here:
https://MistyZaugg.com/Welcome/
for the truth Ojisan is hiding from Kiriai.
&
Leave a sentence or two review!
Your reviews make a huge difference for a new author like me.
Thanks! :)

MY UNDYING GRATITUDE

Do you read reviews before you buy a book?

Me too!

I'm so new that each review makes a huge difference in convincing other readers to take a chance on one of my books.

If you have one minute to write just a sentence or two about Combat Shift . . . I'll do a happy dance here next to my computer in your honor. :)

It's really easy. Here's how:

1. Go to Combat Shift's Amazon Page
2. Scroll down and click the button that says "Write a customer review".
3. Type a little honest feedback about the book. (Even a sentence is enough!)
4. Pat yourself on the back for helping out a new author. :D

Thanks for making my day!

— Misty :)

Thank you for reading COMBAT IMPULSE, the fourth in my World of Combat Series!

Are you curious about Kiriai's beginnings and her real relationship to Ojisan?

Pick up COMBAT GENESIS, the free prequel available to my newsletter subscribers:

https://MistyZaugg.com/Welcome/

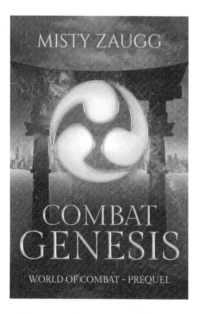

Connecting with my readers is one of the best parts of writing. If you sign up above, you'll receive my interesting and entertaining (I hope) newsletter with first dibs on new content and deals, plus the free prequel. You can opt out easily at any time.

Or come visit us on Facebook:
https://www.facebook.com/groups/MistyZauggReaders

I look forward to hearing from you!

— Misty

facebook.com/MistyZauggAuthor
amazon.com/author/mistyzaugg
bookbub.com/authors/misty-zaugg
goodreads.com/Misty_Zaugg
instagram.com/mistyzaugg

Hi, I'm Misty. :)

I'm a brand new author of the fast-paced, young adult dystopia World of Combat series and love interacting with fans . . .

. . . and eating dark chocolate! :)

I've got a black belt and an M.D., so I can fight off attackers and patch them up afterward. :D

Stop by and say hello on my website or join our Facebook community:

www.MistyZaugg.com

- 🇫 facebook.com/MistyZauggAuthor
- 🅰 amazon.com/author/mistyzaugg
- 🇬 goodreads.com/Misty_Zaugg
- BB bookbub.com/authors/misty-zaugg
- 📷 instagram.com/mistyzaugg

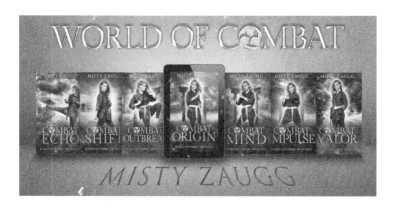

Combat Genesis - Free Prequel and Ojisan's story

Combat Origin - Book 1

Combat Mind - Book 2

Combat Outbreak - Book 3

Combat Impulse - Book 4

Combat Shift - Book 5 (I'd love your review!)

A Few Karate Terms:

- Gi (GEE) — a martial art uniform usually consisting of loose fitting pants and a top that is held closed with a belt.
- Hajime (HAH-jee-may) — Begin. Command used to start a bout.
- Yame (YAH-may) — Stop. Command used to stop a bout.

Name Pronunciations: Most names in this series are drawn from words in the Japanese language and are pronounced accordingly. Here is a short guide to the main characters:

- Kiriai — KEER-ee-iy
- Eigo — ee-IY-go
- Ojisan — OH-jee-sawn
- Sento — SEHN-toh
- Isha — EE-shuh
- Yabban — YAH-bahn
- Sensei Bushi — BOO-shee
- Akuto — ah-KOO-toh
- Jaaku — JAW-koo
- Tsuyoi — TSOO-yoi
- Hoko — HOH-koh
- Jusha — JOO-shaw
- Uncle Kuwashi — koo-WAH-shee
- Auntie Uwasa — oo-WAH-saw

Made in the USA
Las Vegas, NV
11 December 2024